Dragon Lady

AUTUMN BARDOT

Flores Publishing

1

1842
Year of the Water Tiger

Sounds of success rise from below. Voices flow through a ceiling strung with silk lamps. Seep through floorboards covered by costly carpets. Swirl like an eddy into my second-floor office where I can hear whether it is a profitable day or an *exceptionally* profitable day for the gambling house.

Today I hear Spanish silver and credit extensions. And my own impatient fingers tapping the desktop.

I stare at the stack of blank papers, feel my lips sink into my chin, frustrated another day passes without a single word written. This is my burden. It's a weighty task, one anchored by events long sunk into the depths of memory.

I look up from the paper when my youngest grand-daughter glides into the room. Zhenzhen is a beautiful tiny creature with intelligent eyes and a quick smile. She is my heart's delight. Her charm and charisma remind me of my beloved. She has the necessary arrogance to go far, this one. Like me. Like him.

Zhenzhen stands with her hands clasped in front of her. "I've come to accompany you home, Grandmother."

I lay a wrinkled hand on the blank paper. "The words won't come."

"Still?" Zhenzhen furrows her perfect brow. "Maybe they're better left unwritten."

I recoil at her disrespect. "You don't want to know where you come from? How you come to live in wealth?"

"I know you were once a sea bandit." Zhenzhen smiles with the pity the smooth-faced have for the wrinkled. "That life is long over."

"You don't understand." I scowl. "This isn't a story about my life. It's a story about how to survive in a cruel world, how to claw one's way to the top, how one must do horrible things to live another day."

"Ah, it's a confession." Zhenzhen shifts from foot to foot, impatient to leave. "You must tell your story, Grandmother, if for no other reason than as a way to purge the ghosts that haunt your dreams."

"I'm not haunted by ghosts, child." I give her my most withering look. "I have no misgivings. No regrets."

"Then you want to commemorate your accomplishments," Zhenzhen offers with a helpfulness born of sympathy for the stubborn old woman before her.

"I suppose it must be both a confession and commemoration." I pick up the ink stick and point it at her. "You're forbidden to read this account of my life until I'm with my ancestors." I shake the ink stick at her. "I'll know if you do not honor my request. Your lovely face could not hide the shock when you discover the truth."

Zhenzhen's mouth twitches. "Nothing you did would surprise me, GGrandmother."

"Wipe that smug grin off your face. Though you are beautiful and intelligent you did not inherit the *only* thing that matters in this world."

Zhenzhen's smooth brow creases with disappointed surprise. "What's that, Grandmother?"

I tap the blank paper. "It's difficult to explain."

And now I know exactly what to write.

2

Year of the Earth Monkey
1788

I was sold as a slave at thirteen-years-old.

Mama, her face shadowed with shame, called me into the house early one gray humid morning. She wiped a dirt smudge from my cheek, uncoiled my braids, and fanned my hair over my shoulders where it fell thick and shiny to my waist.

"What are you doing?" I squirmed, not because her fingers yanked through my knotted hair but because of the guilt clouding her eyes.

"You're beautiful, Xianggu. We might have found a suitable husband for you if…" Mama stopped trying to detangle my hair. "The gods don't favor us." She examined my arms. "Too much sun. You're too dark."

With a sigh, Mama took my hand and led me into the neglected courtyard. It was a small space made ugly by poverty. The pond was murky with fetid water. A tree sagged in the corner. Only one shrub succeeded to thrive, for it produced a single valiant blossom that unfurled its red petals in search of the sun.

Mama pushed me toward Father, who in turn shoved me toward a stranger, an ugly man with a mole like a peach pit on his left cheek.

"She's not too ugly." The moneylender stroked the long gray strands that hung beneath his chin. "Where are your other children?"

Father swallowed hard, the large lump in his neck moved up and down. "This useless daughter is the only child my worthless wife gave me."

"What about this one?" The moneylender pointed to Mama's distended belly.

Father shrugged. "All my children die at birth or soon after."

The moneylender pointed at my feet, which were dirty and calloused from running barefoot through orange orchards. "She'll make a good slave. Had you bound her feet she might have fetched a better price."

My eyes widened with understanding. "Mama."

Mama hung her head and refused to look at me.

I loved Mama. She was a quiet hardworking woman. From before sunrise until well after sunset she was busy. Cooking rice, making tea, sweeping the hard-packed dirt floor, helping Father in the orchard, weaving baskets, mending our clothes…an endless list of chores. And yet she still had time to sing me songs and tell stories. But never in Father's presence.

Father beat her often. I heard her whimpers. The fault was never hers. Father was an angry man. The gods did not favor him and gave him no luck. He had no sons. His orange trees never produced enough fruit. Blights destroyed a good crop. Every year some misfortune befell him.

Whatever wealth my paternal grandparents once possessed was gone. Or squandered. All but the most necessary household furnishings had been sold. The house itself wore its unhappiness. The clay roof sagged in the middle, the once-straight timbers warped. Mama blamed the house for Father's bad luck. It was not situated perfectly south. The front door not at the precise southerly location. Finding fault and blaming bad luck were my parents" favorite pastimes.

"This settles my debt?" Father rubbed his hands together.

"Paid in full." The moneylender looped a rope around my wrists and gave a quick tug as he walked away.

Too stunned to resist, I plodded behind the moneylender like a reluctant sow to slaughter. I glanced over my shoulders. "Mama."

Mama's head bent like a wilted peony, her tears falling like raindrops.

The moneylender lifted the door flap of a rattan-covered cart and a dozen eyes blinked from the shadows. Slipping the leash from the rope around my wrist, the moneylender grunted for me to get in. I climbed into the stench of urine and feces and sweat. The smell of fear and captivity. I scampered inside, settled in the hay as the door flap dropped into place. Through the wood planks I saw Mama sitting in the dirt, her shoulders shaking as the cart lurched forward. It hurt to breathe the pain in my chest was so great. I stared at Mama until the cart turned the corner.

My parents, my house, my life were gone.

Although the rain-thick clouds emitted only a melancholy light and hot tears filled my eyes, I turned to look at those who shared my fate. Boys and girls sold by their parents to pay a debt. Browned by the sun. Skinny from half-filled rice bowls. Filthy hands. Ragged nails. Calloused feet. Empty eyes crusty with dirt-mixed tears. Mouths slack-jawed with hopelessness.

"What town is this?" whispered the girl slumped beside me.

I swallowed the lump in my throat. "Xinhui."

"Does your family grow oranges?" She ran a tongue over cracked lips.

"Yes." But not enough. Never enough.

"Did the moneylender say where he's taking us?"

Did it matter what becomes of us now that we were slaves? I opened my mouth to snap at her stupidity but stopped when one of Mama's stories swooped into my mind like a swallow. A story that had no meaning until today. I smiled at the girl. "A big house," I lied. "A place where there's enough rice to fill our bellies."

The other children gaped.

"Slaves must eat if they're to be fit for work," I said with false confidence.

The hay rustled and a body uncurled itself from the corner. A pretty girl with a delicate face dragged a slender pale hand across her nose. She lifted her leg and presented a tiny foot encased in an embroidered shoe, a shoe too beautiful and costly for a peasant. "I'll be sold to a brothel or flower boat." Fresh tears ran down her porcelain cheeks.

"What's a flower boat?" I gathered my hair and began to braid it.

The girl scowled at me as though I was the village idiot. "A place where men use women for their pleasure."

I stopped braiding. My hands fell like rocks on my lap. Pleasure women. Prostitutes. There were two in our village. Bad women, Mama said. "I'm Xianggu." I changed the

7

subject. I didn't want to think of *that* possibility. "What's your name?"

"Mei." She smeared a tear across her face.

The young girl sitting beside me scooted closer and her warm body nestled into mine.

I wrapped my arm around the child. "Would you like to hear a story?"

Mei scowled with disapproval, but the child nodded and snuggled closer.

I told the story that had swooped like a swallow into my mind. *The Old Man Who Loses His Horse* was an old tale, one every mother told her children.

"A poor peasant named Sai Wang owned a beautiful horse, a magnificent stallion that filled his heart with pride and his soul with thankfulness. One day, Sai Wang's stallion broke out of his stall and disappeared over the mountain. The villagers, who probably were gloating over his misfortune, said, 'Oh, Sai Wang, you have *terrible* luck. The gods do not favor you *at all*.' But Sai Wang said, 'Who can know what is good or bad.'" I shrugged for effect.

The other children listened. I saw it in their eyes. And their interest emboldened my quiet voice.

"The very next week Sai Wang's horse returned. And not only that, the stallion brought back a magnificent mare. The villagers were amazed and told Sai Wang, 'You're so lucky. The gods favor you.' The wise Sai Wang replied, 'Who can know what is good or bad.'" I looked at each child, each future slave. "Well, Sai Wang had a handsome son who loved riding above all else and rode the new mare every day for hours. But the mare was not as calm as the stallion and when a mongoose crossed the path the mare reared up in panic. The son fell off the mare! 'Ahhh! My leg is broken!' cried the son." I gripped my leg and a few of the children smiled. "The healer came and said, 'I can't fix this. You will be a cripple the rest of your life.' 'The gods do not favor you,' said the villagers. And Sai Wang replied…"

"Who can know what is good or bad," the children said in chorus.

"That's *exactly* what he said. A whole year of sadness passed before the emperor's army marched into the village and commanded all the young men to join them in battle. 'We have no use for lame men,' said the general after seeing Sai Wang's son hobble around. Many months later, a messenger came through the village. 'The battle was lost. All your sons are dead.' The villagers wailed and ranted about their misfortune. They told Sai Wang he was lucky he still had a son. But Sai Wang said, 'do not question or guess at what may be luck or not. Misfortune can be a blessing in disguise that you do not recognize until many years later.'"

Mei frowned and looked away. A few of the older children's eyes brightened with a glimmer of hope. The younger children asked for another story.

Two days, four improved versions of Sai Wang's story, and four bowls of watery *congee* later our journey ended at a great harbor.

Squinting into the sun's glare, we tumbled from the cart one by one. The dock bustled with people. Bare-chested men wearing bamboo *dǒulì* hauled crates and loaded boats. A yellow-haired mongrel sniffed our cart. Rickshaws rattled by. Slaves carried sedan chairs, the rich men they bore on their shoulders kept above the mud and muck. Some chairs were ornately carved wood and had a sun-blocking canopy adorned with tassels. But most were simple rattan chairs affixed between two bamboo poles. Across the way, crude huts encircled a large building that flew colorful flags above its entrance.

"Your life changes this day, little worms," said the moneylender to our motley little group. "Many people are here. Wicked and virtuous. Who will buy *you*?" His loud laughter made his peach pit mole bob up and down.

Who could know what was good or bad?

3

The moneylender's announcement seemed to double the people, noises, and odors. In an instant the dock became my whole world. Anyone could buy me. The old man striking one coin against the other and holding it to his ears. The man and woman who pointed to our little group and shook their heads. The young husband in need of a kitchen slave. Anyone.

"Come." The moneylender jerked the rope tethered at our ankles.

We shuffled behind him.

It was then that I noticed the difference between the straggly gray hair hanging from the moneylender's chin and his too-thick queue black as a moonless night. Only the vainest of men wore a false queue.

The moneylender stopped, held a hand to his brow, and stared into the harbor.

I followed his gaze and my pulse quickened. So many boats! Small crude sampans, ornate long dragons, boats with one, two, and three masts—some so tall they touched the sky.

Boats for fishing. Sampans for carrying cargo. Floating islands of boats, boats, boats.

We waited in the sun while the muttering moneylender tapped his foot. My body had just begun to sway with fatigue when a pale middle-aged woman approached and snapped me to attention.

She was rich; her skin powdered white, her lips dabbed with red, her arched eyebrows plucked thin. Atop a gauzy dress, she wore a red robe embroidered with peonies and birds. Behind her, a young girl held a purple tasseled umbrella over her head.

"What do you have for me, uncle?" The rich woman's haughty tone sounded nothing like the humble quiet voices of Mama and the other women in my village.

"Healthy strong boys and girls." The moneylender pointed to Mei. "This one has bound feet—poorly bound feet —but since she'll spend most of her time on her back it won't matter." He let loose a throaty laugh, dislodged thick yellow phlegm, which he spit on the ground.

The woman's pale hand grabbed Mei's face, and her long, pointed nails dug into Mei's cheeks. The woman clicked her tongue as she turned Mei's head this way and that. "Open your mouth. Ugh, crooked teeth," she said the moment Mei opened wide. "Ugly skin." She patted Mei's breast. "Plum-sized." She pinched Mei's ear. "Are you a virgin?"

Mei's lips quivered. "I'm only fourteen years."

The woman smacked her cheek. "I didn't ask your age." She scowled at the moneylender. "Is she deaf or stupid?"

"I'm a virgin," Mei whimpered, tears welling in her eyes.

The woman shifted her attention to me, her eyes moving downward. "Hideous feet!"

I shrunk back, curled my toes.

The woman gripped my chin, examined my face. "Open."

12

She nodded approvingly as she inspected my teeth. "This one is ugly. Good for nothing but a serving girl. No man will want such an ugly beast, but since her feet are big she'll make a sure-footed slave. I'll buy this one and the one with bound feet."

The moneylender and the woman haggled over the price. Mei's was double mine.

"Don't be afraid," I whispered to Mei as the moneylender untied the rope around our ankles.

The woman slapped my cheek. "That's for your insolence. Slaves must be silent." She next struck Mei with an open hand. "That's for the bad fortune of having a talkative friend." She pulled a red ribbon from her sleeve, wrapped it around our wrists, connecting us together like a double gift.

"I am Madam Xu," she said as we followed her across the quay. "If you're dutiful and not worthless your life will be agreeable enough. If you displease me or show a surly face, I'll throw you into the sea where if you're lucky you'll be eaten by a big fish before you drown."

Madam Xu stopped before a brightly painted sampan covered by a curved rattan canopy strung with red tassels. A girl holding an oar waited at the rear.

Madam Xu stepped into the sampan and sat on a carved chair with the air of an empress. "Get in. Be quick about it."

The girl holding the umbrella pushed us forward. Despite the gentle rock and heave of the sampan, I boarded it without stumbling, my bare feet wide and steady. But Mei, with her tiny bound feet, lost her balance. She tumbled into me and, since we were tied together, I fell down with her.

"You must learn to walk on a boat. Clumsy girls make no money." Madam Xu pointed to the floor. "Sit." She uncoiled Mei's braid and spread it over her shoulders. "Coarse like straw. My girls will show you how to make it feel like the finest silk."

The umbrella-holding slave picked up an oar and together the two girls rowed us into the floating mass of red, green, blue, and and orange. Each brightly painted boat was crowded with possessions. Some were little more than crude barges stacked with bamboo cages and old crates. Others had baskets hanging down the sides. Their rattan roofs went from end to end.

As we glided through the floating throng, we passed two women balanced on a ledge, their posture as natural as though standing on a street corner. On the other side, three naked brown-as-dung children leapt from their boat, splashing and playing. More life was squeezed into this bobbing water town than my village.

"Do you sing?" Madam Xu directed her question at Mei.

Mei nodded.

Madam Xu's face puckered with skepticism. "Do you play an instrument?"

"The lute," Mei said with more enthusiasm than I had ever heard.

Madam Xu smiled and nodded. "Did your mother teach you to dance?"

"Mother died when I was young." Mei's face clouded as she stared down at her hands. "My *amah* taught me only a few."

"Feet too big to be silver lotus and not quite accomplished." Madam Xu sighed. "Why did your father sell you?"

Mei's face colored with shame. "To buy more opium."

"It's ruined many men." Madam Xu picked up a wide fan, whacked it over my head, and then dropped it into my lap. "I'm hot."

I fanned with a steady rhythm until our sampan veered

into a narrow waterway. The smell! I cringed. I was used to the sweet perfume of blossoming orange trees, not the stench of brine, fish, and sweat. My perfect fanning faltered. I would have pinched closed my nose, but I dare not risk offending Madam Xu.

Mei, however, clapped her hand over her nose.

Madam Xu swatted Mei's hand away. "That's the smell of money, stupid girl."

Money!? It was the smell of Water People, wicked worthless sea gypsies forbidden to live with good people on the land. Mama said they had webbed toes and breathed underwater.

I stole a look at Madam Xu's feet, but they were hidden beneath her dress. Madam Xu looked nothing like a Water Person. Nothing like the dark-skinned slim men who wore only short wide pants. And nothing like the tired-faced women in their loose plain tops, not a stitch of embroidery or a button to be found.

Madam Xu was definitely not a Water Person. Those bad people wore *dǒulì* on their heads. Or leaf hats. A few men had turbans. Everyone was barefoot. But I did not see a webbed foot among them. Amid the splashes and clatter, I caught snatches of their conversations, a coarse, vulgar dialect with many unfamiliar words.

Madam Xu pointed. "Your new home."

Mei grabbed my hand and squeezed tight while my mouth hung open in disbelief.

4

M adam Xu's boat was huge! As wide as two boats. Two-stories tall. With a grand three-door entrance across a spacious deck. A red striped awning strung with lanterns stretched across the second story deck. The boat was elegant, a lotus in the midst of ramshackle wood structures bobbing nearby.

Under the lower awning, musicians plucked an enchanting tune on the *pipa, zhong ruan, guqin,* and *liuqin.* Smoke tendrils curled from the pipes of men lounging on couches. A pale-powdered woman wearing a sheer robe and bored expression posed by a carved door.

Madam Xu pointed to the colorful banner overhead. "Heavenly Women." She clapped her hands.

A sour-faced slave girl emerged from the shadows and secured the sampan to a post.

"Take this one to Bright Pearl." Madam Xu gave Mei a push.

This sent me sprawling forward. That was the very moment I knew that being tethered to someone was a double fate, their luck inescapably tied to my own. I did not want my life to be knotted with Mei's clumsiness. If I must be tangled with someone let them ascend to great heights like the midday sun.

"Take the other to the kitchen," said Madam Xu with a wave of her manicured hand.

The slave, noting Mei's tiny feet, extended her arm, the helpful gesture at odds with the jealousy flickering across her face.

The musicians leered as we shuffled past. Though Mei was Madam Xu's latest acquisition I was not invisible. The men stared like hungry wolves at me as well.

"Shhhh," said the sour-faced slave over her shoulder though neither Mei and I had spoken. She opened a door carved with lotus blooms, and a golden ribbon of sunlight brightened the dark hallway. "Most of the flower girls are sleeping. They get angry if you wake them."

Grunts and groans floated into the passage. I knew these sounds. Father made similar noises when he lay with Mama.

"The best flower girls are nearest the saloon." The slave girl inclined her head to the left. "The richest men are fat. They don't want to walk far before entering a girl's chamber."

"What chamber?" Mei whispered.

"Entering the chamber. Fucking." The slave giggled.

Mei's eyes grew wide and her lips quivered.

The slave girl rapped lightly on a door three times. "Bright Pearl, Madam Xu has a girl for you."

The door opened a crack and a sweet-faced girl with full lips and black eyes peeked out. She looked at Mei as though assessing a swath of silk for a flaw.

Mei lifted her dress.

Bright Pearl sighed and shook her head. "Too big. Golden lotus feet bring a rich, fat husband. Silver lotus feet bring a cheap government official." She opened the door wide. Clad only in a thin silk robe tied tight at the waist, Bright Pearl's luminous porcelain face was as beautiful as her tiny golden-clad feet. "You smell like you sleep with chickens." She wrinkled her nose. "A bath first, and then I'll teach you everything you must know to keep Madam Xu happy."

"Madam Xu?" I was confused. I thought prostitutes serviced men.

Bright Pearl rolled her eyes. "Madam Xu's happiness is connected to coin. The more skill you have with men the more coin she makes, and the less likely she beats you or throws your baby into the sea."

"Baby?" Mei's hand flew to her heart.

"You're not so stupid you don't know where babies come from, are you?" Bright Pearl pointed to a bowl on the table near the bed. "The *liangyao* doesn't always prevent a man's seed from growing. You have sex with men every day, you make a baby. I have a son. He stays on the boat behind this one with the other children. It's my greatest sorrow I can't prove he's the son of the rich man who visits me once a week."

Mei blinked, her eyes swollen with tears.

"It's not that bad. Men are stupid, oafish beasts. If you're good, it'll be over before you know it." Bright Pearl narrowed her eyes at me. "You too?"

"This one's a slave." The sour-faced slave tugged on my sleeve.

"We're all slaves. Some on our feet, some on our backs." Bright Pearl dragged a long-tapered nail down the length of my nose and over my lips. "Your lips are too big, your eyes too penetrating—too much *yang*—but your face is all *yin*. How old are you?"

"Thirteen years."

"Fate will mold your face in the next few months. Features like yours either blossom with beauty or sprout into ugliness with a girl's first blood. Either way, Madam Xu will put you to work." Bright Pearl wrapped her delicate white hand around Mei's little wrist, tugged her inside, and shut the door.

I touched my face. Slave or flower girl? Which was better?

"How many flower girls work here?" I asked the slave girl as I followed her down the corridor.

She shrugged. "Many. All the rooms are busy. Always busy. Busy fucking. Busy playing a man's flute. Busy bursting chrysanthemums. Busy gossiping." She bent under a low doorway at the rear of the boat. "This is the galley." She lit a small stove. "Have you bled yet?"

"No," I said confused by all the different types of busyness.

The slave girl looked me up and down. "You're pretty. Prettier than the other one. I'm too ugly to be a prostitute." She crinkled her face and bared her yellow teeth. "No man will pay for me." She dragged a red box from the shelf. "You must learn Madam Xu's ways. Oolong in the afternoon." She placed tea tools—a teapot, a copper bowl, and a porcelain teacup—on a wooden tea tray.

"My name is Xianggu," I said in desperate need of befriending this sour-faced slave.

She tapped her flat chest. "Suyin. Do as I do." Suyin poured hot water into a small clay teapot and closed the lid. "Oolong is delicate. The water must not be too hot. Madam Xu will beat you if you scald the leaves." She filled the blue and white teacup with hot water. "Like this." Using tongs, she emptied the teacup. "If Madam Xu has guests then do this with each cup."

I nodded, fascinated by her tea making. Mama made tea by tossing leaves into an earthen pot.

"I'll teach you the art of tea tomorrow—how to make it when Madam Xu entertains wealthy guests. But today, the basics." Suyin measured the leaves with a bamboo scoop.

The quantity of leaves surprised me. Mama was never so generous.

"Watch me." Suyin poured hot water around the pot, then lifted the pot up and down three times. "To the top." She replaced the lid, poured water into the teacup and promptly discarded the tea. "Never give Madam Xu the first pouring."

Suyin repeated the process, poured the water over the teapot, and folded her arms. "Wait. Not too long."

"How long?" I did not want to fail at this simple task.

Suyin shrugged. "Not enough time to do another task. Too much time to wonder why the gods gave you this fate."

Counting seemed like a better way but I did not say this to Suyin. "What else will I do?"

"Mend and wash clothes. Give Madam Xu foot massages. Show men in and out. Prepare food. Whatever tasks Madam Xu wants. Most important," Suyin glanced at the door, "flower girls sleep. We don't. You'll learn to sleep like a cat. Once the sun goes down the boat is busy and loud. No sleeping then. The best time is just before dawn when the men are gone and the moonflowers are asleep. The sunflowers are busy during the day."

"Sunflowers?"

"The girls who service men of lower status." Suyin poured tea into the porcelain cup. "Say nothing. Be invisible. Follow me."

5

Year of the Earth Rooster
1788

Inconspicuousness was not a talent I possessed. Customers gawked. Flower girls demanded I make tea, bring rice, mend this, and wash that. Madam Xu summoned me hourly to scrub the floor, clean the cabin, wash her hair, rub her feet, show a customer in, lead a customer out.

I prepared meals, rowed the sampan when Madam Xu went ashore, hauled boxes, peeled oranges, shucked peanuts, chopped vegetables, polished wood, prepared meals, dried rain-drenched chairs…an endless list of chores. My days were tedious. Any dull-witted person could complete the tasks.

Evenings, however, filled my head and heart with happiness. I eavesdropped on wealthy customers' conversations while serving tea. I dawdled while the eloquent literati, dressed in long Manchu robes and black hats, quoted poetry and discussed politics. I could have listened to those men all night long.

The flower girls' gossip was equally enlightening. In a few short weeks I learned more about men's appetites than I ever imagined possible. I paid rapt attention to their chatter, served them with a smile, and was rewarded for my charm, their once harsh commands became soft-spoken requests.

"I don't understand why Madam Xu keeps you a slave." Winter Plum patted my cheek. "You're very pretty." Her hand tugged at my sleeve. "This is new. Not suitable for a slave."

"Madam Xu gave it to me." I blushed. "I must wear it only in the evening." The dress was skin-colored silk, embroidered with six cleverly located red lotuses. Though modest in comparison to the flower girls, the fleshy hue and lotus placement accentuated my budding form.

Winter Plum clicked her tongue with approval. "Madam Xu flaunts your wares in hopes of starting a bidding war."

"There's a reason why Madam Xu runs the most successful flower boat in Guangzhou." Bright Pearl reached out and pinched my breast. "Still only buds. Your first blood is late in coming. The moment you begin to bloom, men will be bees for a taste of your nectar, and Madam Xu will demand a high price for the privilege."

Making crude gestures, Bright Pearl and Winter Plum fell into fits of laughter.

I traipsed away on big feet hoping my next chore was challenging enough to keep my mind from worrying about my eventual deflowering. But thoughts were raindrops. You could not control when they fell, and that afternoon while stringing lanterns in the saloon I thought about my home.

I missed Mama. Not Father. I longed for solid ground under my feet and the fragrance of orange blossoms. I did not miss the mud and poverty. Or the village life where the only distractions were the same dull celebrations and tired people.

The flower boat was a hive of activity with interesting

people buzzing about. As long as I did not anger the Queen Bee, I found a drop of honey in my servitude.

This life wasn't *so* bad. I *could* have been sold to a a brutal master who beat and raped me. Madam Xu was demanding and stern, but she was not cruel. Disobedience earned a slave a whack with a bamboo switch. Although once, Madam Xu had yanked a handful of hair from Suyin's scalp for smelling of garlic. I had received two blows so far. One for a stain on my new silk dress, the other for serving lukewarm tea to a guest.

I did not fault Madam Xu. I admired her. She was unlike any woman I had ever known. Her *own* woman. Servant to no man.

I studied everything about Madam Xu. By day, the creases on Madam Xu's face showed her age, but at night, the wrinkles vanished, the moonlight transforming the middle-aged madam into a timeless beauty. With customers, Madam Xu's manner was gracious and serene, her voice sweet as a tinkling bell, her laughter melodious, her every movement graceful.

Madam Xu entertained only one man, a rich government official who visited once a week. Madam Xu told me to wait until two incense sticks burned before I brought their tea. Each week I found Madam Xu's slim body nestled close to his, both their faces serene with satisfaction.

On the day marking my first year on the flower boat, I plodded into Madam Xu's cabin and set the lacquered tea tray on the table.

"Come here." Madam Xu's only customer beckoned me forward. "Are you a woman yet?"

I lowered my gaze and shook my head. I felt his eyes drink in my figure like a thirsty man.

"My friend will pay well for a virgin," he said, but not to

me. "A girl on the verge of womanhood. He prefers a peach picked early while still tart and firm."

Madam Xu draped her long straight hair over his chest, swept the tips over his brown nipples. "I'm saving this one for a very rich man. Look how beautiful she is. Her eyes are as big as apricots."

He snorted. "Her feet are big and ugly."

"My feet are big and I please you." Madam Xu's leg moved under the blanket.

The official made an odd moaning cough. "Show me your hair."

I uncoiled my braid, fanning it to show its thick length.

The official ran his fingers through my hair. "My friend will like this girl."

Madam Xu tugged on his queue. "Silver will secure her for one month."

"You're a shrewd woman." He laughed. "You know I cannot make an appointment for another man."

"Tell him not to wait. She won't be a child much longer." Madam Xu dismissed me with a bob of her head. "Now, let's discuss the fee."

I returned to the kitchen without hearing any more about the value of my virginity. "My kitchen slave days are at an end." I flopped down on the kitchen stool.

Suyin didn't even bother to look up while she chopped bok choy. "I'm not surprised. How do you know?"

"Madam Xu discusses my deflowering fee with her official."

Suyin stopped chopping, the knife held in midair. "Her patron wants a virgin?"

"No, his friend. What's a patron?"

Suyin pushed a small pile of pea sprouts across the table.

"I don't know about all patrons, but this one comes every week for two things. To collect his share of the profits and for a free fuck."

My brows shot up. "Madam Xu gives something away for free?"

Suyin shrugged. "It's a strange relationship. Part business, part love, part obligation, part need."

"That's a lot of parts."

Suyin set down the knife and took a quick peek out the door. "The flower girls say Madam Xu was a prostitute long ago. On this very flower boat. By some luck," Suyin stuck out her tongue and flicked it up and down, "she gained favor with the former madam. One day the old madam disappeared, and Madam Xu took her place."

"Why? How?"

"You ask a lot of questions I don't know the answers to. I only repeat what I heard." Suyin flicked away a speck of dirt on the pea sprouts. "Maybe she killed her. I heard Madam Xu did things with her feet that the girls with bound feet could not. Madam Xu was clever. She turned her bad luck into good fortune."

I looked down at my own large feet. Could I turn the curse of my big feet into a blessing like Madam Xu? If Madam Xu did it why couldn't I?

I was not afraid of working as a flower girl. I was afraid of staying one.

There were no flower girls over the age of thirty. Once their fresh-faces faded, they disappeared. Like Red Sky. Who vanished the day after Madam Xu pointed out a furrow between her brows.

Unless my deflowering proved remarkable, I would begin as a lowly sunflower. These girls worked all day and night in cramped compartments below deck, their services with tradesmen and merchants purchased for a few coins. Sunflowers wore dresses of poor quality and suffered the most sicknesses. I did not intend to remain a sunflower for long.

Moonflowers like Bright Pearl lived on the upper deck and enjoyed larger compartments with lavish appointments and silk robes. Every girl was beautiful and white as a lily. Their customers paid more, and their regulars often brought gifts.

"Make it the best fuck he ever had," Madam Xu always told the girls. "Maybe he will be so enamored he will make you his fifth wife."

That was each girl's hope. Their dream.

Yet Madam Xu did not wait for that luck. She made her own. One where she made the rules and earned her own money. This appealed to me. Made my heart beat faster. Made my mind race with ideas.

I thought of those people who stare at a fruitless orchard and dream of a better life. Like Mama and Father. I thought of those who chop down the fruitless trees to build a temple everyone will pay to visit. I wanted to be a doer, not a dreamer.

I did not want to be a favorite prostitute or a rich man's fifth wife. I wanted to be like Madam Xu. I was fourteen-years-old. Naïve and stupid.

And since I never expected that the winds of fate might blow my lofty goals in another direction, I cultivated my ambitions like a good gardener.

Two months later, while I swept the saloon, my days as a kitchen slave ended.

Madam Xu took the broom away and inspected my hands. "Are you a woman yet?" She squeezed my breasts.

I lowered my eyes and shook my head.

Madam Xu lifted my chin, turned my face this way and that. "Go see Bright Pearl. She'll tell you all you need to know. Your first customer comes tomorrow."

6

The sun was high in the sky before I dared knock on Bright Pearl's door.

"Madam Xu said—"

"I know." Bright Pearl opened the door and, yawning, beckoned me inside.

The afternoon passed quickly while Bright Pearl shared her knowledge about men. She told me ways to determine their appetites, methods to speed their pleasure, and techniques to prolong it. She taught me how to flatter without words and demonstrated expressions and gestures sure to please. She removed a wooden model of a *yīnjīng* —sizes vary, she said—from a drawer.

"Move your hand like this…no…like this. Here too, fingertips only…" She straddled me. Moved up and down. "Some like it this way." She flipped around, lifted her robe to give me a too-close view of her chrysanthemum. "If he likes giving pleasure you must sigh and writhe. If he prefers giving pain let a tear roll down your cheek and quiver your lip."

"How do I know what he wants?"

Bright Pearl pinched my breast.

"Ow!" I pushed her away.

"If he gropes, forces his finger into your chamber, jams his tongue in your mouth, or bites your lips—he gets his pleasure from you *not* getting yours. But if he is slow and gentle," Bright Pearl lifted my hair and ran her tongue across the back of my neck, "then his pleasure increases with your pleasure." She stared at me, her eyes glinting with mischief. "Did that feel good?"

I swallowed and looked away, ashamed of the heat spreading through my body.

Bright Pearl kissed my lips. "Some lewd worms pay for two flower girls." She picked up the wooden *yīnjīng* and held it to my mouth. "Many men want you to play their flute first. A bit of flute playing speeds their pleasure. Drunk men are the worst. You have to work too hard before they let off their fireworks." She rolled away from me. ""That's all I know, Xianggu."

Not true. Bright Pearl shared only the basic information and most obvious positions. We were rivals now. To share all her secrets was foolish.

The following day was busy. I bathed, perfumed my skin. Suyin washed and styled my hair. Madam Xu forbid me to eat. I only sipped jasmine tea.

I waited serenely on the bed in the compartment next to Bright Pearl. She and Madam Xu would watch through a peephole. This was my one chance to prove I belonged with the high-priced moonflowers. Only my clenching stomach—which Madam Xu couldn't see—revealed my nervousness.

From slave to prostitute. This was a stepping stone to a better life. *If I* was shrewd. *If I* made my own luck.

My fingers curled into fists as I compared Madam Xu's life to Mama's. Mama skipped meals so I would not go hungry. Father beat her. Mama wore frayed cotton pants and too-often mended tops. Had to ask Father for money to buy a bit of hemp or a handful of mung beans. No man beat Madam Xu. She wore silk robes. A slave held her shade umbrella. She ate dumplings and pork and sticky rice cakes and pickled eggs. She drank wine and the best quality *baijiu* and asked no one's permission to do anything.

Immoral Madam Xu had a better life than my honorable Mama.

My first customer arrived just after sunset. He was middle-aged and not ugly. His forehead was freshly shaved, his queue long, and his blue Mandarin jacket of fine quality. He stared at me like a hungry dog, nodded his approval to Madam Xu, and closed the compartment door.

I smiled shyly before dropping my gaze, all practiced ploys.

"You're a virgin?" The bed heaved as he sat down beside me. "Not yet a woman?"

My chin dipped in response.

He lifted my chin and dragged his thumb over my lips. "Have you kissed a man before?"

"Never." I clasped my hands in my lap to keep them from trembling.

He touched my hair, let the strands run through his fingers. "You have beautiful hair, like a black waterfall of silk." He sniffed and looped a tendril around his finger.

His breath grew heavy, and I sensed his mounting lust as his fingers continued stroking my hair.

"Show me your hands." His voice was thick, his eyes glazed as though coming out of a reverie.

I unclasped them, palm side up.

His soft thick fingers wiggled between my own. "A peasant's hands." He frowned. "Your feet."

I bit my lip and tugged up my robe. My big feet were

covered with embroidered socks and Manchurian flowerpot shoes that pinched my toes.

"Take off the shoes." He shrugged off his Mandarin jacket. "Stand up."

I willed my legs to stop shaking as he circled about me.

He tugged at my robe. "Take it off."

Naked, he circled me again, this time with a low rumble of pleasure. "Lie on the bed."

I lay down obediently and lowered my eyes in subservience. I felt his stare. Was he looking for an imperfection? A reason to reject me? Finally, after too many long minutes, he leaned over and blew across my nipples. My body responded immediately, my pink buds hardened and lengthened.

"Oooo, you like that." He lowered his head, took a nipple between his teeth and tugged.

I squeaked in pain, but he mistook it for pleasure and attacked the other breast. Recalling Bright Pearl's advice for hastening a man's fireworks, I pretended enjoyment.

He parted my thighs with his knee, grabbed a fistful of my hair, and pushed past my virgin chambers. I yelped, the pain unexpected, and his throat rumbled with a sound between a laugh and a moan.

The man bucked, pulled my hair with each thrust, and for some reason—perhaps because of his earlier bites—I sank my teeth into his shoulder. He let out a long moan and fell on top of me.

It was over. So fast!

I turned my head and aimed an overconfident smile at the peephole.

The man lay on top of me until I squirmed for breath.

"You want more?" He rose up on his elbows and leered. "Good. By the time the sun comes up there will be no part of your body untouched." He laughed. Probably at my shocked expression.

It took all my strength not to vomit my fear. To stop my tears. To play the flower girl.

The man liked to bite. He enjoyed when I bit back. He deposited his pleasure in my hair and in my mouth. He put me in unusual positions. Some of them hurt. By the end of the night I was sweaty and sticky and the entrance to my chamber burned like fire. The moment he left I collapsed into sleep.

Suyin shook me awake in the morning. "Madam Xu wants to see you."

7

Puffy-eyed and heavy-limbed, I rose from the bed and followed Suyin down the hall.

Madam Xu, sitting at the deck, looked up from her *congee*. "He was pleased."

"Happy customers return for more happiness." I forced a small smile and parroted Bright Pearl's words.

Madam Xu laughed. "In *any* business." She lifted the spoon to her mouth, her eyes fixed on me as though coming to a decision. "Until you get your first blood, I'll be able to get a higher fee—girl-women are preferred by many men. You'll remain with the moonflowers. For now. If I receive enough favorable reports, you'll earn your place among them."

I inclined my head and bit back a relieved smile. "You're generous and kind."

Madam Xu placed the spoon in the bowl and picked up a letter. "I'm neither generous nor kind. I'm a businesswoman with a talent for making a profit. The moment you lose your appeal, you will be a sunflower." Madam Xu dismissed me with a flap of her hand, her attention focused on the letter.

"You read," I whispered with amazement.

Madam Xu lifted her chin, the vertical line deepening between her eyes. "Why are you still here?"

I clasped my hands together. "I would like to learn to read someday."

Madam Xu arched one thin eyebrow. "Flower girls need only to read the desires of men."

"I don't want to be a flower girl forever."

Madam Xu's eyes narrowed into slits, the creases made her look tired and angry. "You want to be a rich man's concubine?"

"No." I looked down at my big feet. "I want…I wish to be a woman like you."

Madam Xu set down the paper. "Do you know how I became the owner of the most prosperous flower boat in Guangzhou?"

I took the smallest step forward. "I heard rumors."

"Rumors?" Madam Xu swished her hand back and forth. "I'll tell you the real story of my success. I was sold to this flower boat—not as grand as you see now—when I was your age. I was beautiful, more beautiful than you, and I was a virgin—the old madam profited many times from my deflowering. She took a foolish risk. One night a man came, and he knew—as some men know—that I was not a virgin. I was young and stupid, and did a poor job pretending to be a virgin that day. The man was enraged—he had spent his hard-earned coin for a virgin—and beat me almost to death. Then he beat the old madam even though she returned his money. Foolish woman. Her greed cost her more than a few pieces of silver. It cost her the flower boat's reputation. And it cost her the respect of her flower girls. They didn't feel safe anymore. In time, of course, after her deceit was forgotten, her former customers returned—wary and eager to bargain." Madam Xu tapped her temple with a long fingernail. "I never forgot that lesson. I became the best moonflower. All the men wanted me. I commanded the highest price." She sat straighter, her chin in the air.

"Like Bright Pearl?"

"I was nothing like her." Madam Xu made a sour lemon-sucking face. "The man who now visits me every week fell in love with me and wanted to make me his fourth wife. Fourth wife? *Āi*! It is bad luck to be a fourth wife, the number of death. I told him no and made him a different offer. If he bought the flower boat, I would be his first flower boat wife and give him a share of the profits. He accepted my offer and he gave me some advice. Customers are like jade, merchandise is grass. I worked hard. Night and day. I still work hard."

"What must I—"

"You're a child, Xianggu. Prove your worth as a moon-flower first. Earn your keep. Make me rich. Learn the art of paper cutting."

I cocked my head. "Paper cutting?"

"Is there something wrong with your hearing?"

"No, I—"

"Begin with something simple, the Good Luck or Longevity character. Make a Window Flower for your compartment. Decorations for a festival. Practice. Be perfect. Carelessness is ugly. Your skill will grow if you are diligent and patient. When your skill is supreme, we will speak again. Now go."

Back in my compartment I puzzled over Madam Xu's real purpose for cutting paper.

"Mei is crying again." Suyin came in with a few sheets of cheap paper and a small knife. "She asks for you."

My heart hurt for Mei. My mind was not as kind. Because Mei had bound feet and a privileged upbringing she was placed with the moonflowers. But her constant crying and hysterics forced Madam Xu to send her below with the sunflowers. She didn't earn her keep. Only the most heartless worm wanted to pay to listen to a flower girl weep during sex.

My stomach tightened with sorrow and pity, I descended into the lower deck where the boat groaned and squeaked, where rats scurried into the darkness, and where the air was stale and thick.

I scraped my fingers against the rattan flap hanging in the narrow doorway. "It's Xianggu."

"Come in." Mei's voice was weedy with misery.

The year had wilted Mei's pretty face and withered her spirit. The girl before me was a ghost.

"The gods hate me," Mei moaned. "If father had not smoked away my dowry I would be wedded to a rich man." She moved aside the cheap silk, set her hand on the small swell of her belly. "Look! This child belongs to a thousand men. At first, I was angry, then sad, but now…now I want to die. I want to die before this thousand-customer baby rips my chamber apart and demands to be suckled."

"Mei…"

"I'm not brave enough to kill myself so I'll kill the baby when it's born."

I sat beside her. "Did you drink the *liangyao* every day?" The herbal concoction prevented pregnancy. Most of the time.

"Of course, I did!" Mei patted her stomach. "*Āi*, I will give birth to a slave." She jabbed her finger into her chest. "I come from a good family!" She gripped my hand, her nails digging into my flesh. "I already know how I'll do it. I'll strangle it."

I didn't believe her. "Madam Xu will be furious if she finds out."

"Good. Maybe she'll throw me overboard." She released my hand and punched her stomach.

"Stop." I grabbed her wrist. "Mei, be strong. The winds blow and fortunes change. Don't think of what could have been. Think of the future." For the first time I was glad for my parent's poverty. It had strengthened my spirit.

Mei shook off my hand. "I'm food for fishes. That's my future."

Poverty, I decided, had one advantage. I saw opportunity where Mei found none. I saw hope where Mei found despair. I saw my customers as a way to climb up, not fall under.

Mei had become a ghost. There was no sense reasoning with a ghost. I would never change her despair into hope.

8

Blood streaked down my thigh and I cursed under my breath. Now I would have to prove myself. Had I over-heard enough of the moonflowers' tricks to be as good as they were? Had I listened to all their advice?

Father had never heeded advice. Or, as Mama claimed, he believed the wrong people, those secret rivals bent on seeing him fail. I would not be so foolish.

I listened to everyone and befriended all of the flowers—moon and sun alike—and came to my own conclusions.

I was wary. Moonflowers excelled at faking their plea-sure, which meant they could fake anything. Including 'help-ful' advice.

I made sure to ladle my own bowl of *liangyao* each day. A prostitute with a swollen belly made no money.

Unlike the other flower girls, I did not spend my free time gossiping. I taught myself the art of cutting paper and hoped to master the intricate designs I had seen pasted on shop windows on festival days.

I started with the Double Happiness symbol, which looked easy enough. I was wrong. My first attempts were clumsy. I had no skill with the knife. Some edges were clean, but most were frayed and torn. Suyin delivered my ugly attempts to Madam Xu. It was humiliating but the only way I could get more paper.

One day, Suyin returned with only half the amount of paper. I swallowed the lump of shame in my throat, cut the sheets in half, and doubled my efforts.

After mastering a few symbols, I attempted leaves and flowers, the memories of the blooms and fronds of home my only models. Two months later, Suyin delivered three times as much paper as before—with a few red sheets slipped into the cheap stack. Madam Xu approved!

I tried my hand at zodiac signs. Soon I was able to capture the bristle of a horse's tail and the spikiness of a dragon's scales.

When Suyin brought a stack of good quality red paper I knew I exceeded Madam Xu's expectations.

The moonflowers began making requests—cut a lotus, make a tiger—and soon all our compartments displayed my artistry.

Designing and cutting kept me sane. With each new paper I repeated a promise, today I am a prostitute but one day I will find a way to be free.

"Hand job has a double meaning for you," said Bright Pearl when I presented her with a horse cutting. "With one hand you decorate the flower boat, with the other you pleasure the customer."

The other moongirls twittered and giggled.

"As long as I don't confuse the two jobs one day," I said, giggling with them.

As my skill with paper cutting increased so did my skills of the flesh. I had many repeat visitors. All left satisfied. I made Madam Xu a lot of money. I worked hard. All the while

I imagined a day when I would earn my freedom. Not the freedom found by Mei, who died during childbirth and roamed the boat an angry ghost who made mischief by hiding the moongirls' combs and causing Bright Pearl to lose a rich customer when he found a gray hair on her head.

My relationship with Bright Pearl changed during this time. Each passing year her smiles grew more false, her eyes flashed with more jealousy, and her tongue was coated with more envy.

One afternoon while brushing my hair I paused to study my hands. My skin was soft, the nails buffed and long. A woman's hands. I removed the small mirror from under the bed to inspect my face. It was as white as a lily, plump of cheek and lips, my features sensual and lush. The peasant child was gone. Outwardly. Within, however, the lessons of poverty and physical labor remained. What fortunes would the winds of fate blow at my feet? Good or bad?

"The beauty of youth is fleeting." Madam Xu, standing in the doorway, interrupted my self-indulgent musing.

"You're still beautiful," I said with honesty.

"My beauty lies in the symmetry of my face and refinement of my features. Fresh skin, taut breasts, smooth limbs—those lures are past their prime." Madam Xu picked up a red paper from the table. "Are you content with your paper cutting skills?"

It was a complex question. One which had nothing to do with paper cutting and everything to do with my ambitions. I was certainly not content with being a prostitute. Most customers were repulsive, only three men were handsome enough to bring me physical release. Neither was I content with a servitude I found impossible to escape.

"No," I said.

"Good." Madam Xu crumpled the red paper in her hand

and dropped it to the floor. "I conduct business during the morning while the moonflowers sleep. By the time you girls lift your lazy heads from the pillow I've already made deals, purchased supplies, and acquired new slaves. Do you understand?" She pursed her thin bare lips.

I did.

The next morning, I woke early, lids and limbs heavy with exhaustion—my last customer had left just before dawn —donned a heavy robe and traipsed to Madam Xu's cabin. The rain, which had been no more than a heavy mist throughout the night, pelted the flower boat.

A sleepy-eyed Suyin answered the door.

Madam Xu, whose finger ran down a column of figures, didn't bother to look up. "Maybe I will tell you what I'm doing. Maybe I'll take you with me to Guangzhou. Maybe I won't."

"Much can be learned by being an attentive bystander," I said.

Madam Xu's mouth twitched. "Diplomacy will serve you well."

For the next ten days I watched Madam Xu. I watched her shuffle papers. Watched her barter with the rice supplier, fish seller, and the woman selling herbs for our *liangyao*. Watched her point out slubs in an inferior length of silk to the cloth dealer. Watched her inventory food supplies and strike a deal with the man bringing fresh water.

On the eleventh day, Madam Xu explained the curves and lines on the paper. I memorized the characters for rice, water, fish, and tea. The next day, Madam Xu showed me how to use the *suanpan*, a device for counting. A week later I accompanied her to the Guangzhou markets where she purchased two young girls, *baijiu*, and opium from an uncle.

"You have many uncles," I said one rainy afternoon while we drink chrysanthemum tea under a gazebo.

Madam Xu lifted the cup to her lips and slurped noisily. "Family makes good business partners. Even if the family is not blood. All the flower girls are my adopted daughters. When a man buys one of them, he becomes family. There is opportunity and benefit in acquiring a large family. Loyalty is best attained through *guanxi*, personal relationships."

I needed more than family. I needed to learn to read. Merchants cheated people who did not read. "Will you teach me to read and write?"

"No." Madam Xu set down her teacup.

"I'm a quick student." I pulled back my hair to show her my high ears, the sign of a fast learner. "I won't trouble you to repeat a lesson."

"Why would I teach a baby dragon to breathe fire on her own mother?"

She was right, of course. I changed the subject. "I have an idea for a new cutting, one more fitting for a flower boat."

"Ideas are fleeting. Like a leaf in the wind," said Madam Xu like a Manchu-robed literati dispensing great wisdom. "Show me when your idea has form."

The cutting took a week.

When I brought Madam Xu the finished creation she cackled with delight. "Make more."

So began my paper cuttings of men and women in sensual positions and carnal acts.

SEASONS PASSED. Many seasons. Too many to count.

Each morning, I rose early to assist Madam Xu with her business. I did not mention my desire to read.

"How is my baby dragon, today?" Madam Xu asked one morning when I covered a yawn.

I swallowed a frown. Men were described as being dragon-like. Not women. "I don't have dragon traits."

Madam Xu arched one thin painted eyebrow. "$\bar{A}i$, but you do. Your wood element is strong." She leaned back on the red lacquered chair and crossed her arms. "You have all the ferocity, arrogance, and ambition of the azure dragon. In a few years you went from a clumsy-footed slave to a nimble-footed moonflower who dreams of taking my place." She cocked her head, eyes twinkling with the belief I would fall into her trap.

I didn't.

I neither denied nor agreed. "One day you'll be weary and your eyes tired. You'll need a trusted friend to ease your workload."

Madam Xu shook her head. "You're a naïve dragon."

9

Year of the Metal Rooster
1801

Ten years passed. Spring. Summer. Winter. Fall. No man paid to make me his wife or concubine. It was Madam Xu's fault. I was overpriced. She needed me. Grew to depend on me. I was glad. Being a wealthy man's concubine was just another kind of servitude.

One early morning when the boat swayed more than usual, Madam Xu rushed into my compartment.

"Wake up, lazy dragon!" She tore the blanket from my body.

"What's wrong?" I rubbed my eyes and sniffed the air. "Is there a fire?"

Spilled cooking oil caused fires that leapt from boat to boat, destroying every home, shop, and flower boat in its path.

"The Red Flag fleet is coming!" Madam Xu was wild-eyed with panic. "Hurry!"

I followed behind as she ran to her office.

Madam Xu spread a tattered map on the desk. "The harbor is close, but not close enough to provide us any protection. The Red Flag are not usually this brazen but we can't take the chance. We'll move the flower boat—hide among the hundreds of others—just in case."

I rubbed my eyes, still heavy with fatigue. "What do the pirates want with a flower boat?"

"Women." Madam Xu's face pinched with exasperation at my thick-headedness. "They won't pay for the privilege either." Madam Xu paced her office. "Don't just stand there looking stupid. Don't you understand? They'll come late at night—hundreds of them—with swords and knives and they'll rape every girl on this boat, take the most beautiful for their wives, and make the others their slaves." Madam Xu spread her arms wide. "They'll take anything and everything they want. Then they'll burn the boat."

My fists balled. I didn't spend ten years kowtowing to Madam Xu to be a lowly pirate's wife. Or worse. Their slave! "They only strike at night?"

"Yes."

"Then we will make the flower boat invisible in the darkness."

"I'll lose business and a lot of money." With beads of sweat on her furrowed brow, Madam Xu flopped into the chair.

I gave her a fan. "It's too risky to keep your boat lit up like a thousand lanterns during the moon festival. The flower boat must be as dark and unassuming as a poor fisherman's."

Madam Xu swooshed the fan back and forth. "The girls will want to know why. If I tell them we're hiding from pirates—" She swooshed faster. "I don't want to even think about their panic." Madam Xu reached out and squeezed her cold fingers around my wrist. "You must tell the girls a convincing lie, Xianggu. One not arousing their suspicion. Do this, and I will teach you to read."

Evidently only a pirate raid was more frightening to Madam Xu than my knowing how to read. I patted the hand gripping mine. "Don't worry."

That morning, Madam Xu and I hired men to pull the flower boat into the floating throng of shops, homes, and fishing junks.

"Why did we move?" asked Winter Plum after I gathered the girls in the saloon.

"Madam Xu is getting old," I said. "Long ago, she made a promise to the Sea Goddess, Mazu, and now she wants to honor that promise."

The flower girls looked from one to the other, their brows knotted with disbelief. "What kind of promise?"

"The kind an old woman is shamed about not honoring." I made a show of looking over my shoulder as though worried Madam Xu lurked behind a drape. "She doesn't want us to work tonight. That's all I know."

"No work tonight?" Bright Pearl's nose crinkled. "She'll expect us to work double tomorrow."

"I've been here twelve years, and not once did Madam Xu ever close the business to pay homage to the goddess." One of the moonflowers crossed her arms.

"Is Madam Xu dying?" asked a sad-faced sunflower.

"Is she hiding from creditors?" asked another.

"No." Winter Plum's voice rose over the girls' muttering comments. "The worm whose hairy eggs I sucked last night told me the Red Flag are headed this way."

"Pirates!?" Bright Pearl clutched the moonflower beside her. "They'll rape us all!"

"Rape us and then murder us." Winter Plum pointed her long-tapered nail at me. "You lie to us, Xianggu."

A moonflower dropped to the ground and wrapped her arms around her legs. "Pirates murdered my father."

Winter Plum stepped in front of me. "They'll lock us in the hull and fuck us until we die of starvation." Her voice grew shriller every second. "Then they'll throw us overboard for fish bait."

I spoke with a calm authority I did not feel. "Madam Xu will protect us. This boat will disappear into the night and the pirates will pass us over."

"She doesn't care about us," screeched Bright Pearl. "She's only interested in protecting her own wrinkled neck."

"By saving her own neck she saves yours." I looked each girl in the eye. "If Madam Xu wants us to work triple the next day, we'll do it. Or would you prefer being raped by a hundred lowly pirates?"

Finally, they agreed to the scheme despite whispering their fears to one another.

In the pink-hued light of late afternoon, Madam Xu put us all to work. We removed the Heavenly Women banner, took down the red lanterns, unhooked the drapery, and moved the chairs and couches from the deck to the center saloon.

Madam Xu posted a lookout, the young son of a moon-flower, on the second story deck. All the flower girls hid in the saloon inside. Except for Madam Xu and me.

"The loss of a whole night's profits makes me ill." Madam Xu stared into the distance. "What will happen to our regular customers? I never sent word. They'll think I abandoned them." Madam Xu balled her fists. "I hope the pirates return to Vietnam or whatever stinking place they come from soon. Another night like this and I'll be as poor as that sad excuse for a boat next to us."

The night passed uneventfully. I fell asleep in a chair on

the upper deck and felt no guilt at all. When was the last time I didn't have a customer? I couldn't remember.

The following morning Madam Xu opened for business. Only a few customers showed up. Those earning moderate wages. Rich men and government officials always came at night. Lamp and moonlight were better suited for wicked pleasures.

Madam Xu pointed southward. "The Red Flag attacked a salt junk down river."

The small knot of worry in my stomach unraveled with relief. The pirates wanted salt. Not flower girls. "Maybe they'll leave today."

Madam Xu shook her head. "Not likely. They didn't come in from the Outer Ocean for a single cargo of salt." She rubbed her head. "Unless I hear otherwise, we stay hidden tonight as well."

Madam Xu's instinct proved sound. That night an orange glow lit up the sky. The pirates looted and burned their way up the river.

Madam Xu paced the upper deck, her fingers tight around the wine goblet. "Where is the imperial navy?! Nowhere! Why? Because they're afraid!" She shook her clenched fist. "Who would have guessed how the Tâyson rebellion changed everything."

"Tâyson rebellion?" The name wasn't familiar to me. Neither did I recall it being discussed by any of our customers.

Madam Xu rolled her eyes. "I suppose your family talked about rain not politics." She searched my face and found, as always, my hunger for knowledge. "The rebellion began thirty years ago with three brothers from the village of Tâyson. They formed a rebel force and captured Qui Nhon, the capital city of Vietnam. That was the first step to unite their warring country. There were many battles, wins and losses on both sides—Saigon was captured and recaptured seven times."

I wrinkled my nose. "What does a rebellion have to do with pirates?"

"Be patient, little dragon, the Great Qing is bigger than this harbor. Or the province of Guangdong. Or your little mind." Madam Xu tapped my head. "The money I make—the coin flowing into my boat—is all thanks to power-hungry government officials, self-serving county magistrates, and ambitious merchants clawing their way to the top. Learn this truth now and you'll make good decisions in the future."

"Politics matter." I gave her an obedient smile.

"More than you know." Madam Xu gulped down her wine. "After Quang Trung declared himself Emperor of Vietnam, the Tâyson rebels needed allies for protection and profiteering. They convinced a pirate name Pao to do their bidding. He proved to be such a cunning sea commander they made him a general of their navy. General Pao was savvy. He recruited out-of-work seamen, former soldiers, and poor fishermen. He gave them boats, weapons, and supplies. He even bought wives for the captains. General Pao gave them permission to plunder junks with cargos of silk and opium and silver with one condition—he wanted a small percent of their plunder. So, what had once been a few down-on-their-luck fishermen who stole enough to keep their family from starving became an organized military led by ambitious men."

"Did the emperor do anything to stop them?"

"Not enough." Madam Xu looked into her empty goblet. "The Tâyson gave birth to a litter of fearsome tigers and fed them well. Those tigers birthed more tigers. And now

Vietnam and the Guangdong and Fujian coasts are overrun with ferocious pirates with claws and fangs."

Madam Xu must be exaggerating. This was the first time pirates had come down the river this far. "How many pirates are there?"

"Who knows? Thousands and thousands." Madam Xu shrugged. "I *do* know the Red Flag fleet is the largest."

A few hours later as the sun struggled to peek through somber gray skies, a young eager-eyed boy delivered a message.

"This is from my patron." Madam Xu waved the paper. "The Red Flag were seen sailing back to the Outer Ocean." She pointed at me. "Find men to pull my boat back to its regular location." She rubbed her hands together. "Tonight, business as usual."

That afternoon all the flower girls hoisted the banner, hung drapery, arranged chairs and couches on the deck, and strung red lanterns. Even the musicians returned.

As the sun slunk behind the horizon the flower boat blossomed with color, songs, and enticement.

"I want every girl dancing on the decks," said Madam Xu.

And we did. Business was brisk. Madam Xu's face relaxed into her making-money smile, except when a few regular customers demanded a special deal for being denied their favorite girl for two nights.

I was in my compartment between customers when I heard the first shouts.

Not drunken yells. Not orgasmic bellows.

Fear prickled up my spine. I slipped on a silk robe and stuck my head through the doorway. The boat lurched and I tumbled to the floor.

More shouts. Loud gruff voices. High-pitched frantic cries.

I scrambled to my knees as a scream pierced the clamor. Then it stopped—cut off in mid wail.

Every hair on my body rose. Dread chilled my limbs.

Too many heavy feet. Too much clanking. Pottery crashed to the floor. Chairs smashed against the wall.

Every muscle in my body tensed. I couldn't move, my limbs paralyzed, my mind blank.

The boat rocked again and jolted me from this trance of dread. I pushed my hand against the wall, braced myself. Willed myself to remain calm. All this commotion could only mean one thing.

Pirates!

I swallowed my fear and poked my head into the corridor.

"Pirates," said a wide-eyed customer cowering in the doorway opposite mine. "They'll kill us all."

The door banged open.

A pirate charged in. One hand gripped a cutlass, his other hand behind his back. "Come out and show yourselves! Flower girls *and* customers!" Spittle flew from his thick lips.

Fear-white and weeping, the moonflowers appeared in the doorways. Most were naked.

Thick Lip leered. "This belong to you?" From behind his back he pulled a decapitated head and sent it rolling down the hall.

My limbs froze but my blood boiled.

The head was Madam Xu's.

10

Madam Xu's bloody head rolled past my door. The moonflowers screamed. My stomach heaved, bile rose in my throat.

Pirate after pirate charged through the door into the narrow corridor.

"Everybody out!" A pig-nosed pirate swiped his blade back and forth as though he slashed through over grown weeds.

A younger customer, a sword in hand, leapt from the compartment and aimed his shaking arm at Pig Nose. "I'll kill you all."

Thick Lip burst out laughing. "Stupid boy. You're outnumbered."

Pig Nose snorted with mirth. "Look at him. His cock is still hard."

Though the customer's knees shook, he twisted the blade and glared. "I'm not afraid."

Pig Nose barreled toward him, swiped his blade as he ran past. The customer's cock fell to the floor.

I clapped my hands over my ears as the moonflowers

screamed. I stared as every customer dropped to their knees while the cock-less man writhed like a snake on the floor.

"Bet this one's rich." Thick Lip's foot rested atop the head of our oldest customer, a grandfather of twenty. "There's more men and whores below. Bring them all on deck."

Ten pirates pounded down the hall.

"Help the others out," Thick Lip said before he aimed his evil smile at me.

The pirates 'helped' the customers by kicking the wind from their bellies, slamming their heads against the floor, and driving their foot into their testes. Dazed and in pain, the helpless customers didn't struggle as the pirates bound their ankles and wrists.

Bright Pearl and the other moonflowers looked to me, their red eyes imploring for help. I had none. What could I do? I was a weaponless whore.

As the pirates dragged the customers toward the deck, they ogled and made obscene gestures. We were next.

Horrific screams poured through the wooden floorboards. The pirates had begun raping the sunflowers below deck.

I squeezed closed my fists. I was powerless. Useless as a paper tiger. Rage filled me from toe to top.

Thick Lip jabbed his blade in the air. "I'm coming back for you next." He kicked Madam Xu's head toward me, then dragged his customer by the feet toward the door.

Madam Xu's vacant eyes stared up at me, her silent mouth begging. Little dragon, little dragon.

I studied Madam Xu's decapitated head with all the practical logic of my wood goat sign. Madam Xu's head was my only weapon. I bent down and picked it up.

The moonflowers gasped at my bravery. Or stupidity.

Thick Lip heard the air sucked from the corridor. He looked over his shoulder.

I lifted my chin. "The men you hold for ransom are nothing but worms to us. But Madam Xu," I set a kiss on her cold cheek, "was like our mother. We are moonflowers." I thrust out my bosom. "Her adopted daughters. Favored by her because of our skill."

"Whores have no skill." Thick Lip lobbed a yellow spit glob at us.

"*Cheap* whores have no skill." I stood tall. "But men pay dearly for our talents."

Thick Lip curled his lip into a sneer. "Not my men."

I swallowed the bile rising in my throat. "Save us for your leaders. Your generals."

Thick Lip blinked, as though confused by a clever thought. "Why?"

"You raided *this* flower boat because *we* are the best." I twirled Madam Xu's head. "And therefore, the richest men come *here*. We whores only add sweetness to your raid. Take us to your captain or general. He would want—demand the best. I don't think he'd want such loveliness damaged before he had his fun."

Thick Lip stalked toward me. "You've fucked thousands." He grabbed a fistful of my hair and wrenched me forward. "What's a few more?"

"We pleasure men of wealth and status." I winced, dropped Madam Xu's head as he yanked my hair. "Not commoners."

"Then fucking us adds variety." Thick Lip guffawed and, pulling me by my hair, headed back to the deck.

I clutched my scalp with both hands as the moonflowers stared wide-eyed with terror. "You dishonor your leader," I cried out, "by molesting the finest flower girls in Guangzhou. Do you really intend to deny your leaders the privilege of bedding the most enchanting prostitutes in Guangzhou? Make a gift of our undamaged bodies to your general."

Thick Lick stopped and turned to the moongirls cowering in their doorways. "Who's the best whore?"

"I am." Bright Pearl stepped into the corridor, shrugged off her robe, and hobbled toward him on her tiny lotus feet.

Thick Lip wrinkled his nose. "Your pride and lotus gait will not appeal to our squad boss." He gestured to his men. "Tie up all the whores. Naked. We'll make a gift to Zheng Yi." He stuck his face in mine. "When Zheng Yi is done having fun with his gifts, I get his leftovers. We'll have fun, won't we?"

I looked down. "Yes." I blinked back a tear. My poor negotiating skills only prolonged the inevitable.

The pirates bound our feet and wrists, then dragged us outside where they shoved us next to our shackled customers.

"What's your name?" asked Thick Lip to the oldest customer. "Who's your family? What's your profession?"

Another pirate wrote down the answer. While Thick Lip asked each man the same questions, other pirates ransacked the flower boat.

After an hour passed in this manner, a sampan came aside the flower boat. Thick Lip's demeanor changed in an instant, his superior smirk bending into a worried simper. He straightened up when a well-dressed man sprung like a tiger onto the flower boat.

11

"You were right, boss." Thick Lip swung his arm over his prisoners. "Lots of rich men on this flower boat."

The boss surveyed the deck with disdain, his dark scrutinizing eyes finally resting on the captives. His appearance surprised me. His clothes were clean and of superior quality. His beard trimmed to follow the line of his square jaw. He looked to be in his mid-thirties, with arrogant features that *almost* diminished his good looks.

The boss held out his hand.

Thick Lip snatched the list from the pirate who recorded their victims' assets and raced over to the boss.

The boss's finger ran down the list. "Adequate." He pushed the list back to Thick Lip.

Thick Lip aimed his sword tip at the flower girls. "These whores service only the wealthiest men."

The boss flicked his uninterested and impatient eyes over us. "Where is Madam Xu?"

Thick Lip swallowed. "Dead."

"Dead?!" The boss narrowed his deep-set eyes. "Which useless idiot killed her?"

"I…" Thick Lip winced, his whole body shrunk in on itself as though he expected a blow. "I'm not sure."

"How do you propose we find out where she hides the silver?" His nostrils flaring, the boss shouted, "Extra silver to the man who tells me who killed Madam Xu."

The pirates swiveled their heads back and forth looking for Madam Xu's killer. Except for one.

"I did." A boy threw himself at the boss's feet. "I thought she was an old whore. I didn't know."

The boss growled something under his breath. "Your stupidity cost you your share. And you will bail water until I think you have found your brains."

"Yes, boss." The boy tapped his head on the deck as he kowtowed.

"Boss!" Bright Pearl, tied up beside me, flicked me a devious smile. "Xianggu knows where Madam Xu keeps the silver." It was her customer voice, as sticky sweet as a rice cake.

My stomach lurched. "What are you doing?" I hissed under my breath. Was she trying to get me killed?

The boss shifted his attention. "Who's Xianggu?"

Bright Pearl sat up tall. "Xianggu is Madam Xu's favorite. She knows all her secrets."

"Where is she?" The boss folded his arms.

If eyes were daggers my glare would have pierced Bright Pearl's evil heart. "I'm here." My voice did not quiver too much.

The boss strode forward, looked down his nose at me. "Where's the silver?"

"Where is easy. It's the *how* that I need to show you."

The boss stared at my big peasant feet and stifled what *almost* looked like a smile. He thrust the cutlass in front of my face. "Take me there and walk slowly on those big feet,

Xianggu." He untied my ankles. "Don't jump overboard either because I'll jump in after you."

I tilted my head away from the blade and batted my eyes at him. "You'd save a flower girl from drowning?"

He wrinkled his nose. "Only if she knows where the silver is." He wrapped strong rough hands around my arm to hoist me up. "Lead the way."

I walked to Madam Xu's office, wary of his blade tip only inches from my back. I needed a plan. One where I didn't end up raped or dead.

I walked through the open door and gasped. Chairs were scattered. The bed flipped. Vases, porcelain, statues, clothes, pillows, and bedding gone. Papers strewn across the floor. Only the desk bolted to the floor remained upright.

"Don't do anything foolish." His arm snugged around me, his cutlass against my throat.

"My wrists are tied. I'm a prostitute not a magician." I used my customer voice, soft and meek.

"Where's the silver?"

I recalled Madam Xu's advice. Always deal with the *real* boss in any business venture. I hoped the same was true for captive situations. "Are you the Red Flag chieftain?"

The boss lowered the blade to my heart. "I don't care for your stalling tactics. Show me where Madam Xu hides the silver."

I let my body go slack, as though relieved, and made my pitch. "Before my father sold me, I was poor. Poor but free. I've been a flower girl—a slave—for ten years."

"One more word and I'll cut you." The boss's arousal pressed into my back. His mind was on Madam's Xu's silver, but evidently his body found a naked flower girl equally enticing.

"I'll show you where she keeps her silver." The next words rushed out. "But only if you grant my freedom."

The boss spun me about and stared. "I'll slit your pretty white throat. No exceptions. No deals."

There's *always* a deal to be made. Know what the other person wants. *Really* wants. Madam Xu was a first-rate businesswoman. I learned all her lessons.

I smiled coyly and arched my back to give him a better view of my breasts. "Why kill something you want so much?" I wiggled into his hard cock.

"You talk too much." He touched the blade to my breast.

I looked down at my blade-covered nipple. One wrong move… One misspoken word…. "What's your name?"

"Zheng Yi." His breath was ragged, smitten by lust. "Where's the silver?"

I lifted my bound wrists. "Like I told you, where is easy. How is a different matter."

Zheng Yi grunted as though not surprised. "A puzzle box?"

"Yes." I wiggled my arms. "Untie my wrists and I'll retrieve Madam Xu's stash."

Zheng Yi gave me a hard look, decided I was trustworthy, or at least not a threat, and untied my wrists.

I expressed gratitude by brushing my naked breast against his hand.

Zheng Yi jerked away. "Stop your whore games." He shoved me forward. "The silver."

He was a tough customer. Not easily influenced by a flower girl's charms.

I walked to Madam Xu's desk with an exaggerated sway, then rounded the desk to the front. "Here." I crouched down and ran my hand slowly over the carved desk leg like it was a man's *yīnjīng*.

Zheng Yi followed my every movement, his eyes bright with wariness and lust.

"Mmmm." I made pleasure sounds, as though disengaging the desk's hidden lever brought me sexual satisfaction.

Zheng Yi stomped forward, his cutlass poised for trickery.

I looked up at him, happy to see his eyes were on me and not the desk. "Like opening a woman's pleasure gate. A squeeze here, a twist there, three turns."

A drawer sprung open. Zheng Yi grunted.

I removed the tray of silver, *tael*, and Spanish dollars, and picked up a small satchel containing jade and amber cabochons. I poured the gemstones into my palm. "These two," I pointed to the largest stones, "are recently acquired, a rich man's deposit to buy me." I hoped this lie proved my worth. "He was supposed to buy me tomorrow and make me his third wife." I set the stones in Zheng Yi's hand. "Thank you. Had you not raided this boat, I would have had to endure another kind of servitude." I squeezed out a tear. "He's such an awful man. Ugly, fat, and cruel."

"This is the deposit?" Zheng Yi, his voice barbed with amazement, closed his fingers around the gems. "What was your total price?"

I told him. The amount was excessive enough to pique his interest in my sexual skills.

Zheng Yi's eyes roamed up and down my body. "What do you do that other women don't?"

"I'll show you." I had one chance to change my fate.

12

Seducing a man was easy. Convincing a ruthless pirate leader not to rape and kill you required another kind of seduction.

I drew a light finger down his arm. "Keep hold of the blade. It will add to our pleasure."

Zheng Yi raised the cutlass between us, his gaze following my fingers as they trailed over his hand and up the blade.

"This blade is part of you," I said. "You command its rise, control its course, and wield power with every thrust." I pressed the flat side against my nipple. "A man who knows the art of dominance and practices such control makes an excellent lover." I replaced the blade with his forefinger, leaned into him and nibbled his bottom lip. "My weapon is much like your own." I nudged his blade-holding hand downward. "I control *your* rise, *your* course, and *your* thrust. Cold steel meets soft warmth." I rubbed his hand against me. "Permit me to show you how a flower girl duels."

Zheng Yi moaned a reply.

He was accustomed to less talented women. He

succumbed with ease. I drew him to the threshold of ultimate pleasure only to prolong his fireworks. I built up his urge again and again while I whispered about his prowess. As we writhed together, my body, too familiar with fat old men, delighted in this handsome man with muscled limbs and the strength of a tiger.

Not content to be merely serviced, Zheng Yi was attentive, teased me with fingers and tongue, this duel of ours becoming a fleshly battle to prove erotic skill. When I dared not delay his gratification any longer his fireworks exploded with a roar. My own body joined and rippled with release.

Zheng Yi wiped sweat from his brow. "I'm taking you with me."

"As slave or concubine?" I said as his salty release dripped down my thigh.

Zheng Yi rose from the bed and put on his clothes. "Neither. Both." He shrugged. "You'll make my tea but if my thirst is not slaked, you'll be assigned another duty." His lips curved into a shape that was neither smile nor sneer. "But first you'll burn the boat that made you a slave." He unwound his turban and tossed it at me.

I thought it odd he wanted me covered but I said nothing as I wound the fabric around my hips and breasts.

"Nice." He laughed, picked up the box of silver and other valuables, and led me outside.

I was surprised to find that everyone—pirates, flower girls, and customers—were gone. Had we fucked that long?

"Where is everyone?" And every thing? The deck was stripped bare of all drapery and furnishings. Bright Pearl, Winter Plum, Suyin—flower girls and slaves were gone!

"The skipper is efficient." Zheng Yi lit a torch, passed it to me. "The hostages are already on his ship."

A knot coiled in my stomach. "What about the flower girls?"

"The same." Zheng Yi frowned. "You ask too many questions." He went to the edge of the deck where a pirate waited in a sampan.

The pirate handed him a container. Zheng Yi uncorked it and trickled out the liquid as he walked back and forth across the deck.

"Do it." He gestured to the torch in my hand. "We need to be gone before sunrise."

I threw the torch to the other side of the deck where the flame flared in the liquid before slithering like a fire dragon across the deck.

Zheng Yi was already in the sampan when I turned around. He extended his arm, his rough warm hand helping me me into the gently rocking sampan.

The rower picked up the oars and we glided away. From my seat beside Zheng Yi, I watched the Heavenly Women banner sizzle into nothingness. Ten years of my life was gone, reduced to flame and ash. Swirling sparks all that was left of my previous ambitions.

13

"Where are we going?" It was a sincere question, a reasonable concern.

"To another life, flower girl." Zheng Yi understood my question's complexity.

The flower boat flamed, bright flares licking the predawn sky. My heart lurched even as my soul danced. My fingers tightened around a rail worn smooth by salted time. From farmer to slave to flower girl to....

My future was as dark as the sky.

The sampan wended its way past floating homes, ornate ferries, fishing junks, and cargo boats as we moved ever closer to an enormous whale-shaped ship that sat high in the water. The foredeck resembled a whale's head. The stern, fluttering with streamers, was painted with an elaborate mural of sea dragons and sea creatures.

A thousand questions came to mind but did not pass my lips. I didn't want to annoy Zheng Yi. He might throw me into the bay.

A deckhand tossed a rope ladder with wooden slats over

the side of the great ship, and I climbed up—glad for my unbound feet—after the barefoot Zheng Yi.

Deckhands moved busily about a space packed with wooden barrels, bamboo crates, rattan baskets, water tanks, and mysterious contraptions. Rope was everywhere. Rope connected to rigging. Rope wound in a pile. Rope coiled around two large teak windlasses. Rope netting jumbled in a pile. Except for a few men sleeping against a mast or crate, each crewmember engaged in some task.

Dawn came and with it pink-tinged clouds that glowed against an indigo sky. The river beyond changed from an inky black to a lustrous purple. Deckhands gathered around a large rotating device and, hand over hand, wrapped around its spikes. In unison they hoisted the mainsail.

"The mast weighs several tons." Zheng Yi, noting my wide-eyed stare, pointed to the foreword sail. "A thousand yards of matting."

A thousand yards!?

Zheng Yi's boat was not the only one setting sail. Many boats of all sizes—none as large as this one—prepared to make way. Like a field of flowers opening their petals to greet the sun, more than thirty sails unfurled against a lily-colored sky.

"It's beautiful." My hands touched my cheeks.

"Beautiful?" Zheng Yi cocked his head.

"How did the others know to hoist their sails at the same time?" I could not take my eyes from the blossoming field of sails.

"When my ship hoists sail it's a signal to the others. The headman on each boat go where and when I command."

Ah, so he *was* the real boss. "That's another kind of beauty." I glanced to the sky, smiled as the first rays of light shone on a red triangle banner with white scalloped edges.

Zheng Yi bumped his shoulder into mine. "Having power is both beautiful and ugly."

My heart skipped a beat. He knew what I meant! I snuck a quick peek at him, my pulse quickening for the first time over a man.

"I wouldn't know," I said.

The crisp morning breeze blew through my hair as the ship sluiced through the river.

Zheng Yi nudged me again. "Your talents did not satisfy, flower girl. I'm hungry again."

I turned to him. "I'm not a flower girl any more. I belong to you. And your hunger is now my own."

One corner of Zheng Yi's mouth curled upward in that puzzling half smile half sneer. "Come with me."

I followed him aft, climbed two ladders to an upper deck, and trailed him through a doorway. Despite the ship's crude exterior, Zheng Yi's cabin was lavish. Lanterns of silk, paper, and horn were suspended from the ceiling; the walls adorned with paintings of landscapes, flowers, and zodiac creatures. Above an ornate desk, three windows of crushed oyster shells filtered the early morning light. On the opposite side, Zheng Yi's berth was draped in silk damask and topped with thick pillows. On a table nearby stood an altar for Mazu, Venerable Mother of the Sea. Incense smoke wafted from its silver censer.

"Boss." An old man burning paper money before the altar bowed his head. "I'll see to the other gods in the saloon." He scurried away.

"Tea," said Zheng Yi to a young boy outside the door. He turned to me and pointed to an elegantly carved chair. "Sit."

I sat quietly, hands clasped in my lap until a crewmember arrived with Madam Xu's box of valuables. Zheng Yi exchanged a few hushed words with the man before dismissing him.

"Tell me, Xianggu, how did you earn Madam Xu's trust?" Zheng Yi said after the boy brought our tea.

"I don't know." I shrugged. "She must have found some worthy trait in me."

Zheng Yi scowled. "I don't value false humility."

I sipped the tea. It was too hot, the leaves scalded. I looked into Zheng Yi's brown eyes and tried to decide if it was worth the gamble to tell the truth. "I wasn't content being a flower girl. I wanted to be like Madam Xu—to have my own flower boat—to find, like she did, a wealthy patron to partner with. I'm ambitious. While the other girls slept through the morning, I learned the flower boat business. I went with Madam Xu on her trips to Guangzhou to buy slaves and supplies. I learned how to bargain for the best price and discuss business with men." I paused, afraid of appearing too arrogant.

Surprised interest flickered across Zheng Yi's face. "Go on."

"I'm a hard worker, a quick learner. I want…" I looked away. "Wealth." It was the faintest whisper.

Zheng Yi blinked, his face unreadable. After a few long minutes staring at me, he quaffed his steaming tea, stood, and pulled me up into his arms. His mouth was greedy, his need strong. "Show me more of your tricks."

I had many men but none like Zheng Yi. His hands were rough, grabbed at the soft flesh of my thighs and yet his fingers slid in and out of my warmth with such gentleness I gasped with delight. His kisses were demanding and fierce. Or teasing and soft. Each new position and each new service I offered was met with lusty approval. He slowed his pace when I thought he would quicken it, sped up when I least expected. He grinned at me when my own fireworks exploded.

"Forgive my ignorance." I nestled next to him. "Are you the general of the Red Flag fleet?"

"No." Zheng Yi rolled to his side, propped his head on his hand. "I'm the squad boss who commands the biggest squadron in the fleet."

I drew my long nail over his nose. "How many boats make a squadron?"

He wrinkled his nose, tried to bite my finger. "You ask too many questions."

"Asking questions made me the best flower girl." I wrapped my hand around his *yīnjīng*, which to my amazement grew stiff and long again. "How does one man command so many boats?"

"Fear. Respect." His fingers twiddled my nipples. "Squad bosses and skippers aren't lowly fishermen. Many of us were once Tâyson naval officers."

"Madam Xu told me about the rebellion."

Zheng Yi grunted. "An unproven squad boss may command as few as ten junks, an expert leader as many as forty. More boats, more prestige."

"What rank is beneath you?" My finger danced up and down his shaft.

"Skippers." Zheng Yi's attention roved back and forth from his cock to my breasts. "They command several boats within a squad. Under him, the headman. My ship has several headmen—chief, deputy, and vanguard."

"And beneath that?" I wiggled downward and flicked my tongue across his thigh.

"Helmsmen. Two per boat." Zheng Yi exhaled a long happy breath. "Below that, those in charge of manning cannons and throwing anchors. Deckhands handle many duties. The lowest are slaves and captives."

"The highest paid flower girls had to prove their worth. Is it the same with pirates?" I lapped his length from bow to stern.

"Yes, many times and in many ways." Zheng Yi set his hand on the back of my head while I played his flute. It did not take long. My technique had him thrusting his hips in no time.

"How do you become a chieftain of the fleet?" I licked his sticky release from my lips.

Zheng Yi snorted, either from laughter or astonishment at my question. "Cousin Qi would have to die. After that, the squad bosses and I would compete for control."

"The chieftain is your cousin? Surely he's as powerful as a government official."

"Cousin Qi is *more* powerful than any Mandarin official." Zheng Yi sat up, rolled off the berth. "He picked up his unwound turban and scowled. "Let's see if the headman's wife has more suitable clothing."

"NO," grunted Zheng Yi as I walk towards him in borrowed blue cotton pants and top. "Those clothes are too plain for such a beautiful woman." He gestured to the horizon. "Look."

My breath caught in my throat. A thousand *li* of blue in every direction, the sapphire sea stretched into an azure sky. The wide-open space soothed my spirit. The wind blew away my past. The salty spray soaked into my skin and freshened my ambitions. I was born anew, buoyant with anticipation for a new future.

"Where are we going?" I gathered my hair at the nape of my neck and began to braid it.

"Donghai Island. My birthplace and family home." Zheng Yi cast a critical gaze about the ship.

"A trip to honor your ancestors?" I asked, hoping he might reveal more about his past.

"No," he chuckled and returned his attention to me. "To honor the business of piracy." He wrapped my braid around his finger and tugged. "The southwest winds are favorable at this time; the visit will be brief. But long enough for you to learn to swim." He nuzzled my neck. "You claimed you were a fast learner. Now you'll have to prove it."

My stomach tightened. "How…how do you know I can't swim?"

"On the flower boat I warned you not to escape by jumping overboard. You asked if I would save you from drowning." Zheng Yi pulled on my braid again, our faces inches apart. "Pirates are good swimmers." With the third tug our lips met for a lusty kiss. "You're useless to me if you can't swim."

All my hopes crumbled like a stale walnut cookie. I needed more than just sexual skills to please him. "Well, you're useless to me if you don't satisfy my hunger to learn new things. Like learning about you, which I think, begins with learning about this boat."

Zheng Yi's mouth slipped into that half sneer half grin. "I'm a simple man, this ship is far more complex."

14

By the time the lookout sighted Donghai Island I was familiar with both Zheng Yi's temperament and the ship's layout.

Man and boat were much the same. The iron-like strength of the main mast matched Zheng Yi's unyielding and strong will. The watertight camphor and pine bulkheads were as impenetrable as Zheng Yi's command, his leadership sealed by experience as a former Tâyson rebel leader. The pirates' tiny sleeping compartments on the lower deck corresponded to the size of Zheng Yi's intolerance for laziness and disrespect. Like the giant retractable rudder that controlled the ship's course, so too did Zheng Yi guide me towards a new direction. His squad boss face was as rough and crude as his ship's exterior. His private face—expressive and handsome—much like the lavishly appointed saloon and cabin. His smile-sneer, I decided, was meant to confuse and intimidate.

Zheng Yi was the first man I respected. The first man who made my stomach flutter.

Like today, when he strode into the saloon where Golden

Moon, the headman's wife, taught me how to mend a broken teacup with rivets.

"Donghai Island is just ahead." Zheng Yi examined the teacup's seam. "Excellent. Do you enjoy this sort of work?"

"It's a satisfying way to pass a few hours, although I much rather the helmsman teaches me how to steer."

Golden Moon covered a giggle with her hand.

"That's a man's job." Zheng Yi's mouth scowled but his eyes flashed with pleasure. He set down the teacup, beckoned me to follow, strode out the door, and to the ship's bow. "How long has it been since you set your feet on land?" He gestured to the strip of land in the distance.

"I went with Madam Xu into port to conduct business."

"I'm not talking about the odor and noise of a thousand merchants. How long since you felt sand between your toes, smelled fresh flowers, rested against a tree, and slept on solid ground?" His brow lifted, expectant.

"I don't remember." Memories of fragrant orange blossoms, tall grass, bird songs, insect hums, and comforting stillness rushed into the locked-up place in my heart. I squeezed shut my eyes, willed myself not to cry.

Zheng Yi's thick brows knotted with concern. "Do you miss the life stolen from you?"

My spine rippled with fear. Was Zheng Yi's plan to sell me to someone on the island? I took a ragged breath and met his incomprehensible gaze. Perhaps this was his way of telling me he was getting rid of me. How foolish to think I had any value other than being his concubine. And although my flower girl skills included fawning over a man enough to make him a repeat customer, I knew this was no whore's game.

My life rested in Zheng Yi's hands. His rough pirate hands. He was nothing like the queue-wearing, soft-bodied, rich men I entertained with flattery and false sighs. If Zheng Yi had reason to believe I playacted, that my respect for him was false, he would kill me. My answer must be true, leave no room for misinterpretation, and yet excite and delight him.

"Do I miss my former life?" I twisted my lips. "I don't miss the poverty. If Father hadn't sold me I would be married to another poor farmer and birthed nine children by now. I don't miss the flower boat either, even if I did wear silk. The work was dull and too boring for my curious mind." I touched his hand, which rested on the rail. "For ten years I have merely existed. All joy gone. Until you came. The sea. Your ship. You. I'm alive. You've made my soul sing." I looked out at the sliver of land. "I don't know your intentions. Whether you want to sell me or kill me, but it doesn't matter. You and your ship, for some reason, make me happy. And a little bit of happiness is better than none at all. I thank you, Zheng Yi."

Zheng Yi pushed me against the bulwark, his lust evident, and wrapped me in his arms. "I won't sell you, Xianggu. You're not mine to sell."

My stomach lurched with fear. "What!? Am I the chieftain's property? Your Uncle Qi?"

Zheng Yi's mouth dropped open. "No. No. You're mine. Not as a slave but..." He rubbed his grizzled cheek against mine. "You delight me in ways I can't explain."

My heart leapt. I delighted him! In unexplainable ways! Which meant he liked *me*, not just my flower girl skills. "Is your wife on Donghai?" I kept my voice light. How could he *not* have a wife? Or several.

Zheng Yi rubbed his chin. "Wives are expensive and dull."

"Why do you think the flower boats are always so busy?" My mischievous grin made Zheng Yi laugh.

A few hours later, the ship made anchor. Zheng Yi jumped from the sampan that took us into the lagoon and splashed through the turquoise water up to his knees.

I followed his lead and trailed after him up the wide beach, the white sand soft between my toes. I gulped in the fragrance of earth, bamboo, and azaleas. It was a welcome change from burning incense, unwashed bodies, and brine.

Zheng Yi's village was a safe haven for the fleet. Men kept a wife or two there, careened and repaired their boats, and met with chieftains and other squad bosses.

"My house." He pointed to a large unassuming wood structure.

Waiting at the door stood his sharp-eyed paternal grandmother and lizard-faced aunt.

"We have your favorite Vietnamese rice and sweet bean cakes." Grandmother cast a wrinkled and withering look at me.

Zheng Yi nodded, pleased, and strode like a tiger into the house. He disappeared into a room, leaving Grandmother and Aunt to circle around me as though I was a sow for sale.

"Why does my favorite grandson bring home this whore?" Grandmother asked Aunt.

Aunt shrugged. "She doesn't look as stupid as the others."

Grandmother stared at my coarse smock and too-big pants, then walked into a nearby room.

"Here." She came back out and threw an old silk robe at me.

"Zheng Yi won't like this." I folded the fabric with care and set it on a black lacquered table inset with ivory.

Aunt's caterpillar eyebrows shot up. "He likes only the dirty space between your legs."

I had done business with some of the nastiest merchants in Guangdong. I knew exactly how to deal with these women.

"I was the highest paid flower girl on the finest flower boat in Guangzhou." I lifted my chin, stared down my nose at them. "I demand clothes worthy of Zheng Yi to remove."

"You demand, do you?" Grandmother spit on the floor. "You'll have to earn them."

"Fine." I glided from the room like an empress and went in search of Zheng Yi. I found him drinking tea with an old man in the courtyard.

Zheng Yi frowned. "They don't have suitable clothes for you?"

"They do." I smiled brightly. Wives complained about in-laws. Not easily discarded concubines. "Do you have red paper and a small knife?"

Zheng Yi sent a servant, who I followed back into the house. Once those items were in hand, I sat at the table in the room where Grandmother and Aunt discussed my ugly features. I remained silent and began cutting a familiar design, two cranes in the water among flowers. Grandmother sat beside me, grunting occasionally in approval.

"What else may I make for you?" I pushed the perfect picture across the table.

Grandmother examined my artwork, held it close to her eyes. Finally, she smiled, a genuine smile. "Knife skill like this will make you a dangerous sea bandit. You could carve out someone's heart with precision. Does my grandson know about this?" She flicked the paper.

"No."

"Make more." Grandmother stood, shuffled toward a large trunk, and rummaged through the contents.

I did. Each as perfect as the one before. Grandmother and Aunt were impressed.

Hours later, after bathing and washing my hair, Grandmother gave me a silk *hanfu* embroidered with cranes, lilies, and peonies.

Zheng Yi's stopped eating, his chopsticks poised over the bowl when I walked into the kitchen.

Grandmother placed five paper cuttings on the table. "Your whore made these."

"Her name is Xianggu. She's not my whore." Zheng Yi flipped through the cuttings, his brows raised with amazement. "Beautiful." His soft eyes told me everything. He had fallen in love with me.

The following morning, he took me to a small crescent-shaped cove.

"Pirates must know how to swim." He stripped off his robe and waded in.

I discarded my silk *hanfu*. "I'm a wood goat. Wood floats." I waded up to my knees. "I hope."

"I'm a wood rooster. We're a good match." He took my hand and led me deeper.

I wrapped my arms around his neck when my feet no longer touched bottom.

Zheng Yi was a good teacher. I learned to tread water in no time. Our first lesson concluded with my legs around his hips and double fireworks.

Swim lessons were twice a day. Each lesson ended with pleasurable release.

"Swimming naked is easy," Zheng Yi said on the third day, "but not likely to happen. You must learn to swim in clothes."

Zheng Yi insisted I swim in pants and shirt. I practiced in a silk dress—easy enough when I lifted it to my waist and tied the fabric into a knot. Next, I swam holding a cutlass. Then I swam holding a box. For the final test of my ability, one of the village children climbed on my back and I swam across the lagoon.

"You passed," said Zheng Yi as the little boy ran back up the beach to his mother.

"Why don't I have to swim with two children on my back?" I asked.

"Because the sons you give me will know how to swim before they walk." Grinning, he dove in and dragged me under. Together we emerged from the water laughing, his cock deep inside me.

That night, I tossed and turned.

"What's wrong?" Zheng Yi wrapped me in his arms.

"The bed is too still." Could it be I preferred a boat's soothing sway to unmoving land?

Zheng Yi rolled on top of me. "Then let me rock you."

15

"**A** pirate must know how to fight." Zheng Yi put a *dao* in my hand.

I wrapped my fingers around the hilt, felt the blade's weight. "I can't kill."

Zheng Yi's brows lifted. "I was told you held up Madam Xu's head and demanded special treatment while all the flower girls screamed in terror. Courage like that is courage enough to kill." He held his blade over his shoulder. "This is the ready stance."

Despite my attempts to mirror his agile movements I struggled with this two-handed weapon, and when I tripped over my feet Zheng Yi laughed until tears rolled down his cheeks.

The next lesson was with a saber.

"It's not a club." Zheng Yi cupped his hand over mine. "You control the blade with your fingertips—like a man, yes? Good. Squeeze, release, squeeze, release. See how the blade moves? Use gravity to help swing."

It was the fourteen-foot long bamboo spear I eventually excelled at. My first throw did not reach the target by half.

The second landed on the ground at the target's base. My third impaled the target's outer circle. The spear, however, was a long-range weapon. Zheng Yi insisted I practice with weapons used in close combat.

I was practicing with the spear one sultry afternoon when Cousin Qi paid a visit. The Red Flag chieftain was a robust man with miss-nothing eyes and braided hair. He wore the proud demeanor of a man comfortable with power.

"We need to talk." Cousin Qi's confident tone was that of a man who never had to say anything twice. "Tell your wife to put down her bamboo spear and bring us tea."

"She's not my wife." Zheng Yi scratched his neck, shifted his weight, suddenly uncomfortable.

Cousin Qi clasped his hands behind his back and rocked on his heels. "Why not? She has excellent aim. How does she handle a blade?"

Zheng Yi's eyes met mine before replying. "Like an artist."

I pressed my lips together to keep from laughing. The only skill I had was with small paper-cutting knives.

I went to get the tea. When I returned with the tea tray, both Cousin Qi and Zheng Yi were hunched over a map.

"Dianbai is a ripe peach waiting to be plucked." Cousin Qi slurped his tea. "It has stores of salt and supplies. It's ours for the taking." He tapped the map. "These walls are crumbling—haven't been fortified for many years."

Zheng Yi rubbed his chin. "What about the magistrate?"

"Hung Yuyi? Appointed a few months ago. Young and incompetent. Too busy whoring and playing mmahjong to assess the town's weaknesses," said Cousin Qi. "The time is now." He set down the teacup and folded his arms while Zheng Yi, his brows knotted together, studied the map.

"Are these forts still manned?" Zheng Yi's finger skipped along the map.

"My spies say less than a hundred. And only eight war boats guard their harbor."

"Bold." Zheng Yi flashed his sneer-smile. "But worth the risk." He glanced over his shoulder at me, one brow lifted. "Does this interest you?"

"I had no idea so much planning went into a raid." I couldn't take my eyes from the map.

"Strategy is all." Zheng Yi turned to Cousin Qi. "What are Dianbai's other weaknesses?"

"This part is badly damaged." Cousin Qi flicked his thick finger on a bay-facing defensive wall. "One cannon blast will crumble it."

Zheng Yi rubbed his chin. "We'll need at least a hundred boats to take the city. I have forty."

"Good." A wide satisfied smile crossed Cousin Qi's sun-wrinkled face. "Wushi Er promised three Blue Flag squads."

"Is that so?" Zheng Yi shook his head and laughed. "For a defrocked scholar he's a wily old pirate." He leaned forward, his tone suddenly serious. "When's the raid?"

"September twenty-second—the first day of the Mid-Autumn festival."

I gasped, and Cousin Qi, who had not looked at me since I returned with the tea, glowered at my impudence.

"My plan doesn't meet with your womanly approval?" Sarcasm dripped from his snarling lips.

I had serviced many men like Cousin Qi, arrogant merchants who had little use for women beyond sex and childbirth. I knew how to deal with those men. "It's brilliant." This was the truth. "Everyone will be gorging on moon cakes and wine, or busy making offerings at the temples. They'll be totally unprepared."

Cousin Qi tilted his head, his forehead furrowed, his eyes critical. "Zheng Yi took you from a flower boat a few weeks ago. Today," his hand flapped to the empty teacups, "you serve the most powerful sea bandits in the South Seas. Why do you imagine a whore's opinion matters to me?"

I was not intimidated by the chieftain's demeaning question. I kneeled in front of Cousin Qi, my head bowed in respect. "My opinion doesn't matter because you don't know my worth...yet. I was more than the best whore of the best flower boat in Guangdong, I was Madam Xu's..." I searched for the right word. "Apprentice. I learned the flower boat business. But that's not important." I stole a glance at him. "What's important is that if I, an ignorant whore, find your plan commendable, your crews will be equally impressed. Even this whore," I touched my breast, "knows enough to understand your bold plan needs the full support of its crews to be successful. So, though my single humble opinion is without merit, if you consider it as representative of your crew, then it is invaluable."

Cousin Qi, chieftain of the Red Flag sat back in his chair and grinned. "Yi, marry this one."

A TRADITIONAL MARRIAGE ceremony was impossible. No fortuneteller or matchmaker had decided our compatibility. My parents were not present. There was no wedding procession, no formal welcome and bowing. Fortunately, Zheng Yi declared the bride price paid because I had unlocked Madam Xu's box of silver.

We were not without guests, however. Villagers, friends, pirate chieftains, and even several jealous-faced unmarried young women came to our wedding.

I met Zheng Yi's brother, San—who sailed with Wushi Er—his sister Hesheng, and the chieftains of the Green and Black Flags. Everybody seemed to be related to someone else in a thousand different ways.

After decorating Zheng Yi's home with paper cuttings of *shuāngxǐ,* the double happiness symbol, I dressed in a long red two-piece *gua* embroidered with purple flowers.

With a red sash draped over his chest, Zheng Yi and I paid respects to the Goddess of the Sea and to each other.

Xianggu the flower girl was now Zheng Yi Sao, wife of Zheng Yi. I was almost twenty-six-years-old.

Afterwards, we feasted on fish and rice and vegetables and pastries. And, of course, I ate red dates, peanuts, dragon eye fruit, and melon seeds for fertility. It was while I peeled the outer skin of the dragon eye fruit that I noticed Guo Podai, the Black Flag chieftain and his unnerving stare.

"Guo Podai keeps staring," I whispered to Zheng Yi. "Is he a relative?"

"My adopted son," Zheng Yi beamed. "I kidnapped him during a raid years ago. I made him my protégé when I discovered he could read and write. He's smart. He told me piracy paid much better than fishing. I adopted him after he proved his worth."

"You *gave* him his own fleet?" That would be like Madam Xu giving me a flower boat because I was the best flower girl. There had to be more to this story of how Guo Podai rose through the ranks.

"Like I said, he's smart." Zheng Yi tapped his temple. "He has ninety boats and almost eight thousand men now."

As though knowing we talked about him, Guo Podai approached our table. Although his large forehead and humped nose were signs of a keen intellect, his full lips, square jaw, and liquid brown eyes made him look more like a poet than a pirate.

"*Gong xi.*" Guo Podai offered congratulations. "Father, it's an honor to attend your wedding. I wish you a good match for a hundred years." His eyes slid toward me and flickered with something beyond politeness. He cleared his throat, then returned his attention to Zheng Yi. "Perhaps tomorrow we can discuss business. I need your advice concerning a delicate ransom exchange."

"Of course." Zheng Yi beckoned him closer and lowered his voice. "Have you changed your mind about the Dianbai raid?"

Guo Podai pressed his lips together regretfully. "The date, unfortunately, prevents my joining your ambitious venture. But I'm confident that by the time my ransom business is over, they'll be singing songs of your successful raid." He reached into his robe and withdrew a red-wrapped gift, which he presented with both hands. "A token of my devotion."

Zheng Yi unwrapped the paper and lifted out a jade vase, a dragon and phoenix carved around its graceful shape.

"It's beautiful." I ran my fingers along its surface.

"From the time of the Ming." Guo Podai smiled tightly. "And although I agree it shows artistry, it doesn't compare to your beauty." With that, Guo Podai uttered another wedding wish and left.

"Bao has ninety boats and almost eight thousand men but no wife. The man needs a wife," said Zheng Yi.

I agreed.

That night after the guests had departed, and after I made tender love to my husband, I watched the slow rise and fall of his chest while he slept.

Because of him I was no longer a prostitute. That life vanished like a single raindrop on a sunny day. Today was the first day as a wife of a pirate. AA shiver ran through my limbs, part excitement, part anxiety.

What did I know about pirates and their wicked world of thievery? Very little. I did not even know what happened to the kidnapped flower girls or what boat Thick Lip sailed on.

I did, however, know pirates scorned the morals of respectable people. And yet I knew from experience that the line between villainy and respectability was thinner than silk thread.

Was my father wicked for selling me? Was Madam Xu a villain for earning a living? Were fleet chieftains criminals for refusing to remain poor? The gods, it seemed, gave us few choices. Like me. Like Madam Xu. Like Father and Mama. Like Zheng Yi.

The next morning as I folded the borrowed wedding dress, Yi came up behind me.

His finger traced my cheek, and then rubbed the hem of the dress. "Your skin is as soft as silk, which reminds me of the story about the Yellow Empress."

"Lei Zu? The empress who discovered the silk worm? Why is that?"

"Like the cocoon that dropped into her tea, you fell unexpectedly into my hands. And like the empress wound the silk cocoon strands around her finger, you wrap your silken skin around my body." He nuzzled my neck.

I brushed my lips against his. "I hope to prove as valuable as well."

Zheng Yi held me tight. "They'll finish careening tomorrow. We'll leave the following day, Little Dragon."

"That's what Madam Xu called me." I tapped his nose. "Why?"

"You're wood, its heavenly creature the azure dragon. With your fire and strength of spirit, you, Xianggu, are a dragon." He grabbed my finger, gave it a playful nip, and then pulled away and crossed the room. "Get ready to leave."

I picked up the newly sharpened *dao* from the table. "I'm ready." I sliced it through the air.

Zheng Yi grimaced. "No, Little Dragon, I don't think you are."

16

*Z*heng Yi stuffed salted fish in his mouth. "Your lips are silent, but your eyes ask a thousand questions, Little Dragon."

I shifted in my seat, amazed at my good fortune to have found a man as observant as Zheng Yi. "Cousin Qi is a pirate. All the men at our marriage ceremony are pirates. Your grandmother and aunt bragged about being the first wife of a chieftain. How long has piracy been a Zheng family business?"

"Two hundred years," he said as though eight generations of piracy was common.

My mouth fell open.

"It all started with Jian and Chenggong. They were farmers from Fujian in search of a better life. You know this feeling yourself." Zheng Yi signaled the slave to pour more *baijiu*. "They left their farms and traveled to Dapeng harbor near Hong Kong. With their hands and backs they did some fishing. With their minds," he tapped his temple, "they devised clever ways to convince men to give them copper and silver." He gave me an expectant look.

I chewed on my lip. "Extortion?"

Zheng Yi drank from the newly refilled cup. "Extortion is illegal. Persuasion, however, is a worthy business skill. Jian and Chenggong were excellent persuaders." He grinned, proud of his profiteering ancestors. "My great great grandfather took over their persuasion business, first as a Ming officer, then as a fee-collecting fisherman for merchant boats entering Mirs Bay."

"Fee collector?" I nodded. "Is that pirate speak for extortionist?"

Zheng Yi shrugged. "My father, Lianchan, grew the family business, even built a temple to Mazu on Devil's Peak."

"A temple or a stronghold?"

Zheng Yi chuckled. "You think like a pirate. Yes, the temple's purpose was twofold, worship and refuge. Father taught me well, but after his death, I joined the Tâyson, rose high in the ranks until the political winds required me to return to the family business." His gaze dropped to my belly. "My sons will—" A knock on the cabin door interrupted his wishful expectations. "Enter," he barked.

The headman bowed low. "A drag-the-wind junk is trolling three *li* starboard. Should we approach?"

"Of course. They'll have cargo to share." One corner of Zheng Yi's mouth lifted in that smile-sneer I had grown fond of.

I followed him across the deck, down the ladder, and almost stumbled over a deckhand leaning against a barrel. Sometimes life on this ship overwhelmed me. The cussing loud crew. The boat's constant creaks, pitch, and sway. The ever-blowing wind and the constant spray of water over the decks.

Flower boats were not built for sailing, the only heaving

happened during a monsoon. The only sounds on deck from singing flower girls and lute-playing musicians. Sweet incense masked the briny odors of fish and foam and filth. The greatest disturbances came from a customer bellowing in ecstasy or during a loud party.

This ship stunk of brine and the sweat of a hundred deck-hands, a few wives, children, and slaves. Precious personal space indicated one's rank. The headman had a small cabin. The helmsmen, a tiny one. Deckhands slept in crate-sized berths, slaves and captives slept on decks outside or below in the holds.

Today, it seemed, everyone crowded on deck to enjoy the cloudy cool weather, which meant I had to squeeze around rigging and windlasses, between men playing mahjong and slaves cleaning the floor.

Yi moved about the ship like an undulating dragon in a dragon dance. My clumsy attempt to keep up was impeded by a chubby baby crawling across deck. Golden Moon, the head-man's wife, apologized as she scooped up her child and returned to the other wives sitting nearby. Before I married Zheng Yi, these women did not speak to me. Now they were all smiles and false friendliness.

"Come talk to us." Precious Jade, the helmsman's wife, patted the bench beside her.

"How much longer?" I gestured to her belly, sat down, and wondered if pirate wives were all that much different from jealous flower girls.

Precious Jade set a hand on her swollen belly. "Any day now. I really wanted the baby to come while we were in Donghai but now…" she sighed.

"You could've stayed on Donghai," said Golden Moon, who bounced her son on her knee.

Precious Jade scowled. "I'm not leaving my husband alone. Catch one's heart, never be a part."

"At least not long enough for him to find a second wife." Golden Moon giggled.

"He's not rich enough for another wife. But," Precious Jade gave me a conspiratorial look, "if Zheng Yi made him headman, he would have enough to buy a second wife and then I could live in Donghai and eat pork and dumplings and be content. Let the second wife live onboard."

Precious Jade had just contradicted herself, but I only smiled.

"Wushi Er keeps four of his six wives on his ship," said the quiet wife of the vanguard headman. "Lots of shouts coming from the Blue Flag cabin, I hear."

The wives cackled and wondered aloud if old Wushi Er's cock was as long as his gray beard.

"Long or tiny, he needs a stiff one to—" Precious Jade made little gasping noises, "enough to satisfy all those wives."

Pink Flower leaned toward me. "He's a rather interesting man."

"Not near as interesting as," Golden Moon lowered her voice, "Guo Podai. *Ài*, the man is heaven." She fanned her face with her hand and fluttered her eyes.

I couldn't disagree with that opinion. Guo Podai was exceptionally good looking. But because I didn't trust these women, I simply pretended indifference. "How did you meet your husband?" I asked Golden Moon.

Golden Moon giggled. "Hsiang-shan often came to my village to sell Red Flag cargo. One day as I helped my lazy husband, I saw him stare at me with starving-for-sex eyes. That very moment I decided to change my fate and spoke shameful thoughts with my own eyes." Golden Moon demonstrated her brazen-eyed look. "He was smitten and offered to buy me then and there. Since my lazy husband's boat needed repair and he thought I was barren he sold me cheaply. *Ha*, his oar never went in the right direction. Now look at me, two children in two years."

"Are you glad you changed your fate?" I rather liked Golden Moon, despite her too frequent giggles.

"No regrets. Not a one. For five years I lived with that lazy fisherman. He was always in debt to moneylenders. We never had enough money to repair the boat or buy the best quality rice. When the fish did manage to jump into his boat, he gambled away the profits. Hsiang-shan gives me a better life. One day we will have enough money to open a store." Golden Moon smiled the satisfied smile of one who believes all her dreams will come true. "You're lucky, Xianggu. Luckier than all of us. A great and powerful squad boss married you. Why?" She shrugged. "Maybe he likes how you fuck. Maybe it's your spirit. Be wary though. Luck opened the door, you must offer Luck some tea to stay awhile."

"Yi's lust for you is fresh." Precious Jade nodded as though Golden Moon had imparted some great wisdom. "Give him sons. Be valuable. Or he'll throw you over the side like he did the others."

Fear as heavy as an anchor dropped in my belly. "I...I know how to swim."

Golden Moon gave me a pitying smile. "You can't swim if your legs and arms are in chains."

My anchor-heavy belly dragged up my deepest fears. I looked around to make sure Zheng Yi was not around. "Tell me about the other women."

Golden Moon shrugged. "There's nothing to tell. He fucks them. Tires of them. They disappear."

Precious Jade nudged me in the side. "That's when he usually takes on a new recruit—between women."

My head swam, all my hopes for a happy future drowned. Or was this a trick? Were these wives as vicious as flower girls? Did they have something to gain by lying?

I arranged my face into a mask of confidence. "Yi loves me. He made me his wife, not those other women." I took both their hands. "Let's be friends. Good friends. Friends that comfort and help instead of…" I pretended to search for the right word. "Frighten one another. Envy is not pretty—it ruined many flower girls. It sours speech and causes wrinkles. Sweet smiles and kind words increase our beauty and that makes any husband love his wife more."

Precious Jade and Golden Moon rolled their eyes. "We *are* your friends, Xianggu. We're not lying, but—"

Loud excited shouts had us scrambling to our feet.

Golden Moon sighed. "To be able to join a raid again." She lifted her young son and pointed starboard. "Let's watch *bà*."

17

T en Red Flag boats circled a drag-the-winds fishing
vessel. Its seven panicked sailors scurried around the
deck like mice.

When our ship came alongside, our crew leapt over the
rail and jumped onto the nets attached to the fishing boat.
Shouting, they unsheathed their cutlasses from the leather
strap worn over their shoulders and rushed the terrified
fishermen.

The fishermen were defenseless, their small fishing
blades useless against the long knife-wielding pirate mob.
They fell to their knees and covered their heads with their
hands. All but one.

A young fisherman with the prominent thick cheekbones
of boldness stood on an upended basket and swooshed his
tiny fishing blade from side to side. He was tall and handsome. And stupid. The pirates backed away. Desperate
courage was as dangerous as a trapped animal.

One pirate crept up behind him and smacked the blade's
flat side into the back of his knees. The young fisherman

tumbled off the basket. A second pirate struck his head, knocked him almost senseless.

The pirates laughed at him and shackled his feet. The young fisherman squirmed, any resistance met with kicks to his stomach. Not once did the young fisherman yelp in pain.

The pirates brought all the fishermen aboard in chains. And like the raid on the flower boat, stripped the small boat of any item they could eat, drink, smoke, or sell. The merchandise appraiser sat on a crate, ink stick in hand, and noted every item transferred onboard. Even the fish. Some were given to the cook. The rest to be sold at the next port.

"Well?" Zheng Yi stood over the chained white-faced fishermen like an executioner over his prisoners.

The headman spit. "Poor. Worthless. Not good for anything but cleaning and bailing."

The young fisherman lifted his head and grinned.

"KEEP YOUR EYE ON THAT ONE," said Precious Jade as we watched the deckhands harass the fishermen captives. "He's not like the others. Look at his hungry eyes, not for food either. Tough too. He doesn't collapse from exhaustion."

Captives cleaned toilets, washed dishes, polished, scrubbed, and gave massages. They were kept so busy they were too tired to rebel.

"He's the only one who smiles while working," I added as he scrubbed the ladder to quarterdeck.

The young fisherman's attitude was endearing. Likable. Already he made friends with a few of the more amiable pirates.

I felt the weight of his stare as I climbed past him.

"You stupid?" A deckhand asked behind me. "The boss will throw you overboard if he sees you ogling his new wife."

I looked over my shoulder, saw the deckhand smack the young fisherman's head into the ladder.

He spit blood onto the deck. "Forgive me. This poor worthless fisherman has never seen such a beautiful woman."

I bit my lip to keep from smiling and continued to Zheng Yi's cabin where I found him staring at the map of Dianbai like a disgruntled customer looking for one bad grain in a bowl of rice.

I ran my fingers through his tangled hair. "Let me braid your hair."

Zheng Yi bristled. "Why? Do you want me to look like all the respectable men with their queues and shaved foreheads?"

"No. I don't want your hair to become a gnarled mess in the wind." I kicked off my pants and pulled my silk tunic over my head.

"Mmmm." Zheng Yi grinned. "Well, if that's how you're going to braid my hair..."

"It's the best way."

My conversation with Golden Moon and Precious Jade had been festering like an ugly sore for days. There was only one one way to prevent Zheng Yi from throwing me overboard when he tired of me. Make myself indispensable to him.

I knew men. Pirate, scholar, or government official, it didn't matter. Men were easily manipulated when a woman was naked, warm, and willing.

"I promise, it'll be pleasant." I picked up the comb and began to unsnarl his mane. "Tell me about the business of piracy."

"Why?" Yi pushed away the map and closed his eyes.

"You're only one man. With only two ears and two eyes."
I kissed these four places. "Let me help you. Then you'll have
four ears and four eyes. When I first began as a flower girl, I
spied on the moonflowers to discover their secrets. It's how I
became the best very quickly."

"I have my headmen, helmsmen, and skippers. They're all
the eyes and ears I need." Zheng Yi grunted as I dug my
fingers into the pressure points of his knotted neck muscles.

"But don't you give these men a squadron if they prove
themselves?"

"What's your point, Little Dragon?" Zheng Yi moaned as
I scratched behind his ears.

"Let me help you. I could be your most valuable
crewmember."

Zheng Yi opened one eye, chuckled, and pulled me onto
his lap. "Service me now, Little Dragon."

ZHENG YI SURRENDERED to me after two weeks of my
gentle prodding.

And so, during the White Dew season when the air was as
wet as the sea and thunderstorms buffeted the ship, the
helmsmen taught me how to steer and when to tack. Deckhands showed me how to repair a torn sail, reef the sails, and
load a cannon—and what to use if we were out of cannonballs. The bookkeeper showed me the accounts, but waved
me away when I confessed I couldn't read.

I learned how to predict weather from the vanguard headman. Lightning in the southwest meant clear skies the next
day. Clouds like fish scales forecasted unstable weather. A
school of jumping porpoise meant the winds would blow for

days. I learned the signals for recall and chasing, for safe trading and getting under way.

I suspected that Zheng Yi told his officers and crew to fill my mind with so much information I would be overwhelmed. I was not. I was delighted. My mind, once as limited as the Guangzhou harbor, was now as vast as the Outer Ocean.

"You learn the basics, Little Dragon," said Zheng Yi as we ate supper in his cabin. "The art of negotiation and leadership—the real talent of sea banditry—is not easily learned. Those skills come only with experience."

I filled his bowl with more rice. "The beginning is the best place to start."

There was a quick knock on the door and Headman Hsiang-shan dragged in the young fisherman by his ear. "This worthless worm begs a word with you." He pushed him to the floor.

The young fisherman kowtowed, his forehead to the floor.

"Speak," Zheng Yi growled.

"My greatest desire is to join your crew." His eyes fixed to the floor, he spoke with confidence, each word clear and emphatic.

"You're already a crewmember." Zheng Yi's voice was a loud arrogant rumble like thunder.

"I want to be more than a slave. I humbly beg to learn the ways of the sea bandits. To be a pirate."

Yi folded his arms. "Stand."

The young fisherman stood, eyes still rooted to the floor. "I won't disappoint you, boss. The sea is a money pond for merchants and sea bandits, and yet it gives poor fishermen nothing but misery and pain. My father—he works below— my grandfather—long dead—were also wretched Dan fishermen. My share was only three percent of the day's catch. Not enough for a pound of rice to feed my younger brothers. The day the Red Flag plundered our boat was my lucky day. I want to be a sea bandit. I want to…" his gaze flicked at me, "have wealth enough to buy a beautiful wife one day. I'll do anything to work for such a great squad boss."

Zheng Yi rose from his chair, circled the young fisherman with a thoughtful gaze, then stopped behind him. His hands ran over the fisherman's broad shoulders and down his lean muscled arms. "How old are you?"

"Fifteen years." The youth, taller than my husband, squared his bronzed shoulders, lifted his chin, yet continued to stare at the floor.

Zheng Yi stroked the side of his face. "Smooth as a baby's ass."

The youth held out his hands. "My hands are big and rough and strong."

Zheng Yi glanced over his shoulder. "What do you think, Xianggu? Would this boy make a good sea bandit?"

I shrugged. "He always smiles, so either he's an idiot or he enjoys menial tasks."

"Hmm." Zheng Yi's hand traveled down the youth's back and over his buttocks.

The young fisherman did not flinch at Yi's intimate touch. "I'll do anything to join the great Red Flag."

"What's your name?" Zheng Yi stood in front of him.

"Zhang Bao." He squared his shoulders.

"Remove your pants, Zhang Bao." Yi's tone was emotionless, yet his eyes danced with a familiar look that sent shivers of alarm down my spine.

Zhang Bao untied his tattered pants, dropped them to the floor. His cock was stiff, a mast to the Red Flag. I shouldn't have been surprised, a breeze aroused a a man of his age.

Zheng Yi's mouth twisted into a sneering grin. "Leave us, wife. Bring me *congee* in the morning."

My stomach lurched. What?! Had I already fallen out of favor? Golden Moon and Precious Jade had tried to warn me, but I was too overconfident of my bedroom skills. "What? I...I..."

"Go," Zheng Yi snarled without even looking at me.

My heart battering against my chest, I rushed from the cabin and stumbled outside where rain pummeled the deck. There was nowhere to go. Was I reduced to sleeping on deck like a slave?

The cove we sheltered in provided some relief from the vicious storm on the Outer Ocean but not enough. The rain soaked my skin in the time it took to descend the ladder and slip-slide into the saloon.

I slammed the door against the gusts of pelting rain.

"What?!" Precious Jade jolted awake, disoriented.

"Why are you here?" I was surprised to see her.

Precious Jade patted her great round belly. "My husband ordered me out. He says I toss and turn too much, and it keeps him from sleeping." She yawned. "I'm ready for this baby to come."

I paced the saloon. The beauty of the elegant furnishings, colorful paintings, hanging lamps, shrines to Mazu, and the eighteen-armed Guanyin, Goddess of Mercy, brought no comfort tonight.

"Why are *you* here?" asked Precious Jade.

"Yi kicked me out." I dropped into the chair as though my body was as heavy as a cannonball.

Precious Jade's expression was that of someone sucking on a sour lemon. "Forever or for the night?"

"I don't know." I looked up at the scores of hanging lamps. Small silk lamps embroidered with fire-breathing dragons. Glass lamps with gilded frames. Lamps made of horn. Paper lamps painted with monkeys hanging from trees. But I felt only a darkness descending. "You once said my husband takes pleasure from recruits…" I blinked back tears. "That's why he made me leave."

"The young Dan fisherman." Precious Jade nodded with knowing. "Didn't you hear the gossip about all their not-so-secret secret looks?"

I shook my head and wiped away the tears. "Will he throw me overboard?" I would never survive. Not in a storm-churning cove. I would drown before reaching shore. Or be crushed by one of the other twenty boats in the squadron sheltered in the cove.

Precious Jade's sour face melted. "Don't worry. This is how the bosses initiate recruits. It's a privilege. It means the recruit is worthy enough to join the fleet."

"Initiation? For how long?"

Precious Jade gritted her teeth. "Some enjoy it more than others." She winced. "This baby is an acrobat."

"Does your husband initiate recruits?"

"Of course. How else will he create a loyal bond with a new recruit?"

Madam Xu had also believed in the benefits of *guanxi,* loyalty acquired through personal relationships.

I shifted in my seat. "Does he send you away?"

"Sometimes, but I like to watch. *He* likes when I watch." Precious Jade rubbed her belly. "I don't understand. You were a flower girl. You've seen and done everything. Why are you upset?"

Because I thought I was special. Because my future depended on Zheng Yi. Because I realized I was expendable. I didn't confess this to Precious Jade. I just shrugged.

Precious Jade skewed her lips. "You walk around this ship

with your nose in the air like an empress. You bother the headman and helmsman and deckhands with a thousand questions. How this? Why that? They're obedient to the chief so they humor you. But tonight, you learn another lesson. You learn how and why the men are a family, how and why the loyalty begins and grows." She readjusted the pillow behind her back, closed her eyes, and turned away her head.

I left the saloon, went back into the storm, and huddled in the corner by our cabin door. I heard everything, my husband's groans of pleasure and Zhang Bao's grunts.

Puffy-eyed from tears and sleeplessness, I brought Zheng Yi's *congee* in the morning.

"Did you bring some for Bao?" Zheng Yi sat on the bed and gestured to the young fisherman still sleeping. On my side of the bed!

I set down the tray. "Forgive me. I'll get it right now." When I returned, the young fisherman was in a most subservient position.

Plastering a smile on my face, I set the second bowl on the table. "Can I watch you induct the new recruit?"

Zheng Yi mumbled his consent.

My hands in my lap, I sat down to watch this carnal initiation into piracy brotherhood.

Zhang Bao, who was bent over, turned this head while my husband burst his chrysanthemum. He smiled at me. Not a smile of pleasure but of resolve. A face of ambition and purpose.

Zheng Yi was not gentle, but Zhang Bao bore it with dignity and poise. Proof of his tough spirit.

I smiled back at the fifteen-year-old who used his handsome face and strapping body to join the greatest flag fleet of the South Seas. I did not fault him. I had done the same.

Initiating a new recruit was not a one-time occurrence. Zhang Bao became my husband's lover. I was forgotten. Zheng Yi spent each night with him. I slept in the saloon and continued learning the art of sea banditry, the joy for learning now replaced with fear for my life.

18

Zheng Yi forbid me to join the raid on Shuidong's customs office.

My teeth clenched with annoyed disappointment as I stood on the poop deck with a heavy-bellied Precious Jade and watched while the other wives rowed sampans to shore.

Zheng Yi deployed twenty-two teams. One team invaded the customs office. Eighteen attacked and seized cargo from salt junks in the harbor. The remaining three teams raided the surrounding fishing villages for vegetables and pigs.

I leaned over the bulwark for a long time, my eyes straining into the distance.

The village gong sounded.

"Time to go," said Precious Jade.

"Why?" I asked.

"The village alerted their militia." She wrung her hands. "It's the most dangerous time for us."

All Zheng Yi's men returned high-spirited and unharmed.

The following day as Yi and I bathed in the saltwater bath below deck, I decided to broach the topic again. "When can I go on a raid or scull a sampan?"

"Soon."

I knew better than to ask how soon was soon. No sense angering him. Especially since all his passionate attention was still focused on Zhang Bao.

Just when I had given up hope, Zheng Yi's desire for me returned. I wondered if it it had anything to do with the fleet's gathering near Dianbai for the attack.

Zheng Yi was a slow and thorough lover. He lingered over my curves, relished the scent of my skin and secret places. I lavished him with devotion and coaxed him to pleasure peeks only I could release. Yi roared his fireworks—louder than when he was with Zhang Bao.

"I missed you." Yi's hand glided over my flat belly.

"I missed you too." I wondered if he thought I was barren. A son would strengthen our marriage. Unfortunately, all my offerings and prayers to the gods went unanswered. Perhaps ten years of drinking *liangyao* had ruined me.

"I'm going to adopt Zhang Bao." Yi nibbled my ear. "He's fearless and ambitious. Those Dan are good fishermen but much better pirates."

His casual announcement clenched my stomach. "You've only known him a short time." I swallowed my astonishment, kept my voice composed. "Do you trust him?"

"He'll have to earn my trust." Yi laid on his back and put his hands under his head.

"How?" I rolled to the side and drew circles over Yi's taut stomach.

"He'll cook first. For me. For the crew. If he does the job well, I'll promote him to lookout—that's when most recruits show the first signs of laziness, clumsiness, or stupidity. If he's a good lookout, he'll join a raid."

"He's only fifteen." I sat up and urged Yi to roll over.

"He's man enough." Yi groaned as I worked out the knots

in his back. "This is our way, Xianggu. Do you remember meeting He-song at our wedding?"

"Yes. He gave us a jade carving."

"Well, six years ago, Cousin Qi adopted He-Song when he was only twelve-years-old."

"So young?"

"It's best that way. He-song rose through the ranks and after several years Cousin Qi bought him a wife. He-Song turned out to be a clever businessman—gets local officials to ignore our crimes. Five months ago, Cousin Qi fronted him enough silver to open a store."

"What kind of store?" I dug my elbow into an especially hard knot.

Zheng Yi let out a long growl. "He sells our stolen merchandise and recruits pirates. This is why we win on land and sea. Our reach is long, our family vast, our loyalty bonds strong."

I dragged the heel of my hand up his back. "*Guanxi.*" Loyalty acquired through personal relationships. I had no *guanxi* with anyone on this boat besides Yi.

Yi let out a low rumble of pleasure. "Which reminds me, Guo Podai will join the raid. His ransom business concluded early. You want to learn the business? Listen while we discuss tomorrow's raid."

I hadn't seen the handsome Guo Podai since our wedding. "Thank you, husband."

Guo Podai came aboard later that afternoon. "Honored Father." He bowed his head.

I followed them into the saloon where a large map draped over the table. The men sat down, and Guo Podai raised an eyebrow when I pulled up a a chair next to Yi.

I listened to their every word. Assault tactics. Best time of day. Number of men per vanguard team. Number of sampans needed to take the teams ashore. How close the ships must be for their cannons to breach the wall. I soaked it all in, amazed and impressed. Nothing was left to chance. Was it any wonder that only the most intelligent became chieftains?

"My wife wants to test her sword skill," said Zheng Yi.

Guo Podai frowned. "One cutlass swipe and her beautiful face will be scarred forever."

"She's more than just beautiful," Yi scolded. "She's curious. Asks too many questions. Like you did. She's fearless too. Has the same fighting spirit as Matron Cai Qian."

Guo Podai's fingertips brushed across the map's edge. "As long as as Xianggu doesn't have Matron Cai Qian's same lust for men and opium." He glanced up, one brow arched.

"If she does, I'll kill her." Yi flashed his smile-sneer to me; part warning, part teasing.

"Who's Matron Cai Qian?" I asked with more than a little interest. She sounded like a real pirate, not just a sampan sculler.

"She's Cai Qian's first wife." Guo Podai leaned back and folded his arms, his narrow-eyed stare taking measure of me. "She's fierce and cunning, more *yang* than *yin*. She convinced Cai Qian to give her command of a boat." He lifted his eyes to the ceiling and shook his head. "Her crew is all women. The only men are captives who service her lust."

I gasped. The shameless Matron Cai Qian wielded a lot of power for a woman.

"She and Cai Qian are Fujian sea bandits," said Zheng Yi expecting my next question. "You'll meet them during our next joint venture."

"There's another matter to discuss. And it doesn't bode well for us." Guo Podai removed a letter from his robe and passed it to Zheng Yi. "This is evidence of shrinking Tâyson power. It seems the royal troops are reclaiming their territory."

The discussion turned to the crumbling Tâyson regime before it eventually shifted to other topics: A double-dealing spy. Increased dominance of a certain secret society in Hong Kong. The Guangdong officials who approved stricter punishments for piracy.

My elbows on the table, chin resting on my fist, I paid rapt attention, fascinated by a business with more tentacles than an octopus.

Guo Podai stole frequent glances at me. I knew that look all too well. The look of sexual desire.

Little signs gave a man's yearnings away. Their skin emitted a raw essence of maleness, a subtle scent of desire. Guo Podai's eyes went where they should not and lingered there too long.

Afterwards, Zheng Yi, Guo Podai, and I climbed to the top deck to view a marvelous sight.

The Black and Red fleets had all arrived. Hundreds of ships. More impressive was what we did not see, a hundred more vessels hiding among the islands outside the inlet leading to Dianbai.

The crew was restless. Petty arguments broke out, minor scuffles between deckhands. Everyone was impatient and excited for the raid.

As was the custom, Zheng Yi told the old *xianggong* to burn incense and make offerings of paper money. The afternoon passed with tedious slowness. I watched the sky deepen from blue to lavender to black.

To pass the evening hours—to keep my nervousness at bay—I cut paper in the saloon. I made an elegant design of three tassel-adorned lanterns suspended from a circular border of peach blossom branches.

Precious Jade came to tell me she dreamed her son would be born surrounded by the sea's bounty. She was more worried about her overdue baby than tomorrow's attack on Dianbai.

On deck, slaves hung red lanterns and streamers for the Mid-Autumn festival.

The moon winked behind the gathering clouds as Yi bent me over the berth. He was distracted, his rough thrusts without finesse, sex a way to pass the time and take his mind off the throbbing headache he had for hours. Despite my pleasure moans his fireworks were little more than a grunt.

"Anxious?" I lit the lanterns when the moon disappeared behind the clouds.

"I don't like waiting."

"Well, since we must wait until morning, do you mind if I share one of my greatest hopes?"

"Besides my becoming the chieftain of the Red Flag?" He grinned mischievously.

"You're terrible." I smacked his naked thigh. "I like Cousin Qi. He told you to marry me. No, my other great hope is that you may one day teach me to read."

The boat lurched.

"Women don't need to read." Another swaying lurch caused Zheng Yi to look out the crushed oyster window. "Too dark," he muttered and rubbed his temples.

"Wives of fishermen perhaps. Not the wife of a squad boss. My reading will help you."

Yi donned a thick tunic. "How?"

"I will write ransom letters or messages to storeowners. I can confirm the lists from the merchandise appraiser and supply clerk, which will give you more time to relax or plan other ambitious raids." My plea was as vigorous as the ship's rocking.

"You make a good case." A worried look passed over his face as the ship heaved beneath us.

"You'll teach me to read?" Joy pounded in my heart.

"Not me. A teacher." Zheng Yi stumbled as the ship lurched, grabbed hold of the door.

"A thousand thank you's, husband. You won't regret it. I'll be the best wife a squad boss can have." I slid a thick tunic over my head and followed him out the door.

He stopped, the wind whipping his braids about, and patted my flat belly. "The best wife gives me sons." Yi stared at the sky and grunted.

Churning waves sprayed up and over the bulwark. Storm-black clouds covered the stars and moon.

"Boss." The old *xianggong* waited outside our door. "My elbow's acting up."

Yi nodded grimly. A big storm was coming. The change of air pressure made joints ache and Yi's head throb.

"Wake the headman. Wake everyone. Prepare for the storm." Yi looked over the side into the roiling sea below. "Get inside, Xianggu. Make an offering to Mazu for the typhoon to pass us by."

"But—"

"Don't argue with me, wife!"

My stomach churned as much as the ocean as I returned to our cabin. The ship rocked and pitched. The timber planks creaked and groaned under the strain of wailing wind, surging waves, and hammering rain.

I sat down and held on to the chair bolted to the floor.

Minutes became hours. Each second doused me with more fear as the storm's wrath grew worse. I gripped the chair arm with each rise and plummet. One wave knocked me from the chair. If it was this bad inside the cabin...

"Yi," I whispered and crawled across the floor.

I cracked open the door. A gust ripped it from my hands and smashed it angrily against the wall.

The storm roared its deafening fury, the crew's shouts drowned in the violent union of sea and rain. I was soaked to the bone in an instant.

Slaves clutched the lines and braced themselves into corners. Captives hung on to whatever was bolted to the deck. There were red tatters where the red lanterns and banners for the Mid-Autumn Festival had hung.

"Zheng Yi!" My scream was submerged in the waves that crashed on deck.

"My son!" Precious Jade, hair matted to her face, grabbed my arm.

Even in this dark nightmare, I glimpsed the blood flowing down her legs before a sluice of seawater washed away her crimson misery.

Precious Jade clutched her stomach, staggered, and dropped to her knees. "The baby is coming." She squeezed my arm, her eyes wild with panic. "My son! I can't find him. Did you see him? I'm too weak—" She grimaced as another pain ripped through her womb.

He's probably dead. Blown overboard. But I swiveled my head about to give her hope. "There he is!"

The toddler huddled between two crates.

On hands and knees, Precious Jade crawled toward her son as the ship lurched starboard. A gush of seawater slammed my body into the windlass before I could help her.

"Zheng Yi!" I screamed as I watched Precious Jade drag her wailing child toward their cabin, seawater diluting her bloody trail.

"Damn it, wife! What are you doing out here!" Yi, looming above me, grabbed a rope line and wrapped it around my arms.

I opened my mouth in apology and saw the terrible truth. A mountain of water rushed at the boat. "Yi—"

My ears roared. The sea stole my breath, my sight. An explosion of cold and pressure…of everything and nothing…

I blinked blinked blinked. "Yi!" The squall carried away my scream.

The deck was near empty. Everyone swept overboard. Zheng Yi was gone.

"Xianggu!" Zhang Bao scuttled toward me like a crab and stretched out his hand.

My head exploded with light.

19

I was weightless and cold. The sea roared in my ears. I sank deep, choked, coughed, and gagged.

"Zheng Yi Sao. Wake up. It's not time to sleep. Your husband wants tea."

From far away I heard whimpering…

"Xianggu, Little Dragon."

Warm lips touched mine.

I swam up through the thick warm water, broke through the surface, and forced open my salt-sealed eyes. Pain stabbed my skull.

"Yi, you're alive." My voice sounded like sand against rock.

"Alive and lucky." Zheng Yi squeezed my hand. "Others were not as fortunate."

"How bad is it?"

"We lost many people. Many boats. Not as many as Wushi Er and Podai though." Yi's voice was hoarse, his face scratched, and eyes shadowed with exhaustion. "Bodies and wreckage are washing ashore." He nodded to Zhang Bao who had just entered the cabin with food and tea. "Bao saved your life. Do you remember anything?"

I shook my head but stopped when a searing pain sliced through my skull.

"Bao said a flying crate knocked you unconscious. The rope around you uncoiled. Bao tied your bodies together and dragged you back to the cabin."

Zhang Bao set the tray near the bed. "A dutiful son must protect his most honorable mother."

Mother? I winced. "Is Precious Jade alive? What happened to her baby and son?" I lifted the tea to my lips. The cup shook in my hands.

"She's dead, washed overboard with the boy." Yi rubbed his temples.

Precious Jade's beautiful dream concealed a nightmare, her baby had been born in the ocean's dark depths. "Golden Moon and Pink Flower?" I curled my fists and waited for the worst.

"They stayed in their cabins, like I told you to do." Yi walked around the bed. "Precious Jade shouldn't have left her cabin."

"Her son—"

"Don't make excuses for her. Her death is tragic, but I'll buy another wife for He-song."

My body shook with silent sobs.

Zheng Yi touched my shoulder. "I didn't know you and Precious Jade were good friends."

"The beginning of a friendship." The woman died while giving birth, while trying to save her first-born.

How easily a wife was replaced! Zheng Yi had no compassion. I turned my head and wiped away tears that stemmed more from self-pity than for Precious Jade's death.

Zhang Bao cleared his throat. "I'd be honored to wash the

dried blood from Mother's hair. I'll be back with soap and water." He departed.

Yi paced the cabin, his shoulders slumped with the weight of his responsibilities. "Cousin Qi and I are headed to Guangzhou. We lost a lot of supplies and must recoup our losses." He gently touched the large goose egg on my head. "The time has come to prove your worth as a pirate, Xianggu. Are you ready?"

"Not today. Maybe tomorrow." It hurt to smile.

"It'll take more than a day for that bump to heal." Yi set a soft kiss on my forehead. "I must go. My men need me." With a sad smile he trudged from the cabin.

I drained my teacup and had just scooped out the last spoonful of *congee* when Zhang Bao returned with a basin full of water.

I submitted to the hair wash.

"Sorry for my clumsy hands," said Bao for the fifth time despite his gentle touch while washing my salt-matted hair.

My eyes closed and my body relaxed as he lifted my wet hair from the bowl, wrung its length, and wrapped it in a soft cloth.

"You've done this before," I murmured.

"For my other mother when she was too sick to do it herself. Her hair was not as long and beautiful as yours, but she took great pride in it." He rubbed my hair dry with a cloth. "May I comb your hair? It's very tangled."

I pointed to the tortoise comb on the table. "Why were you on deck last night? Why weren't you below?"

"A man doesn't cower in fear when people need help." Bao picked at a knot with the comb. "Typhoons don't frighten me. And I knew my offerings to Fengbo and Jammu, wind uncle and gale mother, would save me. They also allowed me to save the boss's wife." Bao's logic was naïve and simplistic.

"Those same gods who favored you did not favor those who died in the storm." I sounded like a mother scolding a spoiled child.

Instead of shrinking from my rebuke, Bao squared his shoulders. "I speak for myself, not for others. Because of my actions, the boss promoted me to lookout."

I shrugged, not surprised. Yi was overly fond of the youth. "I'll miss your tea." The water was never too hot.

"Thank you, Mother, but making tea and rice is slave's work." Zhang Bao ran his fingers through my hair with such intimacy I stifled a moan of pleasure. "I have more ambitious goals." He continued raking his fingers through my hair, fanning the locks to dry.

"That's enough." I pulled away and stood, his caressing touch was much too enjoyable. This young man was my husband's lover, his recruit, and our adopted son.

He bowed his head. "As a lookout, I'll be able to admire the top of your head from my lofty perch."

I gave him a hard look. He was too bold.

"Did I offend you, Mother?" He picked up the water bowl.

"No, why do you ask?" Uncomfortable with how close he stood, I crossed the cabin.

"Your lips press together when something displeases you."

"What?"

"Your lips." Bao touched his own. "They form a straight line when you're irritated."

"Go." I flapped my hand. Bao should not be staring at my lips!

He closed the door behind him and left me to wonder at his uncanny people-reading skills.

20

Argh! I could not lay like a pampered empress in bed all day. Not while every crewmember worked to repair the typhoon's damage. Not while the crew mourned the loss of their friends.

My body would ache whether I lay in bed or not. Better to do something than think about my throbbing skull and sore shoulder. I put on clothes and tucked my sword into its sheath. Zheng Yi should not be the only one rallying his grief-stricken crew.

"It's a good day to be alive." I strode across the main deck among the crew. "Venerable Mother favors Zheng Yi's squad. We had less damage than the others."

The slaves, captives, helmsmen, and deckhands mumbled agreement.

Every able-bodied person was busy. They cleaned, swept, shined, and mended.

"Goose egg or quail egg?" asked the helmsman while inspecting the boom on the mainsail.

"A small bump. It knocked good sense into me." I

unsheathed my sword, ran my fingers over the blade. "I'm ready to fight with you in our next raid."

Two deckhands, who inspected a barrel of gunpowder for water damage, shouted their approval.

"Be sure to stab the right sailor, Zheng Yi Sao," said a chubby-cheeked deckhand.

"Then stay on my *left*." I wagged my finger at him.

The crew laughed.

"Right. Left. I'll be safer *behind* you," said a gunner named Three-finger Lo.

"Boss prefers you go first." Chubby Cheeks bumped Three-finger Lo's shoulder. "That way you're not distracted by his wife's ass."

Three-finger Lo shoved Chubby Cheeks to the ground, jumped on this back, and wrapped his hands around his throat. "Zheng Yi Sao, I humbly present this man as target practice."

"Forgive me, honorable Zheng Yi Sao," choked a red-faced Chubby Cheeks. "I'm an empty rice bucket, a stupid worm."

The crew crowded around, pushed one another for a better view.

Yi observed the commotion from quarterdeck.

My stomach knotted. This was a test. I could earn the crew's respect or lose it this very moment. "Three-finger Lo, is this man good with a sword?" I touched my sword tip to Chubby Cheeks' face.

Three-finger Lo, still sitting on Chubby Cheeks, shrugged. "Good enough."

My lips pressed together, and I tapped my chin in thought. "It would be foolish to kill a man simply because he appreciates my ass, especially since the typhoon took some of our best men." I scratched his cheek with the blade. "What's your name?"

"Qing Ping," he gasped with pleading-for-his-life eyes.

"Well, Qing Ping, if my blade touches your face again, you'll earn the nickname, One-ear Ping." A nod to Three-finger Lo released his hold.

Qing Ping groveled at my feet, but I paid no attention. Instead I looked at Zheng Yi. Did he approve?

Yi nodded, his familiar smile-sneer filling my belly with pride. But a prickly feeling that I was being watched made me me look at the crow's nest. Bao stared at me, his expression unreadable from the lofty perch.

The crew roared their approval and my heart leapt. I was on the path to earning the crew's respect. *Real* respect. Not the false respect given because I was the boss's first wife. My small triumph tasted sweeter than any moon cake.

The rest of the day I helped deckhands with tasks and comforted crewmembers who lost loved ones. I learned that Thick Lip, the pirate on the flower boat, drowned in the storm. By evening, I collapsed into bed, head throbbing, body weary, but content.

Zheng Yi was doubly lustful that night—inspired, he claimed, by my bold and helpful behavior this afternoon. I was too exhausted to satisfy him, so he took his pleasures with Bao for the next few days.

THE DARK BLUE sea sparkled beneath a golden sun hovering over an orange horizon. This time of day was my favorite. More beautiful than a field of flowers. It was also the perfect time to close in on a lone salt junk.

The cannons were in position and loaded. The earthenware stinkpots ready in the crow's nest. The crew poised for the leap.

Zheng Yi gave the signal.

Cannonballs shot from the cannon ports. One fractured the salt junk's main mast. The second ripped wide a section of bulwark. Their screaming crew ran for cover.

The Red Flag crew jumped on the salt junk and scuttled spider-like up and over the side. Yelling and brandishing their cutlasses, our men rushed at the petrified sailors.

Our advantage was sheer numbers. Sailors seldom resisted or fought back. What were ten obedient sailors against a hostile pirate mob?

Zheng Yi turned to me. "Ready?"

"I am." This was it. My first act of piracy. With a cutlass in one hand and sword in the other, I followed Yi over the plank that connected the boats.

The sailors sank to their knees on the main deck and begged for mercy. Meanwhile, our captives transferred cargo. According to Mandarin officials, any captive who handled stolen cargo more than twice was complicit in piracy and subject to the same punishments.

Several crewmembers were tying up the last of the sailors when Three-finger Lo dragged a crying woman by her hair across deck.

"No, I beg of you, don't take my wife." The salt junk captain rocked back and forth with misery.

Bile rose in my throat as four deckhands—those I joked with yesterday—held down the young wife. I looked away.

Our men had no cause to rape. Zheng Yi, like all flag bosses, kept several pleasure slaves in the lower deck to satisfy the men.

Yi beckoned me forward. "Your blade is shiny, Xianggu."

I swallowed the sourness burning the back of my throat. "The sailors have already surrendered."

Yi aimed his cutlass at the captain. "Kill him."

I flinched, squeezed my fist around my sword. "Why? He surrendered."

Yi glared at me. "You must prove your wickedness. No crew will respect you if they think you're weak. It also teaches our new captives fear."

This was my initiation into piracy. Murder. I blinked, blinked again, took a deep breath and crossed the deck to stand over the kneeling salt junk captain.

He lifted his head but instead of fear there was only the certainty of compassion. My womanly compassion.

"Beautiful bandit woman, I beg mercy." The salt junk captain dared look me in the eye. "Spare my life and my wife's."

"Don't you care about your crew?" I pointed to the motley group of sailors. Bound and bruised. Frightened. Certain of their death.

A familiar expression flashed across the captain's face. The same look Madam Xu had whenever the flower girls begged for a day of rest. Indifference.

Chieftains, officials—anyone with privilege and fortune —cared nothing for the weak, ignorant, and poor. The lowly were merely stepping-stones to their destination.

"Your face betrays you," I said. All the injustices I had suffered—poverty, slavery—gathered inside me like a storm. It was time to take back my life. "A good captain would have bargained for everyone's life. You care only about saving yourself. Now you must choose between your life or your wife's."

The captain's mouth dropped open, his eyes wide.

Our men stopped looting to watch. The merchandise

appraiser looked up from his list. A hush fell over the boat. I felt Bao's eyes on me from the lookout nest. If I didn't kill the salt junk captain, I would be nothing more than a pretty but useless wife.

"What's your answer?" I used my most seductive flower girl voice.

The captain stared, agape, eyes white with terror.

"Your indecision is your undoing." My voice dripped honey. "Your wife is better off without you."

I lifted the blade.

21

Prostitution required the violation of my body. Piracy required my soul. The first enslaved me. The second set me free.

I swiped my blade across the salt junk captain's throat before the dawn of understanding reached his eyes. He pitched forward and the blood pooled crimson beneath him.

I felt nothing. Not anger. Not hatred. Not pity. Not triumph. Taking his life felt no different than taking a customer's cock in my body or mouth. A job done. A task that brought me one step closer to my dreams.

I recalled Zheng Yi telling Headman Hsiang-shan that if the goal cannot be reached, do not change the goal, change the steps to the goal.

My goal—a life of prosperity and independence—had not changed. The means to achieve it had.

My shiny blade dripping, I spun about. "Release her, or I'll cut all your cocks off." I pointed my blade at the crewmen waiting to rape the wife.

Their pants at their ankles, the slack-jawed crewmen looked to Zheng Yi.

"You heard her." Yi's smile-sneer was wider than usual.

Deckhand Qing Ping pointed to the lifeless salt junk captain. "Slice him! Slice him!"

"Wife? Do you want to do the honors?" Zheng Yi folded his arms.

Slitting a throat was quick and easy, but slicing was better left to bloodthirsty men. "I give that privilege to Three-finger Lo."

Three-finger Lo whooped with glee. He chopped off the salt captain's feet first. Next, the hands. Then he hacked the legs at the knees, cleaved the arms and, with a triumphant cry, severed the head. The men grabbed the blood-slick body parts and threw them over the side. Food for fish. A terrorizing meal for the salt junk sailors. The best way to instill fear.

I lifted my bloody cutlass in the air. "Who will join the great Red Flag?" I shouted to the salt junk captives.

"Me! Me! Me!"

Better a live pirate than a dead sailor.

The Red Flag crew roared their approval.

"Well timed." Yi sidled close.

"We needed more men." I slipped my cutlass beneath my sash.

"We?" Yi's eyes traveled my body, from the blood drops on my cheek to my blood-splattered feet. "You may have been born a farmer and worked as a prostitute, but you, Xianggu, have a pirate's spirit." He swept me up into his arms and we kissed with a lust that took all night to satisfy.

WE ANCHORED in port a few hours later to sell the stolen salt. Zheng Yi returned with more than a bag of coin.

He pushed a slim, solemn-faced man into our cabin. With his hands fettered in front of him and his feet tied together his body swayed with a woman's lotus gait.

Another recruit? Another lover for my husband?

"Here she is." Yi pushed the captive forward.

My lips pressed together. A lover for me?

"*She's* your wife?" The stranger gawked.

"Show respect." Yi smacked the back of his head and the stranger fell at my feet. "If he's not a good teacher slice his throat like you did with the salt junk captain."

"A tutor?! This is my tutor?!" I wrapped my arms around Yi, my heart bursting with happiness.

Yi ran his finger along the edge of my silk hydrangea-patterned *hanfu*. "Worth the expense." He touched the complicated topknot at the back of my head and nuzzled my neck. "Beautiful. Too bad it won't last the night," he purred in my ear.

"Gambling debt?" I asked the tutor after he left.

"Fan-tan, madam. Father refused to pay any more of my debts." He struggled to his knees. "An unfortunate financial arrangement with an unhappy member of the Society for Filial Sons led to my being sold to your husband."

It seemed impoverished children were not the only ones sold into slavery.

"Gambling is the ruin of many men and women." I remembered why Mei's father sold her. "Is opium another of your vices?"

"No, madam." The tutor vigorously shook his head. "My mind is too eager for knowledge to surrender to its numbing effects."

"Good." There were more than a few deckhands with a weakness for opium. "Be careful. There's lots of gambling aboard. If you don't pay your debt here, you'll be thrown overboard. If you value your life, refrain from gambling." I untied the scholar's hands but not his feet. "How long will it take to learn to read and write?" I pointed to a chair.

The tutor wiped his sweaty brow and sat as regally as possible with tied ankles. "That depends on your thirst for learning."

I rubbed my hands together. "There's not a pitcher big enough to quench my parched mind."

By the time we weighed anchor and started for Macau I trusted the scholar enough to untie his feet.

WE STOPPED in Macao for two reasons. First, to buy more tung oil, tar, bamboo matting, gunpowder, weapons, and water from Zheng Yi's favorite merchants. Second, to plan the next campaign with Cousin Qi, Guo Podai, Wushi Er, and other chieftains.

But that's not why my heart leapt with double joy. That morning, my tutor proclaimed I was the brightest student he'd ever had the privilege of teaching. That afternoon while wiggling my toes in the sand, I realized my monthly blood was three months late. Finally!

I would not tell Zheng Yi just yet. Much could go wrong the first few months.

I ran across the beach to the nearby house where Zheng Yi and Guo Podai ate dumplings and discussed a joint venture with the Three Harmonies Society.

Guo Podai, a pork dumpling dangling from his chopstick, seemed especially glad to see me when I walked into the kitchen. "I hear you have a tutor. Are you proficient yet?"

I sighed. "Marginal at best. I'm still too slow."

"Be patient with yourself." Guo Podai's brow furrowed with compassion. "It doesn't matter how slowly you go as long as you don't stop."

"Confucius? Really?" Yi shoved a dumpling in his mouth.

"There's wisdom in his words." Guo Podai fetched paper, quill, and ink from the desk. "Let's test your skill." He pointed to an empty chair. "Write 'The most distinguished, squad boss, Zheng Yi, of the fearsome Red Flag,'"

I raised my brows. "This sounds like the first line of a ransom letter."

Guo Podai nodded and continued his dictation. "'demands one hundred Spanish silver dollars.'"

I put ink to paper. "My characters lack style," I said after finishing.

Guo Podai studied the sentence, every muscle in his face betraying his surprise. "Impressive. You're a quick learner. You'll be exceptional in no time." He set down the paper. "Perhaps by the time the baby is born you'll be able to read one of my poetry books."

I sucked in my breath, wide-eyed with amazement.

Zheng Yi's chopsticks paused in midair. "You're pregnant?"

"I…" I set my hand on Yi's arm. "I wanted to be certain before telling you."

Guo Podai sat back in the chair, his mouth curled into smug satisfaction. "Xianggu blooms with the happiness of motherhood."

"Maybe you should have been a physician." Yi pointed his chopsticks at him. "Or a face reading master." He took a swig of *baijiu*. "Enough women's talk. What news did you hear from Dianbai?"

The typhoon that had thwarted our Mid-Autumn festival attack had been a boon for the townsfolk, but a nightmare for pirate survivors washed ashore.

"The villagers killed any crewmember who resisted arrest. Those who surrendered peacefully, they sent to Guangzhou for trial." Guo Podai shook his head. "Unfortunately, Magistrate Hang is a merciless worm. He condemned two of my men to death by slicing. Banished forty-eight of Wushi Er's men to Manchuria where they'll be slaves for imperial soldiers. Whipped twenty-one of Cousin Qi's men with bamboo sticks before sending them to a penal colony. The rest were beheaded." Though his voice was calm, Guo Podai's eyes flared with anger. "Their heads were sent to Dianbai and the villagers strung them like lanterns over the entry gate as a warning."

Zheng Yi squeezed shut his eyes for a moment. "Any captain who anchored his boat that close to shore was an idiot!" His fist smashed the table. "It's better to drown at sea than endure the horror of slavery or torture by those fucking government magistrates." He stood, paced the room, his face red with outrage. "What did the villagers steal from us?"

I pressed my hand to my mouth to keep from speaking. The Dianbai villagers stole nothing. They salvaged whatever had floated on the sea or washed ashore. It was a detail Zheng Yi would not appreciate.

Guo Podai crossed his arms. "Five boats, innumerable weapons, three cannons, and a valuable bronze seal."

"Fuck." Yi kicked a chair leg. "What else?"

Guo Podai grimaced, shifted his weight from foot to foot. "The villagers brag that *our* lost wealth is building *their* new fortified wall."

"Defeat is a bitter meal." Yi clasped his hands together

behind his back. "Let's raid a few towns along the Han River to add some sweetness."

Guo Podai retrieved the map from the desk, and they talked strategy. Forgotten and ignored, I went into the garden where Hesheng, my husband's sister, sat on a bench.

"Enlighten me, Xianggu." Hesheng twirled a pink peony between her fingers. "Why did my brother marry a common whore?"

I sighed and looked away.

Hesheng snorted. "You lift your head with the haughtiness of a favorite concubine in the Forbidden City."

My head snapped back around. "I'm not a concubine. I'm the first wife and *only* wife to the Emperor of the South Seas."

Hesheng's sneer melted with my compliment. "He does wield a lot of power, doesn't he?" She stuck the peony in her topknot. "Is it true you slit the salt junk captain's throat and recruited the entire crew?"

"Yes, and I saved his wife from being gang raped." I sat down beside her. "Yi ransomed her back to her family."

Hesheng flapped her hand toward my belly. "Give my brother a son and you'll win my favor."

"I don't need your favor when I have his." I smoothed my *hanfu.* "I don't know and don't care that you don't like me. But I do admire your love and concern for Yi's happiness. Maybe one day you'll find me a worthy wife."

Hesheng's suspicious eyes dropped to my belly. "Make offerings for a son."

A FEW DAYS later while I waited on the beach, a sharp pain sliced my belly.

I got in the sampan, winced at another contraction-like pain.

"Are you okay?" The sculler rowed toward the ship.

"Fine." I pressed my hand to my womb, willed the pain to stop.

It didn't. By the time I slammed shut the cabin door and lifted my *hanfu*, my thighs were slick with blood.

22

August 1802
Year of the Water Dog

Zheng Yi sat in the chair and wept. Cousin Qi, Red Flag chieftain, was dead. And piracy had no hand in his early departure from this world.

Through tear-filled eyes, Zheng Yi explained what happened.

The Tâyson leaders needed Cousin Qi's help to defeat Emperor Gia Long's navy. Cousin Qi agreed and sailed his weapon-ready pirate boats to Hue to join the Tâyson forces. They were defeated.

Undaunted, Cousin Qi's ordered his two hundred boats to mount a defensive on the Red River at Hanoi. The gods were merciless. By a wicked twist of bad luck, the emperor's inferior navy commandeered Qi's ship and beheaded him.

Emperor Gia Long, smug after the death of several pirate chieftains, demanded the immediate destruction of all pirate strongholds in Vietnam. Hundreds of sea bandits fled to the safety of Guangdong waters to vie for jobs on the remaining flag fleets.

Zheng Yi pushed away an uneaten plate of salted fish and stared out the crushed oyster window. "We need a new chieftain. Fast. Today or tomorrow is not soon enough."

"Why not you?" I asked, confused by his reluctance to declare himself the new chieftain.

Yi stood and stalked the length of the cabin like a caged tiger. "It's not that easy, Little Dragon. Every squad boss will fight for the position."

I folded my arms. "The squad bosses will bicker and argue for weeks. By then the southwest winds will decrease and less cargo-laden ships will sail into our waters. That's bad business."

"Don't you think I know this!?" His loud voice startled me.

I jumped from my chair and stroked his cheek. "I know you know, it's just...well, wouldn't it be best if you summoned all the squad bosses to settle the matter?"

Yi waved away my caresses. "That act in itself implies my authority."

"Exactly," I purred.

A slow smile washed over his face. "Clever."

I took Yi's hand. "Don't demand the meeting. Suggest it. Once everyone is together, the other bosses will see there's only one man with the Red Flag fleet's best interest in mind."

Yi kissed my palm. "I'll invite the other flag chieftains to come as well."

"Excellent idea. Guo Podai will want to see his adopted father made chieftain. Wushi Er is your good friend. That will be two chieftains' indisputable support you can count on. You, my husband, are the only one worthy of taking command of the largest flag fleet." I knelt down.

"My worth is growing." Yi pushed away his robe.

As is mine, I thought while taking him in my mouth.

THE FLEET CHIEFTAINS met in the back of a Macao shop that sold our stolen goods. The proprietor was a former pirate, Tâyson rebel, and brother-in-law to the Incense Master of the Three Dot Society. He was also one of our spies. And today he reported that the townspeople panicked when hundreds of pirate ships sailed into their harbor.

Zheng Yi had arrived first, accompanied by his forty-boat squadron. The moment our banner-festooned long dragon docked, I hurried into town and paid a visit to the best brothel.

I hired the most beautiful prostitutes to serve food and provide entertainment. Next, I went to the best restaurant and hired the chef to make chicken, pork, dumplings, red bean cakes, and noodle soup.

"Excellent food and beautiful women soften the toughest customer," I assured Yi.

His smile-sneer crinkled his eyes. "You are deliciously wicked."

Guo Podai, the Black Flag chieftain, arrived second.

Eleven-finger Wu, the Yellow Flag chieftain, strutted into the room next. He was a thick-shouldered man with a wide nose, short pointy beard, and a shaved head but for a tufted strip down the center. He had the thin low eyebrows of those with few ideas, scattered thinking, and impulsive actions. He spit red betel nut juice on the floor as he walked past me.

White Flag chieftain, Liang Bao, or General, as everyone called him, strolled in with a cheerful expression. I took an immediate liking to the old bushy-browed, white-haired man.

Deaf in one ear, the General tilted his head toward the speaker, giving the impression your words were like gold.

Wushi Er of the Blue Flag and the bald-headed, braid-bearded Toad Rearer—chieftain of the smallest fleet—sauntered in together.

Cousin An-sang, He-song, and other Red Flag squad bosses and skippers filed in after them.

Once everyone sat down, Zheng Yi dismissed me. I didn't go far, just into the next room where I pressed my ear to the wall. Yi's short speech was perfect. Exactly as we had practiced. He explained the importance of remaining a unified group and asked each chieftain to voice their concerns. Then he asked for everyone's agreement to become the Red Flag chieftain.

That was my cue.

I signaled the prostitutes to serve the *baijiu*, steaming Thai rice, and bowls of spicy broth topped with pea sprouts and fragrant herbs. After the men gorged on food and feasted their eyes on the dancing prostitutes, the meeting resumed. It was quick. The chieftains unanimously proclaimed Zheng Yi the new Red Flag chieftain.

"I'm chieftain in name only," said Zheng Yi when we returned to the ship. "A few failed raids, bad weather, or poor profits is all it takes for one of them to overthrow me."

"The only overthrowing will be the prostitutes I hired to join us in bed tonight." I nuzzled his neck. "You're the Emperor of the South Seas now. Why not partake of its pleasures? Emperors should have…" I whispered what three women could do for him.

Yi swallowed and grabbed his cock. "I'm already hard."

A foursome was a risk. What if he wanted four women all the time? Or found me lacking? But it was a risk I was willing to take to make him feel like a real emperor.

Which he did.

"Little Dragon, you never cease to amaze me," he said after the prostitutes had left the next morning. "My cock is drained." He put one hand under his head. "What would you have done if I wanted to make one of of those girls my second wife?"

I scraped his ear with my teeth. "You're the Emperor of the South Seas. Do what you want. Just make sure she's a strong swimmer."

Yi set his hand on my flat belly. "I need a son, Xianggu. Do you understand?" Though whispered, his veiled threat was louder than any gong.

"Your first son was waiting for his father to become Red Flag chieftain first." My voice was light in tone but tight with worry.

"I'm not good at waiting, Little Dragon."

I sat up and drew zigzags down his hard stomach. "Then give your seed only to me. Nobody else. Not even Zhang Bao."

"Don't tell me what to do and who to fuck." His voice was blade sharp and had the same steely edge he used to criticize the crew.

MY BLOOD FLOWED THAT MONTH. And the next.

All my life I had believed determination and skill were the twins of good fortune. Now I knew better. Those good qualities would never open my womb.

I turned to the gods and made offerings to Chuangmu, goddess of the bedchamber, on the Double Seventh Day.

A barren wife was worthless, which meant I must increase my worth in other ways. I became an excellent reader and writer, wrote ransom letters, and oversaw the bookkeeping. I became Zheng Yi's most energetic and devoted confidant. We discussed everything, from which business to buy to the best way to solve the petty grievances between arguing fleet chieftains.

"We need a set of rules," said Zheng Yi one evening while a slave lit the lanterns in the saloon. "Something all the chieftains will agree on. Something that ends our pointless competition. Some kind of standards where rule breakers are punished and cooperation rewarded."

"A pirate code. That's an excellent idea." I removed paper, inkpot, and quill from the sideboard. "The palest ink is better than the best memory." I dipped the quill into the inkpot and stared at him expectantly.

Yi rubbed his hands together. "Item one…"

23

Year of the Water Pig
1803

*Z*heng Yi and I sat on quarterdeck in our thick surcoats when a messenger arrived with good news. A vessel with a cargo of costly bird nests and rhinoceros horns would depart port within the hour.

I tugged the small blade from my belt. "I'll go with you."

Zheng Yi looked at me like I was an idiot. "No more raids for you, Xianggu."

The New Year brought new happiness. I was pregnant! The new life inside me grew more active every day. Zheng Yi was convinced his first son would arrive in April with the southwest winds.

"I'm still quick and agile." I sprung from the chair like a tiger.

Two nosy deckhands scrubbing the deck turned their heads to listen.

"I forbid it," Yi growled.

"Why?" I swung the blade and arched my back to emphasize the rounded swell of my belly. "Who would attack a pregnant woman? Nobody. My belly is an advantage. I'll cut them down before they realize I am the fearless wife of Zheng Yi." My blade hovered over the neck of a deckhand. "Would you attack a pregnant woman?"

His head quivered back and forth. "Never, madam."

I spun around and jabbed the blade toward Zhang Bao, who leaned against a crate. "Would you expect a pregnant woman to run at you with a pointed bamboo stick?"

Bao scratched his chin and squeezed one eye shut as though pondering a difficult dilemma. "Not unless the woman is giving birth. I hear women are wild tigers then."

The deckhands stopped scrubbing, their eyes darting from me to Bao to Yi.

I patted my belly and spoke to the deckhands. "The chief's unborn child must feel the rhythm of a raid and the tempo of a plunder. That way he appreciates the music of piracy."

The deckhands whooped their agreement.

Zheng Yi flashed an indulgent smile. "My crew won't allow you to fight. Will you?"

"No, chief," the deckhands said in unison.

I pushed out my bottom lip, trudged across the deck, and handed the blade to Zheng Yi. "As you wish."

Yi's arm slunk around my waist, his mouth on my ear. "An excellent performance, Little Dragon. Now all my men will be talking about your courage."

I did not participate in raids for the remainder of my pregnancy. Instead, I read, discussed confederation-building strategies, and drafted a pirate code.

"WHY DO you have to meet him?" I adjusted my *hanfu* and smoothed my hair. "Our fleets never plunder in the Fujian sea."

Zheng Yi had sailed up the coast and out of Guangdong waters to meet with Cai Qian— self-proclaimed Majestic Warrior King Who Subdues the Sea—at his Kinmen Island base.

"Cai Qian found an easy way to increase his income." Yi set a gentle hand on my distended belly. "My son kicks strong."

"He likes kicking my ribs best." I enjoyed every kick, no matter how painful. It was a blessing from the Goddess of Mercy and proof of the power of red bean and barley soup.

We met Cai Qian and his wife on the beach under the harsh glare of a sweltering sun.

Cai Qian was a beast of a man, his face the size and shape of an angry water buffalo. He was in his fifties judging by the silver threaded through his hair and beard.

His wife, a thick-limbed woman with thin arched brows, wide flat nose, and fleshy lips looked to be in her mid-forties. Her sallow face revealed her over fondness for wine, *baijiu*, and opium.

They took us to a rather unassuming house guarded by sleepy-eyed men who wore conical *dŏulì*. Bamboo pikes and cutlasses laid at their sides.

"Armed guards?" I whispered to Yi. It seemed rather excessive.

Then we went inside.

Every room was more elaborate than the last. Costly jade vases, intricate bamboo root carvings, large painted hanging scrolls, detailed ten-panel screens, and finely wrought furniture. All plundered treasure.

After he sent a slave for tea, Cai Qian lowered his girth

onto a throne-sized chair. "To what do I owe the honor of a visit from the Red Flag's new chieftain?"

"Business," said Zheng Yi. "I heard you devised an ingenious way to add to your already substantial wealth."

Cai Qian grinned and tugged on his beard. "You refer to my Safe Conduct Pass."

"How does it work?" asked Yi.

Cai Qian thundered with laughter, his jowls jiggling. "That's what I like about you, Yi. No flattery, no posturing, just right to the point."

The slave brought our tea.

Cai Qian wrapped his fleshy paws around the dainty teacup. "It's simple really. I hire my most trustworthy relatives—or those who pretend to be trustworthy—to sell Safe Conduct Passes to merchant ship captains, fishermen, even British and Spanish traders."

"They show you the Safe Conduct Pass and you don't attack," said Yi.

"Easiest money ever." Cai Qian banged his fist on the table and bellowed with laughter. "The bigger the ship, the higher the fee."

His lips pressed tight with skepticism, Yi rubbed his chin. "Your skippers agree to this?"

Cai Qian nodded. "Everyone shares in the profits. If they don't," he drew his thick forefinger across his throat. "Paid not to plunder. What a racket. Soon I'll be as rich as the emperor."

Matron Qian set down her teacup with the elegance of an empress. "Let's leave the men to their business. Walk with me."

She took me to their garden, a serene plot of well-tended shrubbery, abundant trees, and water lilies that bloomed pink, white, and yellow.

"I don't feel like a sea bandit here," said Matron Qian as we strolled over the bridge to the artichoke-roofed gazebo. "There are no worries about weapons, gunpowder, captives, and Mandarin officials." Her eyes flitted to my swollen belly. "How many men have you killed?"

"I didn't have time to stop and count."

"That few then?" Her thin black eyebrows shot up. "You were a flower girl. How many have you fucked?"

"I didn't have time to stop and count."

Matron Qian snorted with laughter. "I like you, Xianggu."

"I like you too." Although what I really liked was that she captained her own ship. "My husband says you command an all-female crew."

Matron Qian's fleshy lips pursed. "Not just a female crew. Female *warriors*."

"Cai Qian allows you a lot of freedom."

"Freedom? Commanding a ship comes with its own kind of shackles. Not iron shackles but shackles of worry brought on by the burdens of leadership."

"I'd gladly wear such shackles. How did you convince your husband to give you a ship?"

"How does a wife convince any man?" Her mouth slithered into a knowing grin. "Qian's my third husband. The first two fools sold me. Right away, I liked Qian—admired his ambition—liked how he fucked. I proved my worth to him—killed many men in raids and worked alongside his crew. I used my mind, body, and garden of peach blossoms." She thrust her hips forward. "One day we captured a drag-the-wind and I said, 'it's mine.' Qian agreed—probably on a whim—and gave me twenty-eight men. I took half the female captives from our flagship and told them they would share in the profits if they learned to fight." Matron Qian touched my arm. "Men undervalue women. We're fiercer, more resourceful, wilier."

"But with the subtly of *yin*," I added.

"Precisely. We're quicker, lighter, and more agile than men. I recruited more women—what woman wouldn't want a life free from a man's dominance—and returned most of Qian's men but the strongest." Matron Qian toyed with her teal melon bead necklace. "The women grew restless—other women not quite satisfying—that's when we began to kidnap only the most handsome men."

"Cai Qian allows this?"

She shrugged. "We indulge each other's appetites." Matron Qian rose from the bench. "Will you join me in smoking opium?"

I didn't care for opium. It was expensive. Turned energetic men lazy, and imaginative thinkers into muddled ones. I had no desire to sink into an opium abyss.

"Thank you, but not today, its pleasures don't agree with this huge belly."

What did agree with me was being given the fortune to know two independent women. Matron Qian and Madam Xu. Both lived by their own rules and refused to be controlled by a man.

24

W arm water trickled down my legs onto the deck. Beside me, Zheng Yi and Wushi Er finalized plans for capturing a southbound ship with a cargo of silkworm cocoons, raw cotton, and leather goods bound for Guangzhou.

"It's time." I looked at the puddle at my feet.

"No, the raid happens at nightfall." Zheng Yi mistook my meaning.

I set my hand on his arm. "Your baby is coming."

Yi puffed out his annoyance. "Tonight?"

"Babies disembark at their leisure not yours, my friend." Wushi Er flashed his gape-toothed grin.

Yi scowled. "Try to have the baby before the raid. I don't need any distractions."

"I'll do my best," I mumbled under my breath and headed to the saloon in search of Pink Flower and Golden Moon.

Suddenly, a cramping agony buckled my legs. I flung out my arm to grab the nearest thing to steady myself. And latched on to Bao's forearm.

"Breathe through it," he said.

"I didn't think it would be this painful." The contraction

over, I released his arm, felt the heat of embarrassment over my weakness.

"Every woman is different. One of my aunts said it was as painless as taking a shit. The other screamed so loud the whole village heard." Bao's brows knitted together. "I'm sorry. How stupid for a man to tell a woman about labor pains." He gave me a sidelong glance. "Did flower girls have babies?"

"They did everything to avoid it. Bad for business. Thank you for your help. Another pain won't come for—"

The second cramp split my body in two. I grabbed Bao's shoulders.

"This will be a fast labor. You're lucky."

I didn't feel lucky. My knees wobbled and my teeth clenched. I held on to Bao's arms and grimaced. The pain of labor made me as fragile as a wounded chickadee.

"I'll help you to your cabin," said Bao.

I nodded. The ship had never seemed so long, each step I took added to its length.

The third contraction came midway up the ladder. I leaned on Bao until it passed.

"Almost there." Bao offered a reassuring smile.

A few moments later, he opened the cabin door. Although only seventeen-years-old, Bao was a man in every way. He excelled at everything and had been promoted from cook to lookout to deckhand to gunner to helmsman in less than two years. The crew adored him. The women swooned. He was charismatic and wore the traits of a leader like an emperor's *mian*, with royal confidence. Yi planned on giving Bao his own squad soon. But it wasn't these things I thought about as I buried my head in the pillow with the next cramp.

Bao rubbed my back—an inappropriate gesture, too personal, too intimate—and spoke soothing words.

"I'll get Pink Flower." Bao hurried from the cabin.

Another contraction came. I gripped the blankets and prayed for a successful birth.

Pink Flower rushed in as another pain wracked my body. "Bao said your water broke."

Bao stood in the doorway. "Last month we kidnapped a healer."

"Bring her." Pink Flower brushed away my hair from my sweat-soaked forehead.

Bao returned five contractions later with the healer, a young woman with crooked teeth, frizzy hair, and a thick chin. Her close-set eyes meant she was meticulous, her short nose a sign of her hard-working nature, and her small mouth proof of her sincerity.

"Have you helped with childbirth?" I rubbed my rock-hard belly.

"Yes, madam, many times."

"What's your name?"

"Fenfang." She shuffled forward. "May I?" She moved her hand all around my belly. "The baby is in a good position."

A new pain came. Different than the others, its force like an avalanche rushing down a mountain.

"The baby…" I groaned through a clenched jaw.

"The baby comes. Madam, you must squat now." Fenfang helped me into the birthing position.

She and Pink Flower held me up as I bore down.

I cried out as a fiery mountain of rocks plunged to the bottom of a valley.

"Madam, your cries will attract evil spirits," whispered Fenfang. "Focus your energy downward. You're a blooming flower, the petals of your body opening…blossoming…flowering…open your petals, madam…allow the pressure to bloom…you're a peony…"

With Pink Flower holding me steady, I pushed pushed PUSHED the infant into Fenfang's waiting hands.

Fenfang held up the black-haired infant. "A son."

I leaned against Pink Flower until the afterbirth slid out, and then I collapsed on the floor.

Fenfang secured a silver necklace around my son's neck and cut the umbilical cord.

Pink Flower helped me into bed. "I'll tell the boss."

Fenfang lay my son in my arms. My heart swelled with happiness, pride, and relief. I felt as bright and light as a thousand lanterns released into a starry sky. This was joy!

Zheng Yi burst into the room in full warrior dress; thick shirt, armored vest, wide belt, turban, and two swords slung over his shoulder. His grin stretched from ear to ear. He kissed my forehead first, then kissed the top of his first son's perfectly shaped head. "Tonight, I fight in honor of my first son. Tomorrow, we'll make offerings to the gods and hand out red-dyed eggs. Everyone will know Zheng Yi has a son." He lifted the infant from my arms and stared at him with wonder.

"Fenfang was a big help. She's skilled in childbirth and healing." I bobbed my head in her direction. "She was kidnapped a month ago."

"Good to know. I'll increase her ransom." Yi's gaze stayed on his newborn son.

Fenfang clapped both hands over her mouth to stifle a cry.

I winced. Such a stupid error. I had just prolonged her ransom process. I glanced at Fenfang and hope she understood the apology in my eyes.

IT WAS tradition for a new mother to sit for one month. No bathing. No hair brushing. It was awful! Annoying and dull. I felt unattractive and unclean. The long hot days passed slowly despite sipping hot soups and reading the romance novels Guo Podai brought me.

We observed the other traditions as well. Fenfang placed peach tree arrows by the cradle. Bao gave Yi two charms, one for his pants, the other for the bottom of the cradle to distract evil spirits.

The day of the one-month celebration, I shaved my son's head and bathed us both in pomelo to ward off any evil spirits. Yi named our son Ying-shih but called him by his milk name, Little Dog.

Guo Podai and Wushi Er helped us celebrate. We ate *ang ku,* pickled ginger, and red eggs. The crew also feasted. That evening, the sky sparkled with fireworks set off by the three flagships.

Yi sent fast boats to deliver red-dyed sweet cakes to chieftains too far away to join our celebration.

At noon, a Yellow Flag messenger came aboard to deliver news about Eleven-finger Wu's great victories along the Leizhou coast. His fleet had looted shops and homes, kidnapped more than thirty people, some wealthy merchants. Better still, when town officials begged for help the emperor said a few plundered villages did not concern him. Which gave me an idea.

Later, as Zheng Yi and I strolled across the deck awash in twilight's pink glow, I gave his stubbly chin a playful scratch. "Tell me, Yi, if Cai Qian can sell safe conduct passes to ships, why can't we sell the same kind of protection to villages?""

Yi's brows shot up. "Mmmm…"

"Of course, the other chieftains need to agree, but I doubt they'll refuse such easy money."

Yi stopped to examine a tack line. "Maybe making such easy money will make us weak. Fearless nerve makes us strong. Soft leaders lose respect."

I swallowed his rebuke like tough meat. "You can be bold *and* still have safe conduct passes. Diversification is good business."

"You've got a point." He turned his attention across the deck where Fenfang played cards with another slave. "Fenfang's relatives won't pay her ransom."

I pressed my lips together. How awful not to be wanted. "Let's make her Little Dog's *amah*. Fenfang comes from a family of landlords. She reads and writes, knows the ways of the rich, and is a skilled healer." It was a better fate than being sold a slave. "There's another matter…"

Yi's brows knitted together in annoyance. "What?"

I stood on my tiptoes and whispered in his ear, "We can enjoy each other again."

Yi's smirking grin was as vast as the Outer Ocean.

25

"The chief's son wants to know the best way to wash a deck." I squatted down and balanced my plump sixth-month child on my knee.

It was easy to learn about every part of the ship when crewmembers thought they were entertaining the chief's son.

The new recruit looked surprised. "Why? Little Dog will never have to do such a lowly chore."

"The only thing low about the job is getting on your knees. Little Dog must understand the importance of a clean deck. There's nothing more dangerous than a slick one. Or an angry deckhand with a twisted ankle or an irate helmsman with a broken arm because of it. You have an important job."

The recruit's face brightened. "This is a sandstone." He held up the bar to Little Dog. "All kinds of things grow on wet wood that warp and rot the planks. Sandstone scours away the scum. This is the best way." He exaggerated his scrubbing movements.

"Thank you, it's important Little Dog learn from diligent and skilled crewmen."

The new recruit beamed with pride. "I'm honored, madam."

Another day, Headman Hsiang-shan showed Little Dog the book of Water Ways. "He's too young to understand my routes." Headman Hsiang-shan, a man with a long thin nose, perpetual scowl, and the faithfulness of a *chongqing* dog, patted the cryptically written old book.

"Little Dog is exceptionally intelligent. Don't discount his coos, he's secretly memorizing every page."

Headman Hsiang-shan barked with laughter. "Then visit every day, madam. By the time Little Dog walks he should be able to chart our course through the Pearl River. And then I can retire." He picked up the hourglass and compass and gave Little Dog a lesson on navigation.

I hung on every word.

Every day Little Dog and I learned something new. The best way to load and unload cargo. The best methods to furl sails, use oars, repair a tear, predict weather, decide ransom amounts, track extortion notes, store and count merchandise, fire cannons, throw anchors, and tie up a captive. The deck-hands seemed to enjoy teaching their tricks and techniques to the chief's son.

Better yet, the crewmen and I became friends.

Learning the details of Zheng Yi's business was important, especially since our relationship rose and fell like the tides. We argued too often. It was my fault. I was frustrated. He forbade me to go on raids or attend chieftain meetings until Little Dog was weaned.

I missed the heft of the cutlass in my hand, the thrill of a raid, and the excitement of interrogating captives. A woman with leaking breasts was not threatening, so I watched from the upper deck while feeding this child who suckled suckled suckled.

I missed our passion-filled evenings. Little Dog rarely slept through the night. Sometimes Fenfang kept him in the saloon until morning, but guilt kept me from doing this too often. A mother hears—or thinks she hears—her baby's every whimper. I was not a good mother or a good lover then.

Despite feeling inadequate, birthing a son did increase my status. Zheng Yi's grandmother, aunt, and sister stopped criticizing me and pretended to forget my flower girl beginnings. They declared Little Dog the very likeness of his father and credited my milk for his chubby body and happy personality.

My improved status also allowed me to speak more freely about ways to increase Red Flag income. Yi had a new generation's future to consider.

Day after day I witnessed the fear the fleet inspired. Villagers fled. Merchants kowtowed. Captains begged. Mandarin officials stooped. Again and again, I urged Zheng Yi to profit from this fear.

At first, he was irritated. He insisted that it would be impossible to unify all the flag fleets under a single code.

"The chieftains will never agree," said Zheng Yi. "Their arguments are more vicious than a cockfight."

I wagged a paper in front of him. "I wrote a list of benefits."

Zheng Yi flapped his hand. "What? Are you a government official now with your lists?"

"I also wrote a list of every possible objection they might have."

Zheng Yi snatched the paper from my hand. He grunted as he read.

"Well?"

He set the list on the desk. "I have a few more to add."

It was a small victory.

By the time Little Dog took his first wobbly steps across

the teak planks, Yi valued my opinions and trusted my judgments above all others. We talked strategies, created plans, and debated a crewman's promotion. This strengthened our marriage.

Zheng Yi wanting another woman in our bed did not.

I indulged his desire for threesomes until I found him pleasuring a young merchant's daughter in our cabin. Without me.

"Go away, wife," Yi said as the young woman, her face toward his feet, rode him and sang out with every plunge.

I backed out of the room and hoped his lust for the slim-hipped girl named Love Song would pass.

It did not.

Love Song shared our bed every night for the next two months. It was her secret places Zheng Yi doted on, her garden of pleasures he preferred.

Love Song's only talent was her voice. Her moans were loud and musical. Her screams, a song telling anyone within hearing of Zheng Yi's ability to prolong her fireworks. I never hated anyone so much.

"I don't like her," I said to Fenfang as we watched Little Dog toddle across the deck. He walked to the wave's rhythms, his superior balance attained while the boat swayed and lurched. How sure-footed he would be on land—better than all those land-born children.

"Deceit shines in her eyes and dances across her lips," agreed Fenfang.

I shared my true feelings with only Fenfang. A chieftain's wife must be careful whom to trust. Fenfang was loyal and honest, her healing skills worth more than silver. She had become more than my son's *amah*, Fenfang was my trusted friend. She was discreet, and never once repeated a single word she heard after watching Zheng Yi and I disagree. Even when we argued about having a second headquarters on Lantau. She knew it was important that the crew believe Zheng Yi and I were of like minds.

"Yi is too smitten by Love Song's youth," I said.

"Men are controlled by *yang* desires." Fenfang held out her hand to steady Little Dog as he jumped up and down. "You're beautiful and talented, and yet he lusts for a girl with no skill in lovemaking. He believes her ridiculous howling is genuine. A young girl fooled my father by pretending awe of his wealth. Father basked in her adulation. Love Song is awed by Zheng Yi's power. He, in turn, is awed by her awe. The admiration he sees in her eyes is an aphrodisiac. It's like he fucks his own image of greatness."

"I don't know if I can fake such adulation."

Zheng Yi needed more than a worthy wife; he needed a young woman's adoration. One not smart enough to disagree with anything he said.

"Love Song is a merchant's daughter. She's probably not a good swimmer." Fenfang planted the seed. There was no need to say more.

That night while Love Song sung her false fireworks, I tried to muster my initial amazement of Yi. But relationships do not go backwards, the feeling of newness lost to familiarity.

Afterwards, Yi cradled Love Song in his arms and boasted of the cache of bird nests and rhinoceros horns found hidden in the rice junk we had raided earlier. While she cooed with admiration, my mind was on which merchant would give us the best price.

Love Song set her smooth white hand on her too-taut belly. "Your seed is strong. I'm already pregnant."

Liar! That was impossible! She might be pregnant but not

with Zheng Yi's child. But Zheng Yi was too smitten to doubt her.

A new young wife. I knew exactly what would happen. Yi would send me to live with his grandmother and aunt on Donghai Island. Bitterness coated my tongue. I would not be so easily replaced.

26

F enfang confirmed my fears.

"Love Song is ambitious," she said when I told her about Love Song's pregnancy. "She wants to be his second wife and wants you sent to Donghai Island."

I knew it! "Who told you this?"

"Zhang Bao. Yesterday, Love Song visited her brother—he's a gunner on Bao's ship—and he overheard them."

"Why didn't Bao tell me himself?" I shifted Little Dog to my bursting-with-milk breast.

"He said it was safer."

"Safer? For whom? And why didn't you tell me earlier?"

Fenfang glanced over her shoulder for eavesdroppers. "I don't trust Bao's motives."

"Bao is loyal."

Fenfang dropped her voice to a whisper. "Bao wants you in a way an adopted son should not want his mother. He's smart. He knows it's safer for someone else to tell you about Love Song's ambitions."

"Bao is a boy," I said more to convince myself than Fenfang.

"Bao is no boy. He's full man. A squad boss. All the women swoon over him. His crew love and respect him, and everyone thinks the gods favor him."

I shrugged. "It's Love Song I worry about, not Bao."

Love Song revealed her intentions two weeks later.

I found her standing over Little Dog's crib, and though only a three quarters moon lit the cabin, I saw the envy in her eyes. I slid from the bed and stood by her side, while Yi, sated from satisfying two women, snored with perfect rhythm.

My arm snaked around Love Song's slim waist and I kissed her smooth cheek. "A man's first son holds a special place in his heart."

"I hope nothing ever happens to Little Dog. This ship is a dangerous place for Yi's precious first-born. Wouldn't it be safer for him to stay on Donghai with his grandmother and aunt?"

"How good of you to worry about him." I pretended not to recognize her subtle threat. "There's something—a secret—I must discuss with you about Yi."

"A secret?" Love Song's eyes glimmered with curiosity.

"Shhh…" I took her hand and led her to the poop deck. "This is my favorite deck. Look." I stretched my arm into the distance. "Can you see Hong Kong?"

"I see nothing," said Love Song.

A large cloud covered the moon. Such luck! But to throw Love Song overboard was risky. She would scream and splash and wake everyone but the drunkest crewmembers. Then I saw the solution.

I moved my hand down her back and caressed her firm buttocks. "Women please women best."

"I prefer men." She did not remove my hand.

"You're a skillful deceiver." My fingers moved between

her legs. "Your false singing moans won't fool Yi for long." I pushed her against the bulwark, my fingers deep within her soft folds. "You want to be Yi's second wife? Then sing *real* fireworks. I can give them to you."

Love Song sighed, her hips pushing against my strokes. "I prefer... men....ooooh."

I continued my attentions and thrust my tongue into her mouth. As her body tensed with pleasure, I grabbed the hammer propped behind her. With her first moan of fulfillment I smashed the side of her head.

Bone crunched. Blood gushed. Her body fell limp in my arms. Its lightness surprised me. But maybe it was the lightness I felt from her death. Worry had been an anchor weighing me down.

Love Song was dead, or near dead, when I shoved her over the side and into the sea. The splash was soft, anyone awake would assume it was a leaping dolphin. I threw the hammer into the sea, and that too, seemed weightless.

"Goodbye, Love Song," I said to the indigo water.

"I didn't like her either."

I spun around. Hidden in the shadows, Bao leaned against a crate.

"She threatened to kill Little Dog," I said.

"I'm not surprised." Bao walked across the deck and looked over the bulwark. "You know, I would've killed her for you."

I straightened my spine. "What are you doing here?"

"I've been here since morning. Did you forget Father and I planned our next campaign?"

"I thought you returned to your ship."

"I came up here to clear my head from this opium haze." Bao rubbed his temples.

"I forbid you to tell Zheng Yi." It was an order.

"I won't." Bao frowned, his brows like diagonal lines, like the character for 'mankind'.

"Your allegiance is to Yi. How can I be certain?"

"My allegiance is to Yi. My heart is yours."

It felt as though a great gush of air blew into me and yet left me gasping for breath. "Stop it. I don't want to hear anymore."

"Xianggu…"

I stepped back. "If I hear even the hint of a rumor accusing me of Love Song's disappearance, I'll kill you."

Bao's eyes grew soft. "Dying by your hands would be an honor…Mother."

"Good. It seems we must both keep each other's secrets. I promise not to tell Yi that you have lustful thoughts of me." Head held high, I walked away.

Rain pelted the ship the next morning, washed away any trace of blood and cleansed my crime.

"Where's Love Song?" Yi yawned and swung his legs over the edge of the berth.

"I don't know." I lifted Little Dog from the crib.

We ate *congee* and discussed the day's business as usual before he left the cabin. He returned a few moments later.

"No one has seen Love Song. She's not on the ship." Yi stood before me, arms crossed, expectant.

I shrugged.

Yi took Little Dog in his arms. "Did you kill her?"

"Why would I do that?" My voice was too strained, too tight in my throat, like I spoke with a mouthful of lemon juice.

Yi nuzzled Little Dog's cheek. "You have no equal, Xianggu. No one will ever take your place. You're the mother of my first son. My business partner. My heart's desire. We're kindred spirits. Love Song isn't a threat to you."

"You're wrong. She was—is a threat."

Yi set Little Dog on his chubby feet. "Was?"

"If I confess to killing her will you think more or less of me? Will you praise me for protecting our son? Or criticize me for jealousy?"

"Both." Yi chased our laughing son around the cabin.

"That girl had only youth and a tight cunt. Nothing more."

"That was enough." Yi captured Little Dog in his arms.

"She was treacherous."

"All but the dimmest women are treacherous." Yi lifted the squealing child over his head.

"I adore you, Yi. My heart swells with pride when I watch you stride across the deck or plan campaigns. There's no chieftain more respected and feared than you. But men like you are never content with one woman. I know I must endure this but..." I wiped away a tear and turned my head.

"Don't stain your face with tears, Little Dragon. The women I bring to our bed will be gone the next day. I promise." He stroked my cheek. "If I get a second wife, I'll keep her in Hong Kong or—"

"Not Donghai, not where she'll plot against me with your grandmother and aunt."

"Never there." Yi's smirking smile was playful. "If I were a wealthy lord in Guangzhou, I would build you a big house with beautiful courtyards where you would wear a different silk *hanfu* every day, drape yourself in jewels, and eat moon cakes while you lounge on a gold settee."

I traced the line of Yi's jaw. "We would break the settee with vigorous exercises."

"And that," said Yi transferring Little Dog to my arms, "is why no other woman will ever come first in my heart." He crossed the room and opened the door. "You killed Love Song."

"I would kill a thousand Love Songs for you."

"I think, Xianggu, the crew already believes that."

27

Zheng Yi was right. And wrong.

Rumors about Love Song's disappearance sprayed like seawater from boat to boat, each version different depending on the gossiper's rank.

The officers' wives insisted I had her killed to frighten any of Yi's future concubines. The officers, worried their first wives might be inspired to do the same, claimed Love Song committed suicide when Yi tired of her. The deckhands were certain I sliced her to bits and flung her body parts overboard. I suspected Bao had a hand in that gruesome tale but had no proof.

The slicing tale grew grislier with each telling. The crew already thought I was a fierce fighter. Murdering Love Song made me doubly dangerous. Earning my displeasure resulted in death. Or so Fenfang heard the deckhands say.

"THE CHIEF WANTS you to decide this man's fate." Squad

Boss He-song pushed the captured sugar boat captain at my feet.

Zheng Yi, his hands clasped behind his back and a smirking grin on his face, observed from quarterdeck. This was a test, one to determine my courage to mete out harsh punishment. All eyes—deckhands, officers, and captives— were fixed on me.

A soft punishment was a sign I was overly compassionate. Too harsh, that I overcompensated for my own feelings of weakness. I knew these crewmen. They valued justice and second-chances as much as they valued power and practicality.

"You jeopardize the lives of your crew by your foolishness." I studied the sugar boat captain and saw arrogance in his eyes. I next addressed his young skinny crew, all stick men. "Are you strong and fit?"

A few murmured their affirmation.

"Your captain is stupid. That's why you wear chains. He put you in danger—risked all your lives—by refusing to purchase a safe conduct permit—a pass *guaranteeing* the safety of his cargo and crew. If he paid the small fee you would be at your duties now, anticipating your earnings from a successful trip. But your captain," I touched the blade tip to the captain's throat, "thought he could outwit the Red Flag. The Red Flag! The largest fleet on the seas! What sort of fool believes he can outrun and out maneuver the Red Flag?!"

The sugar boat sailors look from one to another, then to their captain.

"I'll tell you what sort of man your captain is. He's cheap, and if he's cheap carrying such valuable cargo, he'll be cheap with you—withhold your full wages. And cheap men cheat."

"That's not true," the sugar captain cried.

"Then prove me wrong. Purchase the permit now."

"With what? You've already seized my cargo!"

"I'm offering a different safe passage now, one which grants safe passage for you and your crew."

"I'm not bargaining with a woman," snarled the sugar boat captain, his lips bent in contempt.

I tapped the blade against his throat. "Even if that woman has the power to excuse your violation."

"Violation?! It's an extortion fee! I'm not paying. Besides, how will I pay? You took everything of value." The sugar boat captain spit on my feet.

I sighed, not bothered by the spittle. "Such arrogance." I shook my head. "Such stupidity." I beckoned Three-finger Lo. "Nail the captain's feet to the deck."

It took three deckhands to hold down the screaming sugar boat captain. He head butted Qing Ping. Kicked another in the groin. Writhed and twisted until a gunner nicknamed Mountain gave him a rib-cracking squeeze and bit off a chunk of his ear.

The first hammer blow changed everything. The sugar boat captain stood still and whimpered as his blood pooled and soaked the deck beneath his feet.

"Next time you're offered an opportunity to correct a wrong, take it." I pretended exasperation.

I could not appear heartless or arrogant. This was business, nothing more. Yet, the power that coursed through me was intoxicating. Better than opium. Better than sexual release. Power was an aphrodisiac for the soul. No wonder men killed for it.

"You'll be whipped until I return." I smiled pleasantly at the sugar boat captain. "Three-finger Lo, ask our captives if they want to swear loyalty to us."

Three-finger Lo glared at the captives. "What if they don't?"

"Cut their throats and throw them overboard. I'm in the mood for shark fin soup." I patted my belly and scuttled up the ladder to join Yi. "Well?"

"What are you going to do with the sugar boat captain after he's been whipped?" asked Yi.

"Nothing. I'm going to ask our new sugar boat recruits to prove their loyalty by slicing off a piece of their former captain."

"Don't ask. Demand. Kill those who hesitate. Timid men make incompetent pirates."

28

Year of the Wood Rat
1804

"Victory is certain." Zheng Yi burst into the cabin after a day spent with Squad Bosses Zhang Bao, Liang, Hsiao, Chen, and Ta. "Every chieftain sends squadrons. With our fleets united nothing will stop us from controlling trade in the South Seas. We'll be no match for the emperor's wretched navy." Yi rubbed his hands together. "Once we take Lantau, we will have two well-situated headquarters."

"Is two enough?" I set down the ivory comb and began braiding my hair.

"No. We need more safe havens and more recruiting offices. Wushi Er, Eleven-finger Wu, the General, Guo Podai, Toad Rearer—they all report the same. Every day more recruits join—some of them the same clerks and *yamen* who tried to arrest our men months earlier."

"Respectable people want to join our fleets?" I pinned up the braids and wrapped a turban about my head.

"Not as pirates, no. They want to be spies and middlemen.

163

What government official doesn't enjoy silver and double-dealing?" Yi pressed his finger into the map. "See? Lantau's location at the mouth of the Pearl River and its proximity to Lintin Island is perfect. From here we'll finally be able to control the entire South Seas."

I secured the strap holding my cutlass and sword. "I'm ready."

"You're not going." Yi slid his cutlass into his belt.

"Why not? Hundreds of men will swarm Tung Chung like locusts over a rice field. They need my leadership."

"You're staying here."

"Why?"

Yi scowled. "I don't need to give you a reason."

"No, the great chieftain of the Red Flag fleet does not *need* a reason other than to satisfy his wife's curiosity." I set a soft hand on his chest. "Are you worried I'll kill more villagers than you?"

Yi burst out laughing. "No, Little Dragon, I need you here. You'll be in charge of the flagship until we take Lantau."

"I'm in charge of nothing."

"Nothing?!" Zheng Yi roared. "My flagship is nothing?!"

"I mean only that—"

"The flagship is the heart of the fleet. Even a vacant and empty flagship! It is a beacon, sanctuary, and temple. It's the crew's lifeblood. Its strength gives them strength. Every plank, every bamboo matting, every smear of tar, every drop of tung oil, every inch of line is fixed in their soul."

"I—"

"Hear me, wife. All my best men—thousands of them—raid the island, which leaves my ship manned by only a few. The villagers know this. And they might use the opportunity to seize the ship—to fire our own cannons at our other boats

—to destroy in minutes what I've worked so hard to attain. I leave the flagship in your capable hands, Xianggu. Your job here is as important as mine."

"Forgive me, Yi. In my eagerness to be by your side, I forgot—"

"Chieftains and squad bosses don't forget to defend their ships."

"I won't make the mistake again. I'll protect the flagship." With help from a few slaves, a couple captives, and a withered old gunner.

Yi usually left a team of deckhands and gunners on board, but the raid on Lantau required every able-bodied man and woman.

"Good." Yi gave me hard look. "We're far from shore. I doubt the villagers are ambitious or sneaky enough to get here without being seen but be vigilant just the same."

"I will." I hurried after him as he strode out of the cabin.

Zheng Yi signaled the deckhand to raise the attack flag.

In the gray twilight, Zheng Yi led thousands of armed pirates in hundreds of sampans to the shore. The Lantao lookout system was efficient, and by the time the first teams stormed the beach the village gong boomed its warning.

I pressed the wood and brass spyglass to my eye in search of Zheng Yi's red surcoat amid the kaleidoscope of colors.

"Women and children flee into the forest," shouted our lookout from his perch. "The village men fight back."

Merchants, fishermen, grass cutters, shoemakers, peddlers, *yamen*, woodcutters—they all fought to keep hold of the precious bit of land—the center for salt, silver, and opium trading—at the mouth of the Pearl River. Which was why Yi was determined to make it our new headquarters.

"To seize such a strategic island is sure to enrage the emperor." Fenfang struggled to hold on to my squirmy child.

"The chieftains don't fear an emperor in faraway Beijing." I trained the spyglass on the undefended Tung Chung fort.

"The emperor has a thousand eyes," said Fenfang. "His punishing arm reaches into all provinces."

"We have a thousand arms and eyes too." I lowered the spyglass. "We're not that different from the Mandarins."

"Yes, but their laws are ancient, written on scrolls hundreds of years old."

"Ours will be written down soon enough." Frustrated that the fighting was too far away to watch with accuracy, I walked from deck to deck, back and forth to make certain the captives and slaves kept busy. There was always repair or cleaning to be done.

Hours later, several loud booms sent me rushing portside. Smoke curled upward from the fort. The town was ours!

I scooped Little Dog into my arms, kissed his fat bronzed cheeks, and stared at the beach.

The old gunner and Fenfang joined me. No villager was foolish enough to cross the harbor to try to commandeer one of our ships.

But I was the foolish one.

The attack came from behind.

29

F ive men in threadbare pants scrambled over the sides. They were seasonal sea bandits, desperate fishermen who banded together during the off-season to commit petty theft. Surely these senseless amateurs knew it took more than five men to sail a ship this size.

The oldest man brandished a rusty sword. "This ship is ours."

"You're crazy. You can't commandeer a flagship." I shifted Little Dog from my left arm to my right. "Chief Zheng Yi will slice you himself when he returns." My eyes flicked to Fenfang.

She blinked her response.

"He won't be returning to *this* ship. It's ours now." The leader stepped forward, it was the small step of a hesitant man.

His three accomplices stayed behind him, their eyes roving from side to side as they scanned the deck for crewmembers. The other, a man missing half his teeth, went to search the cargo holds.

"Nobody but a few slaves and captives," said Half Teeth when he returned.

Without taking my eyes off the sea bandits, I threw Little Dog to Fenfang, then pulled out my cutlass and small blade. "Which of you would like to die first?"

"You mean which of us will fuck you first?" Half Teeth pantomimed the action.

I had to stall. The lookout needed to descend. The wrinkled old gunner needed to sneak around the other side.

"The only fucking will be my blade up your ass." I gave the blade a quick twist.

"Foul mouthed cunt."

"Don't be stupid," I said. "Leave the ship. As a token of my thankfulness I'll give you two gifts. Enough silver to feed your family until fishing season and my promise that I will forget your faces."

"Fuck your gifts." The leader spat on the deck.

I spat back. "Five men cannot sail this ship."

"There are plenty of captives below." Half Teeth stomped his foot on the deck.

"They can't sail the ship either. You've captured a dragon you have no ability to control."

"Is that why this ship is unprotected?" The leader waved his blade about.

"*I'm* protecting it."

"A woman?" The leader snorted with laughter. "Why don't you use that little blade you're holding to make us some food?"

"The wife of Zheng Yi does not tolerate disrespect."

No more negotiating. Enough time had passed for the old gunner to get into position, for a slave or two to find a weapon, for the lookout to come down, and for me to calculate my throw.

My aim was true. The blade skewered the leader's eye.

He howled, pulled the blade out and dropped to his knees as blood gushed over his hands.

The others rushed at me.

Yi had taught me well. I was small and quick, anticipated their thrusts and blocked their blows. With a sword in one hand and a cutlass in the other, my *gung fu*—years spent practicing the art of sword fighting—made me a formidable opponent.

My cutlass carved a wedge of skin from the second bandit's forehead. Blinded by the gushing blood, he wiped it away only to see one of our slaves run him through with a bamboo spike.

I ducked, spun about, and slashed the arm of the third bandit just as our lookout joined the fight.

Half Teeth lunged at me. I executed a move Zheng Yi had made me practice a thousand times and used Half Teeth's own momentum against him. He received the promised blade up his shit-filled bowels.

The old gunner gutted the fifth bandit with his cutlass.

I stood over the leader as he writhed on the deck, his blood-soaked hand covering his empty eye socket.

"Wrong ship. Wrong cunt." My blade slit his throat.

Zheng Yi returned to the sight of five heads mounted on bamboo sticks.

"I pity those who cross you," said Yi with his smirking grin. "Did you punish the lookout?"

"Why? He didn't expect desperate fishermen to come from the sea."

"Lookouts look out in all directions."

"The fishermen's boat was small. It was easily concealed among all of ours." I had had enough blood for one day.

"The lookout expects to be punished." Yi crossed his arms. "The crew expects him to be punished. Punish him."

I had the lookout beaten with a rattan whip until he bled. The boy didn't cry, not so much as a whimper escaped his lips. When I lifted my hand to stop the punishment, the boy fell at my feet and pledged his loyalty.

"If I fail you again," he said. "I beg you to pluck out my eyes."

THE GENERAL BROUGHT TRAGIC NEWS.

"The Mandarins attacked Cai Qian and his wife off the Taiwan coast." His eyes were shadowed from too many sleepless nights. "The navy used our own tactics against us and struck during the night. Cai Qian's crew defeated them but…" He shook his head, "By the time Qian came to help it was too late. His wife and her crew had been slaughtered."

"We're better organized than the Fujian pirates," said Zheng Yi. "The navy wouldn't dare attack us. Our united fleets far outnumber their paltry forces."

"Are our fleets as united as you think? Or is it only the same blue waters we have in common?" The General's question was a valid one.

The Mandarin's victory over Cai Qian upset me. Madam Qian's death felt like a great rogue wave over my spirit. First Madam Xu. Now Madam Qian. My role models. My inspiration. Perhaps women were not meant to be successful, powerful, and independent.

More bad news arrived later that month. Government officials pretending to be merchants arrested Zheng Yi's sister, her stepson, and several Red Flag members for selling stolen wine and oil.

Yi roared like a tiger when the messenger delivered the news. "My sister is too shrew to be caught in a trap. This is the work of rival pirate gangs."

It was a a possibility.

Not all pirates joined a flag fleet. Some, like the fishermen who attempted to commandeer our ship during the battle at Lantau, started their own gangs. These worms were stupid, unorganized, and careless. Even the secret societies refused to make deals with them.

The pirate gangs, however, had two effective weapons, gossip and sabotage. Sometimes all it took to undermine years of a chieftain's *guanxi* with local merchants and middlemen was a few outrageous lies.

"It's time to unite the flag fleets under a formal code," I said. "Merchants are less likely to believe the pirate gang's lies if it means the loss of *all* the flag fleets businesses. It would put them out of business."

Yi quaffed a tall cup of *baijiu* as he sat at the desk. "To cheat or betray one flag fleet is to cheat on them all." He removed the draft of the proposed codes from the drawer and slid it towards me. "Add it to the code."

I did. The list I had started several years ago had become quite long.

I set down the quill after completing the final character. "The time has come, husband. Summon the chieftains. Let them debate the merits of the code."

Yi rubbed his temples. "Debate is good, but I'm worried this debate will open old wounds. That would be a disaster."

30

Year of the Wood Ox
July 1805

We, the Red Flag fleet, arrived in Macao first.

The next morning the harbor was crowded with two-masted fast boats, black-hulled trough junks, drag-the-winds, open-the-waves, and great flagships. Each flew their banner. Our red with white scalloped trim banners outnumbered all the others.

Guo Podai raised a black triangle with white trim. Eleven-finger Wu hoisted his red square with a yellow border. Flapping in the breeze was a red triangle with a yellow border, and Toad Rearer's blue and white square banner.

Portuguese merchant ships anchored nearby panicked and posted extra lookouts and crew on deck just to watch our sampans and long dragons deliver messages from flagship to flagship, from boat to boat.

Our amassing at the Macao harbor also had another effect; it served as a reminder to foreign fleets that our strength far exceeded the Mandarin navy.

The next morning sluggish rain dripped from the sky as Yi and I trod up the wide beach toward the teahouse. Despite the messenger's promise that we meant no harm, the streets were empty. The townsfolk stayed in their homes, their beautiful daughters and young boys hidden from view. A few had no fear. Men too old to be kidnapped and wrinkled grandmothers warily watched the most powerful chieftains of the South Seas walk down the streets. Merchants observed our procession with an eye toward profit. This many men and boats were a boon to any business.

Absent from this gathering was Cai Qian, who currently plundered the north with the rage of a man bent on exacting revenge against his wife's death.

Dressed in elaborate robes, each chieftain brought his first wife—if he had one—his foremost squad bosses, trusted scribe, and a small contingent of armed men.

The chieftains entered the large room and sat at the table. Behind them, sat their squad bosses and wives. Zhang Bao welcomed each chieftain with his usual irresistible charm.

As a show of solidarity, Guo Podai, the second most powerful chieftain, sat next to Zheng Yi. The General sat on the other side. Toad Rearer of the Green Flag flashed me a wide grin and settled opposite. He flicked the small gold bead at the end of his thin braided beard. It was a gift from Zheng Yi and I for his help with a thorny ransom exchange. Eleven-finger Wu of the Yellow Flag took a place beside Toad Rearer. Known for his quick temper and belligerent tongue, Eleven-finger Wu would be the toughest chieftain to convince.

Wushi Er entered last. "About time we form a confederation." A skilled negotiator, Wushi Er made small talk with each chieftain before pulling up the last chair at the table.

"United we are unconquerable," Zheng Yi began.

"Divided we squabble among one another. Divided we compete for the best cargo ships. Divided, seasonal pirates sabotage our interests. United, we thrive. We grow strong. We prosper. Our children prosper."

"Competition makes us strong." Eleven-finger Wu spit on the floor.

"I agree," said Yi. "Competition hones our negotiation and fighting skills. Competition made us all rich. Yet I believe forming a confederation by adhering to a set of rules will make us even richer."

"Rules? Whose rules?" Toad Rearer puffed out his cheeks. "What rule can apply to your large fleet and my small one?"

"The rules will increase our wealth no matter how many boats you command." Yi held up the draft of the pirate code. "These are ideas. We'll discuss the merits and faults of each —add, change, or remove only when we all agree." He pointed to the secretary trusted by all the chieftains. "Wu Shang-te will write the formal code. But first we must put aside our egos and petty differences. Only then can we form a strong confederation and rise in power and wealth."

"Nobody is going to tell me what to do," growled Eleven-finger Wu. "Fuck rules!"

"Rules are for rice bucket government officials." Toad Rearer fiddled with his gold bead.

"Only idiots scorn an idea before they hear it," said Wushi Er.

Eleven-finger Wu spit again. "Only idiots listen to idiocy."

A Blue Flag squad boss stood up. "Do I have to consult a rule book before attacking a salt junk?"

"How specific are these rules?" asked a Yellow Flag squad boss.

"What's the penalty for breaking the rules?"

"Who administers the penalties?"

"Do these rules pertain to safe conduct passes?"

Yi waited for the barrage of questions to die down. "It's all here." He rattled the paper. "First rule: the fleet must register and fly the correct banner on their foremast." He lifted his hand to halt side comments. "There are three reasons for this rule. We can't fool one another. We'll be able to quickly identify banner-less rogue pirate gangs. And the navy can't trick us by masquerading as a flag fleet."

While the chieftains debated the particularities of the first rule—including the need to register every boat—my admiration for Yi blossomed like a field of chrysanthemums. He tempered his forceful personality, spoke without intimidation, considered others' opinions, discussed solutions, and calmed rising tempers.

It took over an hour for the chieftains to approve the first rule. Each boat must display a registration number on its bow and fly an identifying banner on the foremast.

It took another hour to decide the penalty for breaking the rule, which was to seize the offending vessel, its weapons, and any merchandise. Yet it took only minutes for the chieftains to agree that the confiscated property would be distributed among all fleets.

After a much needed break, Yi proposed the second rule. It was a continuation of the first and made it mandatory for each boat to fly its fleet's flag and registration number. This rule forbade one ship or squad from committing atrocities under the guise of another. Punishments for such a terrible breach of trust would be decided by all the chieftains.

I was surprised at how callous the chieftains were when it came to punishments. They demanded harsh penalties for anyone who committed treachery, disobeyed rules, damaged another's vessel, and hindered a campaign. Even pirates had an honor code.

"Nail the headman to the deck and flog him until there's no flesh on his body."

"Slice him into twenty-four pieces."

"Cut out his heart and eat it!"

These punishments were meted out for defiant fishermen, thieving villagers, duplicitous spies, rebellious merchant sailors, and the navy. Not our own men. Until now. The chieftains wanted our men treated with equal cruelty.

"The punishment must be harsh and unforgiving," said Eleven-finger Wu. "Otherwise the rules will be bent or broken. Useless as a lame horse. Minor punishments like flogging or ear-chopping are as hurtful as an ugly whore's rebuke."

"Why are you fucking ugly whores?" Wushi Er stroked his long beard. "Is that all your beautiful wife allows?"

"At least I'm not stupid enough to keep six wives on my ship," said Eleven-finger Wu.

I bit my tongue to keep from laughing. Everyone knew about Wushi Er's six bickering wives.

"It takes six to satisfy my needs." Wushi Er spread his arms wide and grinned.

"You mean six wives to get it hard, old man."

Wushi Er stood, his fingertips resting on the table. "I'm older than everyone but the General. While you were still sucking on your mother's tits, whores sucked my cock." He made a fireworks face, and everyone laughed, and then he turned to Eleven-finger Wu. "I agree with you. The penalty for disabling or impeding another fleet's boat should be severe, but it defeats our purpose if we murder one another for thievery. We're all thieves, aren't we? Well-organized professional thieves. What we need is a punishment causing maximum *monetary* pain."

"A punishment strict enough to discourage us from robbing one another." Toad Rearer puffed out his cheeks in agreement.

The chieftains finally decided the penalty for inter-fleet theft or disabling another's vessel was monetary compensation awarded to the wronged party. If not immediately possible—small boats carried about fifty thousand dollars and large boats almost one hundred thousand—the offender deducted future profits until payment was paid in full. In addition, the offender's weapons would be confiscated until all the chieftains reviewed his case.

The fourth rule was decided quickly. The first vessel to attack a cargo ship laid claim to its goods. Any vessel attempting to overtake the initial captor must pay a fine exceeding the cargo's value—as determined by an impartial accountant—or be subject to the combined fleets' attack.

"Time for a break. We'll meet back here tomorrow," said Zheng Yi after secretary Wu Shang-te finished recording everything.

Toad Rearer, Wushi Er, and Eleven-finger Wu headed to the nearest opium den. The General had business with an uncle with ties to the Three Harmonies Society.

Yi pulled me aside. "Podai, Bao, and I have business with several merchants." He gestured to the chieftains' wives. They were all going to A-Ma temple.

"I'll go with you. But first I want to talk to Kim."

The pretty wives were more prone to mean-spirited chatter than conversation about trade problems and market values. I knew Kim, Wushi Er's first wife, would relay gossip of any real value. She and I often shared stories and drank tea while our husbands planned joint campaigns. She was a quiet but shrewd woman who managed to avoid bickering with her husband's five younger wives by helping him with the banditry business.

Once outside the teahouse, Kim and I found a chance to talk.

"Did you hear the rumors?" I asked not specifying *which* rumor.

Kim's eyes sparkled with mischief. "Mmmm, might that be the rumor about how you murdered Yi's concubine? What was her name…Sunken Lyric?"

"I don't recall." I gave her my most innocent smile.

"Ah, that's right, it was Love Song. Yes, I heard most of the rumors. Tell me, Xianggu, if the other wives ask—and they will—should I confirm or deny?"

I chewed on my lip. Confirmation made me look jealous, bitter, and violent. Denial implied I was ashamed. "I trust your good judgment."

Kim clicked her tongue with approval. "Neither one. Very wise." She looked over her shoulder. "A warning, Xianggu, not about the rumor but something I have seen with my own eyes. Be careful around Yi's two adopted sons. They are two men with one desire."

"Podai and Bao? What do they want besides more ships and wealth?"

"You."

31

"Not making offerings to Mazu with the other wives?" Zhang Bao helped me into the rickshaw. "We can go to to the temple after this business if you like."

"I'd like that." I slid next to Yi.

Guo Podai, both hands extended, presented me with a red umbrella. "To keep the sun off your fair skin, Xianggu."

I opened it up. "It's beautiful." A garden of purple and green painted flowers decorated the umbrella.

Our two rickshaws rolled through the busy Macao streets. No longer afraid of a raid, merchants, peddlers, fishermen, Portuguese traders, and sailors loitered about, gambled in the streets and made deals across makeshift tables. Everyone stared as we passed. Pirates did not blend in. Every man, except for the Portuguese, shaved their foreheads and wore long queues.

Pirates rejected the Mandarin hairstyle, hats, and clothes. Fleet chieftains preferred turbans to conical bamboo hats. And wore bright surcoats and tunics instead of short pants and shirts.

At only nineteen-years-old, Zhang Bao was already the

talk of every town. His flashy purple silk robe and black turban made him instantly recognizable to every pirate and most townsfolk. It seemed everyone, land and sea folk alike, held him in awe. He was a savvy supervisor, athletic warrior, and a skillful strategist who would make an excellent chieftain one day.

But it wasn't those qualities I peeked at under my umbrella. Bao was exceptionally good looking. He was tall and broad shouldered, had an honest face and penetrating brown eyes. Most endearing were his thick straight eyebrows that made diagonal lines whenever he was disappointed.

Yi no longer asked Bao into his bed. The ritual initiation ended when Yi promoted Bao to helmsman. Fenfang said Bao enjoyed the prostitutes on his ship. The women adored him, each wanted to be his favorite in hopes of becoming his wife. His sexual prowess was already legendary.

Twenty-five-year-old Guo Podai was also quite handsome, and nearer my age. He was more muscular than Bao, thicker in chest and limbs—the leanness of youth replaced with a man's bulk. He had a square jaw and the soulful eyes of a poet. It was time he took a wife. As chieftain of the second largest flag fleet he could afford several. When I asked him why he wasn't married yet he confessed his love for a woman he could never have.

My husband's two adopted sons, both equally ambitious, but their differences were as vast as the lands of the Great Qing. Bao was flamboyant and charismatic. Podai, private and serious.

This afternoon, despite the productive meeting, Podai and Bao snarled at each other like two lions vying for dominance. Men! Such fools. Both could learn from each other. Bao's leadership style needed honing. Podai needed to have better relations with his crew—he was too standoffish.

"Podai and Bao act like they're competitors," I said after we left a shop owned by one of Zheng Yi's many uncles.

"They are." Yi glanced at their rickshaw behind us. "It'll get worse when Bao commands his own fleet. Podai is more knowledgeable, but Bao possesses a rare ability, he inspires devotion. Podai is envious of this trait. He knows blind devotion is the difference between a crew ready to die for a risky venture and one merely obeying orders." He patted my leg. "Competition is good. It will make them better chieftains. Push them past their limitations. Force them to take bold risks they might not otherwise. My adopted sons are gems, they need friction to be polished to perfection."

KIM DREW me aside the following morning before the meeting. "The wives have a new name for you. I think you'll approve." One side of her mouth curved upwards with amusement. "Dragon Lady."

"Dragon Lady?!" I wrinkled my nose. "This better not reach the emperor's ears. His imperial dragon will breathe fire on me if he learns such a name was given to a lowly female sea bandit."

Kim's head swiveled about as she checked for eavesdroppers. "I think it's the perfect name for you. After all, you made Yi's concubine disappear and beheaded those five rogue pirates in Lantau." She leaned into my shoulder. "The wives said their husbands are as charmed by your beauty as your daring. Eleven-finger Wu's wife said he told her only a great sea lord like Zheng Yi can subdue such a powerful woman."

"Chieftains have too much *yang*. They control their women, dominate their crew, and want to conquer everything on land and sea," I said despite the pride that surged through my body. "We wives know better ways to achieve our desires."

Kim cocked her head. "Like having another son?"

"Of course." I lied. I wanted more than that. I wanted to be my own master. To captain my own boat. Business and leadership stirred my spirit, gave my life purpose, and filled my heart with happiness.

Our conversation was thankfully cut short when the second meeting day began.

"The next rule concerns the safe passage permit," said Zheng Yi. "You've already discovered how profitable it is. We'll earn more from permits than from selling stolen goods. But..."

"There's always a 'but'." Eleven-finger Wu popped a betel nut in his mouth.

"I like buts. Especially big soft ones," said Wushi Er.

Yi waited for the laughter to die down. "This is neither big or soft. It's critical we honor these permits. If we don't, they become nothing more than a worthless piece of paper. Anyone witnessing a violation must report it. Turn a blind eye and you will be punished as a co-conspirator."

"I agree," said Guo Podai. "If we don't supervise ourselves, merchant captains will stop buying them."

"Who's overseeing this supervision?" said Eleven-finger Wu. "None of us want to give up a ship to play supervisor."

The General, Toad Rearer, and Wushi Er all agreed.

"When was the last time you sailed without an escort?" asked Podai. "We're a thousand strong with lookouts on every vessel."

Eleven-finger Wu snorted. "Lookouts are boys. They wouldn't know what to look for."

"Get better lookouts," Guo Podai snapped.

"Lookouts. Deckhands. Slaves." The General's bushy gray eyebrows merged into a wrinkled web on his forehead. "Offer a reward." He spread one eye wide with two fingers. "They'll see treachery better."

The chieftains growled like tigers until they decided that any man who reported and stopped an unlawful seizure be rewarded one hundred silver dollars. And, if his keen eye for treachery caused a fight that left him wounded, everyone would pay for his medical care.

After they agreed on the fifth article, the chieftains called for a break.

"The sixth article is about sailing into other oceans and far harbors without permission," said Zheng Yi before the chieftains rose from their seats. "Think about the best punishments." He glanced at me.

My chin dipped ever so slightly.

The sixth article struck at the core of the fleets' independence. No pirate wanted to be told where they could or could not sail. Which is why late last night Yi had summoned Podai, Bao, and the General to our ship for a secret meeting. Yi wanted to have a convincing rebuttal for every possible argument.

Guo Podai had reminded us of the obvious. Piracy thrives because it was lawless. And yet it was rules which would help us all grow richer.

"They only understand one thing. Money and more money," said Podai.

"I have a plan," I had said. "Bao, Podai, General, you must be the first to disagree. Cite every reason why it's a bad idea, that way Yi has the opportunity to explain the advantages."

I had a part in the charade as well. And I played my part when the meeting resumed.

"The sixth article will assure our continued domination of Guangzhou," said Zheng Yi. "By making sure fast boats get permission before venturing outside the province."

"Fuck no!" Eleven-finger Wu slammed his hand on the table. "The world is mine for the taking!"

The others harrumphed in agreement, Guo, Podai, and the General the most vocal.

"Forgive me, Father, for disagreeing." Bao rose to his feet. "You taught me well. So well that raiding towns and boats along Guangdong coast is not enough. I will make more money sailing farther away than being confined to a territory like some petty Mandarin official."

"Your own son is against the article," said Eleven-finger Wu, "because he seeks his own greatness. As he should."

"Greatness is only achieved when we stretch our authority to far places." Guo Podai sounded very convincing.

"Is it greatness you want? Or wealth?" Zheng Yi settled back in the chair, the familiar smirk-smile curling the corners of his mouth.

"They're the same," said Toad Rearer puffing out his cheeks.

"I'm too old and too experienced to ask permission of any of you. I'll sail when and where I please." The General ended his declaration with a loud convincing grunt.

"We all agree, we hate article six." Wushi Er stroked his long beard. "Let's hear the next one—hope it's not as stupid as this one."

Showtime.

I rose from my chair.

32

My eyes welled with false tears. "Guo Podai. Zhang Bao. I'm ashamed. Is this how you return the love and loyalty your father shows you? Do you think *you* know more than the man commanding the largest fleet? The man whose veins flow with the blood of generations of pirate ancestors? You do not!" I glared at both Podai and Bao. "I beg of you, listen to your father. Give him a chance to explain how it will help you prosper. You owe him that." I dabbed my eyes with a handkerchief. "I'm only a woman…"

Someone muttered 'Dragon Lady' under their breath.

"But even a woman knows the importance of strategy. Each chieftain here," I spread out my arm, "is great because of Zeng Yi's excellent strategies."

The chieftains nodded their agreement and seemed a bit surprised by Podai's and Bao's opposition. Adopted sons were expected to be loyal.

"Podai, Bao," I continued. "I challenge you to declare why article six is unreasonable."

Each objection was debated. The problem of switching loyalties to another fleet. Of instigating warfare with sea bandits from other provinces. Of risking a vessel and crew. Of stashing treasures and wealth in far off coves. Of maintaining the safety found in a large squad. Of confiscating weapons and goods. And of executing the skippers responsible for insubordination.

Eleven-finger Wu was the last to agree. He finally relented because he hated the thought that one of his squad bosses would hide stolen prizes without distributing the profits.

"I'll be happy to chop off the head of any crewmember who hordes treasure." Eleven-finger Wu aimed a steely gaze at his squad bosses and slashed his cutlass through the air.

The contentious sixth article passed, we moved to the seventh. More controversy followed.

"What? You want me to look away while Wushi Er's relative does business with my enemy?" Eleven-finger Wu banged his fist on the table. "That dog-nephew of his spies for local officials—four of my men were beheaded in a sting operation."

"My nephew shouldn't be penalized because he does business with dishonest fellows," explained Wushi Er. "I have ninety vessels. I am the Great General Who Pacifies the Sea. Blackmail and racketeering along the Leizhou Peninsula make me rich. And *you're* telling me you refuse to do business with a wicked person? If we only bought and sold to honest men, we'd have no one to do business with."

"We all have merchants and officials who've deceived us," said Zheng Yi. "But we need to think more like merchants than pirates. Why do I care if someone deals with my enemy if he gives me the best price?"

"I don't believe what I'm hearing." Eleven-finger Wu pushed the teacup off the table where it shattered across the floor.

"Swallow your pride." Wushi Er scowled. "Think how it is for those pitiful shopkeepers on land—stuck in a town—forced to deal with greedy dishonest officials every day. We can sail away. They can't."

"I'd rather run them through, destroy their shop, and burst their daughter's chrysanthemum."

Guo Podai rolled his eyes. "Stop thinking with your cock."

"He likes ass," said Wushi Er.

"Shut the fuck up," growled Eleven-finger Wu.

Despite Eleven-finger Wu's begrudging approval, everyone agreed to the eighth article. And the ninth.

"We're in agreement then." Zheng Yi, weary but pleased, rubbed his temples. "If a flagship hoists its flag high on the foremast it's a signal we need to confer. A flag on the third mast of the squad boss's ship means all fast boats must assemble to hear new orders." He looked at secretary Wu Shang-te. "Make enough copies for each chieftain and squad boss."

It was finally done. A pirate code! It was *almost* perfect.

Yi refused my pleas for another rule. I wanted to forbid the rape of female captives, but he claimed the chieftains would never agree to it.

After a meal of roasted pork, rice, and vegetables, Yi and I returned to the flagship. He was in good-humor, our new pirate confederation had put him in the most agreeable mood I had seen for months. It was the best time to ask for a favor.

"I want to captain my own vessel." I poured his wine to the brim.

"No." He guzzled the cup down, gestured for a refill. "Give me another son instead."

My womb was a shackle, its own kind of servitude, and prevented me from achieving my goals.

"I can captain a vessel and give you a son at the same time."

Yi peered into his cup as though it contained the answer to the world's mysteries. "You would be too vulnerable. Cai Qian couldn't save his own wife. Or did you forget that? Besides, you can't captain a ship with a baby tugging at your tits all day. Do you really think you can order these men about when they're slipping on a deck slick with breast milk?" He looked up and laughed.

"Perhaps I'll suckle new recruits at my breasts and make them my own adopted sons."

Yi's good humor vanished. "I am not Cai Qian. Fuck another man and I will kill you."

Unruffled by his quick temper, I stroked his rough cheek. "One day women will have the same opportunities as men. Then what?"

"You want more opportunity? Here's one." He set my hand on his stiff cock.

I SHIELDED my eyes from the glare and stared at Kinmen Island, Cai Qian's headquarters. "Another joint venture?"

"I don't know. His message was cryptic." Zheng Yi lifted the spyglass to his eye. "He and Zhu Fen ended their alliance after a vicious argument over the naval defeat."

"Does this mean he no longer proclaims himself the Majestic Warrior King Who Subdues the Sea?" I rolled my eyes at the pompous title.

Yi guffawed. "Watch your tongue around him, Xianggu."

The water buffalo-faced Cai Qian met us on the beach. In the courtyard, a pretty young concubine, bearing a strong resemblance to his deceased wife, served tea.

"Your visit honors me." Cai Qian needed a favor. He was suspiciously soft spoken, his gruff manners replaced with flattery.

"Our visit has nothing to do with honoring you," I said as the Tien Chi flower bloomed in my cup, the tiny buds floating the green sphere to the surface.

"You remind me of my first wife." Cai Qian sighed. "Blunt. No nonsense." He waved away her memory. "I need a partner." He shifted his girth. "It's time I leave this island for a new one. A better one. Taiwan."

Yi cocked an eyebrow. "Your success at Luerman port—"

Cai Qian pounded his thick chest. "I'm a big success! Huge! Thirty-six merchant junks captured last year! Amoy-bound rice junks raided as they left port! I have a hundred and fifty boats and command five thousand men. I am the fucking emperor of Fujian province!" He collected himself, adjusted his surcoat. "The time has come for me to take Taiwan."

Yi rubbed his chin. "You want to rule the island?"

Cai Qian nodded. "As the Majestic Warrior King Who Subdues the Sea, I will form a new empire. The Cai Dynasty. You," he jabbed his chubby finger at Yi, "will join me in this profitable venture."

"It's tempting," said Yi. "Tell me about Taiwan's local militia."

"Weak. Ineffectual. Boys still sucking on their mother's tits and men pulling on their cocks."

"Do all your vessels have cannons?"

"Cannons and ammunition."

The Red Flag had more. More men. More vessels. More cannons and weapons. Three hundred boats and thirty thousand men at last count.

Cai Qian glanced at me. "Xianggu is a beautiful woman.

She deserves to live in luxury, walk in elegant courtyards, wear the finest silks, and drink costly Da-Hung Pao tea. She's a wife of rare skill. Already she gives you a son. Your son and any future sons deserve a secure future, a future where the government recognizes your sons' legitimacy—not as wicked sea bandits but as virtuous citizens—and enjoy a place in society."

"In *your* reign."

"In the whole of the Divine Dominion. Imperial families rise and fall by the mandate of heaven. I will bring harmony and balance back to Taiwan. The people are unhappy with Taiwan's governance. I will unite the divided prefectures."

"Those are excellent and noble ambitions," said Yi.

Cai Qian beamed. "Did you know each day more people move to Taiwan despite the warring clans and invasion by foreigners? Who better to rule than a sea bandit? Who better to unite all the people, promote trade, and repel invasions than me?"

"I'm honored by your offer," said Zheng Yi. "but I'll need to think about it."

"Of course."

We returned to our ship and waited until we were alone in the cabin before discussing Cai Qian's proposal.

"Well?" I asked the minute the door closed.

"Qian minimizes the risk, which is great." Yi removed his turban. "The Mandarin navy will sink some of our boats—they're not *that* inept."

"If he becomes the emperor of Taiwan, we would be fabulously wealthy, and earn status and respect." I unwound my hair from its coiled style.

"From the same Mandarin officials I despise. I don't need their respect."

"Do you want Little Dog to live his whole life on the

seas? To be at the mercy of typhoons and winds? To eat dried fish and red rice all his days? Don't you want a better life for him? He could go to school. Live in a big house that keeps him warm and safe during typhoons. Have a respectable job."

Yi scowled. "I won't kowtow to Cai Qian."

"I don't think he expects you to—"

"Don't be naïve, Little Dragon. If I fight his battle and he becomes emperor, he will be grateful. For a while. Then, after a season passes, his pirate tunic will slip from his shoulders and be replaced by a *chaofu* robe with golden dragons."

"You don't think he'll honor his promises?"

"No, especially since my fleet is superior to his." Yi shook his head. "I would be a threat." He nuzzled my neck. "No, Xianggu, the only knee bending I do is between *your* legs."

"A proper show of respect."

Yi's hand trailed down my neck and under my robe. "I'll decline Cai Qian's offer in the nicest way possible. I don't want him as an enemy, especially when he looks at you *that* way."

I wrinkled my nose.

"Too old for you?" Yi played with my nipples.

"His fifty-four years is written on his face and body. Where you are strong," I squeezed his bicep, "he's gone soft."

"Tell me, Xianggu, if something were to happen to me, which chieftain would you marry?"

Yi wished to be flattered. I indulged him.

"Mmmm…Eleven-Finger Wu is mean spirited and lacks your keen intellect. I'm certain his fireworks will be accompanied by spitting. Toad Rearer has a quick smile and pleasant personality but isn't ambitious enough for me… although his giant ears would make fine handles to hold onto while bouncing on top of him."

Yi laughed so hard, his eyes teared.

"The General is too old, his eggs probably hang to his knees and I'll have to rub his cock vigorously to make it stand—too much work. Wushi Er already has six wives. But Yi, just as you refuse to kowtow to Cai Qian, I refuse to be a second or third wife."

"What about Podai?"

"I cannot marry your adopted son." I removed my clothes. "Anyway, don't talk about dying. You're too clever to be captured. Too alert to be wounded. Too strong to succumb to disease." I grabbed his buttocks, pressed his need into me. "Your life will be as long as your cock and your victories as plentiful as the seed running down my legs. I want no one else."

The next day, Yi told Cai Qian he was a pirate. Not a merchant, not a farmer, not an administrator or scholar, not an emissary or government official. His ambitions, he explained, did not extend to the land.

33

"Good morning, madam." Morning Star, the vanguard headman's sixteen-year-old bride of less than a month, took a seat opposite me in the saloon. Her gaze dropped to my swollen belly. "Motherhood becomes you."

"Motherhood gives me leaky breasts and a thick waist." This pregnancy made me both happy and sad. I loved being a mother, but it also meant I would be milk-tethered to a baby for another year.

"Chou wants a child but…" Morning Star heaved a great sigh, the troubled overdramatic sigh of a woman in need of advice.

"What is it?" I always befriended the officers" wives. Sometimes it yielded valuable gossip. More often their companionship was a pleasant way to pass an idle afternoon. Morning Star was a newcomer. I didn't know her well, but the other wives said Vanguard Headman Chou was love-struck by her heart-shaped face and pouty lips.

"I was a virgin when the Red Flag kidnapped me. I know nothing about…sex." Morning Star's soft whisper made me look up from my teacup mending.

"I need advice. I can't ask the prostitutes. They'll just laugh."

"I won't laugh." I put down the broken teacup and gave her my full attention.

Morning Star's big pouty lips were not as pretty turned upside down. "It *hurts*. Chou says I'm as dry as a scorched field. And when he's in, it...his cock...shrivels like a dried plum." Her heart-shaped face crumpled. "Chou makes me rub it up and down until...well...I do it too fast or too slow... never the perfect rhythm. When it gets hard again, he pushes it back inside...and then..." She looked away.

"And then?"

"Sometimes it works, sometimes not. What am I doing wrong?" Morning Star dabbed away a tear.

"Nothing. It's his fault. He's not attending to your pleasures."

Morning Star heaved another loud sigh.

"It doesn't have to hurt. Before he comes to bed, rub the bud near your entrance chamber to grease your entrance."

"Rub myself?" Morning Star's eyes grew rice-bowl round.

"How can a man pleasure you if you don't know how to pleasure yourself? Some men are brutish and have no skill with women. It's your job to show him without teaching him."

Morning Star's eyes bugged out, her pouty lips forming a little hole in the center.

During my moonflower days, plenty of loutish men had bucked on top of me without grace or skill. They never fondled or caressed the merchandise they paid so dearly for. "Do your best. It might take time." I didn't want to discourage her. Life was long and difficult for a wife who received no pleasure from her husband.

"MADAM?" Morning Star's wispy voice came from above. Her face peered down into the bathing compartment.

Either the girl was stupid or too troubled to understand her rudeness. One privilege of being the chieftain's wife was the pleasure to bathe in the fresh seawater before anyone else. Alone and without distraction.

"I'm here." I waded out of the shadows.

"I need to talk." Morning Star closed the door and descended the ladder. "I...I rubbed myself. I understand now."

I smiled tightly. Her successful masturbation was not a good enough reason to disturb my bath.

"But Chou won't...continue my pleasure. When he's done, I make my own fireworks after he's asleep. Is this wrong?"

"Not at all. But your marriage is new. Give it time."

"Is it wicked to imagine another man?"

I bit back a smile. "No, but don't tell Chou."

"Am I a terrible wife because I don't love him?"

"Fireworks, love, respect, babies, you can't hurry these things. Be patient."

"Thank you, madam, for easing my fears." Morning Star climbed up the ladder and closed the hatch.

The lamplight danced on the water as I floated on my back and wondered what Morning Star was really afraid of.

34

"There's a problem." Zheng Yi barged into the cabin, his voice unnecessarily loud. "Come with me."

"Sounds serious." I wiped my mouth—I threw up every morning—and followed him to the main deck.

Yi rubbed his temples. "Squad Boss Ko kidnapped someone."

"That's not a problem. It's what we're good at. Unless…"

Yi nodded. "Exactly."

We descended the ladder into a sampan where two deckhands rowed us to Squad Boss Ko's vessel. Zhang Bao's sampan was close behind. Guo Podai was already aboard.

"Best person ever kidnapped," boasted Squad Boss Ko as we boarded his ship.

"Show me," said Zheng Yi.

He took us to a group of six bound captives huddled on the deck. Five were dark-skinned men wearing small round hats and belted tunics over white trousers. Except for the thick mustache, each was clean-shaven.

The sixth man was an ugly ghost, a foreign devil with straw-colored hair and filthy beard. Unlike the others, he wore dark stiff-looking pants with a close-fitting jacket emblazoned with gaudy gilt buttons. His eyes, blue as the sea, were wide with fear.

"He's ugly and smells terrible." I stepped back, the foul odor sickening my already sensitive stomach. "Are all foreign devils this giant?"

"The British sailors are big ugly beasts." Zhang Bao strode toward our group.

I stood on my tiptoes and whispered into Yi's ear. "Squad Boss Ko is correct. This foreign devil is the best captive. The best for making problems." Foreign devil problems. Mandarin problems.

Squad Boss Ko's foot nudged the British sailor. "Turrrrn-nerrr." His voice struggled with the word. "First mate of the *Tay*. The others are Lascars, hired sailors from foreign lands."

"First Mate J. Turner." Turner bobbed his head with too much enthusiasm. "First mate." His next words grated my ears, their clipped nasal sounds lacked nuance.

Yi waved over the helmsman lurking nearby. "Scabby Ta, you speak this language. Ask him who he works for."

Scabby Ta spoke to Turner with the same ugly sounds. Turner replied. Back and forth they went. Whether Turner negotiated or begged for mercy was difficult to determine.

"He works for Baring & Company," said Scabby Ta. "Says if we harm him, they won't pay."

"Why are these men hostages?" asked Yi.

Squad Boss Ko puffed out his chest. "When I saw the *Tay* anchored at Shangchuan Island I sent three scouts to find out if we could take her. We used an old ruse— pretended to be fishermen—said the waters were difficult to navigate and offered our services to the captain for a small fee. The captain agreed to pay. That is, until we told him the fee was one hundred silver dollars. My men warned him about the local pirates and pointed out that his two cannons weren't enough to hold off pirates. The English captain bragged they had plenty of small guns and sailors."

"You decided attacking the *Tay* was too risky," said Guo Podai.

"That's right," said Squad Boss Ko. "But a week later the *Tay* showed up and fired on *us*. We got lucky; a northwest wind carried us between islands and hid us from view. At that point, the *Tay* anchored about a mile from shore."

"Get on with it." Yi hated long drawn out explanations.

Squad Boss Ko blanched. "Ah...during a scouting mission, we saw their skiff head for shore—probably a supply run. That's when two of my boats bore down on her and fired from the bow. He," Squad Boss Ko kicked Turner in the shin, "was still loading his musket when my men jumped on board. One of my men killed a Lascar, then took a swipe at Turner but the foreign devil jumped overboard."

"Coward," Yi muttered.

"We scooped his body out of the water and he started babbling. Then he saw all the cannons on our ship. That shut him up real quick." Squad Boss Ko turned to Scabby Ta. "Tell the chief what Turner told you."

"I asked Turner about the firepower on the *Tay* and he lied —claimed she had twenty mounted guns and one hundred and fifty able-bodied men to shoot us down. We knew better." Scabby Ta grinned and kicked Turner in the stomach.

"Why didn't you take the *Tay*?" Zhang Bao's nostrils flared.

Bao's question was surprising. Sea bandits never attempted to commandeer a vessel if uncertain of success. They knew when they were outmanned and outgunned.

"Still too risky." Squad Boss Ko looked at Zheng Yi for approval. "But Turner will fetch a fine ransom." He glanced at Turner, who still writhed from Scabby Ta's kick. "Should I send Turner's finger to the *Tay's* captain as proof?" He unsheathed his cutlass. "Or an ear?" He nicked Turner's lobe with the blade's tip.

Yi grabbed Turner by the hair and yanked him to his knees. "You'll die if the ransom isn't paid, First Mate Turner." His blade crossed Turner's throat without drawing blood.

Scabby Ta did not need to translate. Turner's eyes bugged out, his skin turned the color of ash.

With a disgusted grunt, Yi released Turner with a shove, then stomped towards Squad Boss Ko's cabin without a word.

"The Lascars are worth nothing," I said to Bao as we hurried after Zheng Yi.

"Not nothing. Baring & Company will pay some small token." Zhang Bao closed the cabin door and turned to Squad Boss Ko. "Kidnapping Turner is a big problem."

"When is easy money a problem?" asked Squad Boss Ko nervously.

"When there's layers of clerks, supervisors, bosses, and owners to deal with." Zheng Yi sat down at Ko's desk. "None of them have any authority to make decisions. Which means we'll need to deal with the Hong merchants, who will negotiate with Guangzhou custom officers—and every single greedy intermediary will demand a percentage. I'll need my best negotiator." He rubbed his forehead. "Transfer Turner to my ship."

"But—" Squad Boss Ko's eyebrows knitted together in dismay.

"Turner needs to be separated from the Lascars," said Podai.

Ko knew better than to disagree.

"CHOU CAUGHT Morning Star with Fat Lu." Fenfang announced while drawing a needle through a tear in my pants.

Fat Lu was a cheerful, fun-loving gunner. He was not fat, far from it. But his cock, the women claimed, was as thick as a man's fist. He left no woman unsatisfied, he often boasted.

"What?" I looked up from the romance novel borrowed from Guo Podai. "Where is she now?"

"Chou tied her to his berth then smashed in Fat Lu's face."

"Stupid girl." My stomach tightened. "I told her intimacy took time."

Yi stomped into the saloon. "Did you know about Morning Star?"

"Only that she had no fireworks with Chou." I grabbed Yi's hand. "Morning Star is young and foolish. Don't be quick to judge her. Don't make her pay for her stupidity."

"Chou and Morning Star are idiots." Yi squeezed my fingers. "Grandmother told me to marry a virgin, but I knew better. A virgin may satisfy an inexperienced boy but not a man."

"I disagree. Flower boat customers pay dearly for the privilege."

"Virgins have no imagination or skill," said Zheng Yi. "I pity the stupid girl, but she knew the cost. Come. You too, Fenfang. Everyone must witness her punishment."

"I'm not feeling well." I laid my hand on the swell of my belly.

Yi pulled me from the chair. "You'll feel better after you condemn her."

"Me?!" My stomach flip-flopped. "Why?"

"Because it'll be better if you do it."

"But it's a man's rule not a woman's." I swallowed the bile in my throat.

Yi looked at me like *I* was the idiot. "All rules are men's rules."

"Do you want me to chop off Fat Lu's head as well?"

"Fat Lu's gone. Jumped overboard, I'm guessing."

Many *li* away a thin sliver of land met the blue sea. Fat Lu would rather drown than have his head cut off.

With a sour stomach I followed heavy-footed behind Yi.

Morning Star stood on quarterdeck, tears running down a face swollen from Chou's beating. Between bruised lips, she pled for mercy with a phlegm-choked wail.

Everyone was there; deckhands, slaves, gunners, cook, slaves, pleasure girls, headmen, steward, incense burner, bookkeeper, even First Mate Turner.

The crowd parted to let Yi and I pass.

I embraced Morning Star, smoothed her hair from her face and whispered, "I'm sorry." I stepped back and spoke to the crew. "Morning Star, you dishonored yourself, dishonored the chieftain, dishonored the crew and your husband."

Morning Star wailed to the heavens. "Noooooo."

35

Morning Star gulped air. "Please, no. Please. I promise to be a faithful wife. I'll never do it again. Beat me. Tie me to the mast. Nail my feet to the floor. Anything, anything but that!"

I peeled off her robe, her small breasts exposed to every gawking man and woman.

"We wives are fortunate." I looked each wife in the eye. "Our men protect us, feed us, bring us gifts, and give us children."

The wives bobbed their heads, a few embarrassed faces glanced from one to the other. Who else made fireworks with another man?

I removed Bright Star's pants, every inch of her skin now uncovered. "This ship is large but not large enough to conceal deceit. We can't run away and hide in another village when we wrong someone like those who live on land. At sea, we must guard our actions and words. Morning Star committed a shameful act. She knew the penalties for adultery. Lust overcame good sense. Just as rage or jealousy might one day overcome your own good sense."

The crew was still, their eyes flicked back and forth from Morning Star to Chou.

"Morning Star is a friend. I call many people friend on this ship. But friendship doesn't matter when you break a rule —a rule made for our safety and happiness. If you break a rule you suffer the consequences."

I bound Morning Star's ankles with a chain and attached the weight. "Don't hold your breath," I murmured in her ear. "Morning Star," my voice was loud again, calm and resigned, "there's a a small kernel of honor in your death. It serves as a reminder for the women to obey the rules and remain faithful to their husbands." I signaled Mountain to pick her up. "*Zài jiàn*, my friend."

Mountain released her.

Morning Star hit the water with a splash. My task accomplished, I hurried through the crowd and to my cabin where I let the tears run down my cheeks.

Stupid stupid Morning Star! She did not appreciate her good fortune. She had it too easy. From kidnapped virgin to vanguard headman's wife. She never was a slave, never spread her legs for thousands of men, never sucked thousands of cocks. Never stooped to a boss to earn favor, never proved her worth to her husband. Instead Morning Star found fault with her life because her husband did not give her fireworks.

Hardships and misfortune made a strong person stronger. Morning Star did not treasure her good fortune and died because of it.

I CAME up from the cargo hold, strode past ten mounted cannons—the two biggest shot eighteen-pounders—climbed another ladder, and crossed the main deck in search of Headman Hsiang-shan.

"He refuses to eat." Headman Hsiang-shan stretched his hand out to Turner's uneaten bowl of red rice and fried silkworms. "He wrinkles his nose at our good food."

I inspected the bowl. "He eats the rice. Give him only silkworms next time. If he's hungry enough he'll eat them."

"Spoken like a mother," said Yi, strong-arming a Malay hostage whose terms of ransom were almost complete. "This one speaks English." With one hand he pushed the Malay hostage forward, with the other he thrust paper and quill at Turner. "Tell him we have new demands. It'll cost three thousand dollars for his safe return."

Turner appeared confused, his mouth gaped like a fish. The Malay hostage translated. After what seemed like too much repeating of ugly-sounding words, Turner gawked at Zheng Yi with understanding.

"You write," Yi tapped the paper. "We'll deliver the letter to the *Tay*."

Turner wrote. Midway down the paper he paused to speak to the Malay hostage.

"He wants to write two letters," said the Malay. "One to agents for the Baring & Company in Guangzhou, and one to Greig, the *Tay's* captain."

"Good. I want this business over with quickly." Yi's mouth curved into the familiar smile-sneer that intimidated and confused his enemies.

Turner passed the completed letters to Yi. The English script was ugly, all curves, coils, and circles. A childlike scribbling.

"These better not be lies." Yi unsheathed his blade and whisked it above Turner's ankles, knees, wrists, elbows, and neck. Then he pantomimed picking up the severed pieces and flinging them overboard.

All color drained from Turner's face. He knew slicing was a common form of punishment.

Yi stalked away and I followed him to quarterdeck where he stared at the sea.

"I don't trust the Malay captive," said Yi. "Bao has an Armenian who speaks better English. He'll be here tomorrow."

"The healer speaks English? Good. He can look at Crazy Eye's leg. It smells foul and it's green with pus. It would be a pity to lose such an excellent gunner."

Yi ripped Turner's letters lengthways, ripped it crosswise, and ripped it twice more. "We're lucky no one will pay the Armenian's ransom. He's proved his worth several times over." He tossed the shreds overboard, where they looked like moths, the wind lifting and fluttering the fragments in the air.

The following morning, Zhang Bao, dressed in a brilliant purple robe and black turban, brought us the Armenian.

As Bao cross the deck, I watched him greet the deckhands and officers. Despite Bao's quick rise to squad boss he enjoyed a warm rapport with the crew. They held him in awe. Believed the gods favored him. Bao was pleasant, well mannered, and showed self-control far beyond his age. Had he been born to a wealthy man his natural charm and leadership ability would have catapulted him into the upper echelons of the government.

"Good morning." Bao's gaze dropped to my thickening waist. "I hope you're feeling well." He tilted his head toward the Armenian behind him, a skinny man with a mango-sized nose and eyebrows like black caterpillars.

Mountain brought First mate Turner to us.

"Ten thousand dollars for your return," said Yi. "Or we'll nail your feet to the floor and beat you until you die."

The Armenian translated and Turner, eyebrows shooting up to his hairline, put his hands together in prayer. This time, Yi ordered a fast open-the-waves junk to deliver the letters.

During the Armenian's stay he tended wounds, cured ills, and befriended Turner. He even convinced Turner to eat the fried silkworms after he devoured a bowl himself.

"Maybe the white devil would prefer rat," said Bao as First Mate Turner picked up a single silkworm, squeezed shut his eyes, and swallowed it whole.

"We don't eat rats," said the Armenian. "I mean…western sailors do not know the delicacy of a fatted ship rat. I haven't tried it myself, but the crew say they're delicious."

"If well-prepared," said Bao.

An hour later, Turner threw up the undigested silkworms while watching deckhands chop the limbs off three captive fishermen caught mid escape.

SQUAD BOSS KO strutted into our cabin like a rooster. "I spoke to a customs officer and an agent of Baring & Company." He lifted his chin. "I had them by the balls." He pumped his fist. "And increased the ransom to thirty thousand dollars."

"What!?" Zheng Yi leapt out of his chair. "That's too much!"

Squad Boss Ko reeled back. "But, chief, that's how you barter. Start high."

Squad Boss Ko was a good leader but lacked the subtle art of making a deal.

Yi stomped out of the cabin in search of the Armenian, who we found on deck with Turner.

"The ransom's been increased to thirty thousand." Yi shoved a paper and ink stick at Turner.

The Armenian translated. Turner dropped his head into his hands, took a strangled gasp of despair, and wrote.

I looked at the unintelligible scrawls on the letter. "What did he write?" I asked the Armenian.

"He says you will chop him into pieces and throw his body parts to the sharks. He says he's cold and the sleeping compartment on deck is too tiny. He says you make him eat worms."

I winced and turned to Turner, my voice silky soft. "We give you food and water. A two-foot compartment is big enough for everyone else. You're as big as a giant but as weak as a kitten. You have a friend, the Armenian. Life is good on this ship, foreign devil. Most hostages suffer worse treatment."

Turner shrunk back, my honeyed tone more frightening than my husband's loud threats and limb-severing gestures.

Yi transferred both Turner and the Armenian to Squad Boss Ko's ship despite my practical reasons for keeping them both on the flagship. I loved Yi with all my heart, but he often dismissed my opinions simply because I was a woman.

36

Year of the Fire Rabbit
1807

Two women rowed Yi, Fenfang, and I toward the Macao shore. Three-year-old Little Dog squirmed, his chubby legs kicked, and his arms flailed. He was a happy, hardy, and energetic child, never content to sit still.

"He's excited to see the New Year's festival." Zheng Yi wore a proud smile.

"If we don't get there soon, he'll jump out and swim to shore," I said while Little Dog arched his back as though ready to launch himself out of the sampan.

The moment we hit shore, the child sprung over the side, loped across the beach and tossed fistfuls of sand into the air.

Zhang Bao and Guo Podai, who waited on the beach, joined us for the short walk to Macao. Shops and homes were strung with paper lanterns and red paper cut outs. Pasted on doors were two-line poems wishing good fortune, long life, and prosperity.

We arrived in town during the lion dance. The paper-mâché beast shook to the rhythm of the drums, its feet dancing in beat. When the red lion stood on two legs and jumped on a platform Little Dog squealed with glee.

Most of the crew and all the officers were here to celebrate. Only an unlucky few remained onboard to guard the hostages. Everyone else over indulged. Crewmembers spent their money, gambled away their earnings, sang bawdy songs—one about our victory at Lantau—smoked opium, drank too much, paid for prostitutes, and started street brawls.

We filled our bellies with sweet rice balls, bean paste dumplings, rice cakes, and fish. Next, we watched the dragon dance. Little Dog was spellbound, at times he gasped at the dragon's sharp white teeth, at others he clapped as the long green body and glittering tail undulated through the pavilion.

As usual whenever I was in a town, I studied the faces in the crowd in search of the moneylender Father had sold me to. I would never forget his face. Never forget the peach pit mole in the middle of his cheek. What would I do if I found him? Boast of my success? Slice off his hands? Probably both.

The day passed quickly and by the time the orange sun drifted towards the horizon my belly felt as heavy as an anchor.

"This baby steals my energy." I yawned. "I'm going back to the ship." I kissed Little Dog's cheek. "Do you want to stay here to watch the fireworks with Fenfang?"

Little Dog jumped up and down. "Yes! Yes! Yes!"

I walked back to to the beach where Qing Ping and Mountain waited by a sampan.

"Leaving so soon?" Bao hurried towards me.

I climbed into the sampan. "I'm tired."

"Where's Yi?" Bao glanced back at town.

"He, Wushi Er, and Podai are trying to stop Eleven-Finger Wu from killing his in-laws."

Bao laughed. "That man gets stupid when he drinks too much."

"Doesn't everyone?"

Bao stepped into the sampan. "Not me. I become the best lover in Guangdong province. The women gasp with pleasure and their backs arch with fireworks." Bao picked up an oar. "I'll take Madam Zheng to her ship," he said to Mountain and Qing Ping.

In the pink glow of twilight, his eyes twinkled with a feeling better left hidden. I almost ordered him out of the sampan, but that would appear very odd to Mountain and Qing Ping.

I rested my hands on my blossoming belly. What mischief could come from Bao rowing me to the ship?

37

"Tell the chief where I am," I said to Mountain as he waded into the surf to push out the boat. "I don't want him to worry about me."

"Worry about the Dragon Lady?" Bao grabbed the oars. "No one would dare lay a hand on you, especially since you send your friends to the bottom of the sea without a tear."

"That's not true." I winced, the memory still painful. "I wept for Morning Star. Alone. In my cabin. You know the crew disrespects weakness."

"Compassion is as important as emotional strength."

"I'm not taking advice from you." I closed my eyes, the rhythmic splash of the oars striking the water soothed like a lullaby. "You need a wife."

"I agree."

"Why aren't you in Macao flirting with all the beautiful girls?"

Several silent moments passed. I opened my eyes. Bao stared at me in a way that heated my skin despite the crisp air. I looked away and into the dark water.

An uncomfortable silence descended. He rowed toward the flagship and we climbed aboard without speaking.

Because the crew followed the tradition of cleaning one's home before the New Year's celebration, the flagship gleamed double in the moonlight. I didn't stop to admire their work and walked quickly to the cabin, Bao at my heels. I caught whiffs of his distinctive scent, a blend of sweet grasses and spices he wore in a red silk perfume pouch.

Bao locked the cabin door behind him. "I need to tell you something."

"Be quick about it. I'm tired." I wrapped my arms around myself.

Bao lit the small brazier. "You're my adopted mother, and yet I'm twenty-one-years-old, only a few years younger than you."

"Eleven years is not a few." I was glad my surcoat was thick. I needed armor to protect me from Bao's confession.

"What's eleven years? A grain of sand on the beach of time." Bao cast an envious glance at the bed piled with furs. "I remember the day I was captured. The day I first saw you." He stepped forward. "That's the day I fell in love with you."

"Bao—" I moved away.

I wasn't fast enough. Bao wrapped his arms around me and touched his lips to mine.

I pushed him away. "I love Yi."

Bao licked his lips. "You taste like heaven."

"Stop this nonsense. You're my adopted son." I grabbed his silk robe and yanked. "Such flashy clothing. You want everyone to see you, but you've done nothing worth noticing."

"Not yet," he grinned. "But one day I'll be the most powerful chief in the South Seas."

I bit back a smile. "Not while Yi still lives." I warmed my

hands by the brazier. "Yi has power on the sea and in the bedroom. Do you understand? I'm happy with him."

Bao moved close, his eyes soft with lust. "I know my heart. And now that I know the taste of you, I want you more than ever. I'll never wed anyone but you."

"You're too young to make such a promise."

"Oh, I may fuck other women, Xianggu, but it's you I imagine. It's you I dream of while I stroke my pipe. It's your face I see in my dreams." He traced the curve of my cheek. "One more kiss."

My heart pounded. Excitement and fear and desire churned like a typhoon inside of me. I wanted to kiss him. Wanted to run my hands across his chest, stroke his face, feel his length inside me. My body *wanted* his.

I leaned forward, pressed into him, and bit his lip. Hard. Then I stepped back and smacked him across the face. "How dare you dishonor Zheng Yi. I will have you killed for this."

Bao touched his finger to his lips, studied the bright red drop of blood. "What will you tell him?"

I adjusted my surcoat. "The truth. That you tried seducing me, but I fought you off." I drew a small blade from my inner pocket. "Get out."

"If I don't?" Bao did not look intimidated in the least.

"I'll slice off your ear first. Your cock next."

Bao laughed, sank to his knees, and leaned back and presented his bare throat. "Kill me now if you must, my beautiful Dragon Lady."

"I'm not 'your' anything."

Bao's adoration was enthralling, more potent than any aphrodisiac. I removed his turban, ran my hands through his hair, soft as silk strands and straight as sea grass. "I love you as my adopted son."

Bao sighed and his eyes closed as he reveled in my brief caress.

"I'm going to insist Yi find you a wife before this infatuation of yours goes any further," I said.

38

*Z*heng Yi entered the saloon with a pleased look. "First mate Turner has a new friend."

"Who?" I pinned up my hair.

"Afoo."

"Doesn't he help the Keeper of the Treasury?"

Yi nodded. "For almost a month now. He has a head for business."

"Should we separate them?" I set my ivory comb on the table.

"Not this time. They write letters on each other's behalf begging Guangzhou officials and British merchants to pay their ransom."

"Pardon the intrusion, chief." A messenger entered the saloon. "I've come from Squad Boss Ko's ship. There's a problem."

Yi's good mood receded like a wave breaking on the surf. "Go on."

"A deckhand overheard two hostages planning to escape, but instead of reporting it to the headman he blabbed about it to the crew. By the time the headman sent the message to Ko, the crew was pretty worked up. Ko came aboard and told the headman to flog the hostages and put them in irons. The crew argued with Ko—they wanted the hostages killed and…" The messenger swallowed and looked down.

Yi and I exchanged a horrified look.

"I'm waiting." Yi crossed his arms.

"They attacked Ko."

My mouth dropped open. Ko's own crewmembers attacked him?!

"Where were Ko's men? Where was the headman?" Yi's face tightened with anger.

"Ko's men were overpowered. Several were wounded."

"And Ko?" Yi clenched his fists.

"He retreated to his ship." The messenger stared at the floor. "Squad Boss Ko humbly begs your help."

Yi walked around his desk. "Bring Ko here." He threw the chair across the cabin the moment the messenger left. "Useless idiot! How can he allow such defiance?"

"You need to hear Ko's explanation." I picked up the jade vase wedding gift before Yi decided to break that too.

Yi paced back and forth. "What do you think?"

I set my hands over my belly, which with three months to go, would soon triple in size. "I think Ko's crew no longer respect and fear him. Power is like a riverbank. It can erode over time or be damaged by a typhoon. Ko's rogue crewmen are like rushing water. Ko didn't fortify the walls of his riverbank by asserting his power with frequent visits."

"Yes, but what would you *do*?" Yi picked up the broken chair leg.

"Ko is no longer fit to be squad boss. He's a good pirate and a good sailor. He's courageous and quick with a sword. It's true his decision to kidnap Turner was bad but eventually Baring & Company will pay."

Yi flipped the chair leg in the air. "I need an answer not a lecture."

"Ko rose higher than his ability. Relieve him of his position."

"I agree; however, he must come to the same conclusion otherwise there'll be bad feelings between us."

Rain pelted the deck when Squad Boss Ko arrived. He left a trail of wet footprints as he crossed the length of the saloon where Yi and I waited to pronounce judgment.

"What happened?" Yi settled back in the chair.

Squad Boss Ko told his version. There was only one difference. The would-be mutineers, he insisted, were not typical of his usual well-behaved crews.

"Why is that?" Yi scowled.

Ko shifted nervously from foot to foot. "I don't know. Maybe just a bad group."

"Who's at fault?" Yi's voice was devoid of accusation or anger.

"Those stupid idiots who dare try to kill me." Ko thumped his chest.

"Who's at fault?" Yi asked again.

"The…" Ko paused, his brows knitted together in confusion. "The headman. He can't control his crew. He allows insolence."

"Who's at fault?" Yi's stoic tone remained the same.

"I told you, chief, the headman." Ko stopped, looked down at the table and pinched the bridge of his nose.

Except for creaking planks and a gull's caw the saloon was quiet. Silence was an effective strategy. Yi used it often and would wait a long time for the answer he wanted.

Ko lifted his head, his face shadowed with defeat. "I'm at fault."

"Why?"

"I'm responsible for every crewman on the boats under my command." Ko spoke clearly and with an authority he had been too late in exerting.

"And?"

"The headman is my responsibility." Ko exhaled. "I should have noticed his men did not respect him. Which means they did not respect the squad boss over him. Me." Ko took a deep breath. "Without respect, without fear, my authority is worthless. I failed you, chief. I'm unfit to lead a squadron."

"The ability to command men is a gift," said Yi. "Not all men have it. You're still valuable to me, Ko. You're loyal, a good sailor, and a first-rate warrior. But your mistake is severe. It encourages insubordination and riots."

"How do I make it right?" Ko was hopeful, he had no idea his question just sealed his fate.

"Your question reveals another failing."

Ko's brows furrowed until understanding dawned. "I don't know how to fix the problem. I failed you again." He hung his head.

"You haven't failed me," said Yi with compassion. "You have many business contacts, loyal spies, and good relations with important government officials. I'm reassigning you to one of our headquarters where you will oversee the administration of safe conduct and protection permits."

Relief washed over Ko's face. "Thank you, chief."

"Don't go back to your ship." Yi nodded like an emperor bestowing favors. "You're dismissed.

"Who's replacing him?" I asked after Ko left.

"Bao will absorb Ko's squadron."

My teacup hung in the air. "Bao will have the largest squad in your fleet."

"He's more than capable." Yi looked surprised by my

surprise. "His crews believe he has some kind of supernatural ability. He's a born leader, adored by his men. Who better?"

I set down my teacup. "Me."

"You?! A woman can't command a squad." He shuddered. "What would you have done in Ko's case?"

"I would raid my own boat, chop off the head of every sailor who joined the attempted mutiny, and display their heads from atop bamboo poles. I would gut the headman, rip out his heart, and throw him overboard."

Yi's face beamed with pride. "Too bad you're a woman, you would've made a fearsome squad boss."

Within the hour of Bao's being told he now commanded Ko's squad, he sent a team to kill the rebels and insubordinate headman.

The following morning under rain-heavy clouds Ko was rowed to shore to begin his new position in Hong Kong. Yi and I watched his sampan disappear into the mist when my belly cramped. I raced back to the cabin and found my thighs smeared with blood.

39

"I'm bleeding," I said from the bed when Fenfang arrived.

Fenfang laid a cool hand on my forehead. "Rest and make offerings to goddess Pi-Hsia Yuan Chin. I'll make a warming tea to fight the cold from blood loss. Don't worry, we'll restore balance."

Yi shrugged when I told him the remainder of my pregnancy must be spent in bed.

"No bedroom activities either," I said.

Yi blinked. "We'll be in Donghai soon." His face revealed no emotion. "The boats need to be careened, and we need to buy more fresh water, tar, tung oil, and matting." He gave me a tight smile. "Grandmother and Aunt will take good care of you."

I sat up in bed. "Don't leave me on Donghai."

"Don't argue with me, Xianggu. My mind is made up." Yi stalked out of the cabin.

Yi did not spend the night with me. Nor the next. Fenfang confirmed my fears. Yi found pleasure with a young woman on Bao's ship.

The day we arrived in Donghai, Yi lifted me from the bed.

"Don't carry me," I said. "I'll look sick and weak. I don't want the crew's pity."

Yi's mouth twisted in exasperation. "How do you expect to get off the boat?"

I pointed to the chair. "Two men will bear me like an empress to the village. Tell the crew Zheng Yi Sao conserves her strength for more important tasks."

Yi chuckled. "You're a demanding wife."

Mountain and Qing Ping bore my chair across deck, down the ramp, and through the white sands. With my hands atop my large belly, I joked about my makeshift litter to the crew. I told them the chief's unborn child demands transportation befitting the son of the Emperor of the Seas.

My litter bearers stopped beside the British hostage.

"Foreign devil Turner," I said to the bare-chested man with pink-scorched skin, "Baring & Company bicker with Guangdong customs officials. You'll be old before they pay your ransom."

Turner stretched his hands skyward and beseeched his sky god.

"Do you think he understands?" I asked Mountain.

"He understands that he's fucked." Mountain laughed so hard the chair shook.

Grandmother and Aunt greeted me with scolding concern for not taking better care of myself. I was relieved when Fenfang arrived with Little Dog. They were so delighted by him, they forgot to criticize me.

Guo Podai visited the next afternoon.

He set an armload of books on the bedside table. "I figured you needed a way to pass the hours."

His thoughtfulness made me smile.

"What types of books did you bring?"

Podai selected one from the stack. "This is poetry by

Yuan Mei. It's elegant and full of supernatural sentiments. This one," he picked up another, "was written by Pu Songling. It's a collection of stories with magic foxes, vindictive ghosts, and vampires."

I took both books from him and flipped through the pages. "Do you believe in those things?"

"I believe in the sea's magic and in the mystical lure of a lotus flower." He pulled a chair to my bedside. "I believe there's magic in books. How else can you travel far and wide or learn from long dead scholars?"

"What about the supernatural?"

"We pray to Mazu, she's supernatural. We burn incense, make offerings, ask for blessings. Are any of our gods less mystical than shape-shifting foxes or demons?"

"Well, now that you've put it that way." I always enjoyed our conversations. Podai made me look at the world in new ways.

"You've seen the strange creatures we pulled from the depths of the oceans. Eyeless fish, transparent squids, and creatures as hideous as demons." He flung out his arm. "Far south of here lives a great lizard twice your length, Xianggu. Not nearly as fierce, though." Podai's eyes glazed. "Maybe I'll write a story about magical sea creatures."

"How do you manage to order men to their deaths while dreaming of the fantastical?"

Podai leaned forward. "I'll tell you a secret, but you must promise not to tell anyone."

"I don't keep secrets from Yi."

"It's not that kind of secret. It's about me."

"Then your secret is safe." My curiosity was piqued by his intense expression.

Podai pressed his hand to his heart. "Two souls live here. They don't fight but live amiably side-by-side. One is a sea bandit who thrills in the strategy, mayhem, and violence of our profession." He lifted his chin, narrowed his eyes, his mouth set in an intimidating expression. "The Black Flag chieftain." His arrogant face melted into one of kindness. "The other is an aspiring writer who loves novels about unlikely lovers, evil creatures, and benevolent beings. When my bones are stiff, I'll quit piracy for a quiet life reading and writing on a beautiful secluded island. For now though, my inner chieftain relishes every raid and fight."

"You're a poet pirate," I said. "I won't tell anyone."

"There's great risk in revealing one's true nature."

I looked away from his soulful eyes and tender expression. "What other books did you bring?"

Podai sorted through the stack. "This one has ancient love stories. My favorites are *The Butterfly Lovers* and *Niulang the Cowherd and Zhinu the Weaver*. I'd like to write a love story." He scratched his chin. "But not one with a tragic ending." Podai shifted in his seat. "Xianggu, if you need anything just ask. I'm here for you and my heart—"

"Xianggu!" His face flushed and holding a small pot, Bao raced through the doorway.

Fenfang ran in after him. "I'm sorry. Boss Bao did not wait to be announced."

"Look!" Bao held the small pot under my nose. "Fat Lu's heart!"

"Fat Lu?" I looked from Podai to Bao. "Morning Star's lover? He's alive?"

"Not anymore." Bao tilted the pot to give me a better view.

"Fat Lu is a fool. He knows Donghai is Yi's home base." I took a quick peek.

"He was visiting his dying father, and obviously didn't

expect us to career the flagship at this time." Bao signaled Fenfang. "Get some wine."

I wrinkled my nose. "Do you have to?" The ritual was morbid and disgusting. I pushed away the pot. "Why did you have to cut out Fat Lu's heart?"

Bao's brows knitted together with disappointment. "I had to. My men expected me to cut him open. And there's no better way to remind them all of the punishment for treachery." Bao poked the heart with his finger. "I disemboweled him first," he said as though that was somehow less barbaric. "We'll make a sacrificial offering to Venerable Mother. Do you want some of Fat Lu's heart?"

I nodded. "I'll drink mine with Yi."

Consuming a victim's life force was my least favorite ritual, but it had to be done. The crew's morale would soar and bind them together. Bao knew the importance of uniting his crew with Ko's. You couldn't buy loyalty, but sometimes you could drink it.

Bao turned to Podai. "You bring our adopted mother books. I bring her magic."

"There is magic in both," I said.

Podai looked unimpressed. "Eating Fat Lu's heart doesn't make you a better squad boss, Bao."

"You're wrong. It makes me the *best* one." Bao lifted his chin. "One day, Podai, I will command a flag fleet that rivals your own."

Podai balked. "I command nine thousand men and almost one hundred ships. The Black Flag is second only to Yi's. You'll need to eat a lot more hearts before achieving anything close to my success." He pointed, his forefinger making little circles at Bao. "You'll command the Purple Flag to match your clothes."

Podai's insult bounced off Bao like a ball.

"Purple is the color of spirituality, healing, abundance, and strength," said Bao without a trace of annoyance. "All elements leading to good fortune, luck, and fame."

"Rely on your wits and skill, not the color of your flag." Podai stood, his body tense.

"Wits and skill are useless if the gods despise us," said Bao.

I crossed my arms. "If I wanted to see a cockfight, I'd attend one. You shame Yi with this squabbling. Your rivalry is stupid and goes against the pirate code."

Despite my scolding, Bao and Podai looked like two cobras poised to strike.

"Get out. Both of you. And you better hope I don't tell Yi."

Chastened, they took their leave.

"They need wives," I muttered after they left.

40

Zheng Yi left me on Donghai Island with Fenfang and Little Dog. I filled the long hours with paper cutting and reading. Once a week a messenger delivered Red Flag updates.

While sailing southwest, Zhang Bao was pursued by the imperial navy. He thwarted the attack by hiding his squadron among the atolls. He's shrewd and knows when to engage and when to hide.

Zhang Bao flogged the deckhand in charge of the Lascar hostages after one of them escaped. I'll be glad when this business with the English devil Turner is over.

Afoo acted as a translator and go-between between Baring & Company and me. I don't know what Afoo said but the customs officials boarded the ship and begged for a reduced ransom fee. Turner is more trouble than he's worth.

On the last day of April while the rain beat against the house and flooded the courtyard, Yi, drenched from turban to feet, strode into the bedroom.

"I missed you, Little Dragon." He untied his robe, took my head between his hands and guided me to him.

I obliged him, played his flute, and prolonged his pleasure until he moaned for release.

"I'm taking you back to the ship." Yi scooped me in his arms. "Ugh, you weigh more than a water buffalo."

"I missed you too." I didn't ask why Yi changed his mind. Better flute-playing skills than his mistress couldn't be the only reason. Could it?

To my relief Yi needed my other skills. He talked of nothing but business.

"I agreed to lower Turner's ransom to twenty-five thousand dollars but only if they include six chests of opium and ten pieces of sail matting." Yi tucked me into the bed. "My demands must remain high. Any decrease will be seen as weakness." He thrust a cup of tea into my hands. "But a first-rate negotiator makes everyone feel like a winner. Even the loser."

"The man with the biggest eggs wins," I said, my heart warmed by his unusual attentiveness.

Yi grabbed his crotch. "That's why no woman will ever be a fleet chieftain. Mandarin officials will never negotiate with a woman."

THE TURNER EXCHANGE took place May 22nd off the Lantau Island coast. Nothing could keep me from staying in bed that day.

Every Red Flag ship and boat was there. Scores of

sampans bobbed in the water. British ships waited opposite. A wide swath of empty blue separated us from them.

A large British rowboat from the *Discovery* left the ship's side and headed into the middle. It was weighed down with two thousand dollars, three opium-filled chests, and five thousand pieces of sail matting—the cost split between English and Guangzhou officials.

"What trust does one unarmed rowboat inspire when all their English ships are battle ready?" I scratched my too-big belly.

"A show of their good faith, nothing more," said Zheng Yi before he descended the ladder to the lower deck.

An unfamiliar hush fell over the ship. Every crewmember watched the British for signs of an impending attack. British deckhands preparing weapons, a ship's altered position for improved cannon range, hoisting a signal flag, a horn blast—any of these indicated an offensive position. Our gunners stood ready by our cannons.

The British rowboat had just reached the midpoint when one of our own long dragons fired upon it. The shot fell far short.

"Fuck!" Yi shouted into the wind as two armed English cutters raced toward the ransom-laden rowboat. "Hoist the recall flag. Now! Now! NOW!"

Our deckhands were quick. Our men in the long dragon saw the recall signal and changed course toward us.

"What the fuck are you doing?" Yi roared as the long dragon came aside. "I'll flog you myself!"

Through the spyglass, I saw Bao also calling commands. The English captains, looking through their own spyglasses, pointed to our recall flag. Months of negotiations were doomed if the English thought we duped them.

Below me, the long dragon crew all spoke at once and pointed fingers at their crewmates.

"One at a time!" Zheng Yi's face contorted with rage.

"Chief, we didn't know! We've been up Guangzhou River all week collecting protection fees from the villages. We saw the armed English vessels and—"

"Idiots." Yi pointed to his eyes. "Look around before you start firing. If your stupidity fucks up the Turner exchange, I'll'll rip out your hearts with my bare hands!"

The long dragon crew dropped to their knees and begged for their lives. Which was good. Because the English officers witnessed their groveling through their spyglasses. A few tense minutes passed...

They gave the order for the rowboat to proceed to Bao's ship.

"I imagine Turner will lie and exaggerate his misfortunes," I said to Fenfang as we watched Turner scramble into the rowboat.

"I don't trust foreign devils," said Fenfang. "They're ugly, clumsy, and smell terrible."

"Uncivilized too. Turner gagged on his food, puked up the silkworms, spit out the *bee-chew*, and refused to bathe when given the opportunity. Ooooh." I touched my rock-hard belly. "It's time."

41

The baby did not come that day. Or the next. The unborn child preferred doing somersaults in my womb and tightening my belly with false contractions. I gritted my teeth through yet another false labor pain when Guo Podai arrived in the saloon with grim news.

"Cai Qian's headquarters are demolished. Naval commander Li Changgeng burned it to the ground and destroyed his boats. Qian claims he still has thirty boats, but I think he's too humiliated to be honest about his losses."

"He can't mount a counter attack with that," said Yi.

Guo Podai nodded. "Moreover, my spies say he's lost support in Taiwan. With a reduced fleet and little financial support, Cai Qian's imperial aspirations are as sunk as his junks."

I set my hand on Yi's arm. "You made the right decision not to help him become Emperor of Taiwan."

"Perhaps." Yi had a faraway look in his eyes.

FENFANG STUCK a thick twist of cotton between my teeth to keep me from screaming. The first real contraction had dropped me to my knees and hadn't let up.

Usually, the creaking planks, rocking motions, and splashing water against the ship soothed me. Not this time. The familiar sounds were maddening. Even more maddening was the absence of noise. No deckhands shouted, argued, laughed, or sang bawdy songs.

"Where is everyone?" I said between pains.

"The crew waits for the newborn's cry." Fenfang dabbed my brow.

"Bring the girl who plays the *pipa*. Tell her to play outside my door. I need—" I curled into a ball and groaned.

Fenfang waited for the contraction to subside, then rushed out the door. Moments later the plucky sounds of the four-stringed lute seeped under the door.

The *pipa* player played for hours and hours. Too many hours. But the music gave me something to focus on.

The pressure to push came late that night.

"I see the head. One more push." Fenfang clutched my hand.

I spat out the cloth and howled like a demon, but the babe retreated inside.

"The baby enters the world looking up at the heavens." Fenfang brushed my sweat-drenched hair from my face. "You need to squat."

She helped me into position, feet on the floor, knees bent, back braced against the side of the bed.

"Let your body blossom," whispered Fenfang. "Imagine the petals of your womanliness greeting the morning sun. You're a field of blooming flowers, release the fragrance of new life, unfurl your leaves, spread the calyx of your womb."

A surge of pressure burst forth, and I didn't hold back. I

231

screamed into the pain's weight, felt the infant emerge slowly slowly slowly until the crushing weight was gone.

"A son." Fenfang held up the newborn.

My second son blinked and squinted, eager to take in his new world. After the warm sluice of afterbirth discharged, Fenfang helped me to bed. I set my son, born in the lucky Year of the Rabbit, at my breast, where with a little encouragement he latched onto my nipple.

Fenfang cracked open the door to speak to the slave girl waiting outside. "It's a boy."

The thunder of joyful whoops made me smile. Yi entered moments laterr, his eyes shadowed with worry.

"I love you, Xianggu." He laid down next to me until I fell asleep.

"MORE GIFTS." Yi set a red lacquered box, a large flat package, and a cloth bag on the table.

Chieftains, squad bosses, skippers, and even Cai Qian sent presents to celebrate Second Son's one month.

"This is from Bao." Yi ran his hands over Second Son's newly shaved head.

"Another one? He already sent money," I said, my good humor restored now that I had a bath.

"This one he said is especially for you." He pointed to the red lacquered box.

Nestled inside was a small celadon bowl of exceptional beauty. I lifted it up to the light and marveled at its translucence and finely etched dragons.

"It's beautiful." My fingers glided over the paper-thin curves.

"Bao seized a ship filled with porcelain and other rare treasures. This bowl was in a crate stamped Song."

I gasped. "This bowl is six-hundred-years-old."

"Both Podai and Bao appreciate beauty in all of its many forms. They keep only the most exquisite."

"Shouldn't they sell those treasures in Guangzhou?"

"Rarities aren't as easy to sell as rice and pepper. Now this," said Yi and showed me a square of hodgepodge twigs the size of his forearm, "is beautiful." He twisted the frame of crisscrossed sticks bound by twine strung with random tiny shells. "Do you know what it is?"

I set down the celadon bowl and studied the object. "It's not art. There's no beauty, no form, no attention to detail."

"You're wrong. This is art of the most practical kind. It's a rebbelith, a navigation map." He pointed. "These shells are islands. These sticks show the sea currents. Crude but practical. We took it from the Kuijlen slave on the Taiwanese merchant junk captured yesterday."

I propped the rebbelith on the table. "I suppose it'll be useful if we venture into the Outer Ocean."

Yi peered into the cloth sack. "Books from Podai's library. But I think you're tired of reading." His hand slid under my shirt. "It's been too long."

I opened my robe, bared milk-swollen breasts. "I ought to find Second Son his own *amah*. Little Dog is too active for Fenfang to take care of both."

"We have slaves enough." Yi sighed and cupped each breast.

"Not just *any* slave. Second Son's *amah* must be kind, intelligent, and loyal." And really ugly.

"If people with those excellent traits were easy to find I'd have a thousand boats by now." His thumbs brushed against my nipples.

"All I want is one boat."

"Not that again. Anyway, more important duties require your attention." Yi flicked his tongue across my nipple. "I want more sons." Hisis lips latched around my nipple and sucked. As my milk flowed into his mouth, his hand slid up my thigh and into my garden.

42

Yi hung his wet surcoat over a peg. "The Tâyson want me to help them recapture Vietnam."

A weight dropped into my belly. "Cousin Qi died when he tried to help them retake Hanoi."

"I can't refuse them."

"Why not?" Second Son gulped greedily at my breast.

"You're a woman. You won't understand."

I detached the babe, and his furious cries were louder than the squall that raged outside.

"I'm the woman who gave you two sons. The woman who plans campaigns with you and fights by your side." I pushed the red-faced babe into his arms, my breasts squirting milk like a fountain. "I'm the woman in charge of this flagship while you fuck concubines ashore. I'm the woman who listens to you day and night while you smell like another woman's cunt." I wrapped my robe tight about me. "For seven years, I've written letters and read documents that you're too busy to care about. I've given you seven years of pleasure. Your excuse is feeble. I know you too well, Yi. You conceal the real reason."

"Take the boy." Yi pushed the wailing baby at me.

"His cries mirror my pain. The Tâyson don't concern us. Let them fight their own battles. You no longer need to answer their summons."

Yi set wailing Second Son on the bed. "Feed him and I'll tell you why I must help the Tâyson."

I put Second Son to my breast where he nursed with angry gulps.

"You're right," said Yi. "I don't need to fight their battles. But I owe them *jên-ch'ing*—resources, my expertise, my fleet. Tâyson money outfitted the Red Flag—most of the fleet's weapons and cannons are from them. They trained me, made me who I am today. My success is due in part to them. If they succeed in taking Vietnam, I will be respectable. We'll have a home. A people who welcome us. Respectability cannot be bought, Xianggu."

"Is respectability that important? Our fleet already rules the oceans. Villagers flee when they see our boats. Government officials pay us protection fees. Merchants sell us their goods at a reduced price. Brokers and dealers are eager to do business with us. Young men form long lines at the recruiting centers. We rule the salt trade and have more ships, sailors, guns, and ammunition than the imperial navy. While Emperor Jiaqing is busy fucking thousands of concubines in the Forbidden City, you—the greatest chieftain of the South Seas —have conquered his islands and towns, stolen his profits, and raided his rivers. How can you wish to live in Vietnam when you have already conquered a part of the Divine Dominion? Vietnam is too small for you."

Yi's frustration blew past a frown. "I have two young sons. I want to give them an honorable future. I don't want them to live like me— despised by virtuous people, always looking over their shoulder for an enemy's blade. I want my sons to take their place among society, drink wine with wealthy men, and stroll in fragrant courtyards."

My fury deflated. He was right. Our sons' future was at stake.

WITH A FLOTILLA of our best-armed boats, we sailed toward Vietnam to help the Tâyson.

Guo Podai and Zhang Bao did not join us. Each was engaged in their own piracy projects.

We arrived at the appointed location under fish-scale clouds, and brooking no delay, we met Squad Boss Ha and nephew Pao-yang on the Tâyson general's ship. We finalized tactics, planned for contingencies, and relayed messages to skippers.

The late afternoon sky was gray when we returned to our flagship to double check ammunition supplies with the Keeper of the Armory.

"Sails! Sails! Twenty warships!" The lookout shouted from his perch.

Yi rubbed his temples. "Not only do I have an awful headache, the Tâyson's intel is bad."

"Chief!" A deckhand pointed at the water. "A goose feather."

A hundred and fifty faces tilted to the sky to confirm the omen.

"This is lucky. No one fights in a storm," I said while thick dark clouds amassed above us.

"We need to be ready anyway." Yi grabbed Qing Ping and pointed to the uncovered gunpowder. "Cover it! Now!" He pulled me aside. "Stay in the cabin."

"No, it will worry the crew."

Yi squeezed my wrist. "Do what I say, woman." He dropped my hand and studied the navy's approach through the spyglass. "They intend to engage."

I returned to the cabin and wound a turban around my head. "Don't let the children out," I told Fenfang. "The Vietnamese navy is so cocky they're going to fight us."

"In this storm?" Fenfang took Little Dog's hand. "They're crazy."

I kissed my sons' cheeks and went back outside. The wind blew stronger now and the churning water made it difficult for our ship to stay in position.

As the Vietnamese warships bore down on us, Yi called out commands. "Ready the cannons! Prepare the stinkpots!"

The Keeper of the Armory handed out bamboo spikes, pointed javelins, bows and arrows, and rattan shields while the ship heaved and rocked. Such pointlessness! Those weapons required accuracy.

The Vietnamese warships and typhoon arrived together.

The typhoon attacked first and released a torrent of needle-sharp rain. A Vietnamese warship attacked next. Luckily, their cannon shots fell short.

The typhoon discharged its main artillery. Hail the size of quail eggs plummeted onto the deck and pummeled the crew. The ice balls bloodied and bruised several men.

Buffeted by the wind, I fought to stay upright, looped my arm through the ladder's rungs, and tried to see through the murky veil of sea spray. I ducked as a chunk of debris hurdled toward me, slipped, and lost my balance. The next wind gust flung me into a crate. I crawled sideways. Grasped a chain.

Our ship crested and fell. A single wave lifted our ship beside a Vietnam warship. It was close enough I saw the black maw of their cannon.

"Yi!" I called into the rain and wind.

Our ship tilted…rose high out of the water…the swell of the wave lifted us toward the sky. The Vietnamese warship disappeared, left me staring into gray mist. Our flagship teetered, wobbled as though airborne, and what seemed like a thousand lifetimes passed before we dropped back into the sea. A bright flash cut through the gray haze. Not lightning. Cannon fire.

An odd sensation, an awful intuition clawed at my throat, tore at my heart. Yi stood in the cannonball's path. Every inch of my body felt it.

"YI!" I screamed.

Lightning lit up the sky. Yi stood tall. Not seeing. Not knowing.

The cannonball shaved the side of his head. The force knocked him off his feet, into the wind, and hurled him over the side.

"YI!" I crawled to the side and screamed into the churning black sea. "YI!"

Another swell lifted the ship. I reached out, grabbed for the line. The ship dropped and tossed me into the air.

43

"Madam Zheng!"

Tugs. Pulls. Shouts...

"Madam Zheng! Where's the chief?"

I blinked. Helmsman He-song's face swam into consciousness.

"Are you hurt?" His shouts seemed to come from far away.

"No." I sat up, pushed wet hair from my eyes and wondered when my turban blew off. My eyes flew open. "Yi..." I braced myself against the bulwark, my mind a whirlpool bent on dragging me under.

"Where's the chief?" Helmsman He-song shouted again.

Gone. The most powerful and feared flag fleet chieftain was dead. It took both a typhoon and cannon to kill him.

"Madam Zheng?" Helmsman He-song stuck his face inches from mine. "You okay? Can you understand me?" He assumed I had been knocked senseless. He was wrong. Every sense was flooded with despair.

I pulled myself up and looked over the side. Angry water spewed high and drenched my face. There was no sign of Yi.

I turned towards the Vietnamese warship—where it should have been—but it was gone, lost in the sodden curtain of gray.

Helmsman He-song aimed his thumb skyward. "Lookout's gone."

I blinked. My lips quivered. Tears ran down my cheeks. "I…" My lips refused to make the words. Refused to tell Helmsman He-song the chief was dead. Refused to admit the worst.

Yi *might* yet be alive. Maybe he clung to a floating plank...

I wanted to crawl back to the cabin. Wait out the storm. Bury myself under the blankets and weep. Decide what to do. Whom to tell.

"Go back to the cabin!" Helmsman He-song pointed aft.

I shook my head. "I stay here," I shouted into the storm. "Get everyone below! Everyone! Slaves and captives too! Get our bearings! If the wind blows toward land don't anchor!"

Helmsman He-song had seen us through many such squalls. He already knew what to do. But somehow giving this command gave me a sense of control over the mayhem.

"Done!" He shouted.

I looked up. The sails were partly reefed; Helmsman He-song had already decided heaving-to was the best course of action.

He begged me to go back to the cabin. I refused. He asked me to go below. I refused again. How could I go below where more than three hundred eyes would look to me for reassurance? How could I hide in my cabin where my sons would ask about their father and expect comforting words and reassuring arms?

I remained on deck and faced the storm.

Hours passed. Hours wet with tears and cold with pain. The storm matched my grief. *Was* my heartache. Its wind, my anger. Its waves, my despair. Its fury, my own.

Wind blew. Waves surged. Rain poured. And I planned my future.

Eventually the clouds parted, and the sea calmed. Bright stars twinkled and winked in a moonlight sky, cloud wisps stretched thin across the blackness.

The Vietnamese warships were gone. The Tâyson fleet was gone too. Only a few of our boats drifted nearby. I knew what I had to do. Must do.

I waited until sunrise.

I stood on quarterdeck under a humid morning sun, wet clothes molded to my flesh, hair matted, and ordered Headman Hsiang-shan to summon the crew and light the lanterns.

"I hope you enjoyed your rest below deck." I stood on top of an ammunition chest.

Mountain laughed first. "Just like when my mother rocked me to sleep."

Experienced crewmembers and officers chuckled next. The newer ones joined in.

"There's a lot to do. Repairs to make. Friends to console." I paused for a moment. "A chief to mourn." The sorrow caught in my throat. "Venerable Goddess Mazu claimed Zheng Yi's life. A Vietnamese cannonball knocked him overboard."

Shocked dismay and horrified gasps rippled through the crowd.

"Zheng Yi was no common chieftain," I said. "It took a cannonball *and* a typhoon to kill him."

"What'll happen to us?" The question came from the rear.

"We must make repairs, then we'll sail to Lantau to meet

all the squad bosses. From there, I'll send word to the other chieftains."

"I don't take orders from a woman!" The voice was unfamiliar.

I was ready for this argument. Ready for more than one mutineer. "Come forward. Make yourself known."

The deckhand pushed his way through the crowd. He was a surly shifty-eyed deckhand who always avoided me. He turned to Headman Hsiang-shan. "I will only take orders from you."

I gave a quick nod to Headman Hsiang-shan. His beefy fist slammed into the deckhand's gut. He dropped to his knees and struggled for breath. Too dazed to resist, Headman Hsiang-shan bound his wrists.

"Madam Zheng, how do you want this rude worm punished?"

"Rules are rules." I crossed my arms. "The chief's death changes nothing. You all know the penalty for defiance."

Headman Hsiang-shan swung his cutlass and the deckhand's head dropped to the floor.

"Does anyone else have trouble obeying my orders?" I jumped down from the crate, lifted up the bloodied head by its matted hair. "I'm acting commander of this fleet now. If this is a problem for you, I'll arrange for your swift removal from the ship."

Silence. A long silence of crewmembers looking at each other, at the sky, and at their feet.

"Good." I tossed the head to Three-finger Lo. "Stick it on a pole." With a calm face that belied my pounding heart, I moved through the wide-eyed crowd toward my cabin.

Fenfang sat on the berth next to my sleeping sons. She rubbed her eyes. "They're finally asleep. It's been a long night."

"The longest night of my life." I collapsed with the full weight of my grief onto the bed. "Yi is dead."

Fenfang wrapped her thin arms around me. Like a shattered dam, my despair gushed forth in a torrent of tears. I cried for a life ended too soon. I cried for my sons' future. I cried for my own. I sobbed until I was filled with emptiness.

I peeled off my salt-sodden clothes.

"Will you take me with you?" Fenfang brought me clean pants and tunic.

"Where am I going?" I slipped on the pants.

"To another chieftain's ship."

I tugged the tunic over my head. "No. I can't do it. I *won't* do it. Women are just as capable as men. Some even better. Our female scullers row faster than men. And you and I both know which wives throw stinkpots and spikes with better aim than their husbands." I went to Yi's desk and stared at a map of the South Seas coast. "I never went to school and don't know our history. Has a woman ever ruled the Divine Dominion?"

Fenfang nodded enthusiastically. "Quite a few. My grandmother told me about them." She sighed. "You would've liked her. She took charge of the household when myFather was distracted with his latest concubine—which was always —and my mama cried in her tea." She sighed, then shook off the memory. "Almost every night Grandmother told me stories about dragon gods, monsters, magical places, and creatures."

"Real women," I interrupted. "Not fantastical ones."

"When I was older Grandmother told me about the ruthless and brave women who ruled the Divine Dominion. Let's see if I can remember…" Fenfang tapped her chin. "During the time of the Song, there was an emperor named Zheshon who was too young to rule, so his grandmother, dowager

Empress Gao, held court and decided state matters for him. In the Tang reign, Wu Zetian ruled for sixteen years after her husband died, and thwarted many wicked plots against her. When the Jin ruled, Empress Jai Nanfeng controlled her weak-willed husband." Fenfang scratched her head. "There are others, but I don't remember."

"Then it is possible." I sat down at Yi's desk, folded the map, and opened the drawer. "Women *can* rule as well as men."

"Those women had noble ancestry. Pirates are wicked."

"You think pirates are the only ones who murder and commit treason?" I slammed the drawer.

Fenfang's eyebrows shot up. "I only meant——"

"Treachery is everywhere." I flung out my arms. "In wealthy homes, shops, markets, and teahouses. In fact, I think treachery is more common among members of the imperial court and the Forbidden City than in a poor village. Government and court officials are cunning. They betray with flowery words and false documents. They hire others to do their murder and create confusion. And they call themselves 'respectable.' Silk clothes and jade jewelry don't make you respectable. Virtuous society is a farce—the people as false as actors in the play. We sea bandits are not false. We don't hide behind insincere stooping and double-meaning words. Those respectable people partake of the same violence we do, but their violence is done through laws and edicts. They call it justice. I call it cruelty."

Fenfang wrung her hands as I ranted. "What can you do? That's the way of the world."

I sank into Yi's chair. "Sometimes old ways need to change."

44

Helmsman He-song opened the saloon door. "Pao-yang's ship approaches. He'll want to talk to the chief. What do I do?"

"Welcome him aboard," I said.

The moment the new lookout—a slave girl I promoted—identified nephew Pao-yang's ship in the distance, I retreated to the saloon. Preparation was the key to success and I had a lot to prepare for. But a journey of a thousand *li* begins with a first step.

Today's first step involved nephew Pao-yang. He had twenty-seven boats crewed by seventeen-hundred men, a formidable squad.

Nephew Pao-yang, who had joined us against the Viet-namese navy, was inspecting our damaged mizzen sail when I joined him on deck.

"Good morning, aunt. I've come for new orders from uncle." Nephew Pao-yang clasped his hands behind his back. "The Tâyson are cursed. Or Emperor Nguyen's gods are more powerful." His head swung from port to starboard. "How much damage?"

"A few crates of gunpowder on deck are soaked because the idiot deckhand didn't seal the lids."

"We lost several crates too. If it isn't water, it's air."

The coarse grain and sulfur mixture was fragile. Ironic considering how dangerous it was when lit.

"I hope the navy lost more than gunpowder." A twinge of worry nestled in my belly. "Hungry? They caught a rat this morning. The cook did an excellent job preparing it." Inwardly I cringed. This conversation took me backward not forward.

"I'm starving." Nephew Pao-yang swiveled his head about. "Where's uncle?"

"Follow me." I turned away and headed for the saloon. After I dismissed the incense-burner, I sat down in Yi's chair.

"Did something happen to Uncle Yi? Is he hurt?" Nephew Pai-yang sat opposite.

I folded my hands in my lap. "Yi is dead. A cannonball knocked him into the the sea during the storm."

Nephew Pao-yang put his hand to his forehead and closed his eyes. "He had no equal," he said after several silent moments.

"Yi was a respected ally and a feared enemy." I cleared my throat, tight with sorrow. "He spoke highly of you and always praised your successes."

"He was a good teacher." Nephew Pao-yang's eyes were water-filled when he opened them. "What will you do? Where will you go?"

"This is my home. My life." I stood and circled the table, my heart racing with excited tension. "For seven years I've been at Yi's side while he led the Red Flag to greatness. Together, we decided to expand the business by purchasing gambling dens in Macao and Hong Kong. Together, Yi and I persuaded local officials to overlook our illegal businesses.

We have hundreds of gambling dens now—Nanhai County alone has more than eighty." I circled the table again. "Together, Yi and I planned raids. Your uncle, the greatest flag chieftain of the South Seas, trusted my opinion and valued my advice. He consulted me about a captive's trustworthiness or a new skipper's loyalties. Your uncle and I were more than just husband and wife, we were business partners." I held my breath and waited.

If Nephew Pao-yang caught my meaning he pretended not to. "We've all grown rich because he diversified."

"Only with excellent leadership will you grow richer." My words were a subtle dance, crafty footwork meant to move him into position.

The nodding nephew Pao-yang, however, had two left feet. "Which squad boss would Uncle Yi choose to replace himself? Liang, Po-pao, Hsiao, Chen, Ya, Ta, Zhang? Me? Which one?"

I opened the red-lacquered chest and removed my paper cutting supplies from the drawer. "There's only one person capable of leading the Red Flag." I returned to the table with my supplies and began to cut. "Only one person knows every skipper and boss. Only one knows the leaders of the secret societies. Only one knows the name of the favorite concubine of the Three Dots Society's leader, has done secret business with the Three Harmonies Society, and smoked opium with the leader of the Heaven and Earth society. Only one understands what it takes to manage such a large fleet. Only one is able to seamlessly assume the mantle of leadership." I looked up from my cutting and stared into his disbelieving eyes.

"You?" Nephew Pao-yang blinked, blinked again, as though his eyes could not believe what his ears heard.

"Me."

"No." He shook his head and leaned back in the seat. "Impossible. Women can't be chieftains."

I was ready for this argument. "Why not?"

"Because." He scratched his head, searching for a reason. "Because it just doesn't happen."

"Nobody thought pirates would control the salt trade either. Nobody thought merchant ships would buy our safe passage permits. Nobody ever imagined that all but four Mandarin naval vessels pay a safe passage fee. Four! Out of hundreds. No one thought we would sail into the Pearl River's thousand branches. No one ever dreamed that the South Seas and Pearl River waterways would be under our control. All those impossibilities became realities." I exchanged scissors for a small thin blade. "Yi never said 'this cannot happen.' Because if he had, you would not be wearing a silk robe and have trunks of silver stored in a cave. If Yi had the short-sighted attitude you have now, you would not be profiting from protection permits and safe conduct passes. You would not be sitting on this one hundred and fifty-foot cargo carrier with ironwood sides mounting forty cannon and carrying three hundred and fifty crewmen." I returned my attention to paper cutting. "Yi had vision. And courage. He did what others said could not be done. It's what made him great and you…" I shrugged.

Nephew Pao-yang, his face taut with anger, pulled a knife from his belt. "I'd be careful what you say next, *aunt*."

I placed a finger atop his blade, my touch as light as a feather. "I learned candor from Yi. Blame him." I moved the blade away. "You know what inflicts more pain than this blade?"

"What?"

"Wealth. It buys government officials, loyalty, respect, and gunpowder. More importantly, it buys fear. The

Mandarins fear us. Villagers fear us. We are the emperors of the sea. The Mandarins grow fat and lazy, too secure in their power. One day people won't put up with their self-serving proclamations. They won't tolerate a tyranny that keeps them hungry, ignorant, and poor." I made quick precise slices across the paper. "Yi wanted a better life for his sons, family, and crew. That's why he joined the Tâyson's fight. Yi wanted respectability. He wanted a place in society. Dignity and prestige were important to him."

"We sea bandits will never be part of noble society, not even in a Tâyson court." The lines on Nephew Pao-yang's face pinched tight. "I didn't know uncle had such grand aspirations."

"Not grand. Attainable. Achievable." I slid the completed paper cutting of the flagship—wind filling its masts—across the table.

He picked up the paper cutting. "Quickly and skillfully executed. You've cut this design before."

"Thousands of hours of practice are necessary to master any skill." I hoped he understood my comparison.

Nephew Pao-yang rubbed his chin—a Zheng family trait —his focus on the paper cutting. "I saw the head on a spike. What happened?" He slid the paper cutting across the table.

"He refused to take orders from a woman."

Nephew Pao-yang snorted with laughter.

I shrugged as though decapitation was an everyday event. "May I count on your support?" My heart paused mid beat. His answer would be a step up or a fall down.

Nephew Pao-yang studied his nails, his lips pursed as he picked at a cuticle with his thumb. I didn't rush him. He had a lot to consider. A more experienced pirate would have needed a day at least to ponder the implications. But nephew Pao-yang was not an especially analytical man. He dropped his hand, squared his shoulders, and looked at me. "Any person, man or woman, who deals with insubordination with such efficiency is able to command the Red Flag."

"You honor me with your support."

It was the first step. But I needed to climb a steep stairway before becoming the chieftain. I needed the approval of every Red Flag squad boss and every flag chieftain.

45

*Z*hang Bao arrived a week later. He leapt from his ship to mine, his surcoat fanning out behind him like a purple heron in flight. He was lightness and agility, nimble of body, mind, and spirit.

"Mother." He stooped before me in a public show of humble respect. "Your adopted son is here to command."

I bit back a smile, marveled at his instinctive understanding of my precarious position. Over two hundred men—the crew gathered to greet him the moment the lookout sighted his sails—witnessed his deference.

My crew would pay great attention to each squad boss's arrival. They would note their respect. Keep an eye out for any sign of scorn. If a squad boss disrespected me, so would they. Bao saying 'command' was no accident. He had crafted his entrance and submissive greeting for greatest effect.

Bao's obeisance warmed my heart, but I had to tread carefully. Everyone loved and respected Bao. Charismatic and lucky, Bao would have no trouble persuading everyone he should be chieftain. I needed Bao's loyalty and obedience. And there was only one way I knew to secure it.

"I wept when I found out," Bao confessed the moment I locked the cabin door behind the servant who brought our tea.

"I haven't stopped." I sipped the tea, recalled the night Yi inducted Bao into his pirate family.

The master-student initiation was a brutal rite of passage into sea banditry. Even all these years later, I still saw Bao's face as Yi penetrated him. Bao's eyes had twinkled, one side of his mouth curled up with grateful resignation. He knew this act—this relationship with a powerful squad boss— meant he had a chance of escaping his lowly Dan fisherman status.

Bao, his eyes soft with concern, set down his teacup. "What will you do now? Will you go to Donghai to live with Yi's grandmother and aunt?"

"I can't imagine anything more horrible."

Bao laughed, but after that too much awkward silence passed.

He picked up the celadon bowl he had given me for Second Son's one-month celebration. "Do you know why I gave you this?"

I shook my head.

"It reminded me of you." With lust-glazed eyes he cupped the bottom of the bowl with the same enjoyment as holding the weight of a woman's breasts. His index finger skimmed around the rim. "Beautiful. Exquisitely formed."

A familiar heat coursed through my limbs. I remembered the taste of his lips.

"It's practical." Bao's finger traced the pale swirls, his touch a lover's caress. "Purposeful. Forged by fire. Shaped by skilled hands."

Our eyes locked, and I did not—could not—look away.

"It's a pity to own such an object and not use it as intended. To keep it on a pedestal to be admired when its true purpose is to hold something." Bao set down the celadon bowl, slid it towards me. "How will I fill your bowl, Xianggu? I'm yours to command."

I took a ragged breath—part desire, part guilt—and circled the table to stand behind him. I rested my chin on his shoulder. "In all ways?"

Bao trembled and turned his face toward mine. "You already know my feelings for you."

I tugged off his turban and ran my fingers through his straight black hair. "Remind me."

"I love you," he whispered.

"Love. What does a young man know about love?" My fingers caressed the nape of his neck.

Bao relaxed into my touch. "Only what you'll show me."

My hand brushed across his shoulder and down his torso. Despite the heavy silk surcoat I could feel his muscled chest. "You'll let me command you in bed?"

"I'll obey every order." His voice was thick.

My fingers floated below his waist, his desire prominent. "Will you obey my orders outside of this cabin?"

"I await your first command." He leaned back, his hips tilting upward to meet my hovering hand.

I stepped away from him. "Stand and remove your clothes."

Bao discarded his clothes with a swiftness found only in young men. He was superbly formed, with the lean tautness of a body ripe with vigor. Squad bosses rarely engaged in hard labor, but the cut of Bao's shoulders proved he did strengthening exercises. His arousal was impressive, both in girth and length. With a narrow-chiseled waist and tight rounded buttocks, his body was built for pleasure.

"I'm still grieving," I said after a thorough inspection.

"I'll mourn Yi's death my whole life." Bao's eyes dilated with pleasure. "I don't know how I'll bear his loss."

"We should comfort one another." I untied my robe and shrugged it off.

Bao drank in my body with thirsty eyes. His gaze lingered over my milk-heavy breasts and a stomach soft from childbirth. His self-control surprised me. He did not pounce on me like a man eager to hurry the act. Instead, Bao reached out and gently traced the curves of my face. His light touch left my lips tingling. His fingers teased the tender skin below my ears. Yi never touched me this way. Neither had any of the flower boat customers.

Bao was unhurried, deliberate in his caresses. My nipples stiffened under his touch, the tingle caused milk to flow.

"You're my adopted mother and yet I never suckled at your breasts." He lowered his head and licked off the rivulet of milk.

I gasped, drew him close, eager to have his mouth on me. Instead his tongue continued flicking across the rigid buds. Back and forth. Until I moaned.

One hand drew small circles on my inner thigh. Each loop came closer to my core.

"Bao…"

"Not yet." He lingered at my gate. "I've waited too long to hurry." His fingers brushed against me. "I've dreamed of this moment for many years."

Bao kissed me. A soft kiss. Teasing and darting and nibbling. He tasted as sweet as a red bean cake.

He dropped to his knees to kiss my belly and began his slow descent to my pleasure gate. His fingers parted the moist folds, my pleasure core exposed for a moment before he covered it with his lips. His fingers glided inside as he sucked. My fireworks came at once and I sighed with pleasure, but he did not stop until another shook my body. Only then did he lift me in his arms, set me on the bed, raise my legs high into the air and take his pleasure.

He was insatiable, rose again and again, left me gasping and sweaty. And eager for more.

My chamber was sore and my milk-laden breasts ached when I summoned Fenfang to bring Second Son.

"I can't call you my adopted mother anymore." Bao stretched out on the bed, his hands behind his head.

"Call me chieftain then."

One eyebrow shot up. "You think thousands of men, rough pirates, will take orders from a woman?"

Relief flooded my body and I burst out laughing.

Bao rolled over and up on his elbow. "What's so funny?"

"It's not funny. It's wonderful! You don't doubt my ability. Only the crew's loyalty."

"There's no doubt in my mind that you you are able to command the Red Flag. It's the bosses and skippers you'll need to win over. And the other chieftains."

"I'll convince them." I put Second Son to my breast. "Do I have your loyalty?"

"You have more than that. You have my heart." Bao ran his hand over Second Son's shaved head with affection.

"How do you want me to reward your allegiance?"

"Mmmm…Let me enjoy this dream before thinking about the next." Bao's answer was playful but shrewd. I already knew what he wanted. He wanted to be chieftain of his own fleet.

46

Second cousin An-pang was the third squad boss to visit. A hefty young man with a large chin and jutting jaw, he was known for his quick temper and furious tirades. Yi had often warned him of the consequences of unjustified outbursts. For his sake, I hoped he learned to control his rage before his crew mutinied. His only saving grace was his terrible card playing. He was a good loser and always paid his men what he owed.

Although I already had nephew Pao-yang's and Bao's promise of allegiance it was not enough. I needed cousin An-pang's support. Would I get it?

Cousin An-pang paced the saloon. "The news about Yi's death is spreading fast. Everyone will know soon. Including Mandarin officials who will waste no time attacking the leaderless Red Flag. A new chieftain must be chosen immediately." He spoke as though this had never crossed my mind.

"You're wise beyond your years." A bit of flattery goes a long way with young men.

Cousin An-pang wore a self-satisfied grin. "Yi was a good teacher. The best. I learned everything from him."

"Not how to win at cards." I smiled.

"No, he didn't teach me that." He leaned forward. "I'll tell you a secret. I lose on purpose. It builds camaraderie and makes my crew happy."

"Clever." I did not know if that was true or not.

"Wise and clever, am I?" Cousin An-pang stroked his hairless chin. "I'm not so young I don't know flattery when I hear it."

"You call it flattery. I say, compliment. As for the new chieftain," I adjusted my sleeves, "I'll announce the new chieftain when all the squad bosses arrive."

"What?!" Cousin An-pang's loud voice shattered the tranquility of the saloon. "A decision's been made!? By whom? Why the fuck wasn't I consulted?" His face turned beet red, his nostrils flared.

I folded my hands in my lap. "Who is your choice?" Soft words were best for calming someone's anger.

"Me." Cousin An-pang thumped his chest.

My face revealed nothing. Not amusement. Not pity. "Your squadron is the smallest."

He glared from under heavy brows. "Today it's small. Tomorrow it will triple."

"A chieftain comes from a position of power. Yours is still growing."

Cousin An-pang snorted. "I'll appropriate boats from other squads."

Despite nodding, I disagreed. "You plan to take away boats from the same squad bosses you want loyalty from? A chieftain *gives* boats—increases their squads' wealth. A thousand lost card games won't make up for taking their ships."

Cousin An-pang flapped his mouth soundlessly open and closed, a man so unsure of himself even his lips didn't know what to do.

"There's only one person with the experience and influence to lead the fleet," I said, my voice still calm and even.

With furrowed brows Cousin An-pang pondered all the squad bosses.

"I'm the only suitable replacement," I said after several long minutes.

"You? A woman?!" Cousin An-pang sprang from his chair. "The great Red Flag led by a woman!? What squad boss or skipper will follow you?"

"Nephew Pao-yang already pledged his allegiance."

"What?!" He stomped around the saloon. "One man's allegiance is not enough."

"Zhang Bao also pledged his loyalty."

"Bao? He's…he is…Fuck! Fuck! Fuck!" Cousin An-pang smashed his fist on the table.

"He's what?"

Cousin An-pang snorted. "You know what he is! No man can compete with Zhang Bao. Luck drapes over him like an emperor's robe. The gods favor him! The miracle in Huìzhōu is evidence of that! Did you hear? No? Bao told his men to take the statue of Mazu from the temple, but it was too heavy for anyone to lift. His men said it was a sign the goddess didn't want it removed. When Bao heard this, he went to the temple and picked up the statue as though it weighed no more than a feather." He plopped into the chair, defeated and deflated. "Fortune clings to him like wet clothes. Nobody will side with me if he pledged loyalty to you." Cousin An-pang suddenly straightened up, his eyes narrow slits. "Why doesn't *he* want to be chieftain?"

"He's happy to serve under me." I crossed my arms.

"Under you? Or on top of you?" He smirked.

Sometimes I wondered if seabirds spread gossip from boat to boat.

"Bao promises to serve in *any* capacity." My reply was steely-gazed and unruffled. "Do I have your support?"

"Yes," he grunted. "but the three of us still aren't enough. And the flag chiefs would sooner give away all their hidden riches than agree to let a woman be Red Flag chief."

GUO PODAI ARRIVED a few days later. It seemed word of Zheng Yi's death spread faster than dandelion seeds in the wind.

"I came as soon as I heard." Guo Podai glanced over his shoulder at Bao's ships bobbing nearby. His body visibly stiffened. "Tell me what happened."

I did. I left no detail out, even though Little Dog sat in my lap. The four-year-old did not comprehend death. When he asked for *bà*, I told him his father now lives on a celestial plane where he guides his sons to prosperity. My heart clenched just thinking that soon six-month-old Second Son would have no memory of his father, and that Little Dog's memory of him would dry up like dew on a leaf.

"What will you do?" asked Podai.

"Do?" I tilted my head and pretended confusion. Though I stroked Little Dog's silky hair with seeming composure, my mind sizzled with a single purpose. Getting Podai to back my bid to be chieftain. He was a very steep step to climb. If I couldn't convince him none of the others—Wushi Er, tthe General, Toad Rearer, and Eleven-finger Wu—would even consider it.

Podai's eyes softened with compassion. "I know this isn't the right time because you're mourning—"

"Grief has no time limit. I'll mourn Yi's death as long as I live."

"Yes, but today your sorrow is fresh, still raw." Podai picked up the celadon bowl, turned it about, not to marvel at its beauty but because he fiddled with objects when thinking. "Xianggu…" His eyes, warm with emotion, sought mine. "When your heart is ready to love again, I want to marry you."

I lowered my head. "It's too early for such an important decision.." I had expected his proposal, just not so soon.

"I understand." Podai set down the bowl. "Do you know why I'm not married?"

I had an idea.

"Because no woman is your equal. Not in bravery or beauty or intelligence."

"Thank you. I'll keep your kind offer in mind." One never knew how the winds of change might blow.

"I don't want you to just 'keep it in mind.' I want you to seriously consider it." Podai rose from the chair. "It's not pity. My heart belongs to you." He gestured to Little Dog. "I'll love Yi's sons like they are my own."

"You're a good man, Podai. My first priority, however, is leading the Red Flag."

Podai nodded. "Of course, but only until someone assumes command. Did Yi ever discuss a successor?"

"Never. He never imagined he would not die of old age."

Podai's brows lifted. "Really? That's an odd assumption in our business, although Wushi Er and the General are alive and well."

"Don't forget Cai Qian. Maybe Yi's assumption was not so odd. Once a deckhand rises to an officer position his chances for a long life greatly improve."

Podai spun the paper-cutting scissors I had left on the table. "Which squad boss do you think will make the best chieftain?"

"Someone already familiar with the responsibility. Someone intelligent, fearless, and practical."

Podai broke out into a small smile. "I'm flattered, but the Black Flag and Red Flag are too large to merge. There would be too many logistical problems with managing that many ships, people, and businesses."

My heart saank. Podai overlooked all my qualifications. He was too traditional, too stuck in the old ways. Worry fluttered in my stomach like a moth stuck in a web.

I set Little Dog on the floor. "Go find Fenfang."

The moment he ran out the door I went to Podai and touched his cheek. He looked down, his eyes soft—which many mistook for compassion and leniency—and smiled sadly.

Guo Podai was a man of opposites. The angles and curves of his handsome kind-looking face were deceptive and masked an iron-hard will. He looked and often spoke like a poet, not like a Black Flag chieftain who commanded seven thousand men and hundreds of vessels.

If I wed Podai I would be the first wife of the second most powerful flag chieftain. I would bear his children and be by his side. Just as I was with Yi. Nothing would change. I would simply trade one man for another. Or as Madam Xu used to say, different cock, same man.

I wrapped my hands around the back of Podai's head, drew him close, and set a kiss on his yielding lips. His arms circled my waist and the kiss deepened. I could love this man. I would be safe. He would provide for my sons. He would treat me well.

But that wasn't enough anymore.

47

G uo Podai kissed me again. "Be my wife, Xianggu."

Pangs of guilt and shame scratched at me like a cat at the door. I had just had fireworks with Bao and now I was kissing—and enjoying it—with Podai.

Love was the uniting of two souls. Sex, a merging of two bodies. Marriage was business. Commanding the Red Flag, the biggest business of all.

"What are the terms?" I gave him my most seductive flower girl smile. "Besides love and passion."

The vertical line between Podai's brows deepened. "What other terms are there?"

"Yi promised I could be a skipper of my own boat." It was the tiniest lie, smaller than a rice grain.

"Did he? When did he promise that? After your child-bearing years were over?"

Men! Did they think that was all we were good for? Determined and undaunted by his misconceptions, I caressed the back of his neck. "Each child has an *amah* to attend to their needs. Besides storytelling and game playing are not…"

Podai tilted his head, the vertical line deepening further. "Not what?"

"Those things don't satisfy me. They don't fill my soul." I appealed to the poet. "You understand that. Your books and writing fill that void in you."

"That's true, but I indulge, *indulge* in those things during quiet moments. You can't compare your desire to command a boat with reading. Before you fill your soul, you must fulfill your wifely duties."

I pouted, pulled away, but let my fingertips graze his chest— a practiced flower girl gesture meant to convey sexual yearning. I could not alienate Podai. I needed him.

His eyes shone with love. "I'm sorry. You shared your dream and I point out the reality of motherhood. If Yi promised to make you a skipper, so will I. But you must promise our ships will sail as entwined as our bodies will be each night."

My outward face beamed with affection. Inwardly, I cringed. Why would I agree to a future as a skipper when at this moment I was already chieftain? "I won't make any decisions today."

"You have another offer of marriage?"

"Not yet." More proposals were certain to come. None worth considering. A better alternative was available. That of being no one's wife. That of commanding the largest fleet in the South Seas. "I've summoned all the Red Flag squad bosses. I hope you'll stay until then. I'd appreciate the Black Flag chieftain's support."

Guo Podai inclined his head. "I'd do anything for you."

We'll see about that.

SQUAD BOSS YU dropped anchor before sunset. He was a surly disgruntled ex-government official who embraced the lure of the sea and its easy wealth. I disliked both his brusque personality and cruel punishments but needed his loyalty.

"Who will be chieftain?" Squad Boss Yu said after he offered his condolences.

"There's only one best choice. As the largest, most feared fleet it's critical we maintain that power. Which requires a person with expertise." I waved in the slave, showed her where to set down the long bamboo opium pipe and oil lamp. "Tell me, Yu, how do you think the Red Flag should expand its business?"

The slave girl held a droplet of melted opium over the oil lamp's flame while Yu inhaled the vapor through the pipe. Afterwards, his body relaxed into the chair, his eyes fluttering. Yu was a frequent opium smoker. An inhalation or two encouraged him to swap surliness for affability.

"The fleet's land offices require structure." He opened his eyes. "They're disorganized, run by either fools or thieves who steal our money and make side deals."

"They stare at the profit and step in the pitfall."

"Yes, an ancient and true proverb. I complained about this to Yi. I told him we had grown so large we needed standardized procedures and scrupulous accounting. Safe conduct permits, fishing fees, harbor fees; all these permits must be regulated and codified. Sloppy bookkeeping and mismanaged offices reduce our profits. The fleet loses revenue, which in turn affects the pay of every boss, skipper, and deckhand. A happy crew has coin in their pockets."

I changed my opinion about Yu. "What do you propose?"

"More people to work in our land offices. A bookkeeper, a printer, and enough men to form a collection bureau."

"Yi often mentioned your disgust with ineffective and stupid government officials."

"Idiots all! Empty rice bowls." He lifted the pipe to his mouth.

"I tried to persuade Yi to put your talents as a former government official to use, but he insisted you preferred the sea life."

"You did?"

"Many times," I lied. Not wanting Yu in an opium stupor, I rose from the chair and walked towards the door. "You could organize and improve our tax bureaus. Make us all rich. But I understand why you prefer the sea to land."

"I can do both." Yu stood, wobbled, and braced his hands against the table. "There's plenty of time when we careen and during typhoon season to manage offices."

"Do it." It was my first official order as chieftain pro tem.

"I'll visit the most fucked-up bureau offices first." Yu took one last forlorn look at the opium pipe and followed me on deck. "I have a few dependable relatives in mind."

"Good. Keep me posted on the changes. Now, tell me about the troublemakers in your squadron."

Yu and I continued our discussion over a meal of red bean soup, fish, and rice cakes. He confided about his meek mother and overbearing father. By the meal's end we talked like old friends, which made me glad because I could no longer rely on Yi's *guanxi*. I had to build my own.

"I'm honored by your faith in my administrative ideas," said Yu. "I'll do everything in my power to make the tax bureau a well-oiled money-making machine." Before leaving, he paused in the doorway, turned around, his eyes twinkling. "You're a sly one." His laughter filled the vestibule.

I MET with each squad boss. All one hundred and fifty of them.

After they offered condolences and bemoaned our chieftain-less fleet, I plied them with wine, *baijiu,* and the best food my crew could buy or steal. I asked their opinions about ways to expand or improve the fleet. Each had their own answer, their own ideas. A few were good, most terrible, and some founded on personal desires. Several simply required more matting for their boats. One demanded a third wife. Several needed help with botched ransoms, sick captives, or greedy spies. I advised and helped each one. I summoned a doctor. Promised a wife. Modified a ransom demand. I commended their victories and lamented their defeats. Each squad boss returned to his ship benefiting from our conversation.

I did not ask for loyalty. Did not discuss a new chieftain. I acted as though I already was.

ONE HUNDRED AND fifty Red Flag squad bosses crowded in the saloon. Guo Podai stood among them. As Yi's adopted son, nobody questioned his presence.

"Thank you for your prompt arrival." I stood on top of a makeshift platform—Bao's suggested it as a sly way of making the men look up at me—in one corner of the saloon. "Especially those who came from a great distance." I waited a beat, another of Bao's suggestions. "We all loved Chief Zheng Yi. We respected him and valued his shrewd business expertise. He made you rich, gave you wives, celebrated the birth of your children and mourned your losses. It's due to Yi's leadership that the Red Flag is the largest, most profitable fleet in the South Seas. He handpicked each of you because of your abilities. Yi once told me, a chieftain is only as successful as the men he leads."

Distracted by Second Son's cries outside the door, several bosses turned their head.

My jaw tightened. I had told Fenfang earlier to keep the boys out of sight and hearing. They would remind the squad bosses of what they perceived to be my flaw—my gender. "You are the best men."

Second Son's cries grew louder and broke my concentration. The squad bosses' frowns said what their mouths did not.

My fists clenched, my anger at Fenfang and my sons gathering like storm clouds. They ruined my speech!

And then I had an idea.

My fingers relaxed, and I sighed a mother's exasperated sigh. I raised my hand to silence the men's mutterings. "Bao, open the door and bring me Zheng Yi's second son."

Seconds later, Bao returned with my squalling baby.

I took Second Son in my arms and quieted him with a kiss. "I watched many of you rise in the ranks. We fought side by side. We've feasted together. Drank the tonic made from Fat Lu's heart together. Together we planned raids and campaigns. I've been at Yi's side for seven years. I know this fleet as well as he. I understand the fleet's problems better than anyone. There's only one person capable of leading this fleet. Me."

The saloon was silent for a heartbeat, then it exploded with objections. Guo Podai stared, his mouth open, the line between his brows etched deep with shock. Zhang Bao beamed at me.

"A woman?! I refuse to be led by a woman!" Spike-foot

Ma, nicknamed for his glee at nailing Mandarin naval commanders' feet to the deck, bellowed the loudest.

The odds were not in my favor. But I was not one for waiting on a hill for roast duck to fly into my mouth. I was bold.

"Don't let this child cloud your good judgment. My being a woman is a benefit." My voice was loud, each syllable enunciated. Another of Bao's suggestions: Speak slowly. Raise your voice but never let it get shrill. "I have more *yin*. You, more *yang*. *Yin* is nurturing, its strength in finding options and choices in all situations, all problems. *Yin* is caution and devotion. *Yang* is protective. Its strength is aggression and pride and energy. Together my *yin* and your *yang* are complete and make the fleet unconquerable. No other fleet can boast of this perfect harmony."

"I refuse to be led by a fucking woman!" Spike-foot Ma spit on the floor. "Dragon Lady or not. I've watched you in battle, Zheng Yi Sao. You're courageous and have skill with a blade, but I cannot—will not—take orders from a woman."

"Do as you must." I mimicked Zheng Yi's smile sneer.

Spike-foot Ma elbowed his way through the crowd toward the door where Headman Hsiang-shan blocked his disrespectful departure.

"Get out of my way," growled Spike-foot Ma.

He did not anticipate a response to his insolence. He did not see the blade's glint. Headman Hsiang-shan slashed him across his ungrateful throat.

Spike-foot Ma dropped to the ground with a thud, blood bubbling up from the gnash.

"The penalty for desertion, as you all know, is death." I lifted my chin and searched the faces of my squad bosses. "Now, who chooses an indomitable fleet?"

"I do!" Bao stepped forward.

Nephew Pao-yang and cousin An-pang swore loyalty next.

"Anyone else?" I asked this with a soft voice.

48

The saloon was hushed. Even Second Son was wide eyed with expectation.

Squad Boss Yu, thrilled with his promotion as overseer of the collection offices, pushed his way through the crowd to pledge his loyalty. Four down. One hundred and forty-five to go, Spike-foot Ma having already declined.

Guo Podai moved through the crowd. "You have my support."

The rest of the squad bosses followed suit, some more enthusiastic than others. Their loyalty was provisional. I had to prove my worthiness quickly before one of them challenged my command.

"Shall I send my fast boats to tell the other flag chieftains," Guo Podai asked after the squad bosses returned to their ships.

"Yes, and thank you," I said. "For everything." I took his hand in mine and hoped he did not mistake the gratitude in my eyes for love.

Later that night, Bao came to my bed. "Xianggu." He kissed my cheek. "Wake up."

My eyes, thick with sleep, struggled to open. "Mmmm, I don't need to open my eyes to enjoy your body."

"I just came from a secret meeting."

I sat up with a start and rubbed my eyes. "The squad bosses?"

"Yes. They like you, respect you, but don't think you have what it takes to be chief. You must start a campaign." Bao jumped on the bed. "You have three hundred junks, one hundred forty-nine squad bosses, and thirty thousand crewmen sitting idle. Which gives them time to plot against you. You need a campaign with fast results."

"What time is it?" I slung my legs over the bedside.

"Two o'clock."

I grimaced. "It's not much time." I wrapped a thick robe about me, lit the oil lamp, and laid a sheet of paper on the desk.

Bao nuzzled the back of my neck. "It's plenty of time for this." His hand slipped under my robe.

"Not now. I can't afford to waste a minute." I dipped the quill into the inkpot. "They want a leader? I'll give them a leader who hands them orders for the next campaign before they've had their morning *congee*."

Pink and orange light shredded the dawn when the sleepy squad bosses staggered onto my flagship the next morning.

My campaign was simple yet ambitious. The hundreds of villages along the Pearl River who refused to pay protection fees were in need of persuasion.

I spread open the map of the Pearl River delta. Like a banyan tree, the tributaries branched wide and far from the river's base. "I assigned each of you a tributary. You will remind the village officials who refuse to buy a protection permit with an example of our firepower. The same goes for those that are late with their bi-annual payment."

After Bao helped me distribute their assignments, I promoted Spike-foot Ma's headman to squad boss, then made an offering to Goddess Mazu for a successful campaign.

"Can we talk in private?" asked Guo Podai when I came out of the saloon.

"Of course." I turned to my cabin.

"My ship…please."

"Fine." I climbed over the bulwark and down the ladder to one of the many sampans. Rowers were fast. Sometimes too fast. I had no time to compose responses to any of a number of things that unsettled Podai about my new role. A foreboding scraped at the base of my neck as I boarded the Black flagship and accompanied him into his cabin.

Guo Podai's cabin reflected both his violent and poetic sensibilities. Costly paintings, intricately wrought furniture, dragon-embroidered silk pillows, and vases shared space with exquisitely crafted cutlasses, swords, and javelins. In front of a floor-to-ceiling bookcase stood a carved teak desk arranged with paper, a carved soapstone container, several brushes, an inkstone, two water droppers, and a brush rest.

Podai sat at the desk and indicated the plush silk embroidered chair opposite. "So…you insist on trying to command the Red Flag." He lifted an ivory brush from the pot and brushed the hairs back and forth with his finger.

"Try? No. I will."

"Without a man."

"I don't need a man." I hid my clenched fists in my lap.

"Hmm." Podai set the brush down, aligned it with the edge of the paper. "I love you and will not lie to you. I know Bao visits your cabin every night."

My jaw tightened. "You're spying on me."

"Every evening since I arrived. I'm worried about you, Xianggu. Your crew might decide to murder you while you sleep." He toyed with the brush, spinning it on the desk. "Of course, they would have to kill Bao too."

"I don't need to explain my choice of lover to you." My voice was knife-sharp.

Podai placed the brush back in the pot. "Bao is young. Inexperienced. Too ambitious. Too charming. Do you trust him? How do you know he won't slit your throat while fucking you?"

"I—"

"Bao has grand ambitions. He wants to be the Red Flag chieftain. It's one of the reasons we don't get along. He's always been jealous of me, of my position." Podai leaned forward. "He takes advantage of your grief. Bao's more likely to throw you overboard than remain content as a squad boss of a fleet led by a woman."

"Bao loves me. He always has." I said this even as Podai's warning planted seeds of doubt.

Podai grimaced. "He thinks a stiff cock means love. He's a boy. He knows nothing of love. I will give him credit though, he knew exactly how to comfort the grieving widow."

My eyes narrowed, my blood pounded in my ears, my nails dug into my palms.

"Don't play the fool. He's using you and you're too busy enjoying the false adoration of a younger man." Podai settled back in his chair, chose another brush, and twirled it between his fingers. "You can't trust him. He's superstitious...illiterate...fanciful."

"He's never given me a reason *not* to trust him."

"Has he offered to marry you?"

I looked away. For all his vows of love Bao never mentioned marriage.

"He can afford as many wives as Wushi Er," said Podai.

"There's rumors he keeps treasures hidden in a secret cave, treasures he should've shared with his squad, with Yi and you." Podai frowned. "I've shown my devotion to you. Bao has only f—"

"Enough. You've made your point." I grabbed the inkpot, poured ink over the paper, selected a large brush, and dragged it across the paper, blackening the page with several sweeps. "I don't want to be married. I don't wish to say 'yes, husband' and 'no, husband.' Even if Bao did ask me to marry him, I'd refuse. I'm content to lead the Red Flag, to have my own cave of stored riches. It's time to make my own rules, not follow others. I've had enough of obedience. I obeyed my parents and they sold me. I obeyed the moneylender—didn't attempt to escape his wagon of slave children—and was sold as a kitchen slave. I obeyed Madam Xu and was made a sex slave. I obeyed the men paying for pleasure. I obeyed Yi." I pointed to the paper where only a few patches of white remained. "This is my soul, Podai. It's covered with the blackness of obeying. No more. No more."

Podai studied the ink-dark paper as though it was an ancient text. Then, with a thin brush he wrote in one ink-free corner 'A Soul in Need of Freedom'." He pushed his seal into red ink and pressed it onto my soul-black paper. "I'm going to keep this. It'll remind me why you rejected my marriage proposal."

I stood, relieved this meeting was not about merging our fleets. "I appreciate your concern and your warning about Bao. You're a good friend and you'll always be my adopted son."

"I doubt that. There's too much animosity between your lover and myself to remain on familial terms." Podai showed me to the door.

I stood on my tiptoes to kiss him. It was a bittersweet kiss that tasted of his devotion and my indifference. I was not ready to be a wife again. Particularly the kind Podai wanted. That woman was gone. She died with her husband.

49

Year of the Earth Dragon
1808

Three hundred boats. One hundred and fifty squad bosses. Thirty thousand crewmen. The Red Flag fleet. All looked to me for guidance, leadership, food, water, and supplies.

My command was more fragile than a stem of orchids. Easily snapped off. A single unsuccessful campaign, one severe storm, or a Mandarin ambush would cost me my position. Or life.

Still, the time was right. Red, Black, White, Yellow, and Green fleets ruled the water. We dominated the coast and rivers despite newly appointed Governor-general Na's feeble attempt to destroy our ships. We out maneuvered and out gunned the navy every single time.

The flag fleet confederation had more boats, more cannons, more weapons, and more men than the imperial navy. For every warship they built, we sank two. Yet this did not stop the governor-general's water war.

"My gambling den informants heard that Mandarin officials are petrified by the size of our fleets and beg for special funds to weaponize rice carriers," said Bao as we lay naked and warm beneath blankets on a lazy afternoon.

"Rice carriers? They aren't able to carry more than eighty men and a few cannons." I traced the solid curve of his muscled shoulder. "They really think a rice carrier will take down an ocean ship crewed by three hundred men and mounted with forty cannons?" I laughed. "Anyway, those rice carriers will never chase us into the Outer Ocean."

Bao rolled on his side, propped his head on his hand. "Brigade-general Lin Fa vows he'll stop at nothing to capture me."

"He can vow to the moon if he wants. You're too clever and lucky to be caught."

"Not with everything." Bao ran his hands over my belly. "I haven't put a child in your womb yet."

The day after taking Bao as my lover I began drinking *liangyao*, the soup that prevented pregnancy. "Try harder."

Bao laughed and rolled on top of me. "Be my wife."

"No." The word shot out of my mouth with the force of a cannonball.

Bao frowned. "Why not?"

I could not tell him the truth, that I worried that Guo Podai's warning about Bao might be true. "I'm your chieftain. I don't need a reason."

Bao moved his hands between my legs. "As your lover I'm entitled to an answer."

"You're entitled to nothing." I flung off the blankets and sprang from the bed.

"You're using me, Xianggu." Bao jumped up, his arousal obvious. "You use my cock and tongue and fingers to satisfy yourself. You use *my* loyalty to strengthen *your* power." Bao grabbed my arm. "Without me the squad bosses would have turned against you. Without me, you'd be nothing more than a…" Bao exhaled long and loud. "You need me. You need me to help you manage a fleet of this size, to be your champion, to be your link to the thousands of men at your command."

Bao was right. His rapport with squad bosses proved invaluable this past month. We made a formidable team, and my first campaign was successful because of our combined strengths.

"I do need you. Your loyalty, your faith in me, your love." I shook off his grip. "But if I become your wife, the squad bosses and chieftains will say I'm weak and need a man. If we marry, they'll assume *you* are the Red Flag chief."

"You didn't earn the name Dragon Lady because anyone thinks you're weak."

"Exactly. A dragon is powerful on its own. It doesn't need anyone's help to breathe fire. It doesn't need help to spread its wings and soar. If I marry you it would be like sending a message to every deckhand, skipper, chief, and Mandarin official that I need a man to command my fleet."

"Fine," Bao sulked.

"Is it? Less than a year ago you said you wanted a fleet larger than Podai's."

"One day, not today. Today, I'm satisfied to be by your side."

"What about tomorrow?"

"Not tomorrow. Not the next day. I can't read or write. Which means if I were a chief, I'd be at the mercy of those who can. I'm uneducated but I'm not a fool. It would be too easy for someone to cheat me." Bao raked his hand through his hair. "There's another reason I'm happy to be by your side. You have a talent for long-range planning. Your body is on this ship, but your mind is at the top of the mountain assessing the view. I need to learn from you. My best decisions are made in the moment."

Warmth flooded my body. Any doubts about his true motives ebbed like low tide. "That kind of loyalty requires a distinguished title and elevated position. Today I make you Great Generalissimo of the Red Flag."

"Thank you." Bao grinned. "My first duty as Great Generalissimo is not a pleasant one. Skipper Vo has done a terrible thing." Bao held my hands. "He captured and raped twenty virgins last week while in a town that refused to pay the protection fee."

"What?!" All warmth left my body and cold fury took its place.

"It gets worse."

"He assaulted three daughters of a wealthy merchant."

"I'll slit his throat myself."

"There's more. He set their ransom sky high, then when negotiations were almost finalized, he raped them. The merchant no longer wants his despoiled daughters returned. Vo abused them, Xianggu. He forced them to perform acts they'll never recover from. One already tried to slit her wrist. The other huddles in a corner and weeps. The youngest finds whatever sharp object to cut herself."

I squeezed my eyes shut, did not want to imagine the horror those sisters endured. Enough was enough.

I opened my eyes. It was time every chief opened *their* eyes to the crime of rape. "Remember when we met in Macao to write the pirate code?" It seemed like a lifetime ago. "I begged Yi back then to include a rule punishing any man who raped a female. Yi refused to even discuss it with them. He said it would never pass." I opened the desk drawer, removed a sheet of paper. "Here's a list of all my suggestions Yi omitted because he said it was not the right time."

"Yi is dead. You're the chief. You decide the right time." Bao sat in the chair opposite. "What are they?"

I unrolled the sheet. "Anyone caught disobeying a superior will be beheaded. Anyone caught issuing commands above his rank will be beheaded."

"Severe penalties, but an effective deterrent."

"Anyone stealing from the common fund will be killed. No one is permitted to steal from a village or store that supplies us with goods."

Bao shook his head and laughed. "We're sea bandits, Xianggu. To punish us for stealing is like punishing a fish for swimming."

"We're not sea bandits. We're sea merchants and brokers."

"Pretty names don't change our profession."

"All business requires a bit of thievery. Buyers haggle to get an item for less than it's worth. Sellers haggle to get more. If a merchant ship owner is stupid enough to sail without buying a safe conduct permit, he asks to have his merchandise confiscated. We don't steal. We merely appropriate and transfer goods to our vessels for quick sale. We're expedient brokers of goods."

"You'd have made a fine government official." Bao tapped the list. "What's the penalty for withholding money and goods?"

"Death."

"Too severe. It's better to teach the thief a lesson than kill him."

"What? Chop off his hand?"

"No, then he's useless to us," said Bao. "Good pirates are difficult to find. Flogging would be better. It's an unforgettable lesson for the others and gives the wrongdoer a second chance. Now, if he steals from the fleet a second time he must be killed."

I made a few notes on the paper before continuing. "Female captives will be assigned separate accommodations from the men. Any man who violates a woman will suffer death. Rape is abhorrent and bad business—especially when there are willing women on board each boat to satisfy their needs."

"It's about domination not lust."

"Well, now it's about defiance to my rules and results in death." I smacked my hand on the desk. "The final rule is that a man must be faithful to his wife."

"You can't demand faithfulness." Bao's face looked like he had stepped on a sharp nail. "What's the ultimate purpose of these rules?"

"To add to everyone's wealth and encourage honesty." I mimicked his pained face until he stopped wincing. "If a deckhand steals from the helmsman, or a skipper steals from his squad boss they damage the bonds of loyalty we strive to build. Theft, no matter how petty, is the first step toward bigger offences. Do you recall what happened to Chen Yasheng after he repeatedly raped a female captive?"

"I remember. She incited the other captives to mutiny. They beheaded Chen and chopped off several crewmembers" limbs before the riot was broken up."

"It was an unnecessary bloodbath and all because Chen enjoyed abusing women. My new rules will promote respect and justice."

Bao didn't look convinced.

I tried another tact. "Why did you work so hard to become a squad boss?"

"Riches. Respect. Nobody dares call me a poor lowly Dan fisherman now."

"My new rules will encourage that kind of ambition."

"But how do rules that forbid rape and adultery increase Red Flag wealth?" Bao held up his hand. "I know that look. Your lips always purse before you let someone have it. I ask because it's what your crew will ask."

"We'll make more money because we will be able to demand higher ransoms for daughters not defiled. And those girls who don't have rich relatives to pay their ransom are more apt to join us. Content women make excellent crewmembers. Fearful ones are dangerous in a quiet way. Their fears grow into hatred, which in insidious ways destroys the goodwill we want. Angry women are like rotting wood in a ship or a vine that smothers a tree."

Bao nodded in agreement. "I've seen one woman sour a whole group."

"I'll make copies of my new rules. One for each boat. Tell the officers to tack them up next to the galley."

"You'll have to inform the other fleet chiefs. They'll be raging mad if all their women join the Red Flag."

"Good." I smiled. "Then they'll have to adopt my rules as their own." There was more than one way to skin a cat. I rolled up the paper. "There's a personal matter I want you to help me with."

"Anything."

"Find out if my mother is still alive. My sons need their grandmother. They aren't safe on this ship while the governor-general hunts us down."

My boys deserved a better life. One safe from naval attacks and typhoons. One where they could run through fields, play in courtyards, and be doted upon by their grandmother.

There was another reason. A selfish one.

Being a chieftain consumed all my waking hours—and sometimes my sleeping ones. My two energetic curious sons were in my way. Always underfoot, always fussing, falling, running, demanding my attention. Yes, I was their mother. But my first obligation was to thirty thousand crewmembers.

"Spare no expense. Find my mother."

Mama would lavish my boys with the attention they deserved. She would give them what Fenfang could not, unconditional familial love and devotion.

Bao tapped his chin. "I have the perfect man for the job." Bao shifted uneasily in the chair. "We need to talk about ways to improve relations with the chieftains who..."

"Hate that I'm a chieftain." I rested my head on my hands. Without their acceptance, my command was tenuous.

50

"Fuck no!" Eleven-finger Wu smashed his fist on the table.

The meeting with all the flag chiefs was not going well.

"Don't you mean 'no fuck'?" Toad Rearer's laughter brought tears to his eyes.

"Be nice to women," said Wushi Er in a falsetto.

Guo Podai leaned back in his chair and remained silent.

The General turned his head to hear. "You've posted these new rules on all your vessels?"

"I have." I sat up straighter, lifted my chin.

"I'm not following any rules made by a woman, even if it *is* Zheng Yi's bitch." Eleven-finger Wu spat on the floor.

Bao leapt over the table and charged across the room. "Speak about my chief that way again and I'll slice your throat." He set his cutlass across Eleven-finger Wu's fat neck.

Eleven-finger Wu peered down at the blade. "Dragon Lady blowing fire on your cock, Bao?"

Bao pressed the sharp tip into his skin.

"Stop!" I dashed around the table.

The room was silent, the chieftains poised for a brawl. Their hands hovered over the hilt of their blades.

I set my hand on Bao's forearm but glared at Eleven-finger Wu. "I might have blown my dragon breath on *your* cock, but I hear it's only as big as your eleventh finger."

The chieftains erupted with laughter. Eleven-finger Wu chuckled to save face.

"Put down the blade, Bao," I said. "Eleven-finger Wu is no threat to me. His foul attitude is the reason for my new rules." Palms flat on the table, I leaned toward him. "You and Zheng Yi —and now me—are joint owners of several recruiting centers. We also have a joint venture in a gambling house and opium den frequented by members of the Heaven and Earth Society."

"Yi and I share profits." His eyes narrowed. "What of it?"

"No, you *shared* profits. Sixty-forty, yes? Now you share profits with me. Since you publicly refuse to partner with a woman then it's in both our interests to end our business alliances."

Eleven-finger Wu grunted, ran his hand over the column of cropped hair across his head.

Fleet businesses were intertwined. We shared recruiting centers, fantan parlors, and gambling dens. We employed the same spies and bribed the same officials.

Our land network was a spider web, each strand sticky with connections, allies snared in a lattice of family bonds. One less business meant fewer contacts. One less recruiting office meant fewer able-bodied young men.

"As majority shareholder I'm happy to buy you out." I gave him a smile, one almost like Zheng Yi's sneering grin, and just as confusing. But mine was part devious, part seductive.

Eleven-finger Wu lifted his substantial bulk from the

chair and looked over my head to address the chieftains. "Fuck this bitch. Who'll join me in cutting her down? I'll slice off her tits first."

Wushi Er jumped up and aimed his blade at Eleven-finger Wu. "Sit down and shut up, you deficient-brained fuck head! We're a confederation! All linked by marriage and blood. My cousin's daughter sucks your cock—"

"My second wife has no place in this discussion!"

"Yes, she does, you chicken ass!"

Eleven-finger Wu, remarkably agile for a large man, bound over the table blade first and rushed at Wushi Er.

Bao was quicker. He stuck out his foot and sent Eleven-finger Wu flopping to the ground, where his blade skittered across the floor. Bao jumped on his back, straddled him, and pressed a knife against Wu's kidneys.

"You need an extra brain not an extra finger." Wushi Er nudged Eleven-finger Wu's head with his foot. "Piss Brain, before you destroy years of friendship, think! Your intolerance will rip apart our confederation. My cousin, your nephew, sons, adopted sons, grandmothers, and fathers. Just as it takes a thousand silkworms to make a shirt it takes thousands of associations to maintain our dominance. This is why Cai Qian sails the Fujian seas and still cannot conquer Taiwan. He doesn't have enough silkworms to weave his robe of power."

"Who knew Wushi Er was a poet?" Podai tossed me a quick grin.

Toad Rearer puffed out his cheeks and let go of his frustration with a throaty rumble. As chieftain of the smallest fleet he needed every alliance. "I'm content with our joint ventures, Xianggu. I'm richer because of Yi. I expect you learned from him so I'm okay with your rules."

I inclined my head, then signaled Bao to release Eleven-finger Wu.

Wu rolled onto his back and put his hands behind his head as though resting under a beautiful sky. "Podai, you and Yi shared many recruitment centers, fantan parlors, and quail fighting venues. You're rich enough to buy out Xianggu. Why don't you?"

"Family or femininity isn't the issue," said Podai. "Profits are."

Eleven-finger Wu grunted his disgust. "Podai's mouth is smeared with cunt juice from his new wife. It's addled his brain. What about you, General? You and Yi sailed together. Are you going to join Red Flag campaigns?"

The General grimaced, his forehead a maze of creases. "Yi was practical. He took no unnecessary risks. Under his command, few junks and men were lost." He tugged the lobe of his bad ear. "What this ear doesn't hear, my eyes see double, and my double-seeing eyes have witnessed Xianggu on deck during every attack. My good ear listened while she and Yi planned campaigns. My double-seeing eyes saw into their hearts and found two souls of equal ambition. Unless Xianggu makes bad decisions that cost me boats and men, I'll continue to sail with the Red Flag. I might even ask for a copy of her rules."

Eleven-finger Wu sprang from the floor. "I'm surrounded by cunt-loving dogs!"

Wushi Er waved his cutlass. "Fuck your ancestors to the ninth generation."

"Eat shit," said Eleven-finger Wu, "because that's all any of us will be doing if Xianggu fucks up the fleets with her cunt-shaped rules."

"Is that an offer to buy me out?" I crossed my arms.

"No." Eleven-finger Wu stomped to the table and gulped down his *baijiu*. "We'll remain partners. For now."

"I refuse to continue a partnership with a person hostile to my authority."

Eleven-finger Wu's face was as red as a red-dyed egg, and he huffed and puffed like a bull. He did not have enough silver to buy my shares. And I knew he did not want to forfeit such easy profits. He glared at me, humiliated.

"I'll buy Eleven-finger Wu's portion," offered Guo Podai.

"I need another opium den," said Wushi Er. "In a few years, it'll be time to rest these old bones on a little island where I plan on counting clouds, concubines, and all my money."

"My portions are not for sale." Eleven-finger Wu put his hands on his hips and stretched his bulky chest wide. "Not yet. Our confederation is strong. Strong enough to weather my opinion. I don't think Xianggu can manage the Red Flag. Maybe I'm the only one who thinks this. Maybe you don't want to piss off the Dragon Lady. Maybe her beauty clouds your good sense. Maybe you know her better than I do." He aimed an ugly glare at Bao. "Time will tell, eh?" Eleven-finger Wu stepped toward me. "I want to continue our joint ventures. For the good of the confederation."

It was as close to an apology as he could muster. I accepted it.

"I expect to be judged. One incompetent chieftain weakens the entire confederation." I waved my hand as though Eleven-finger Wu's outburst was no more annoying than a buzzing bee. "Now, there's a more important matter to discuss. Brigade-general Lin-fa vows to destroy us. Here's my plan."

51

That same night while a crescent moon winked between the clouds, Bao strode into my cabin.

"Did Eleven-finger Wu's fleet leave Macao?" I asked.

"Yes, but that's not why I'm here." Bao grinned. "I found your mother."

Suddenly, it felt like I sat on a carpet of needles. Twenty years had passed since FFather sold me to the moneylender. I was a different person. Would Mama recognize me? I was thirteen when I had left. Mama, fourteen years older. She was forty-seven-years-old now.

"Your father died from gangrene two years after he sold you," said Bao. "Your mother got a job as a servant for a rich government official in a neighboring town."

"Buy her back." I dropped my head in my hands and wept. Mama!

A few weeks later Bao told me Mama had been purchased for a few coins. Several more coins paid for her comfortable trip to Lantau Island where I had a fine home, many allies, and where the north bay had ample space for a large squadron.

My stomach was in knots as I sailed into the bay to visit her a week later. I had to look perfect. I bathed in fresh water, wore a sweet-smelling sachet, and styled my hair in a flattering manner. I wore my best silk *hanfu*, an embroidered surcoat, and an elaborate headpiece.

I alighted from the long dragon like an empress, my two sons scrubbed and dressed behind me. My Lantau house was not lavish but everything in it was of the best quality. I employed two servants, one cook, and two guards. It was a small staff but enough for one grandmother, two boys, and Fenfang.

"Stay here with the boys until I get you," I told Fenfang as we walked into the outer courtyard.

The Dragon Lady was gone, a nervous child in her place when I opened the door to the inner courtyard.

Mama sat on a bench and sipped tea. She lifted her head and I immediately saw the deep creases on her face, the slump of her jowls, and a wariness behind the eyes. The look of one haunted by poverty. Despite our near identical features, I would never wear this forlorn face. Mama had no control over her life, her subservience carved into her down turned mouth and drooping jaw.

"*Néih hóu.*" My voice was bright and clear with welcome.

"Xianggu?!" Mama stood, her eyes wide with happiness.

"Mama!" I wrapped my arms around her thin body. "It's been a long time."

"A lifetime." She sniffed, her nose running, her eyes tearing.

"You were pregnant when I left. Did I have a sister, a brother?"

"A boy. He didn't live past his second birthday. You're my only child." Mother stroked my surcoat. "You're rich."

I nodded.

"Are you a rich man's concubine?"

"No."

"A second or third wife?"

I swallowed, my mouth dry. How was it possible to be proud of my success yet fearful of telling Mama the truth? "I was the first and only wife of a great businessman. He died before the new year."

"I'm sorry for your loss." She frowned then swept her arm about. "Is this your house? It's very fine."

I lowered myself on the bench and folded my hands. "Mama, I need you. I manage my husband's business now and don't have enough time for my sons—"

"Sons?!" Mama's eyes widened and her smile was the brightest I had ever seen. "How many? Where are they?"

"Little Dog, his real name is Ying-shih, is almost five, my other son is almost a year. I would like you to live with—"

"Yes! Yes! Yes!" Her palms flew to her cheeks. "Grand-sons! Oh, Xianggu, you make me happy." Mama grabbed my arm. "All these years I thought…oh, Xianggu, I begged your father not to sell you. I begged on my knees, my tears drenching his feet. But today I cry tears of joy to see how successful and rich you are. Your father was right to sell you."

I winced. "Don't say that." I could never tell her what I had done to earn that success. Hurt wrapped its hand around my throat and for a moment I could not speak; could not swallow her absurd belief. But it was probably better she did not know the suffering and struggles I endured. "It's time you meet your grandsons." I rose from the bench and opened the gate where the boys and Fenfang waited.

Mama swept Second Son into her arms and smothered him with kisses. Little Dog, saucer-eyed with curiosity, gripped Fenfang's hand.

The visit passed quickly. Mama shared stories of the family she worked for. I told her as little as possible about my life.

When the sun was low in the sky, I scooped up Little Dog and sprinkled his rosy cheeks with kisses. "I have to go, but I'll visit often."

"Will you bring gifts?" He nuzzled my nose.

"Only if you're an obedient boy and listen to Grandmother and Fenfang."

"Grandmother talks funny," he whispered.

"It's you that talks funny, not Grandmother. Learn her way of saying things." Sea bandits spoke a crude unique dialect, one that bound them together like the twisted twine of a rope.

"How long will I be here?" asked Little Dog. "I miss the ship already."

"Ship?" Mama's sparse eyebrows rose to the top of her forehead. "You live on a ship?"

"A ship as big as a mountain!" Little Dog spread his chubby arms wide. "The flagship! Ma is chief and everyone says yes, chief, and no, chief and—"

"Was your husband a captain of a merchant ship?" asked Mama.

"Yes. Many merchant ships, in fact." I was a merchant, just not the lawful kind.

Mama stared into my eyes. "When you were young and told a lie, your left eye narrowed. Still does. What sort of sea captain makes a flower girl his first wife?"

I stiffened my spine. "A man who loved me, never beat me, and would never ever dream of selling his children because of his troubles."

Painful memories crumpled Mama's face. She wiped away a tear. "For twenty years I was empty inside, childless and husbandless. You made me whole. Gave me grandsons. Bought my freedom to live here in this beautiful home, with the front door perfectly placed. I owe you gratitude, not suspicion. I'll take good care of your sons while you engage in whatever business you manage. I'll protect them with my life." She put a hand over her heart.

"Mama," I squeezed her other hand. "I want you only to be a doting grandmother. The servants have other skills beyond cooking and cleaning." They wielded a kitchen knife as easily as a cutlass. "And Fenfang will teach them to read and write."

Tears ran down Mama's cheeks. "I thought about you every day, Xianggu. Every day."

I rubbed my thumb over her calloused gnarled knuckles, then hugged her goodbye.

"I'll miss you," I said to Fenfang as we stood in the outer courtyard to say our goodbyes. "I consider you a loyal friend."

Fenfang blushed. "It's an honor to serve you, madam."

"I want to release you from service when the boys are older."

"No. That time is long past. I'm a pirate now. My family will never take me back. You're my family now." She sighed. "I'm glad the Red Flag kidnapped me, otherwise I'd be a burden to my father—no one would have married me, I'm too ugly." She shrugged. "If not for you, I'd be serving my father and mother and my brothers' wives. This is much better. I'm wanted." She blinked back a tear. "I am valued and respected. It was good luck to be captured."

"Like that old story about the man and the horse. Who can know what is good or bad?" I took a satchel of coins from my pocket and pressed them into her hand. "You've earned a raise with your promotion."

"Promotion?"

"Manager of my house and sons."

As I headed toward the quay, I wondered at our odd fates, destinies opposite of our original stations in life. Piracy offered opportunities neither of us would ever have had on land.

52

Free from the demands of two energetic boys, I filled my days with piracy and my nights with pleasure. Free from the demands of a husband, I rejoiced in my independence.

Of course, there were many times I missed discussing campaigns with Yi. But with him, I had felt as yoked as an ox plowing a field. As chief of the Red Flag I spread my wings wide and soared like a bird.

My freedom had a price. Shame and guilt. Shame for not feeling more misery over my husband's death. Guilt for leaving my sons with their grandmother and Fenfang. Fortunately, my days and nights were too busy to dwell on these thoughts for long.

Diplomacy and strategy were my greatest strengths. Arrogance and Zhang Bao, my greatest weaknesses. And yet these things worked in harmony. To plan a campaign, lead a raid, and negotiate a kidnapping stimulated my senses. A pleasurable night with Bao kindled ideas and stirred my body. Success improved everything. Food tasted better. Seabirds swooped more elegantly. The crew's bawdy songs were funnier. Sex felt better. Even a harbor's briny smell made me grin.

I pondered these surprising benefits of success while lying in bed one morning after a multi-firework, take-me-to-heaven romp with Bao.

Bao made circles around my breasts. "I built a special boat. It's due to arrive today."

I smiled at his enthusiasm, which was like a child with a new toy. "You didn't need to build a boat when you can take any one you want." I stretched my legs out on the bed, flexed my calves, and wiggled my toes. It was wonderful to be alive.

"Not this boat. It's one of a kind." Bao scooted down, spread my legs, and lowered his head. "It's *almost* as divine as this."

My hips tilted forward and once again I let sensation overpower me.

A little later someone knocked on the cabin door. "Great Generalissimo." Three-finger Lo's voice was urgent. "Your boat's here."

"Be right there." Bao kissed me hard and leapt from the bed. "Come on." He tugged me up. "It's the most amazing boat in the world!"

"You haven't seen the whole world," I laughed and wrapped a robe about me.

Bao put on his pants. His bronze muscular chest bare, he threw open the door and bounded from the cabin like a playful tiger.

Bao was obsessed with warships, especially the British, French, and Portuguese. I followed from the cabin expecting a flamboyantly outfitted artillery-laden battleship. I never expected... *this*.

My jaw dropped. "A temple!?"

The two-tiered Tianhou pagoda was a marvel, resplendent

with tasseled red lamps, gilded lion sculptures, and ornamental woodwork.

"The Dragon Lady keeps the Great Generalissimo very busy," Bao said as we crossed the plank to his floating temple. "It doesn't leave me enough time to make the proper sacrifices to Mazu." He pushed open the sanctuary door and pointed to a a human-sized statue of Mazu. "Camphorwood. The finest quality."

"You spent far too much money," I whispered in his ear to make sure the ancient-looking, incense-burning specialist didn't hear.

Bao shook his head and sighed. "Your eyes see expenses; my soul sees devotion. Look with your heart, Xianggu. We live on the sea, do business on the sea, pray for favorable winds and tides, and yet our shrines are puny. It's an insult to Mazu. The goddess will find obeisance far more superior when done in a temple worthy of her blessings. Mazu favors me, protects me. I pray she'll continue to do so."

"Bao…"

Bao stared at Mazu, his eyes watery with devotion. "I never told you this, Xianggu, but one day while I made an offering at Changzhou temple, I heard Mazu's voice. It sounded like orchids and sugar and sunshine. Mazu told me to build a floating temple."

"Is that so?" I wondered if Mazu spoke after he indulged in opium.

As if reading my thoughts, Bao turned away from the statue. "I was sober, Xianggu. I swear it. Come, there's more." Bao led me under an ornate arch where small compartments arranged in a circle housed more shrines.

"Did Mazu say it was okay to share her floating temple with other gods?"

"She's the one who suggested it. Look, here's Beidi, god

of the north. And Longwang and Longu, dragon king and dragon mother. They've all been good to me and need their own shrine."

"And what of Fengbo?"

"Of course, wind uncle and gale mother, Jumu, have shrines as well." He crossed the circular room to adjust the draped tinsel.

I adored Bao but thought his belief that gods determined our victories a bit naïve. "Do you give the gods credit for *all* your success?"

Bao scowled as though I had asked a stupid question. "Gods. Ambition. Decisions—good or bad. Fate. No single thing guides our life."

"I think it's effort. One's force of will," I said.

"I'd rather be favored by the gods and inept than skillful and unlucky."

I brushed my hand across his cheek, rough with stubble. "Luck is the offspring of skill."

"Two beliefs. One outcome." Bao kissed my hand and together we left the sanctuary. "Look." He pointed into the endless blue horizon where the water sparkled like thousands of gemstones. "From this deck to the horizon is more than three miles. A measurable distance." He stomped his foot. "The depth beneath is unknown, immeasurable. Above us the sky melts into an infinite heaven."

"What's your point?"

"The emperor's robes have three panels. Sea, land, and sky. Each is distinct and separate. This is wrong, Xianggu, a false image of our world. Fishes leap from the depths into the sky. Birds dive into the ocean for food. We plunge into the water and swim down until our lungs force us back to the surface. Our ships connect all three elements. Sea. Land. Sky. That horizon out there is not *really* fixed. The lookout sees farther than we do, the man atop the mountain farther still. There's no real separation between *this* and *that*. The separation is our way of understanding something—of seeing the division between land, sea, and skysky. This blending—like tea leaves steep flavor into water—is everywhere and in everything. Luck and skill are not separate. Not divided. They're brewed together."

"Mmmm…an interesting philosophy."

Bao wrinkled his nose. "Philosophy is for men like Podai. I'm a simple man. The world is my school. Look at us. Man and woman. We're happy, you as chief and me as Great Generalissimo. Where others see two separate people, I know we're one ambition and one spirit. Together, both our strengths and weaknesses—though yours are few—make us unbeatable. You think of a unique strategy for a campaign, I add to it. You improve it again. We build on the other's ideas. *Yin* and *yang*. Together we're complete."

My throat tightened with emotion. It wasn't appreciation or admiration. It was not the wifely affections I had for Yi or the nurturing love for my sons. This feeling was something different, and it made me uneasy. It wasn't love. No. Love made me vulnerable, prone to making decisions based on heart not head. Caused poor judgment. A fleet chieftain could not afford to make bad decisions. Not with more than thirty thousand people and three hundred and fifty vessels.

"I don't need a man to be complete." I cleared my throat. "Tomorrow I'm joining Cai Qian's campaign. You will take your squad to Weizhou and rally our men's spirits." I was worried about the two hundred men and fifty-six hostages that had been captured by the imperial forces. Not to mention the one hundred farmers and four Red Flag go-betweens also arrested.

Bao flared his nostrils but did not argue. He wanted to

raid villages not smooth over a defeat. I wondered how long he would obey me without question.

Would Guo Podai's warning about Bao's ultimate ambitions eventually prove true?

THE GODS SMILED upon the Red Flag fleet. Perhaps it had something to do with Bao's floating temple. My squads seized junks with cargoes of textiles, rhino horns, sugar, pepper, indigo, tin, hides, rice, peanuts, betel nuts, salted fish, opium, pepper, sugar, and dates. My crew shared in the profits and my command was secure. My power grew. More boats. More crewmembers. Even Eleven-finger Wu accepted my authority.

It was seven months since the typhoon and cannonball killed Zheng Yi. Seven profitable months planning campaigns, solving problems, resolving disagreements, distributing merchandise, making deals with the triads, earning riches, visiting my sons, and enjoying pleasures with Bao. I had never been happier or more confident and secure in my future.

The winds, however, never blew in the same direction for long. The first two weeks of July brought imperial gusts that blasted devastation upon the fleet.

I was sailing with Bao and Podai on a joint venture near Macao when a fast boat delivered the grim news. The imperial brigade-general's armada of twenty-five warships headed straight for us.

"We're too vulnerable, too big a target." From the poop deck, Guo Podai studied the advancing warships through a spyglass. "We need to split up. Sail in different directions. Divide our squads."

Bao crossed his arms. "I'm not afraid of a limp-dicked senile brigade-general. I have a better idea." Bao explained his plan.

"You can't do that," I said, horrified. "You sentence those men to certain death."

"It's a good idea, Xianggu," said Guo Podai in a rare show of support for Bao.

"A few deaths will protect many lives." Bao looked through his own spyglass. "We don't have much time."

It was decisions like these that I detested most, that cost me many sleepless nights. "Do it."

Podai and I ordered most of our ships to sail into the hidden bay nearby, where its tall limestone islets and grottos provided perfect concealment. The other boats, our most derelict, waited to engage with the brigade-general's flotilla.

We sent the smallest, stealthiest fast boats to peek around the tall atolls and report back. The battle happened like Bao predicted.

The twenty-five imperial warships quickly sank a few of our boats with cannonballs and stinkpots. We lost a hundred and twenty crewmen. The remaining boats fled as arranged—in the direction opposite our hideout. The arrogant brigade-general took the bait and chased after them.

A hundred strong, we emerged from the bay, cannons loaded and stinkpots ready. We raced after the brigade-general. Pirates are masters of the sea, we caught up quickly. Together, my Red Flag fleet and Guo Podai's Black Flag fleet surrounded the imperial armada.

The brigade-general underestimated our numbers and tactics. Stupid man. A hundred of our finest ships closed in around him.

"You senile idiot," Bao shouted at the brigade-general's

warship. "You can't kill me!" Bao stood on the bow, his purpled robe billowing around him.

"Get down. You're an easy target from there." I said from the safety of the other side of the deck.

Bao looked over his shoulder and grinned. "Yes, but this is the best view of my victory."

"The battle's not over. Don't tempt the gods."

"I want the brigade-general to see me. Pompous idiot. Always after me. Vowing to kill me." He turned his head back. "Here I am! Fuck you!"

"Bao—"

The imperial warship's gun ports all opened at once.

"Get down!" My warning was lost to noise and smoke.

53

"**B**ao!" I raced into the gray cloud, tripped over debris and cursed the smoke. "Bao!" I threw myself on top of his fallen body. I looked for blood, set my hand on his chest, felt its slow rise and fall. "Bao!"

Bao opened one eye and coughed until he vomited. "Xianggu," he wiped his mouth. "We'll fuck later. There's a battle to win now."

I rolled my eyes at his bravado. "Are you hurt?"

"I felt something brush past me." He inspected his sleeve as though expecting to see scorched cloth. "He missed!"

Bursting with anger and relief, I smacked his face. "He didn't miss." I pointed to a charred breach destroying a good portion of bulwark.

Bao was lucky. Flying debris and wood shards were as lethal as a cannonball.

"Like I said, he missed." Bao leapt up, pulled me up with him.

The crew shouted his praises, and Bao ordered the vanguard to commence fire.

A barrage of cannonballs bombarded the brigade-general's ship. Blast after blast. The imperial flotilla was trapped, unable to break through our ring of ships.

We disabled several vessels. Set fire to another. A fifth lost a mast. When the brigade-general's own ship finally began to list, Bao and a hundred knife-wielding pirates scrambled up the sides to slaughter the sailors.

From the safety of my deck—a chieftain's flagship was the last to engage in battle—I watched the fighting. The salty breeze carried the screams and shouts over the water. Enough to know the warship's deck was blood slick and terror thick.

Bao lifted a severed head high into the air. We had taken the imperial warship. The fight, however, raged on. Pirate against sailor, blade against blade, the fighting lasted for hours. It ended only when every sailor either surrendered or died.

Across from the hundred-pirate ship belt of death, Podai's and his father's squadron blasted the imperial warships. Like cornered animals, the imperial navy fought back with desperate ferocity.

But pirates were fiercer. When Mountain held up the seventy-year-old brigade-general's head the rest of the sailors immediately surrendered. All that remained of the navy's twenty-five-ship armada was seven vessels more derelict than sea worthy.

The winds changed again and blew in our favor all summer. The Mandarin's doubled their efforts to subdue us but their efforts proved disgraceful. They retreated every single time.

In September, Bao's squad obliterated Lieutenant Colonel Lin Fa's motley fleet of salt and fishing boats. Stupid Mandarin officials. Did the lieutenant colonel really expect run-down boats crewed by cowards to defend the entrance to the Pearl River?

We dominated the Pearl River delta. In celebration, the flag chieftains met to discuss how to best divvy up the river's tributaries. There were still many villages that needed to be taught the folly of not buying our protection services. The navy tried patrolling. It was laughable. Their old boats had rusty weapons manned by common soldiers with no sailing experience. We sank or seized them with ease.

"We think too small." Bao addressed the chieftains at our monthly meeting. "What's stopping us from overtaking the province?"

"We need to capture Guangzhou first," said Eleven-finger Wu patting his bristly ribbon of red-dyed hair.

"Easily done. The city is defenseless. Their soldiers, cowards," said Bao.

"Easy victories make you reckless." Guo Podai downed a cup of *baijiu*.

"My recklessness is the reason we all sail freely into the Pearl River." Bao folded his arms, leaned back in his chair. "My recklessness fooled an experienced brigade-general and a lieutenant colonel. My recklessness profits the confederation."

"Hmph." Podai poured another glass.

"Taking Guangzhou would be a daring move." Wushi Er stroked his beard. "If we do this, we each need a stake in it."

I remained silent. I needed to hear all sides of an argument before making a decision.

"What happens if we do capture Guangzhou?" asked Podai. "What then? Who will rule the city? We're not government officials. We're sea lords. Warriors of the ocean. Not administrators. We'll have to hire the same magistrates and yeomen we bribe. How long would our control last? All the Mandarins need do is slide enough silver into a few dishonest pockets to sabotage our clumsy attempts at governing. No. Taking Guangzhou brings more problems than it's worth."

Eleven-finger Wu, the General, Toad Rearer, and Wushi Er agreed.

"We already lord over villages and islands," said Bao. "This is no different."

"The emperor doesn't care about a few insignificant villages and secluded islands," said Wushi Er. "Losing them to us doesn't threaten his dominion. Capturing Guangzhou is. He'll consider it an act of rebellion."

"Punishable by death. Slicing or beheading." The General shook his head. "If we lose—"

"The imperial navy is incompetent." Bao spread his arms wide. "I sit with the greatest naval generals of the Tâyson rebellion. Your combined military expertise and experience increased our wealth a thousand-fold. More young men flock to our recruitment centers than imperial forces. We employ accountants, storekeepers, traders, appraisers, guards, religious experts, physicians, acupuncturists, brokers, fee collectors, cooks, stevedores, carpenters, blacksmiths, sail makers, certificate makers, and chandlers. We employ as many people as the Mandarins. We are *already* an empire."

"We were generals in Vietnam, a small realm with less people." The General appeared unconvinced. "The Divine Dominion is vast. The populace too large to count."

"You give me excuses," said Bao. "I give you a dream!"

"Your dream is excellent but impossible," countered Wushi Er. "Our strength is the water world. On. Our. Ships. The land we do control is tiny, a grain of rice compared to the Great Qing's coastlines, forests, valleys, and plains that stretch north and west for months. Guangzhou is conquerable, but what then? We have no land forces, Bao. And whoever might join our rebellion will be a farmer not a fisherman."

"Farmer, fisherman, what does it matter?"

"I'll tell you why," said Podai. "The farmer in the Center of the World doesn't know us. Never heard of us. We know nothing about their way of life. And they don't care about ours. Allies and weapons win wars, not dreams."

"Government workers are poor. Even the top officials." Toad Rearer puffed out his cheeks. "I don't want to rule Guangzhou, push paper all day. I just want silver enough to give each of my three wives their own set of rooms."

"You'll need a mountain of silver for that." The General laughed. "Those women fight like quails. Too bad you can't make any money from their bickering."

Toad Rearer burst out laughing. "The crew does!"

Bao's face tightened, the muscles in his jaw shifting with barely controlled anger. "When people work with one mind they can move Mount Tai."

"And it's easy to find a thousand soldiers but hard to find a good general," said Guo Podai. "Ancient sayings don't win revolts. Allies and silver do."

"Imperial silver hasn't conquered us yet." Bao rose from the chair. "I've other business to attend to. Please consider your futures and the future of the Divine Dominion."

After Bao departed the room all eyes turned toward me.

"The Great Generalissimo aspires to lofty heights," said Podai in a low voice. "Are they yours as well?"

"I'm a business woman. It's wealth I want."

The General cocked his head, his good ear angled for listening. "You made Bao the Great Generalissimo. Is he taking over your command?"

"Bao is Generalissimo because he commands the largest squad and enforces my orders. I *am* and will always *be* the chieftain." No trace of annoyance escaped my lips. "Bao is the son of a Dan fisherman. He did what he does best—

weave a strong net in hopes of catching fish with the same aspirations."

"I think," said Podai, "Bao wishes to shed his lowly Dan fishermen ties, particularly as the Dan are known for being mighty dragons on water but worms on land."

"There's nothing wormlike about Bao."

Wushi Er sidled next to me. "Don't allow your close relationship with Bao to cloud your good judgment."

"It's too late for that." Eleven-finger Wu spewed a stream of betel nut spit. "She's gone all soft for his hardness."

"No one, lover or otherwise, muddles my mind. Now, I suggest we proceed to the next item on the agenda: how to reprimand those towns refusing to pay protection fees."

Later that day, Bao paced my cabin.

He picked up the celadon bowl, circled the rim with his finger. "Such a thing *is* possible, Xianggu."

"Taking Guangzhou?"

"Not just Guangzhou, the Great Qing, all the lands under heaven."

How could I tell my lover his ambition was too great? That no gentry or farmer or shopkeeper wanted a lowly Dan fisherman for an emperor? It did not matter if he inspired the crew's devotion and obedience. Or had a reputation for fairness. Or possessed dignity and poise. Nothing would convince fleet chieftains to join his ambitious campaign. It was not about whether we could, but if we wanted to. The other chieftains didn't want to.

Who was I to ruin Bao's dreams with reality? Bao had already risen faster than a wish lantern during the Mid-Autumn festival. He had attained more power and wealth than all the other chieftains. Who knew how far he could go?

"Bao." I wrapped my arms around him.

Bao's body stiffened. "You doubt me. You think taking control of Guangzhou is impossible."

"Capturing the city will not be a problem. Not for you."

"I see doubt in your face. Your left eye narrows. You think I'm incapable of ruling." He pulled away and set down the bowl.

"You would be a better ruler than those dogs roaming the halls of the imperial palace."

"Of course, I would. The emperor's advisors don't care about people like us. They don't understand our struggles or the disgrace of being born into filth, living with hunger, and dying in misery."

"Is this why you want to capture Guangzhou? To help the poor?"

Bao rubbed his forehead. "Change like that will take many generations or a great revolution. Probably both. The Mandarins have no desire to improve the lives of common folk. I do. Perhaps I will be the spark that lights the fire of change."

"I believe you will."

"Then you'll give me the ships and men to take Guangzhou?"

"No."

"What?" Bao jerked away. "You're a two-headed *naga*. One dragon head nods yes, the other shakes no."

"Capturing Guangzhou isn't like capturing a rice junk. It's not the right time for such a bold act of rebellion."

"Why not?" His nostrils flared.

"Last year was a good year. No famine. The first time in many years. Rice was cheap, food prices low. Last year everyone filled their bellies and had extra coin in their pockets. *This* year we have a famine. Rice prices are high, the people are hungry."

"Then it's a good time."

"No. The people remember last year's time of plenty. Strike when people are furious. Wait until the second year of famine when there's another year of fear, another year of rising anger toward the fat landlords eating moon cakes while their own children starve."

Bao sat down, his fingers drumming the desk as he considered my advice. "You're right. Timing is everything. Mildly upset peasants don't revolt. Will I have your support when the time *is* ripe?"

"Of course." This was neither a lie nor truth but a murky space between. Although we ruled the sea, I doubted we could dominate on land. Our combined fleets were not large enough. The emperor would retaliate with military aid from Portugal and England. With limitless imperial wealth. With a web of Qing familial connections stretching back for twenty generations.

"Be patient. The time will come." I set his hand on my belly. "There's another matter requiring your patience. I'm not certain. I've only missed one month but—"

"A son?!" It was as if the sun shone on Bao's face.

"Make prayers to the gods." I would never tell him the *liangyao* had failed.

Bao's hands wandered over my belly. "I was jealous when you were pregnant with Yi's children." His hand moved around my hips.

I leaned into him, set my fingers on his head, and massaged his scalp. He groaned, pushed the folds of my robe back and began his descent. I marveled at this man. He never tired of my scent and taste. Claimed it brought him to the edge of his fireworks. I reveled in his technique, the way he gazed into my eyes, eager and adoring.

My body, heart, and soul responded to his devotion in a

manner transcending mere physical release. My first fireworks released, I craved his length and girth, and we dropped to the floor.

Love was not an emotion, not a feeling. It was this. A desire made flesh. A yearning made physical through the vibrations and sounds of our pleasure.

I have had many men, but Bao achieved what no other man—not even Zheng Yi—had. He made me forget everything but the feel of his touch, the push and pull of his body. He was the surf and I, the beach. I was at the mercy of his rhythms. At the mercy of the waves of pleasure coursing through me. This total abandonment of body and soul fused us together. In the end, we rode the same crest, bodies joined, eyes locked on each other. His pleasure was mine, and mine, his.

Later, while rain beat against the ship, I considered the excessive price of finding this physical and emotional contentment. Another child was the last thing I wanted.

54

The pregnancy was difficult. I was nauseous, a cup of tea and a spoonful of *congee* all I managed to swallow most days. I hid my queasiness from the crew. Only Bao and my servant girl saw me retching.

"You're thinner each day." Bao fastened his belt. "You must eat more."

"It'll pass and then my belly will be so large you won't find me attractive anymore."

"That's not possible."

I swished tea in my mouth, spit it out, pat my lips dry. "Tell me what happened with the deckhand named Liu. Everyone has a different version."

"Liu wanted to kill me." Bao picked up the long black cotton cloth. "The recruiter claimed Liu waited in line at the recruitment office for hours begging to join the Great Generalissimo's squad. No other one would do. The recruiter was impressed by his determination and assigned him to my squad." Bao folded the fabric in half. "Of all my one hundred and twenty vessels, Liu was assigned to mine. I noticed an odd expression—a peculiar glint in his eye—when I met him.

I know that look. It's how an enemy looks at you while fighting. *That* look. His eyes told me everything." He carefully creased the material lengthwise twice more, prolonging the story. "I ordered Liu's feet and hands bound, and found a hidden knife strapped to his chest under his shirt. The knife was wrapped in cloth."

"He had soaked it in poison?"

Bao nodded. "I was curious. Why does a new recruit want to kill me? I asked him. Liu's answer proved enlightening." Bao paused as he positioned one end of the cloth at the back of his neck and began wrapping his head. "He told me he joined to avenge his father's death."

"You killed his father?"

"No. But one of my skippers did, well, not directly. A few months earlier, Liu's father was kidnapped. Before the skipper arranged the ransom, his father died. I explained, quite calmly, that my skipper was responsible for his father's kidnapping and death, not me. I explained who reports to who and why. Then I told Liu I admired his bravery and gave him four silver dollars as a reward."

"You rewarded him? Why?"

"I turned an enemy into a friend." Bao spread out the cloth folds of one end and finished by tucking it into place. "His apology, his eyes, and his posture convinced me he understood I am not responsible for every officer's actions."

"You're a good judge of people." I was better at calculating sums than people's intentions.

The rest of the the morning we spent reviewing provisions with the steward and protection permit accounts with the bookkeeper. I enjoyed these tasks, loved looking at the ledgers of neatly written numbers. It was proof my command was secure and profitable. In fact, the Red Flag was more profitable than it ever had been before.

The other flag fleets benefited from my improved methods. Improved financial offices. Efficient management of permits and passes. Standardized ransom procedures and amounts. Allocated Pearl River tributaries. All these systems enhanced the confederation's cooperation and coordination.

I was living my dream.

"WHY DO YOU DOUBT ME?" Bao passed me the spyglass.

The *Peng-fa*, sailing from Vietnam loaded with goods, rode low in the water.

"Too risky," I said. "If there's a cannon behind every portal we're outgunned. Anyway, a ship that big won't let us get close enough to launch stinkpots, let alone board."

Bao's grin was irrepressible. "Our ships won't be going anywhere near the *Peng-fa*. Here's my plan."

It was a good one. Simple and devious.

We hid an armed team inside two nonthreatening ferryboats. On deck, six of our most innocent-faced men would pretend to be terrified of the pirates they saw earlier.

"I'm a poor, stupid ferryman." A crewman called Rathands—he had superior rat catching abilities—practiced his part in the charade in front of the crew. "I'm too poor to pay the protection fee. My wife and children are starving. Oh oh oh, the sea is full of wicked pirates. I beg of you, let us sail near you until we reach the safety of port."

The gathered deckhands applauded Rat-hands performance and joined his play-acting. It was a funny bit of theatre. More entertaining than festival plays.

"I think our crew is better suited to acting than banditry," Bao grinned.

"They've had lots of practice at deception." I laughed out

loud as Rat-hands wept real tears and slumped to the deck in mock despair.

We ordered our squads into position and used a common tactic, hiding in plain sight among hundreds of fishing and cargo boats.

The lookout shouted updates as the ferryboat approached the *Peng-fa*.

"They're hailing!"

"*Peng-fa* lets them approach!"

Bao gave the order and our boats closed in. Like a flock of birds spreading their wings and rising into the sky, the boats unfurled their sails in a graceful synchronization I never tired watching.

"Rat-hands is boarding!" The lookout hollered.

The armed team sprung from their hiding place and climbed the sides of the *Peng-fa* like ants up a tree.

The unarmed and surprised *Peng-fa* sailors put up a valiant fight.

Bao ordered the second stage of the attack. Three open-the-wind junks arrived. Each was manned with crewmen possessing a lethal talent, throwing eighteen-foot bamboo spears with deadly precision.

"Ten sailors down," the lookout hollered.

"Works every time," Bao grinned.

By the time my flagship came aside the *Peng-fa,* the captain had been murdered and the sailors dealt with in the usual manner. Those refusing to surrender, we stripped naked, bound their hands and feet, hung from the mast, and beat with rattan-twisted rods. We chained the submissive sailors together.

"I am Zhang Bao, Great Generalissimo of the Red Flag. I'm a patient and kind man so I'll give you a choice. Any man wishing to become a sea bandit will take an oath before Mazu before being assigned to a vessel and receiving a share of future profits. Any man not inclined will be held hostage until your family pays the ransom. Those whose family cannot finance their ransom become our slaves." Bao tilted his head to peer at the sailors hanging overhead and begging to be let down. "Volunteers?"

"I do, I do," shouted ten enthusiastic sailors.

"Good choice," I said coming to stand beside Bao. "I am—"

"The fearsome Zheng Yi Sao," said one sailor.

"Dragon Lady," said another.

It took all my self-control to keep from smiling. It's a heady feeling to realize everyone in the South Seas knew my name and reputation. I was giddy with pleasure.

THE SUN SHONE warm the day I visited my sons to celebrate the New Year. I concealed my bulging belly beneath clothes, but Mama was not fooled.

"You're with child." She sipped tea. "Did you marry again?"

"I don't need a husband."

A hundred tiny lines creased around Mama's disapproving mouth. "Maybe not for money but it seems you need a man for other things."

I folded my hands in my lap and glanced at Fenfang whose lips twitched with amusement.

Mama set the teacup down. "You're a wealthy woman. A woman of some power, I think. But it's not good for a child to be fatherless."

"The child has a father."

"Why doesn't he marry you then? Is he married? Wicked?"

"He's a good man. An important and powerful man. He wants to marry me but there are complications. Matters you wouldn't understand."

Mama scowled. "Business matters?"

"Yes." It was the truth, after all.

"I'm not stupid, daughter." Mama's eyes bore into mine. "Let me tell you what I've figured out about you and your... business. You have plenty of money, enough to find me, buy me, set me up in your home—a modest-looking but fine home designed not to attract attention. Fenfang is no peasant. She's too educated, too knowing of rich men's ways. Too secretive. She refuses to tell me your true occupation. Little Dog tells me stories about battles and fighting and events too horrid to repeat. I know who you are. You're the chieftain of the Red Flag fleet."

I nodded. "I am."

Mama pressed her hand to her heart as though it hurt and pushed away the teacup. "Pirates are wicked. They rape and murder and steal and burn entire villages. How can you do this, Xianggu? How can you dishonor me this way?"

"Dishonor?" My voice was tight, anger rising like a rain-gorged river. "Father sold me to pay his debts."

"I begged him not too. I had no choice but to obey him. You don't remember our arguments. He beat me." She bared her teeth. "Two teeth I lost in one quarrel over his selling you."

"I was a whore for ten years. I sucked thousands of cocks and opened my legs to thousands more. Would you rather I remained a whore? Is fucking more honorable than stealing?"

"Such vile talk!" Mama covered her ears, rocked back and forth. "Flower girls don't hack the limbs from good folk.

Flower girls don't order villages burned to the ground. Flower girls don't drink their enemies' blood or drive nails through fishermen's feet."

I pulled her hands from her ears. "Flower girls don't become rich either. They work until they lose their beauty, and no one will pay for their services. Then they're cast off the flower boat to starve or beg or work as slaves. Zheng Yi saved me from this fate. My flower girl skill opened the door of his love, but it's my sharp mind that earned me respect on his ship."

"There's nothing respectful about severing heads and mounting them on poles." Mama dabbed at her wet cheeks with the edge of her sleeve. "You trade respectability for wealth."

"It's my wealth that gives you this life, your silk clothes, good food, and fine tea. If my business is loathsome then leave."

"My daughter is dead." Mama turned her head away.

"Yes, the girl Father sold to the moneylender is dead. In her place is the most feared and respected pirate of the South Seas." I rose from the bench. "I'll expect your decision in the morning."

"What are you talking about?"

"Either enjoy the comforts I provide without insulting me or leave."

Mama fled the courtyard in tears.

55

I muffled sobs in the pillow. My grief was baffling. Did I weep because I needed Mama's approval? Because she did not admire my accomplishments? Because she scorned the woman I had become?

Rejection, resentment, frustration. Such feeble emotions! I purged them before they weakened my spirit.

Like foul water that soaks into rice kernels and makes them inedible, my brutal water world had saturated my soul. I rolled onto my back and studied the moonlit ceiling. The wood planks were straight, each side grooved into the other. A well-built home. Not like the roof in the house I grew up in that dripped water when it rained.

Mama was wrong, her opinion founded in poverty. Being a pirate chieftain did not make me a wicked person. My crimes were no worse than those of the Mandarin officials, except their punishments were called laws, whereas ours deemed atrocities.

Mandarins valued wealth and power over decency. Just like us. There was one real difference between wicked water people and 'respectable' Mandarins. Mandarins valued the prestige and privilege of their ancestral lineage whereas we struggled to make enough money to last through our old age.

Except for Bao. He aimed higher.

The next morning, I awoke with fresh resolve and a new purpose.

"What was the name of the moneylender Father sold me to?" I sprinkled scallions and mushrooms bits over my morning *congee*.

"Tao." Mama, her eyes dark from sleeplessness, was as skittish as a young colt.

"How appropriate. He certainly provided *the way* into prostitution. Was he from Xinhui?"

Mama chewed on her lip, her eyes darting about as she searched her memory. "I think he was a relative of someone in our village. That's all your father told me. Did he…" Mama peered down at her bowl of *congee*, "hurt you?"

"A good businessman never damages his merchandise. My virginity was sold at a high price. Twice."

"What?" Mama's sparse brows jumped to her forehead.

"Maybe three times. Maybe more. I don't remember. Flesh merchants are in the business of deception."

Mama looked up, her face pinched with emotion. "I couldn't sleep last night. All I thought about was the horror you must have gone through. But you endured, Xianggu. You grew tough. And now you're healthy and prosperous. You succeed where I failed, where your father failed. Look at me. My body and spirit are older than my age. Too much poverty and misery. I'm tired. My only desire is to enjoy my grand-sons and live in peace." She paused, sighed. "I made my deci-sion. I don't care how you make your money. I just have two questions for you. Was your pirate husband kind to you?"

"Zheng Yi treated me well. We were lovers, friends, and business partners."

Mama's face relaxed into a relieved smile. "Is the father of this third child good to you as well?"

"He's the most wonderful man I have ever known. He adores me."

"Your father was considered a good person, yet he beat me and gave me no pleasure...*that* way. It seems pirates are better husbands."

I spit out my tea laughing. "Not at all! They make terrible husbands. I was lucky Yi raided our flower boat. Had it been Eleven-finger Wu...well, I was lucky that night."

"A man brings a woman either pleasure or pain. I'm happy your husband brought you happiness."

Yes, I thought, a husband either tramples a woman's spirit or encourages her dreams.

Husbands should not have so much power.

FAMINE STRUCK GUANGDONG PROVINCE. The worst in ten years. Rice prices tripled. With thousands of crewmen and slaves and captives to feed I was forced to make new agreements and deals. I paid loyal merchants double for food and provisions. We stole from everyone else.

I sent only my most trusted men to deliver packages of rice, pork, and vegetables to my family in Lantau. Growing children suffered the most during times of famine, insufficient food stunted body and mind. I would not let my sons suffer even a moment of hunger.

Lack of food made deckhands irritable. Which in piracy was often a good thing.

I divided each squad into three teams. The first traveled up each watercourse in search of paddies with unharvested yellow rice stalks or unguarded rice drying in the sun. The second lurked in the harbors and waited to attack vessels carrying pigs, chickens, dried fish—any food they could find. The third team confiscated the day's catch from small fishing boats.

It wasn't all thievery. The fishermen-turned-pirates mended their nets and fished as well.

Most days we ate plain congee, a few fried silkworms, and a meager ration of salted fish and dried vegetables. Yet, somehow, Bao always found pork, chicken, cabbage, and watercress for me. When I protested, he said he fed his unborn child not me.

My body shrank as my womb expanded. My breasts didn't swell, and I feared skimpy rations would produce weak milk.

Bao made many offerings to the gods. When that didn't work, he took grander actions. He had three Tainhou temples built, two in Hong Kong and one on Changzhou Island. Like the temple built for Mazu on Devil's Peak by Zheng Yi's father, Bao's temples were similarly situated. Each one was near a rendezvous point.

These temples were more than just camouflaged hideouts. They were a convenient location for making prayers and offerings before embarking on campaigns.

We had a lot to pray for. We heard the newly appointed Governor-general Bai Ling wanted every pirate dead.

BAO and I anchored in Amoy harbor.

"My spy says Governor-general Bai Ling demands the local gentry gather a militia," said Bao. "I'm not worried. It will just be a bunch of young boys and old men with rusted farm tools."

I winced and set my hand over my belly. The painful spasms began this morning. This was the worst one yet.

"Is it time?" Bao started from the chair.

I nodded, rubbed my rock-hard belly.

"I'll summon Headman Huang Cheng-sung's wife. She delivers babies."

"It's too soon. Hours probably. Tell me more about the governor-general's tactics."

Bao settled back in the chair. "He tells officials to fortify their villages."

"I've a bad feeling about this man. He attacks us on many fronts. Increased naval assaults, blockades, local militia, fortified villages." I counted off each on my fingers.

Bao shrugged. "Another incompetent official. He'll suffer the same death as the brigade-general."

"You misjudge—" I clutched the table. The contraction stole my breath. The moment it stopped another followed. No pause, no rest. The third made me growl in pain.

White with fear, Bao bolted from the chair. "I'll get the headman's wife."

"Yes, quickly." I held out my hand.

The next contraction came and with it a familiar sensation.

"The baby's coming," I gasped.

"Now?! Let me get someone." He started for the door.

"There's no time." I began to pant, pressure like a mountain made my legs weak.

Bao strode across the cabin and flung open the door. "Get Huang Cheng-sung's wife! Now! Hurry! You," he shouted to someone outside. "Get clean water, blankets, and scissors." Bao closed the door. "I can't be here. It's not proper for me to attend the birth."

"Proper? You're worried about the crew's opinion?

You're not leaving. I'm not having this child alone. I order you to stay. At least until—" I moaned and knelt down on the floor. I pushed, lost in the agony of a pressure heavier than any cannon.

Bao sat behind me, his palms ready to catch the baby. "What do I do?"

"I—" I screamed. Bore down hard.

"I see the top of the head," said Bao, "oh, it's gone."

I panted like a dog under a hot summer sun.

The. Baby. Must. Come. Out.

Bao studied my bulging female parts as though it was a treasure map. "My child has a head like a turtle. In and out. You must push, Xianggu. You must push hard."

I cursed at Bao. Cursed him again when he laughed and was about to curse a third time when the next contraction stole my breath.

"Here comes the head...push...wait. There's..."

"What's wrong?" I said after the contraction subsided.

"I don't know. I'm a man. This is woman's work."

"Tell me what you saw!"

"I see the head and another part next to the head."

"What?"

"A finger?"

I was too tired to curse, needed to save my strength to push out a child who wanted to come into the world with his hand on his head.

I bore down with the next pain.

"The head," cried Bao.

I pushed pushed pushed. The world went away. I felt only an unbearable pressure, like a tidal wave that struggled to erupt through my body. I pushed...

The infant slithered out.

"A son! My son!" Bao, babe in both hands, wept.

"The headman's wife is here," I said surprised he did not hear the knock.

"Come in," he shouted, his eyes locked on the tiny squalling infant in his arms.

The headman's wife entered the cabin with towels and water. "A fast birth. You're lucky." She cut the cord and checked the afterbirth, all while urging Bao to leave.

Bao helped me to bed. His hand cupped the baby's head, thick with dark hair, and counted the tiny toes and fingers. "Our son." He kissed my cheek. "This is the best treasure of all. More valuable than anything I hide on," he leaned close and whispered, "Changzhou island."

I smiled at Bao. I did not tell him that he too gave me a valuable gift. The gift of freedom. Of accepting my refusal to be his wife. Of being my most enthusiastic and devoted crewmember.

Bao loved me with no expectations. I adored him the more for it. But I didn't tell him that.

I set the child at my breast and closed my eyes. A chieftain did not have the luxury of resting for a month. Tomorrow I had to drag my weary body on deck.

56

Year of the Earth Snake
1809

We fought two great enemies for the next two months: famine and Governor-general Bai Ling.

The governor-general was smart. Too smart. First, he ordered all salt be transported over land instead of by sea. He prevented all salt junks from leaving port. The commodity we controlled for years—gone! Second, he fined shopkeepers who sold our stolen merchandise.

I was infuriated. All it took was the governor-general's signature on an edict for us to lose income and partnerships!

My crews were hungry, angry, and broke.

"Supplies are low, and we've eaten every rat we can catch." Bao cradled our son in his arms.

"Fill sampans and long dragons with armed men. Order them to steal food from the fields and plunder the villages."

The following day we raided a small harbor not far from Guangzhou. Our crew ran into the fields and grabbed all the food they could carry. Hunger made them bold. Fear of starvation made them violent. Fortunately, they returned with enough food to last a few days.

Day after day, I had nothing but problems.

"I found this scum trying to board." Headman Hsiang-shan forced a young man onto his hands and knees.

I stared down at the thin-faced wretch. "You're either very brave or very stupid."

The boy touched his forehead to the floor. "I'm stupidly brave. I must speak to Zheng Yi Sao, the one the foreign devil's call Dragon Lady. I have important news."

"I am Zheng Yi Sao."

The wretch lifted his head, a lock of hair falling over his eyes. "Forgive me, I thought…you'd be…ugly."

"My temper will be ugly if you don't tell me why you tried boarding my ship without permission."

"The Red Flag fleet is in great danger."

I glanced at Bao. "Who are you and why should I believe you?"

"My name is Jian, son of Gen Gang, one of your spies."

"Go on."

"Father died last night. He complained of a headache and went to bed early. He never woke up. But before he fell asleep, he told me the commander-in-chief of our province sails south to battle the Red Flag—to kill the Red Flag chief and her Great Generalissimo. After Father died, I knew it was my job to tell you. I ran to the harbor and rowed as fast as I could."

"How many are in the commander-in-chief's armada?"

"I don't know. I told you only what Father told me. Madam Chief, I want to fight with you."

Bao and I exchanged a glance.

"Your father was a good man. Trustworthy." I smiled at the boy. "However, I know Gen Gang did not have a son."

Jian dropped his head. "I'm his adopted son. His brother's child."

"Did your real father die?"

"I wish he would. He spends all his money on opium. Uncle took me in."

"Very kind of him." I turned to Headman Hsiang-shan. "Bind Jian's legs and arms. Send messengers to alert the others. Tell them to ready the stinkpots and gunpowder. Post the best lookouts. If Jian is telling the truth, he will scrub the decks. If he lied, kill him."

"I'm not lying," said Jian with remarkable composure.

"You think it's a trick?" Bao said after Headman Hsiang-shan led Jian away. "Why prepare us for battle? It doesn't make sense."

"False intelligence keeps us on edge. Enough, and we disregard the real report." I sat down, the tingling in my breasts a reminder to feed Third Son.

"Are you going to kill the boy?"

"I don't know. It's more important he thinks I will." Jian had what my sons never would. Respectability. Though my sons would know wealth and power, they would be seen as villains, their stations in life never rising as long as they lived on the sea. This angered me. I wanted better for my children.

As sons of notorious sea bandits, they would assume command at a young age. And yet in the dark place where a mother's fears and aspirations intertwine, I wanted my sons to have a respectable life. But unless my circumstances changed my sons were doomed to be outcasts. It was a humbling and miserable thought.

Bao's brows made diagonal lines of concern. "If that boy's information is false let me question him first. Information is bad through no fault of the spy. The commander may have issued new orders, or his superior changed his mind."

I sighed. "I suppose if I kill every spy passing incorrect information, we wouldn't find anyone willing to spy for us anymore."

Bao peered through the spyglass. "Xianggu…"

Jian's information was accurate. And too late.

57

I mperial warships on the horizon did not worry me too much. We had evaded them before and would again. But the governor-general's relentless pursuit was worse than a toothache that wouldn't go away.

I climbed down the ladder and passed the men getting their weapons from the armory. They shouldn't need them. Bao's squads would fight. The flagship stayed beyond the fray and never engaged unless attacked. It was the single greatest reason why the Mandarin's could not conquer us. They might sink a hundred vessels, but unless they sank the flagship their victory was pointless. The flagship *was* the Red Flag.

That wasn't the only reason they could not destroy us. Mandarin tactics lacked imagination. We were masters of resourcefulness. Like today. They made no attempt to conceal their numbers, their highflying banners spotted many *li* away.

I watched those banners from poop deck. Assessed the wind's direction and strength. Felt the heave of the sea. Considered my fleet's location. Noted the clouds and the position of the sun. Heard my crew's readiness. All these things sifted and sorted in my mind as I watched the warships bear down.

Bao believed a great commander sensed more than calculated the perfect time to attack. I agreed.

And the time was now.

I ordered the attack flag raised. Every vessel went on the offensive.

We sank the Mandarin's vanguard ships first. Our stinkpots set their sails ablaze in moments. Our cannons ruptured their broadsides. Our bamboo spikes and arrows speared their sailors.

Our crews were more disciplined than Mandarin sailors. Each pirate, deckhand, gunner, and wife knew their task. Even slaves and captives had jobs—they cleaned the deck of spilled gunpowder. We were efficient, experienced, practical, and inventive.

I kept vigil on poop deck. It had the best view. Zheng Yi had always stressed the importance of a good view to strategize. Predict and prepare, he had said. Be ready for all outcomes.

One after another, we burned, sank, or made derelict the Mandarin ships. They were out manned, out gunned, and out smarted.

Governor-general Bai Ling made a common government mistake. He stupidly believed that poorly paid sailors would show the same bravado and determination as pirates with a monetary stake in their success.

With half the governor-general's fleet destroyed and adrift, the Mandarins fled, the other half listing behind them.

I did not give chase, instead I ordered the main sail hoisted. Over a hundred boats responded, their sails filling with wind as they followed me toward the Yai-Men Channel.

Later, my officers told me Third Son's wailing during

battle inspired the deckhands. His hungry cries mirrored their own ravenous fury. Odd, as I had heard nothing but the sounds of men and cannonballs.

Energized by success I told the crews to raid rice paddies, fields, and unfortified towns for food and supplies. Once their bellies were full, I sent squadrons to remote villages. Those who paid the protection fees were safe. The others we burned to the ground.

News dribbled in about Governor-general Bai Ling. Despite his humiliating defeat he vowed, again, to defeat us. He sent fifty-three converted salt junks to patrol the same waterways we sailed.

"Isn't Governor-general Bai Ling tired of losing?" I asked Bao after hearing another report. "Will he ever stop?"

Bao shrugged. "Eventually. Anyway, we should rest a few days. I saw lightning from the northwest. The navy sleeps during a storm."

Bao's forecast proved correct. Heavy rains and whipping winds stopped most waterway travel.

But never pirates.

While rain blew like sheets of fabric across our decks, Bao and I sent out four river junks to reconnoiter.

"I have a bad feeling." Bao watched the boats disappear into the gray haze of needle-sharp rain. His brows met at a point, the outer ends lifting at a too-steep slant.

I set a hand on his arm. "What's wrong?"

"Every year the Mandarins tighten the noose. Every year they build more junks or commandeer more old vessels to fight us. Time and time again we sink their boats and behead their captains. Then they build more boats, hire new captains. And make the noose tighter."

"We should cut the rope."

Bao grinned. "Or swing from it."

Two river junks returned in the afternoon with news that eighty-eight Mandarin boats were riding out the storm at Wei-chia-men Bay. We sent boats to warn the General and Guo Podai, whose fleet was much closer to the Mandarin's than ours.

It was near midnight, the torrential downpour finally easing into a steady shower, when our messengers returned with the news. The General and Guo Podai planned on surrounding the Mandarins by morning.

I did not sleep. Tossed and turned most of the night. Except for a blissful hour when Bao brought me to heaven with his cock and tongue.

Bao rose before dawn. "I'm going back to my ship."

This wasn't like him.

"You look nervous. What's wrong?"

Bao wound his turban around his head. "I consulted the gods. Their responses confused me."

I placed Third Son at my breast. "Stone and clay speak to you?"

"In a way." Bao tugged a small leather pouch from his garment. "Ashes from the temple of Mazu. They're heavier than usual and smell like death."

"You're predicting defeat based on a satchel's weight?"

"I predict nothing. But the temple's ashes are heavier. It's a sign from the gods." He kissed my forehead. It was an earnest kiss, not a kiss of promise or lust. The kiss of a warrior. The kiss of a man with the weight of thousands of lives on his shoulders.

Worry slithered up my spine and lodged in my throat. "We don't have to help them," I said. "Let the White and Black Flag come to their aid this time. The General and Guo Podai rely on Red Flag strength too often."

Bao's jaw dropped in shock.

My attitude weakened the confederation. But I was torn. Which was wiser? Protecting my fleet and crew or destroying the Mandarins? Did motherhood make me fearful? Did wanting to keep Bao safe diminish my boldness? Thousands upon thousands of people depended on my strength of spirit. The Dragon Lady could not afford to be selfish.

"Take three hundred junks. Don't engage unless necessary." I pulled Third Son off my breast and looked at his milk drunk expression. Was I a weaker or stronger person because I was a mother?

Bao looked relieved. "I'll do it." He slipped his cutlass under his belt.

The ship buzzed with busyness as I walked the decks. Two deckhands hauled tubs of rainwater to the galley. The helmsman checked the sails for damage. Headman Hsiang-shan reprimanded a deckhand for having left a chest of gunpowder uncovered.

I looked into the sodden, unusable black powder. The deckhand kneeled beside the crate.

"You spent the night drinking," I guessed from his red eyes and puffy face.

He hung his head.

"Whip him," I said to Headman Hsiang-shan.

"Chief, this lowly deckhand and his husband argued last night," said Headman Hsiang-shan. "He drank from sorrow."

The poorest deckhands, those unable to support a wife, took other male crewmen as lovers. The relationships satisfied their lusts and lasted until one earned enough to buy a wife. But lovers' spats did not concern me.

You fool! You risked the life of Bao's only son. Your negligence might undo all I work for. You risked thousands of lives because you failed to control your own sorrow. Weak pitiful man! Had I the ability of my dragon name I would breathe flames and incinerate you on the spot.

I did not say this. My rebuke was more logical. "One less chest of powder may lose the battle. Lost battles become lost wars. Where you see only one chest of wet gunpowder, I see forty thousand destitute crewmen. Whip him."

"I'm not worthy of your leniency," the deckhand whimpered. "I've disgraced myself and put the crew in jeopardy."

"The next time it rains give this man the same task," I said to Headman Hsiang-shan. "If he fails the second time, slice him into seventy-two pieces and feed him to the fish."

A mistake made once was pardonable. Made twice it revealed a man's character. There was no room on a crowded flagship for feeble-minded men. Or women.

I ordered the mast hoisted. Time to go. The General, Guo Podai, and Bao counted on my ships for support.

We arrived too late.

58

Disaster and death met us at Wei-chia-men.

Flames swallowed the General's masts. Devoured the sailcloth. Sparks fell like rain on the water. The General's boats listed, sank, and smoldered. Wounded crewmen flailed in the water, their anguished screams more horrifying than the obliteration of the entire White Flag fleet.

An explosion—flames met a store of gunpowder—blew a boat apart. People and wood blasted into the air like fireworks.

In the chaos of derelict vessels, smoke, and floating debris I couldn't find the General's flagship.

I did see Guo Podai's squadron. His vessels tried to maneuver into an offensive position. The wind made it impossible. The same gusts also kept the Black Flag's long bamboo spikes from reaching Mandarin decks. Each throw fell short or blew wide.

"Madam Chief!"

I looked down, surprised one of my sampans managed to approach without my notice. "What news?"

"The General is dead. The White Flags are destroyed."

I gripped the ledge, knuckles white with fury. How did such an inept navy defeat the General?

"What about Guo Podai? How many boats did the Black Flag lose?"

"His father's boat was burned. His father with it."

Podai adored his father, always spoke of him with affection and respect. Podai must be raging with grief.

The wind suddenly shifted in our favor, and the navy went on the defensive.

Bao seized the advantage and his men unleashed a barrage of stinkpots. Several ignited and in moments flames engulfed the stern of the imperial flagship.

Squad Boss P'o-pao jumped onto the fiery vessel. Bao followed and led fifty men.

I ordered Helmsman He-song to get as close as possible without putting ourselves in danger.

"Send sampans to rescue the survivors," I told the deputy headman. "Pick up anyone out of the line of fire."

The Mandarin flagship continued to burn. Above, the air was thick with smoke. Below, the water crowded with bodies.

The winds shifted again, its strong gusts gave us more advantage. Without their flagship, the Mandarins would not rally for another attack. Their vessels fled. In their wake they left a watery graveyard of charred sinking vessels.

Arms lifted in victory, Bao stood on his ship's bow as it sliced through the water. Disgusted, I turned away. This was no triumph. The White Flag fleet was decimated, the General dead. The Black Flag vessels were damaged. Too many crewmen dead or injured. Boats could be mended and replaced. There was no replacing the people we love.

That evening as my crews feasted on food and drank

themselves into a stupor, Bao burst into my cabin drunk on victory.

"No one can defeat us!" Bao shed his clothes. "One day we *will* take Guangzhou." He scooped me up, dropped me on the bed, and pushed my thighs apart with the superiority of an emperor. As though I was his plaything and not his chieftain.

I kicked him away. "The White Flag is destroyed. The General is dead. Guo Podai's father is dead. The losses to the confederation are catastrophic! And you want to fuck?!"

"We're victorious. The Red Flag lost not a single man. Only a few had bruises and knife scratches." He grabbed my leg, moved it aside. "Time to celebrate."

"I'm grieving, Bao. Grieving for the loss of Podai's father, for the General, for the hundreds of men and women at the bottom of the river, and for all those maimed and wounded and suffering."

"Mourn while I celebrate." He attempted entry.

I slapped his cheek. "Stop!"

Bao's face darkened. He glared, nostrils flaring, then rolled off, crossed the room, donned his robe, and opened the cabin door.

"Bao. Come here. Don't leave this way."

He turned around, his expression lost in the shadows. "Is that a command?"

"Yes."

"Do what you will, I will not obey." He slammed shut the door.

I hurdled a vase at the door. "Come back!" I screamed. My rage turned to sorrow. My hurt to worry. Guo Podai's warning about Bao loomed like black clouds over my sea of feelings. Rain and wind must be endured, but storms of the heart are not easily weathered.

I woke before dawn and sent two fast boats with messages. The first returned while I drank my morning tea.

"Great Generalissimo is gone," said the captain. "He took his squad up river toward Guangzhou as you ordered."

My anger rose like a raging river. I gave no such order!

"Ah, very good," I said, my serene face a mask hiding the anger and fear churning my stomach. If even one crewman thought I lost control of Bao, my command would be in jeopardy.

The second boat returned with a letter from Guo Podai.

Zheng Yi Sao,

The murder of my beloved father consumes me with great sorrow and a greater rage. Confucius says, when anger rises, think of the consequences. I think of little else. Not of my wife, not of my child, only the ways I will use this rage to avenge my father's untimely death. I've lost supplies, men, vessels, and worst of all, a piece of my heart. I'm headed upriver to the county seat of Hsiang-shan. My rage will carry me to Guangzhou where I will do what Zhang Bao once suggested. Yes, Xianggu, I will take Guangzhou. Should you have need of either my fleet or me I'll do all in my power to help you.

I remain ever your faithful friend, ally, and admirer,

Guo Podai

Two men. One purpose. Winning Guangzhou. One man overcome by grief and rage. The other glutted with victory.

Despite the heat, a chill ran through my body. Zhang Bao

and Guo Podai had a fragile relationship. Egos and jealousies prevented their forming a real alliance. Guo Podai was jealous I chose Bao over him. Bao envied Podai's position as fleet chieftain. They were two chests of gunpowder waiting to explode.

59

I missed my sons. I was tired. My spirit weak. My balance needed to be restored. And my sons needed to meet their little brother. All good reasons to sail to Lantau Island.

It was a stress-free trip, the Mandarin navy still licking their wounds in some bureaucratic harbor.

When I arrived, my sons raced toward me squealing with excitement. I scooped two-year-old Second Son into my arms and sprinkled his plump cheeks with kisses. Then I knelt down and enfolded Little Dog in my arms. He smelled of boy, of warmth and weeds and earth.

"Who's that?" Little Dog pointed to Third Son cradled in his *amah*'s arms.

"Your brother."

Both boys laughed and stroked him as though he was a pet.

After giving them sweet treats and explaining why Little Brother was too young to play, I told the slave to take the stolen sow I brought with me into the kitchen. It was while Mama left to tell the cook how much to allot for the officers and their families when I had a chance to speak to Fenfang in private.

"How's everything going?" I asked.

"Your mother is wonderful. She's kind, discreet, practical, and thrifty, and spends no money unless necessary. She hates the name Dragon Lady and thinks everyone should call you Pirate Empress of the South Seas instead."

"Empress, Dragon Lady, or chief, it doesn't matter. I'm a businesswoman. My job merely redistributing food and supplies." I strolled around the courtyard lush with flowers and plants. "The gap between rich and poor is too vast—the same distance as the bottom of the sea to the stars in the heavens. Yet who knows what the future holds? Today I ride the ocean waves, tomorrow I may float on the clouds."

"Clouds?" Fenfang saw my meaning at once. "The gossip is true? The confederation wants to seize control of Guangzhou?"

"Bao and Podai do." For different reasons. Podai for revenge. Bao to change the world.

"What do you want?"

"I bore three sons. Both fathered by ambitious outlaws. My sons will never be accepted by respectable people. How long will the Mandarins be on our backs and weigh down my sons' futures? They'll be considered pirates, the burden of discrimination as heavy as farmers bringing fresh cut tea leaves to market. I want better for my sons. I want them to be respectable people."

"You think taking Guangzhou will give your sons respectability?"

"It's a first step."

"Bao and Podai are rivals. How will they agree on a strategy?"

"I don't know." I broke down and told Fenfang everything. About my quarrel with Bao. About how he left without permission. About my fear that I misjudged his true intentions. "He disobeyed me and intends to attack Guangzhou without my consent. Officer insubordination is punishable by death."

"Bao loves you. I've seen it in his eyes. He's angry. He won a great victory and expected praise."

"He left without asking permission. He defied me, his chieftain!"

"Bao didn't disobey his chief," said Fenfang. "He ran from his lover."

"Better he leaves, then beat you." Mama strolled into the courtyard and pretended she had not been eavesdropping. "You've been a stranger to me more years than you've been a daughter, but I'm no stranger to the minds of men." Mama's rough hands clasped mine. "I worked in the house of a rich man and his spoiled son and his more-spoiled wives. I'll tell you this, if Bao loves you, he'll come back. Maybe not for many months but he will come back. If his desire to be chieftain is greater than his love for you, you'll know soon enough. Don't stay here long. Men always assume women are lost without them. Don't give him that satisfaction. If he truly loves you, then he loves everything about you, particularly your fiery spirit and independent nature. Breathe fire, dragon daughter, and scorch your man with your blazing spirit."

I hugged Mama tight and took her advice.

I sailed away a few days later after purchasing much needed bamboo matting, tar, rope, and tung oil. I also issued new orders to the squad bosses. To Bao, I sent a map circled with the towns late in paying their protection fees.

The fourth week of August, I received a detailed letter from Guo Podai that left me stunned. He torched the county seat's fort then demanded supplies and silver. Upriver, he slaughtered sixty villagers when they tried to stop his men from stealing food. He burned to the ground a customs house near Guangzhou. He sent groups of armed men into nearby villages to collect protection fees. Those villages that refused to pay, his men raided at night. Podai offered his men an added incentive: ten Spanish dollars for every head severed from a rebellious villager.

Resistance is everywhere, Podai wrote. Only one thing stops me from reaching Guangzhou. Forty-five-armed fishing boats and fourteen hundred men. Courtesy of Mandarin Lieutenant Ho Ting-ao.

The other flag chieftains confirmed Guo Podai's brutal rampage. Wushi Er reported seeing hundreds of severed heads hanging from a Banyan tree on the riverbank. Toad Rearer swore Guo Podai's vengeance reached typhoon-like proportions. A dispatch from Eleven-finger Wu claimed the Black Flag's killing spree exceeded ten thousand.

Meanwhile, Bao's squad burned and looted village forts up and down the inner waterways. Even a fleet of imperial warships fled when Bao overwhelmed them with cannon fire and stinkpots.

"Bao is unstoppable." I boasted to Wushi Er when he came aboard to share gossip and news.

"Not for long. British and Portuguese merchants are tired of paying protection fees and seek to join forces with the Mandarins. There's no way we will withstand that. The foreign devils have superior weapons and better gunpowder."

Wushi Er was right. We needed a new plan.

Eleven-finger Wu, Wushi Er, Toad Rearer and I met in the back of a a Macao furniture store on September fifth. Each chief brought their top squad bosses.

"Where's Great Generalissimo?" Eleven-finger Wu licked the juicy seeds from a pomegranate with a lecherous grin.

"Exactly where I tell him to be." I glared at him. "Does anyone have news about Guo Podai's latest exploits?"

"He's mad with grief." Toad Rearer shook his head. "Every burnt village bears the brunt of his sorrow."

"We will start the meeting without Podai and Bao." I folded my arms and got right to the point. "We must unite against the Mandarins."

"Don't forget the fucking Portuguese," said Eleven-finger Wu.

"And idiot British." Toad Rearer puffed out his cheeks.

"And those shit-eating Spanish," added Wushi Er.

"Good, then we're all in agreement." For once.

Eleven-finger Wu spit out a mouthful of pomegranate seeds. "What fire do you want us to breathe on them, Dragon Lady?"

"Flames of intelligence. We need to pool our collective information about their agreements with local officials." I dipped the quill into the inkpot. "The best fuel makes the hottest bonfire. We need to share information. Wu, what do your sources report?"

The meeting lasted for days, and yet our crews and vessels were never idle. While we discussed schemes to conquer our enemies, our skippers ambushed three Siamese junks, intercepted five American ships, and captured a two-masted vessel transporting the governor of Timor Island.

One the final day of the meeting, Bao burst through the door. Eyes bright with mischief, he gave me a stiff welcome before taking a seat.

"Forgive my late arrival," said Bao. "I would've been here earlier in the day, but I thought it'd be amusing to drag the Portuguese ship I captured across the harbor."

"Fucking brilliant," said Eleven-finger Wu.

"Very risky," scolded Wushi Er.

"Why didn't you sink it?" asked Toad Rearer.

"They'll follow you out of the harbor when you leave and attack. What then?" Wushi Er stroked his mustache.

"I'll lead them astray." Bao grinned, his eyes bright with confident bravado.

Bao left later that day. Without saying goodbye. Without talking to me. Without visiting his infant son.

With the help of three squads, he lured the two heavily armed Portuguese vessels away from the harbor and on a chase that ended with his ship vanishing around the cape.

I hoped his luck lasted.

60

Bao did not show up again until September.

"I destroyed the Portuguese vessels at Whampoa." His voice was cold and formal, his face without emotion. Bao's gaze shifted to the bed where his son slept atop the blankets. "I didn't come to brag. I came to tell you Mandarin officials and Hong merchants formed a fleet of sixty warships against us. The Portuguese are currently planning to join them."

My heart sank. "I'll warn the other chieftains."

Bao puffed out his chest. "Also, the terms of ransom for those seven kidnapped Englishman from the *Marquis of Ely* aren't finalized yet."

Our eyes met.

I should have scolded him. Kidnapping English soldiers at a time like this was foolish. But I was too busy thinking of how we would combat the combined forces of the Mandarins, Hong, and Portuguese.

"Conduct negotiations with speed." My voice was as chilly as his. "We held the Englishman Turner for too long and too many people demanded a share."

"Of course." Bao went to the bed and struggled to remain stern-faced as his five-month-old son sucked on his toes. "He's hungry."

I stepped forward. "Bao…" I missed him. Missed his smile and laugh. Missed his arms around me. Missed my best friend. "Why are you acting this way? I refused you only one night."

Bao stroked the side of his child's face. "For a whore you understand nothing about men."

Angry flames spewed past my lips. "This whore—chieftain of the Red Flag—commands you—an illiterate Dan fisherman who would be nothing without Zheng Yi—to collect protection fees upriver."

"I'd be nothing? Is that what you think?" Bao's voice cracked with disbelief. His nostrils flared. "I'm too clever and too ambitious to *ever* be nothing." Bao set a kiss on our son's forehead and strode from the cabin.

Guo Podai was right. Bao wanted to be a chief. He was biding time now, waited for an opportunity to commandeer the flagship.

I lifted the baby from the bed and hurried after Bao.

The headman intercepted my heated march across the deck. "A deckhand left the ship without permission."

"Are you certain?" I kept an eye on Bao, who was deep in conversation with one of my officers.

"He came back and begged for leniency," said the headman. "His father is ill and—"

"Take me to him."

The deckhand was a young recruit, fresh-faced and reed thin. The crew gathered around as I approached. Bao joined the curious crowd.

Bound at his wrists and ankles, the young recruit kneeled before me, his forehead on the deck. "I beg forgiveness,

Madam Chief. Take pity on this stupid wretch. My father is dying, and I had to—"

"What's the penalty for leaving without permission?" I said with my babe in my arms.

"Cutting off my ears." His voice choked with fear.

"Why didn't you ask for permission?"

"I was afraid I wouldn't be allowed to—"

"Afraid?!" My voice was loud enough everyone heard. "There's no room for fear on this ship. A frightened skipper, a terrified sculler, a panicked gunner—a fearful man endangers everyone here. The crew depends on men and women with courage. A coward is useless to me. Cutting your ears is too lenient. I may as well kill you."

"I have no fear of death," said the boy.

I bit off my smile. "Take off one ear," I told the skipper.

I locked eyes with Bao. At that moment, I hated him and loved him at the same time.

BAO TERRORIZED THE PROVINCE.

On October first, he and five hundred men raided a village, burned homes, and captured two hundred and fifty women and children. The income from ransoms alone put coins in everyone's pocket.

On October fifth, Bao raided the village of Lan-shih and burned their fort to the ground. Their militia fled into the fields, but Bao blasted them with cannon fire. By day's end, Bao's men burned more than four hundred homes, slaughtered scores of villagers, and killed the militia leader.

The other flag fleets were not as lucky.

The combined imperial and foreign forces attacked the

flag fleets again and again. They sank and burned our boats and slaughtered our crewmen.

Imperial forces shot a cannonball through Cai Qian's cabin and splattered his brains all over the room. With Cai Qian dead, the Fujian fleets collapsed, their squad bosses and skippers arguing amongst themselves. Without unifying leadership, the unruly Fujian fleets sank under the weight of bickering and pettiness.

Disorganization and defiance did more damage to a fleet than any Mandarin cannonball. I was worried. More worried than ever before. Fear slithered up my spine and into my limbs. I had to find a way to save myself, my children, my crew, and even Bao. Because the fate of the Red Flag was precarious as long as Bao and I were at odds.

Our dominance over the South Seas was ending. I felt it in my bones. Too many forces conspired against us. The Mandarins, British, and Portuguese hunted us down, wanted to blow every flag fleet to charred bits. We could win the battles, but the war?

Our confederation was expansive, with almost as many layers as the government. With the General's White Flag fleet decimated and the rift growing ever wider between Bao and Podai and me, we were a confederation divided.

If the Flag Fleets were annihilated, thousands upon thousands of men, women, and children would be homeless, poor, and hungry. I would not let that happen.

I stared at the waving fields of rice stalks onshore while rain pelted against my leaf *dǒulì* and wondered how to end this water war once and for all.

"Madam Chief." Three-finger Lo handed me a letter. "A fast boat delivered this. It's urgent."

I read the letter. Suddenly those thousands and thousands of people under my command didn't matter anymore.

Zheng Yi Sao,

First Son is ill. He may not live the week.

Fenfang

I pressed the letter to my breast and ran to the headman. Within the hour, the flagship and a small contingent of boats sailed south toward Lantau.

As we raced through the sea I made offerings and prayers to the gods, burned incense and gilt paper, and begged on my knees for the gods to spare my son.

I paced the decks. Urged the helmsman to go faster. Implored the wind to blow harder.

Once we arrived in the north bay, I urged my scullers to row faster faster faster.

I leapt from the sampan, splashed through the surf, and raced across the beach toward home.

I burst into the house. "Little Dog! Little Dog! Fenfang! Mama! I'm here!"

Mama stuck her head out from the far doorway and beckoned me with a silent hand.

"Is he—" I ran to his bedside, anguish crushing my heart like a vise.

Little Dog was the color of a ghost, his face pale, his closed eyes sunk into dark shadows.

I set my cool hand over his small burning one. "Where's the healer? How much will it cost to heal him?"

Fenfang dropped her head. "Ten thousand silver pieces."

It was hopeless then. No amount would cure my son. "No! I refuse to believe that. There must be something I can do."

"There's a way." Her face pinched with grief, Mama stood in the doorway. "An ancient way."

"Do it."

Mama scuffled back into the room an hour later with a steaming pot of fragrant soup.

"Old ways are best." Mama pulled a knife from her dress. "I need your arm."

I tugged up the sleeve, held my palm skyward like a beggar. Today I *was* a wretched beggar pleading for my child's life.

With a swift deftness, Mama sliced off a mushroom-sized piece of flesh. I would have let her cut me into a thousand pieces if it saved Little Dog.

Mama dropped my flesh into the pot. "Little Dog was born in the Year of the Pig. You, the Year of the Goat. Goats are seldom sick. Little Dog needs your strength." She stirred the soup, my strength and fears infused with liquid hope.

I spooned the broth through Little Dog's dry cracked lips and massaged his throat to encourage swallowing. It took hours to give him all the broth.

Afterwards, I spoke to Zheng Yi's ghost. I had felt his presence since I arrived.

"Forgive me, Yi. I failed you. I brought your sons to Lantau to be safe, away from the dangers of ship life and enemy attacks, and the gods cursed me. Forgive me for expanding the fleet at the cost of your first son."

Zheng Yi's ghost was silent.

That night I curled around Little Dog's fiery hot body, placed my hand on his chest, and willed him to continue to breathe, even though the missing flesh had stolen all my physical and emotional strength.

"Ma."

My head jerked up. "Ying-shih?" I used his real name.

A sheen of sweat glistened on his forehead and his face bloomed with color. "Ma, I'm thirsty."

I felt his cool forehead. "Yes, yes. Healthful tea. Are you hungry?"

"I could eat a whole pig."

"Fenfang," I shouted.

Fenfang raced into the room, eyes bright with relieved joy when she saw Little Dog sitting up. "You're such a naughty little boy the gods did not want you." Tears ran down her cheeks.

"Then I'll be sure to disobey more, *amah*," he grinned.

"Bring tea." I kissed his cheek a hundred times. "Mix in those healing ingredients to restore balance."

I stayed by his bedside for three days. On the fourth day Qing Ping arrived huffing and puffing from his run across town. "Three Portuguese warships and an imperial fast-boat formed a blockade." He gasped for air. "We're trapped."

61

My face was a mask of calm, but my stomach churned like an eddy between rocks. The blockade was my fault. In my rush to reach Lantau I left the flagship vulnerable to attack.

After a quick goodbye to my sons, Fenfang, and Mama, Qing Ping and I ran back to the bay. The Portuguese and imperial ships waited like crouching tigers. My flagship and small contingent were not prepared. I was outmanned and outgunned, a lone fish without my school of hungry sharks.

The moment I climbed on deck Headman Hsiang-shan was there. "Our informer says the Portuguese ships wait for forty more Mandarin boats."

I scratched the large scab over the wound on my arm. "The imperial navy is too eager for fame and glory. Those foreign captains underestimate our strengths." My voice was light and confident.

Headman Hsiang-shan handed me the spyglass. "They expect you to summon help. You're the bait, chief."

"I'm not bait. I'm the shark. They have no idea how fast we sharks race through the water." I counted the cannons on the ships. "The difference between them and us is as vast as the sky. Move as close to the shore as possible. Summon my squad bosses. Guo Podai too."

"And Generalissimo?"

"Of course." Dread coiled around me. When the tree falls the monkeys scatter. If Bao refused to come to my aid—no matter his excuse—would my men join Zhang Bao?

With false bravado I made my way aft to confer defensive tactics with the vanguard headman and the armory steward. "I want a thorough accounting of our catties of lead shells, iron bullets, and all old lead and iron to pack cannons," I said. "Shields. Spears. Iron-tipped knives. Long blades. Sickles. Chains. All of it. An exact number. Count every-abled bodied person aboard this boat. Everyone will have a job to do when the time comes. And triple the lookouts. If our enemies sneeze, I want to know."

Later, Pink Flower, wife of the vanguard headman, set Third Son in my arms. She had nursed him while I was ashore tending Little Dog.

"He's a good boy with a big appetite," Pink Flower whispered, mindful the gods might hear her bragging and steal Third Son from me.

"Like his father." Cradling him in my arms, I marveled at his resemblance to Bao. He had the same wide bright smile. Similar head shape. Miss-nothing eyes.

I longed for Bao's eyes now. He would find any weakness in the Portuguese ships' defenses. He would see all their limitations. Most of all, I longed for Bao's eyes to once again look at me with love.

I tossed and turned in bed, the night a blur between dreams and wakefulness. I strategized in my sleep, worried while awake. Asleep or awake, a thousand different scenarios played out in my head. Burning junks, misfired cannons, listing warships. Sometimes we lost. Sometimes we won. Sometimes I flailed about in the sea. Sometimes Bao's body floated face down in debris-clogged water.

I rose before dawn, agitated and tired, my dreams exhausted both spirit and body. A cup of tea in my hand I leaned over the side to stare at the Portuguese ships. "You don't frighten the Dragon Lady."

Daylight struggled to appear. Black clouds blocked the sun. The air was thick with mist, yet the doubts that soaked my spirit were thicker. The blockade did not over worry me. We *would* push through. It was Bao I agonized over. I lost his love because of my arrogance, because I questioned his love and mistrusted his motives. Worse still, if Bao did not answer my summons, I had to kill him.

An imperial cannon blast broke the calm of the too-gray morning. The shot fell far short.

"You want to fire back?" asked Headman Hsiang-shan.

"Retreat in the bay."

Headman Hsiang-shan snickered. "Good plan. They'll get stuck in a sandbar when they try to close in on us."

Those foreign ships were foolishly designed with conical hulls. They often got stuck.

The crew gathered around me, anxious and in need of a task.

"Don't pay any attention to those warships. They're about as annoying as a few bees. I think they intend to frighten us with their incompetency."

The deckhands laughed and aimed their crudest insults— all referring to the sailors' mothers—at the enemy ships.

"Reinforcements are on their way," I announced. "Once they arrive the Portuguese will scurry away like a beaten dog. For now, let's not waste time. The flagship needs to be scrubbed, the saloon cleaned, and repairs made." I turned to

Headman Hsiang-shan. "If the Portuguese fire another cannon, send fireworks into the air. Fly all our banners. Order the musicians to play. Sing songs—I like the one about Zheng Yi and I."

Squad Boss Huang Cheng-sung was the first to answer my summons. Bao's squad boss, P'o-pao, second. Both anchored their ships across the bay. There was no word from Bao.

On the third day, an armada of Mandarin boats joined the Portuguese warships. Still outmanned and outgunned, I told the skippers to fly all their banners and make repairs. Bao was still a no-show.

On the fourth day, as the sun began its red-hued descent, Bao's squad finally arrived. His ship came alongside, and the deckhands set down the plank for him to cross.

"I bring a gift." Bao signaled a new recruit behind him, who stepped forward with a tall red lacquered box.

My face remained emotionless as we crossed the deck, the gift-bearing recruit trailing behind.

"A pretty boy. Have you adopted a son?" My words were as smooth as the finest silk.

"I don't need to adopt a son." Bao sounded hurt. "Bing is a cousin."

Once in the cabin, Bing set the box on the table and scurried away.

I didn't know what to say but had to say something. "Bao…"

"Open the gift."

"The gift isn't important—"

Bao's eyes grew wide with pretend shock. "You dismiss my humble gift?"

"No, of course not." I opened the lid and lifted out a green vase. "It's exquisite. Jadeite?"

Bao moved near, his body close enough to feel his heat. "There are eight dragons around the vase. Each on a cloud. The ninth one curls around the rim. Here." His finger skimmed the bottom. "A fish lifts his head above the sea."

I tilted the vase to admire the craftsmanship. A tiny scroll of paper fell out. I looked at Bao. "What's this?"

"The real gift." His grin was as bright as his eyes.

I pulled off the thin silk cord and unfurled the paper. "Hu Tao. Guangzhou. House of Peony." A thousand joys filled my heart. "This is the man who sold me to the flower boat? Hu Tao?"

"Yes, and where he spends his time and silver."

"How did you find him?" I gazed into Bao's eyes, liquid with love and desire.

"I've searched for a while. Silver opens a lot of doors and mouths." Beaming with happiness, Bao rocked back on his heels. "We do business with the House of Peony."

I set down the vase and threw my arms around Bao. "How can I thank you enough?"

"Marry me."

I rested my head on his chest. "I can't."

"Zheng Yi Sao can do anything she wants. Nothing binds her will." Bao stroked my hair.

"Duty binds me, Bao. Responsibility is my shackle. I'm a great pirate and yet the rope of responsibility is *always* around my throat. I can't marry. Not now."

Bao exhaled. "We've shared much. Zheng Yi. Ambitions. Secrets. You're my adopted mother. My lover, mentor, and friend. You watched while Yi initiated me into his crew. You're the most respected and feared pirate in the South Seas. You gave me a son. We've shared all these things. Don't you think I also know your deepest fear—that I use you to fulfill my ambitions."

My gasp was too loud.

"You've underestimated me. I could have murdered you with the swiftness of a praying mantis anytime I wanted."

"You forget, it's the female mantis that beheads its partners during sex."

Bao burst out laughing. "I don't doubt you would. You're not my prey, Xianggu. You're my love. And you must remember that even though the mantis is considered the dragon of all insects, a bird easily swoops down to devour it." He nuzzled my neck. "Together we're both bird and mantis. Together we're strong. Together we have the fighting skill of the mantis and the speed of the bird. Together our ships will be as still as a mantis lying in wait and as graceful as a bird in flight." His kiss was feather light and sun warm. "When I received your summons for help my heart folded like a fan. If something happened to you because I wasn't there—"

"I forgive you."

"I didn't ask for forgiveness. I'm not a misbehaving child."

"You *are* my adopted child and you *did* misbehave by avoiding me."

Bao hands moved inside the folds of my silk dress. "Choose, Xianggu. Am I your adopted son or your lover?"

My body answered.

We tumbled to the floor, and I realized a man like Bao could not be controlled. Should *not* be controlled. He did what he wanted. And despite his large crew, cannons, and wealth he had chosen to remain my generalissimo. Because he loved me more than power or prestige.

There was no greater aphrodisiac than a man sacrificing his own ambitions for that of his lover's.

We clung to one another until late in the evening. The Portuguese ships and Mandarin boats anchored nearby added to the frantic pace of our coupling. The threat of cannon fire increased our passion. As I slung my legs over Bao's shoulders, I realized there was no greater proof of our supremacy than enjoying wanton lovemaking in the midst of an incompetent siege.

62

Above a liquid ink sea, silver-dipped clouds drifted across the moon, its beauty disguising a dangerous darkness.

Three lookouts kept vigil through the night, six eyes straining to see across the bay. On deck, the Portuguese warships appeared peaceful, inside they plotted death and destruction.

"What will you say to Hu Tao when you see him?" Bao stood beside me while we studied the Mandarin and Portuguese ships in the morning twilight. "Will you thank him for selling you to a flower boat?"

"Thank him?" I grimaced and huddled inside the fur blanket.

"If not for Hu Tao you wouldn't be the Dragon Lady. Rich, feared, and powerful."

"The man deserves to be sliced into a thousand pieces." Or worse. "He deserves no credit for my fortune. Luck and ambition are my twin companions."

"Before you embark on a journey of revenge, dig two graves."

"Confucius was neither a flower girl nor a pirate." I rested a fur-warmed hand on Bao's cool cheek and changed the direction of our conversation to a more important one. "What do you want for our son?"

Bao answered immediately. "Wealth and respect."

"Wealth is possible. But not respect."

Bao's head snapped around. "Why not?"

"Because we fight the people who give it. Our son, and our future sons, will never be respectable unless we are."

Bao's jaw tightened. "Am I supposed to get this respect like Guo Podai, by accepting the governor-general's offer to negotiate a pardon?"

"What!?" I recoiled. "Podai would never do that. He swore to punish the Mandarins for killing his father."

"Well, sometime between then and now, he made plans to abandon his men for the chance to scratch his ass under a banyan tree." Bao's voice oozed contempt.

I clutched his coat. "Podai told you this?"

"Of course not, you know Podai and I don't confide in one another. He made the mistake of telling Eleven-finger Wu. Who told me."

"I don't trust anything Wu says."

"Who *do* you trust?"

Until Bao's arrival I did not put complete faith in anyone. "Only you, Bao."

"Good," he grinned. "Then let's figure out how to get us all out of here."

"I have a plan." I tapped my forehead. "Mind games."

I ordered more boats beached for careening and repair. Then, with a large entourage, I disembarked to visit my sons. Four days in a row.

Each day a Portuguese warship fired a cannon. Each shot fell short. Winds and currents continued to favor us. More

Red Flag vessels arrived. We were now many, the Portuguese and Mandarins few. Their reinforcements were long overdue.

The easy days gave Bao and I plenty of time to indulge in sensual pleasures and intimate conversation.

On the tenth day since Bao's arrival, Headman Hsiang-shan rushed into the saloon. "Chief. Generalissimo. Sixty boats joined the Portuguese warships. We counted twenty cannons, and thousands of men swarm their decks."

A cannon fired.

I sprang from the chair when I heard its too-close splash. "Send this message to each boat: Organize the armory for fast distribution. Ready the cannons. Prepare the stinkpots. But, and this is very important, they must do these tasks without hurry or alarm. Our enemies are watching for signs of panic."

The Portuguese fired cannonballs for two hours. Their vanguard fired first, then withdrew to the rear to reload as another row of boats took their place. Most of our boats were beached for repair so I did not return fire. Not yet. For now, the wind kept our enemies at bay. After several near misses, I ordered the men to throw stinkpots at their front line. None reached their mark.

I looked up at the masthead to my stinkpot throwers in the cage. "The person who sets fire to the biggest ship gets a handful of silver."

No sooner did my offer leave my lips then Pink Flower hurled a stinkpot with perfect accuracy, better than perfect accuracy. It was spectacular. Her stinkpot crashed into a barrel of gunpowder. The boat exploded! Wood and debris and fire and limbs and heads and torsos shot into the air like gruesome fireworks.

The Portuguese ships tacked away. The gods favored us again. The north wind blew them back farther, the strong gusts thwarted all their attempts to advance.

"We should engage tomorrow morning," said Bao in my cabin that evening. "Whether your beached ships are ready or not, we need every big gun to defeat them."

I tilted my teacup and watched the chrysanthemum bloom, its leaves swaying as it steeped. "Give the order. I want two hundred sampans accompanying them. We attack at dawn."

Bao departed and left me alone to wonder if and how we could permanently end this war. I did not want to die by imperial or foreign hands. I certainly didn't want to be captured and tortured. My sons needed a mother. Third Son, his father.

"When will the Mandarins and foreigners accept our superiority?" I asked when Bao returned.

"When I restore the empire." Bao unwound his turban.

"The Great Qing is vast. Our supremacy comprises only a small fraction of its lands."

Bao leaned over, his silky black hair tickling my cheek. "The gods favor us. I'm equal to the emperor. Greater even, because the sea is a whet stone and I'm the blade, sharpened to perfection." His finger traced the curves of my lips. "You're a far greater ruler than any empress. You command forty thousand men and four hundred boats. You have more than a thousand cannons. You're fierce and shrewd and have won more battles than they can count. Together we are unstoppable. No one can defeat the Red Flag."

Bao was wrong.

They had already defeated my sons' chances for having a respectable life. That was defeat enough for any mother.

63

The Mandarin and Portuguese warships left in the middle of the night.

Bao insisted the gods had intervened on our behalf because the unfavorable morning winds would have made it impossible for us to attack.

While our crews celebrated the navy's departure with song, food, and drink, Bao and and I tried to predict the Mandarin's' next move.

We never expected they would return with reinforcements.

The Portuguese fired. Every shot fell far short. They were afraid to advance.

I ordered fifteen more boats to stop repairs and join us. Two days later, more Mandarin warships joined the blockade.

The real battle began with their first cannon blasts. This time we fired back. A volley of iron balls ensued. Every single one splashed and sank to the bay's sandy bottom.

My spirits rose and fell with each update.

"The Mandarin commander blocks the bay in every direction."

"Great Generalissimo captured a Mandarin vessel."

"A hundred of our boats escaped to the east."

"Great Generalissimo hoists his mainsail and prepares to attack Lantau's fort with two thousand men."

"Wind Uncle prevents our attack!"

"The Mandarin commander stuffs his oldest boats with hay and gunpowder."

"Governor-general Bai Ling arrived from Guangzhou and said he isn't leaving until every Red Flag vessel burns."

"The wind favors the Mandarins!"

"The tide keeps us from leaving."

"A Mandarin fireboat approaches!"

I put on my fearless dragon skin and blew flames of encouragement and praise to the crew. They needed it. Our odds of escaping unscathed were ugly.

I watched the Mandarin's thirty-ton fireboat drift toward us, all the while thanking the gods for the helmsman's skill at booming away from the floating flames.

"Look!" Mountain pointed.

A bright flower of flame blossomed from the Mandarin's fireboat, long white petals of smoke shooting skyward. It looked like a water dragon blew fire from the sea.

My crew cheered.

"Extinguish the fire," I said to Headman Hsiang-shan. "Tow the Mandarin's boat ashore. Salvage anything useful."

The Mandarins sailed another fireboat toward us.

This time the straw on the deck lit a tack line. Like a wick, the rope carried the flame from boom to yard. My crew jumped up and down. They taunted and jeered and hurled obscenities at the Mandarins and Portuguese.

The Mandarins launched the third fireboat.

Then a fourth.

Each time the wind or current prevented the fireboat from

reaching us. Each inferno, a futile effort. The Mandarins destroyed their own boats.

The next big gust blew the Mandarin's fireboat back into their own line up and ignited several boats. My crews went crazy with happiness!

The Mandarin and Portuguese vessels withdrew in disgrace after that. After wiping tears of laughter from my eyes, I ordered my crews to drag the derelict vessels to shore and break them up for firewood.

That evening, Bao and I met in my cabin where Bao sipped on his celebratory third cup of wine.

He leaned toward me. "Will you write a letter to the Portuguese for me?"

"What?" I almost choked on my wine. "Why?"

"I want to offer them a chance to share in my success." Bao grinned, but something behind his eyes gave me pause.

"You're joking."

"I'm not." His voice was earnest, the curves and angles of his face set with seriousness. "I have ships, supplies, crews. All I need is a few of their warships to defeat the Mandarins."

Not again. My body grew heavy with the weight of his dream.

"Once I take Guangzhou and destroy the Mandarin navy, I'll restore the Divine Dominion." Bao glowed with confidence. "But first Guangzhou, eh? After the provinces are in my possession, I'll reward my foreign Portuguese friends with provinces of their own."

"Do you want me to write the letter now?" I loved Bao. I would not spit on his unrealistic ambitions.

"No, the sting of their defeat is too fresh. Maybe in a week or so they will be able to see the great opportunity I offer."

I had hoped time might dilute Bao's heaven-high dreams,

but it had not. He stretched his arms to touch the sky. His overreaching could kill him. And me.

How does a person prevent a tiger from stalking its prey? How does a woman silence the squawking rooster? How does a lover tame her young stallion? The answer was the same. It could not be done.

"One day, Xianggu, we will be Emperor and Empress." Bao pretended to adjust a crown. "Rulers of the Center of Civilization that is ruled by hardworking merchants, farmers, and craftsman."

I enclosed his hand in mine, stroked his skin, salt rough and sun brown. "I don't want to be an empress. It's too much trouble. Bao…" I had to speak the truth. "Wealth is my goal, not power or glory."

"More power, greater wealth." Bao's grin did not fade. "Anyway, goals are like the shoreline, ever-changing with the ebb and flow of the tides."

I withdrew my hand. "Very poetic, you sound like Guo Podai. But I don't want to share my bed with a poetic dreamer."

Bao's fingers curled into a fist. "Overthrowing the Qing isn't a dream."

"Dreams are like fruit. Picked too soon it's bitter and hard. You're only twenty-three-years-old. Give your ambitious dream time to ripen."

"You mean rot." His face darkened.

I rubbed my temples, sore with frustration. "When I recall my younger self—first a slave, next a flower girl, then a young wife—I marvel at my ignorance. I was fearless like you. I had nothing to lose and everything to gain. I would stab a man a hundred times, watch his blood stain the deck under his feet, ignore his cries of pain, and not fear his ghost. Not anymore. Now I know fear. I fear for the forty thousand men and their families who call me their chieftain. I fear for my sons' lives and for their future. I fear Mama may one day be enticed by imperial silver and deliver us into our enemies' hands. I fear Eleven-finger Wu and Toad Rearer and Wushi Er will meet the same end as the General. I fear our confederation has grown too large to control." I sighed. "Our supremacy won't last forever. One day it will end. Our crews, alliances, ships—all these assets are a few grains of sand compared to the thousand *li* coastlines under Mandarin control. My fear is the same fear every leader has for their people. Eight years ago, I was fearless and ignorant, concerned only for today. Now as a chieftain I fear tomorrows. For tomorrows affect not just me but the welfare of forty thousand people."

Bao lifted my hand to his lips. "That's why you'll make the best empress in the world."

I smiled sadly and shook my head. "No wonder you inspire such devout loyalty in your crew. I share my fears and weaknesses, and you find advantage in them."

"*You* are my greatest advantage, Xianggu."

Our lovemaking that night was tender. Slow and deliberate. Made perfect by our mutual release. Afterwards I listened to his breathing, felt the rise and fall of his smooth chest. To love a man like Bao was both a privilege and a misfortune. He was not easily swayed. Refused to take advice contrary to his lofty agenda. He lived and loved with a confident dignity of a man born to wealth and privilege. But were these qualities assets or liabilities?

The next morning, I ordered the mainsail hoisted. As I watched the magnificence of all the Red Flag sails unfurl, I thought about the story, *The Old Man Who Lost His Horse.* Little Dog's near death and my frantic dash to see him resulted in proving our indomitable supremacy to the

Mandarins and Portuguese. Bad things could work out well. And then I thought of the moneylender Hu Tao and his peach pit-sized mole. His luck was about to change.

We sailed out during low tide and then waited for Bao's squadron to join us. They were stuck. Weighed down with supplies, they could not clear the shoal. They waited for the tide to come in. Still, Bao's ships wouldn't budge. If the Mandarins found out Bao's ships were stuck, they would come back and blow them to bits.

Since my squad was already loaded down, Bao sent a fast boat asking Guo Podai for help. He even offered his share of the cargo.

On the fourth day, Bao took a fast boast to visit me in the Outer Ocean. He stalked back and forth like a caged tiger. "I'll have my revenge on Podai. I'll rip out his heart with my bare hands." His fingers curled into claws.

"There must be a reason he won't help."

Guo Podai's refusal to help Bao widened their rift. The two of them might well destroy everything we worked so hard to achieve. The confederation was dominant *only* because the chieftains worked together.

"Podai *knows* I'm vulnerable to attack, yet he does nothing! My ships are like a lame beggar unable to escape the two-legged thief."

"Maybe something happened to him. And don't forget, his own fleet's safety comes first. We need his alliance." I poured Bao a cup of wine.

Bao stopped pacing. "You and I are enough. We don't need anyone. Podai might as well have spit on my face with his snub. We don't need those kinds of alliances." He guzzled the wine. "I'm going to kill Podai and destroy the Black Flag."

64

I should kill the man sitting opposite me. Ought to string him from the masts and whip him until dead.

Guo Podai risked his life with this visit. Particularly as it came after several bloody victories over Bao's squad.

I had begged Bao not to engage in battle with Podai, but he ignored my pleas. And suffered the costs.

The first defeat happened in the inner river. Bao lost three ships, six hundred men, and two squad bosses from Podai's strike. The next battle in the Outer Ocean near the narrow Humen Straight proved more disastrous. Bao lost a thousand more men, had sixteen vessels seized, and three hundred and twenty-one Red Flag captives abducted. Devastated by the beating, Bao sailed to the Tainhou temple in Hong Kong to consult the gods.

Now, hands folded in my lap, I regarded the victorious and gloating Guo Podai who sat with confidence in my cabin. He was the Black Flag chieftain of the second largest fleet. Zheng Yi's adopted son. Second most feared pirate. The man who once asked to wed me. A man I thought I knew.

"You dishonor your adopted father Zheng Yi," I said.

"Don't talk to me about honor. You fornicate with your adopted son."

"Really? Because if I had accepted *your* offer of marriage it would be the same. I'm not cowed by your insult." I crossed my arms. "Why did you risk life and limb to talk to me?"

Podai's arrogant smirk melted. He looked down and drew circles on the table. "I've always loved you, Xianggu. I still love you." He met my eyes. "I loved you so much I never tried to take the Red Flag from you. I supported you. Believed in you. You rejected my love and yet I continued loving you. That love grew into admiration and respect. Even awe. You grow and bloom like the lotus. Your beauty and intelligence bring grace to the muck of our depraved world. Even as I sit here now, I want you, even though I love my wife." Podai traced the edge of the desk with his index finger. "Were you and Bao lovers before Yi died? Is that why you rejected my marriage offer?"

"I considered marrying you. I refused because you are too much like Yi." It was the truth. "You didn't come to discuss love, did you?"

Podai sat up. "I did. I want to discuss the maternal love for your three sons, the familial love you have for your followers, and the material love you have for wealth."

"You have my attention."

"You've seen Governor-general Bai Ling's notices at the ports offering pardon?"

"Of course, they're nailed up everywhere."

"It's genuine, a full pardon, even to chieftains. All he asks is that we show our sincerity by surrendering our ships and crew."

"Who told you this?" I always suspected tricks.

"An emissary of Governor-general Bai Ling's came to me in person. A brave man, I'd say."

I guffawed. "Not brave, stupid, and evidently expendable since the governor-general sent him on such a dangerous errand."

"A gamble, yes, but still impressive, and one worth my listening to." Podai's face softened. "You, me, Bao, and many many squad bosses and skippers had piracy thrust upon us. Zheng Yi was born into the profession. Knew nothing else. But Bao, a Dan fisherman's son, knew the only way to a better life was to become a criminal. And you...your father sold you to pay a debt. What would your life be like now? More respectable, that's for sure. For many different reasons thousands of men find thievery their best, their only, option. A life of piracy changes us for the worse. Its salt causes us to grow the hard shell of a turtle. The winds bite at our good-ness. The tides erode our spirits."

Disappointment sagged my shoulders. "You're aban-doning your men and duties as Black Flag chieftain."

"I'm not abandoning anyone." Podai shook his head as though I had misheard. "I'm giving them the opportunity to leave a life of thievery and murder. The governor-general *will* pardon us. All of us. My children, brothers, and wife are already safe in Haikang."

"Is that why you attacked Bao's squad? To prove your sincerity to the governor-general?"

Podai looked away.

"How foolish of me. That was the terms of your pardon, wasn't it?" I rested my forehead in my palm and closed my eyes. It was over. Everything we had worked for was over. I felt like stabbing Podai. I wanted to vomit. I wanted to scream until my voice was hoarse.

"I'm the second greatest chieftain because I'm shrewd,"

said Podai. "Think about your future and your children's future. Consider how you might use your substantial wealth to open a respectable business. A business you will bequeath to your sons."

My forehead rolled back and forth in my hand. "Bao and I have humiliated the Mandarins in a thousand ways. They'll never pardon us."

"Don't be the frog who dies as he is slowly boiled to death. Jump out of the pot."

I lifted my head when there was a loud knock on the door.

"The lookout spotted Great Generalissimo's ship," announced Headman Hsiang-shan giving dagger-eyes to Guo Podai.

"You need to go." I rose from the chair.

"Surrender," said Guo Podai after the headman departed. "Surrender before the Mandarins' generosity evaporates."

I ushered Podai from the cabin and watched him board his flagship. Within minutes, his armada melted into the throng of trough junks, river junks, drag-the-wind vessels, and cargo boats anchored at Amoy port.

Amnesty. A better life for my sons. Podai's invitation was a long-wished for melody in my heart.

Bao would never surrender to the Mandarins, especially since a condition of pardon meant destroying his former allies.

Hours later Bao strode into my cabin, his hand on the hilt of his cutlass. "Why didn't you kill Podai when you had the chance? He cost us a thousand good men and many boats."

My eyebrows shot up. "You keep a spy on my flagship?"

"I keep spies everywhere." His fingers closed around the hilt.

"The only weapon I want to see of yours hangs between

your legs. Sit down. Take your hand from the sword and I'll tell you why I didn't kill Podai."

Bao dropped onto the chair with an irritated grunt.

"The Mandarins offer amnesty," I began. "Podai accepted and begs us to do the same."

"Surrender?! Why? They can't beat us."

"It's better to surrender in strength while the Mandarins fear us than when we're weak."

"We will *never* be weak." Boa's palm smacked the table.

"Podai defeated you!"

Bao's nostrils flared. "I misinterpreted signs from the gods."

I pinched the bridge of my nose and puffed out my frustration. "Is this the life you want for your son? Do you want him to be called a wicked person and a worthless fellow? Do you want him to live his entire life on the water, always running from Mandarins and foreign forces? Do you really want our son to have to hide his riches in a cave? To live his days in violence and blood?"

Bao's eyes hardened.

"If we're caught, they'll execute us. They'll hack off our heads and put it on a stick for everyone to laugh at. There's no honor in that. Put aside your jealousy—"

Bao started from the chair. "I'm not je—"

"Listen. Podai thinks it's important to accept the governor-general's amnesty while he's strong. While he still has the negotiating power to protect his family."

"Fuck Podai! He's nothing. A coward. His victories against me were luck, not skill." Bao stood and paced the room. "I will not abandon thousands of people to save myself. Tonight, I came to lay in my lover's arms, but it seems she's swayed into cowardice by my enemy."

"Don't mistake shrewdness for weakness." I stretched out

my arms. "We already have a lot of money. We could open a legitimate business. Like a gambling house."

"What?" Bao recoiled. "Surrender my power to watch fat rich men with limp cocks throw dice and play mahjong? I'm twenty-three-years-old! Iron strength fills my limbs!" Bao flexed his arm. "Boldness strengthens my spirit. My mind never gets tired. I'm a crane standing among chickens."

Men and women view life differently. Women are *yin*— our energy finds a smarter and less aggressive way to achieve our goals. Men are *yang*—all bravado and blood. Luckily, my experience as a prostitute, wife, and chieftain gave me skills for managing hot-blooded men.

"You possess the rare ability to lead and inspire," I said employing my most seductive smile. "But why settle for inspiring chickens when amnesty can grant you the chance to lead cranes?"

"GUO PODAI SURRENDERED." The informant delivered this news on the evening of January thirteenth. "He turned over five thousand men and eight hundred women and their children. He gave Governor-general Bai Ling one hundred and thirteen vessels—several that once belonged to Zheng Yi —all his cannons, and more than five thousand weapons. Podai also released all the hostages captured from Great Generalissimo to the governor-general."

Bao's nostrils flared but he kept his anger checked. "Anything else?"

"Guo Podai agreed to join forces with the Mandarins to destroy the flag fleets. They made him a sub-lieutenant in the imperial navy." The informant took a deep breath. "There's more. Feng, headman on the Yellow Flag's flagship also negotiated a pardon."

"Just the headman, not Eleven-finger Wu?" Bao asked with feigned composure.

"No. Wu swears he'll chop any man to pieces if he suspects they even think about surrendering."

"Thank you." Bao dismissed the messenger. "The time has come to demonstrate our power."

"I agree." But not for the reasons he assumed. A show of our domination would make any future deals with Governor-general Bai Ling that much more persuasive.

65

Two hundred and eighty Red Flag vessels sailed up the Pearl River to collect protection fees. Any village that refused to pay suffered our wrath.

Bao was a typhoon and the crew, embracing the tempest inside him, was swept up by his victories. Only one incident soured his successes, one so demoralizing he sought refuge in a cloud of opium for a week.

"Build another floating temple. A bigger one." I stood over his woozy form reclining on the bed. "Show the Portuguese that burning your floating temple has no effect. It's time to come out of your opium fog."

"Not fog but the mist of admiration," Bao murmured through closed eyes. "The Portuguese are a formidable opponent. The only ones with enough skill to conquer us. Their weapons are superior, their gunpowder, better."

"Get up." I nudged his leg.

"I'm not wallowing in self-pity." He pointed to his head. "I'm thinking of ways to crush them. Maybe I'll start by interrogating Glasspoole."

"What would a British sailor we hold for ransom know about Portuguese warships?"

"A lot." He reached for the opium pipe.

I moved it away. "I need you, Bao. I have an important task for you."

One cloudy eye opened. "Business or pleasure?"

"Both. We're going to pay a visit to Hu Tao."

HU TAO'S peach pit mole was bigger. His face, uglier. Fewer strands of hair hung from his chin. His false queue was the same, which made him look even more ridiculous. He did wear better clothes. Selling children made him rich.

Dressed as wealthy merchants, I sat with Bao, Headman Huang Cheng-sung, and cousin An-pang in the elegant House of Peony.

"It's time," I said.

Bao rose from the table, crossed the room, and introduced himself to Hu Tao. Bao pretended to claim kinship with a mutual acquaintance and, after what seemed like too much talk about gambling and government bureaucracy, said he wanted to buy some children. He asked Hu Tao to join our table.

He did.

I poured the man who sold me into slavery the very best quality *baijiu*. He did not recognize me. I didn't expect he would. There was no resemblance between the skinny thirteen-year-old girl and the elegant woman seated opposite him.

"All my chattel comes from good families who fell on bad times. No street urchins. No sickly children. Good quality children." Hu Tao smiled a missing-tooth smile. "Good quality costs more. They're a better value."

Hu Tao paid scant attention to me as I slid the glass of *baijiu* toward him. He merely grunted his thanks and took a sip.

"You don't remember me," I said, "but you bought me from my father, an orange grower in Xinhui."

"Eh?" Hu Tao scratched his chin and really looked at me for the first time. "You've done well for yourself. Your father made a good choice."

"My father had *no* choice. You sold me to a woman named Madam Xu."

"Sounds familiar."

"She was the owner of a flower boat where I eventually became a prostitute."

Hu Tao's eyes narrowed into slits as he sipped.

"I worked for ten years but then had a piece of good luck. The flower boat was attacked by pirates. The Red Flag."

Hu Tao peered into the glass, frowned, and set it down.

"I married the chieftain of the Red Flag," I continued. "Several years later I became chieftain."

"You?" Hu Tao's eyes widened. "Are you the one the foreign devil's call Dragon Lady?" He scratched his neck.

"The same." I stared into his ugly evil eyes.

Hu Tao cleared his throat. "You come to thank me?"

"No. You see, it took ambition, determination, and luck for me to succeed. Other children you sell are not as lucky. Their spirits are weaker than mine. Their body is alive, but their hopes and dreams are dead. Like the girl with silver lotus feet, the other one you sold to Madam Xu that day. She died giving birth to a baby conceived by a thousand different men."

Hu Tao swallowed, coughed, and rubbed his throat.

"You wronged thousands of children," I said.

"W-w-hhaaaat?" He pointed to the bottle of *baijiu*, pushed himself up.

Huang Cheng-sun and cousin An-pang set heavy hands on Hu Tao's shoulders, forced him back down. Bao pressed a blade against Hu Tao's back.

"Poison is better." I pointed to his glass. "It's an appropriate death, yet sadly it's not commensurate with all the innocent young lives you poisoned by selling them into slavery. I'm showing you more mercy than you deserve."

"You…you…" Hu Tao tried to spit but his throat closed up.

"I'm not killing you out of revenge, old man. I have more money, power, and *guanxi* than you can imagine. In fact, the owner of this place is a good friend. I kill you for those who cannot. I avenge the pains, torments, horrors, and deaths of the weak and unlucky."

Hu Tao pawed at his throat while his face bloomed red and purple.

"Do you think your wife would like to be a slave on my flagship? She's a widow now."

Hu Tao's head fell forward.

66

Year of the Metal Horse
1810

We engaged the *Sir Edward Pellow*, killed the officers, and seized three silver-filled chests worth more than thirteen thousand in Spanish dollars. Bao and I shared the prize with the crew who spent their portion at Tanchou celebrating the New Year.

While the gongs clanged and fireworks flared, small squads of industrious crewmembers collected protection fees from nearby counties.

Week after week we rode a wave of good fortune. Only news of Guo Podai's victories over the other flag fleets spoiled our good mood.

Guo Podai's defection had unexpected consequences. Ten thousand abandoned Black Flag crewmen flocked to the Red, Yellow, Blue, and Green fleets. This mass exodus caused fights, resentment, and malicious competing for prestigious positions.

We struggled to absorb the slew of helmsmen, deckhands,

gunners, and stewards pledging loyalty to us. The new crewmembers, feeling displaced and angry, lashed out by brawling and betraying others in an attempt to regain their old positions. It became bad enough the squad bosses begged for a meeting.

"Our deckhands are worried," said Squad Boss Tsung-fu. "They're afraid for their lives. And not just the new crews from Bao's fleet. They're all afraid that the officers will abandon them like Guo Podai."

Foremost Squad Boss Hsiang-shan spoke next. "I hear Governor-general Bai Ling gave Guo Podai the rank of sublieutenant and that his victories against us already earned him a peacock feather. My men don't fear much, but they do worry that you and Bao will abandon your fleet family."

Squad Boss Tsung-fu handed me a list. "These are the defectors."

My eyes ran down the too-long list. "Feng Yung-fa? Kuo Chiu-shan, Chang Jih-kao? Their crews, too?" I kept my voice soft, controlled. "More than a thousand men and fourteen ships?"

"More plan on surrendering," said Squad Boss P'o-pao. "Why are we surprised? Governor-general Bai Ling offers pardons without punishment."

"They're fools." Bao scowled. "What kind of life will they have as poor fishermen, grass cutters, and peddlers? We give them wealth."

"A full pardon is its own kind of wealth," said Squad Boss P'o-pao.

I glanced at the list again. Deckhands and helmsmen behaved like a school of fish, their course dictated by predators, prey, and currents. The Mandarins were all three.

Since my squad bosses were shrewd men capable of

smelling fear better than any dog, I stood tall and offered confident encouragement.

After the squad bosses returned to their ships I went to my cabin. "If our crew begin to surrender, I'll be a chieftain of ghost junks." I cradled Third Son in my arms. "Confucius says, when it becomes obvious the goal cannot be reached, do not modify it but rather adjust the steps to achieve it."

Bao kissed my cheek. "My goal hasn't changed. Has yours?"

"You want to be a respected leader on land. Maybe this pardon is a way of achieving it."

Bao scowled. "The Mandarins will never propose any terms agreeable to us."

"You don't know unless you ask."

"I refuse to kowtow to them."

"Put aside your ego for the benefit of our son and our future."

"Our future?" Bao tilted his head. "Our future together? You'll marry me if we're not pirates anymore?"

I exhaled too loudly.

Bao turned away, but not before I saw the hurt in his eyes. "You want me to adjust my steps but you yourself are unwilling. You talk about opportunities for your son yet refuse to wed his father."

"We both have a lot to think about." I put Third Son to my breast.

"We need to do more than that. We must ask the gods."

THE TAINHOU TEMPLE columns wore a fresh coat of red paint and the roof was strung with new paper lanterns. Bao, with the Spanish silver he had confiscated, had financed the temple's restoration.

"Mazu will give me a sign," said Bao as we passed under the awning and through the sea-facing door.

I hoped so, I thought while we approached the gold-painted goddess seated on a pedestal among flowers and offerings.

Bao lit incense and bowed his head before the goddess. I stood behind him and stared at the beautiful new flooring. How much had that extravagance cost?

A loud *pop* startled me. I looked up.

Fire shot into the air above Mazu.

"Bao!" I grabbed his sleeve and jerked him back.

Flames engulfed Mazu's head as the inferno shot to the ceiling. The fire blazed once, twice, and then simply vanished.

Bao lay prostrate at the foot of Mazu, his forehead against the tile floor. Silent and stunned, I watched for another flare up.

"You saw it?" Bao, on his knees now, spoke in a whisper.

"Of course, I saw it. The flames blackened the ceiling above her."

"It's a sign."

Mazu, Beidi, Longwang, Longmu, Jinghaishen, and Fengbo. These gods remained silent in my presence, perhaps because my prayers and offerings were done by habit rather than conviction. Bao had real faith. To him, the gods whispered warnings and encouragements. I did not doubt this was a sign. I felt certain Mazu warned me that my fleet would perish by flame.

Bao got to his feet, poked his finger in the thin line of black ash left from the charred incense. "Venerable Mother made it clear my ambition is too great for piracy. I'll have to join the Mandarins to achieve the highest positions." He studied the scorched ceiling. "Nothing will contain the burning aspirations within me."

A hundred questions danced on my tongue, but I was silent, too shaken by the goddess's sign, too in wonderment at Bao's interpretation, too relieved by his announcement.

Finally, I found my voice. "We need to be very careful."

Bao nodded. "I'll send Squad Boss Tsung-fu to determine the sincerity of the governor-general's offer." Bao led me from the temple. "I don't think our pardon will be as easily negotiated as Podaai's. The Red Flag are a tidal wave compared to the Black Flag's ripple."

"That's not what I meant." I stopped in the courtyard to face him. "How do we explain our plan to surrender to forty thousand crewmembers?"

ONCE GOVERNOR-GENERAL BAI LING assured Squad Boss Tsung-fu of his sincerity, we employed Chou Fei-hsiung, a longtime friend, self-proclaimed physician, and peddler of dubious medicines, to act as a liaison to arrange the first meeting.

"I won't lie." Chou Fei-hsiung slurped his tea. "The emperor would rather see you both dead. Villagers too. They'd slice you both into a thousand pieces given the chance. The only reason the governor-general offers amnesty is because he believes your influence will encourage the other flag fleets to surrender." He set down the teacup. "Zheng Yi Sao, your beauty increases with each passing year. Unfortunately, the officials refuse to negotiate with a woman, even if that woman is the most powerful chieftain of the South Seas."

I crossed my arms and huffed my irritation out through my nostrils. "Stupid old men."

Chou Fei-hsiung ran his finger along his long, wilted mustache. "I agree. Tradition and partiality fog their minds, but their misguided opinions will not be changed. I'll tell Governor-general Bai Ling the Red Flag promise to anchor at Sha-chiao where the Great Generalissimo Zhang Bao will discuss terms of surrender."

Bao and I exchanged a glance.

"Only if Magistrate Arriaga is present," I said. "We trust him to uncover any government treachery."

"Of course, of course," nodded Chou Fei-hsiung. "Several magistrates will be present. The governor-general is as eager as you to make sure no misunderstandings or assumptions are made by either party."

After we finalized the arrangements, I returned to my cabin and stood before a small statue of Mazu.

"I'm frightened." I lit incense for the goddess. "Much may be lost that will never be regained. On the sea, I'm honored and feared. On land, I'll be just another woman, another widow and mother. Everything rides on Bao's ability to negotiate favorable terms. My fate and the future of my sons lay in his hands. My future rests on the charm and diplomacy of my young lover. Is this a wise course of action?"

Mazu was silent.

67

"**R**aise the banners!"
"Salute the governor-general with cannon fire!"
"Light the fireworks!"

With furrowed brows, wary eyes, and clenched teeth Red Flag crews watched Governor-general Bai Ling's ship approach.

I would surrender but only if the governor-general guaranteed the pardon of every man, woman, and child in my fleet. Bao and I promised our crews we would not abandon them. Bao's charisma, my accomplishments, and our combined triumphs convinced the crews of our sincerity.

Not for the first time, I was amazed by Bao's ability to charm with the perfect words. Had he been born to a wealthy family he might have amassed millions of adoring followers, might have built an empire rivaling any who came before him.

Bao, dressed in his most elaborate purple silk surcoat and black turban, stood beside me while waiting for Squad Bosses P'o-pao, Hsiang-shan, and Tsung-fu to arrive.

"It begins," he said.

"Let's hope it's the right beginning. Whether the negotiations go well or not, we have an opportunity to form a new alliance with the British captains tomorrow. Any agreements we make with them increase our future bargaining power." I touched his arm. "Be careful."

"Maybe. Maybe not." Bao winked and then descended into a long dragon carved and painted with such precise ornateness it could have been the emperor's.

I summoned the deputy headman. "Is the best lookout posted?"

"Yes, Madam Chief. The boy has the eyes of a falcon."

I glanced up. "Are his eyes as good as his head?? What good is seeing if he doesn't recognize danger?"

"He's a smart boy," said the deputy headman. "So smart I'm thinking of making him my adopted son."

"Even intelligent boys cannot remain sharp-sighted for long. Sun, clouds, and sea play tricks on the eyes."

"I took the best lookouts from your other ships. Each lookout will work a half day shift. No opium. No betel nut. No *bee-chew*. No fucking. Just sleep, eat, watch."

"Well done."

"Madam…" His brow furrowed and his gaze slid to Bao's long dragon almost halfway to its destination.

"Don't worry." My face was a mask of serenity. "Generalissimo negotiates for all of us. All. Not a few. All." I swept my arm from one side of the deck to the other. "You're a commendable headman, the Mandarins need men like you in the navy."

Relief flooded his face. "I hope so."

I wanted to go back to my cabin where I could pace the floor and agonize in private. I did not. The crew needed me on deck. Needed to see and hear my confidence. Anyway, there was another way to pace.

I walked the length of the flagship and made sure my crew was prepared for any outcome, good or bad. I told the musicians to play and summoned the wives to take tea with me. I wanted the Mandarins' lookout to report that Zheng Yi Sao and the officers' wives drink tea while their children play at their feet. The illusion of confidence was more important than the reality.

The sway and heave of the flagship marked the passing time, and with each movement I relaxed more. A long meeting was a good sign.

"Great Generalissimo returns," shouted the lookout.

I remained seated and smiled serenely with the expectation of success. When Bao and the squad bosses boarded, I rose to greet them, then bid them to follow me into the cabin.

"Governor-general Bai Ling wants an accounting of all vessels, crewmen, gunpowder, cannons, and weapons," said Bao the moment the door closed.

"They were very eager to negotiate," Tsung-fu added.

"Good." I sat at the desk. "We'll draw up a list. Not an accurate one. The Mandarins would never stoop to providing us with an exact account of *their* assets."

The following afternoon Bao and I met with British captains, Austin and Campbell. We feasted on sticky rice cakes, pork-filled dumplings, oranges, and peanuts, and kept their wine glasses filled.

After the meal and with help from an interpreter we offered our terms. By the time the twilight sky glowed red and gold we reached a truce. The English captains swore not to collude with Spaniards or Mandarins. We vowed not to attack their merchant ships. Once we signed the documents guaranteeing their safe passage permits, Bao asked questions about the British man-of-war vessels. In the midst of the conversation Headman Hsiang-shan came in with a young American boy we captured over a year ago.

"To prove our sincerity, we release this boy into your care," I said. "He's very valuable now because he speaks three languages, Dutch, English, and our own superior language."

The boy, with large moon-shaped eyes and hair bleached white from the sun, bowed low, and thanked Bao and I before scurrying behind the English captains.

"As you see, he's fit and strong. Life at sea suits him," said Bao. "And he learned the art of true seamanship."

With this proclamation the boy nodded vigorously, and the meeting concluded with this happy event.

The next morning, Bao—with our less-than-accurate boats and weapons list—and five squad bosses returned to Governor-general Bai Ling's ship to complete the negotiations. Although we now had English allies, I took no chances and prepared for all possibilities.

An hour later Headman Hsiang-shan rushed toward me. "Ten boats flying Portuguese flags prepare to leave the harbor. They're all headed toward the governor-general's ship."

An ambush! Did the governor-general kidnap Bao and my squad bosses?

I leapt from the chair and thrust Third Son into his *amah*'s arms. "Sound the alarm gong. Hoist the flag. We're leaving."

Mountain, posted on the governor-general's ship, heard the gong and alerted Bao.

"Great Generalissimo and the squad bosses are getting into the long dragon," shouted the lookout.

The moment the last grim-faced squad bosses boarded my flagship we made way.

"Shit-eating insects," Bao growled when he reached my

cabin. "They collude with the Portuguese. Not only that, their terms are insulting." He poured a cup of *baijiu*. "They want every single one of our vessels. Every drag-the-wind, open-the-wind, long dragon, every insignificant rotting sampan. Even your flagship—this beautiful vessel. That's not the worst of it." He guzzled the cup, poured another. "They demand we live on shore. They insist our squad bosses and headmen never go into the seas again." Bao held out his arm. "Salt water runs through my veins, Xianggu. I inhale the sea with each lungful. My heart beats to the rhythm of the tides."

I took off his surcoat. "What was your counter offer?"

"I told the governor-general I require eighty vessels and five thousand of my best men if he expects me to defeat the other pirate fleets."

"That's only a fraction of the boats and men under my command. That's more than fair. Governor-general Bai Ling needs to be reminded who he's dealing with. Let's give him a reason to reach a fair compromise."

I had a plan. I didn't want to do it, but it was the only way. Strength through fear.

Bao downed the second cup and rubbed his hands together. "What's the plan?"

68

I lifted the green celadon bowl. "Do you still wish to surrender?"

"Do you?" Bao narrowed his eyes and tried to gauge my intention.

"My desires haven't changed. But we will not stoop to the Mandarins." I traced my finger around the bowl's rim. "This bowl's beauty is in its craftsmanship. Its exquisiteness and worth found in its fragility. We are the bowl, our position just as delicate. Like this bowl we are valuable, worth more whole than broken into pieces." I turned the bowl over. "Just as the artist's *kung fu* crafted this bowl, so we will show our patience and skill with the Mandarins. Just the right amount of pressure. A show of humility. A display of pride. A reminder of our dominance."

An hour later Governor-general Bai Ling sent a message. He claimed that the small fleet of Portuguese ships that had passed was a coincidence and he looked forward to renewing negotiations.

It was too little too late.

I put my plan into action. One that would prove both our sincerity and dominance. I wanted to surrender and begin a new life, but I would not be rushed into a bad deal. Impatience was a poor negotiator. Neither would the Red Fleet float like dead fish on the water.

First, in order not to jeopardize a pardon, I forbid my vessels from attacking navy or merchant ships.

Next, my fleet sailed into the Inner Passage, where I sent in a team to demand protection fees from uninsured towns. Unfortunately, my men torched hundreds of businesses and homes. Bao, worried their violence ruined any chance of pardon, whipped them until they bled.

The second team proved incompetent as well. Somehow, the villagers, armed with only farm tools and bamboo spikes, sent our men fleeing back to our boats like beaten dogs. Fortunately, the third team was more successful.

Governor-General Bai Ling and his officials did nothing. No message. No summons. No retaliation. The British, however, sent us gifts and letters of gratitude for upholding our truce. We responded by granting them protection passes to enter Macao.

Next, Bao and I met with the commander of the British ship *Antelope*. The commander promised the British would no longer interfere in our business as long as we didn't attack their ships.

Imagine that! The British made truces with pirates rather than deal with Mandarin officials.

Yet still the governor-general sent no word.

"WE NO LONGER ACCEPT PROTECTION MONEY," Bao

said as we stood on quarterdeck. "We sent our agents ashore to surrender at Macao, Hsin-an, and Guangzhou as proof of our sincerity. We sacrificed one hundred and fifty cannons and ninety-eight men, and still the governor-general remains mute."

"We humiliated him, that's why." Rain plop-plopped on my bamboo *dǒulì*. "I have a plan to force him to restart negotiations, but you won't like it."

"Is it dangerous?"

"Maybe." I nestled against him. "There's only one way to soften the hard hearts and stubborn minds of the officials."

Bao lifted my chin and stared at me with his miss-nothing eyes. "Soften?"

I stroked his cheek, rough with stubble. "Women have a gentle touch."

"No." Bao's face grew taut. "You're not coming with us. I'm not handing over our chief on a platter. That would be stupid. The governor-general will cut us all to bits rather than negotiate amnesty. With no leadership the Red Flag will sink. As will all our promises to the crew."

"You won't be coming with me. Neither will any of the squad bosses."

"No, Xianggu." Bao clutched my shoulders. "I forbid it."

I laughed. "You have no authority over me."

Bao breathed hard, frustration puffing through his nose like a bull ready to charge. "I forbid you not as a subordinate but as your lover. Do not go into the nest of vipers alone."

"I won't be going alone. I'll be accompanied by the officers' wives…and children…unarmed."

Bao stepped back and gaped. "You're mad! No wife will go with you, let alone take their child."

"Don't you see the beauty of my plan?" I said as the rain fell hard, the large drops bouncing off the deck.

"I see nothing but Mandarin officials slicing my beloved into a hundred and twenty pieces."

"Don't look through the eyes of a worried lover. Look through the eyes of the cunning Great Generalissimo." I rose on my tiptoes and set a soft kiss on each eyelid. "I won't look like a cruel pirate chieftain when I am accompanied by the officers' wives and children. Governor-general Bai Ling will look into the faces of young mothers and innocent children and see people in want of a better life. He will see a family. Your fierce faces remind them of razed villages and cannon fire. A delegation of harmless women pleading for an honest life will remind them of soft thighs, warm lips, and domestic life."

"You're not taking my son on a fool's errand."

"I'm the chieftain. I do as I like."

Bao snatched the *dŏulì* from my head and flung it into the sea. "And I am the Great Generalissimo and I do as I like."

I glared at him while rain soaked my face. I was like an empress who proclaimed commands and issued orders from her throne. But commands and orders were only effective if a trusted chancellor carried them out. Bao was that chancellor.

Lightning flashed in the distance, the white streak striking at the same moment I saw into Bao's heart. I bit my lip to keep from smiling. How difficult for a man like Zhang Bao to be subordinate to a woman, to wait for her approval when he might have been a chieftain. He did this for me, for the Red Flag, for my fleet. With grace and dignity this formidable man stayed by my side, my most ardent supporter.

I looked at my *dŏulì* afloat in the water. "We made our dynasty on the seas, but our reign has come to an end. Too many things work against us. We've grown too large, like a top-heavy vase easily tipped over." I brushed wet hair away from my face. "I've done what no woman ever has, achieved more success than I ever dreamed possible. I am the chieftain of the most powerful fleet in the Divine Dominion, perhaps even the world. Forty thousand men do my bidding." I placed Bao's hand against my rain-cold cheek. "I wear the face of a warrior and an empress at all times. The *yin* in me is tired of this face. My heart yearns for new adventures, new mountains to climb, new waves to ride. My best decision was making you Great Generalissimo. But I believe you also seek new ventures and greater status, a profession worthy of your excellent talents."

Bao looked years younger as the rain plastered down his hair. "Do you think the governor-general would give me a military post?"

"They should. They'd find no better commander." I gazed toward the distant shore, one blurred by sheets of rain. "I want to live in a beautiful home with glass windows and many rooms, where my sons play in a garden and splash their hands in the pond swimming with *koi*. I want to walk on solid ground. I want to drink from a spring well anytime I choose. I want to live in a place where my days and nights are not consumed with solving problems, with government officials, faulty cannons, and finding food for thousands of people."

"You won't like doing nothing all day."

"I never said that. I'll open a business. A gambling house or a brothel. Maybe both. Very exclusive. Only the most beautiful girls. Only the wealthiest customers." I licked a sweet raindrop off my lip. "I *will* go to Governor-general Bai Ling without you. You can't stop me."

"Xianggu, don't do it."

"Don't ever tell me what to do." Shivering, I stomped toward my cabin. My soaked surcoat felt cold and heavy. I shed it, dropped it on the rain-soaked deck. Beneath, my thin silk tunic was drenched and clung to my body.

The cold wind invigorated my spirit. Brought clarity. Before climbing the ladder, I lifted my face to the sky, opened my mouth to receive the gods' gift. When I no longer felt the water, when I became one with its cold wetness, I looked back at Bao. He waited nearby, mouth agape, hand holding my discarded surcoat. Lust shone in his eyes.

I turned around and climbed the ladder. Bao followed close behind, rushing inside before I shut the cabin door. He stared at my silk-drenched figure, grabbed me, clutched my buttocks, and tore at his own wet clothes with one hand. I smacked his face, but this inflamed him. His rough-passionate kisses demanded more. Much more.

We fell to the floor. I wrapped my legs around him and slapped him again. And again. And again. He pinned me to the floor and drove into me. Brutal thrusts without kindness. Devoid of sensuality. He heaved like a boat during a raging storm. We punished each other, our bodies saying what we dare not. My nails raked over his back. Drew blood. He bit my shoulder. I was furious. Angry I could not control the Great Generalissimo. Angry he questioned my plan. Angry I needed him to manage my crew. Angry his charisma surpassed mine. Angry his men idolized him. Angry I had to kowtow to the shit-eating Governor-general Bai Ling.

Bao was angry for different reasons. His subordinate position. His futile efforts to negotiate a pardon with Mandarin officials. My refusal to wed him.

We fucked violently, released all those frustrations and jealousies long simmered inside. We raged with hurtful words and cruel torments. We wounded each other until we healed ourselves. It was painful and glorious, and our raw emotions erupted through our naked flesh.

When it was over, when our quivering release cleansed us, I tracked the bloody trail my nails had scratched on his arm. We gazed at each other with fascination and horror, as two lovers with no secrets between them.

Lovers cannot hide when they have revealed everything. Lovers must only accept and love the flaws.

"I will go to Governor-general Bai Ling," I said.

"I will do my best to stop you."

69

Bao was true to his word. He summoned all my squad bosses to the flagship for the purpose of persuading me to give up my plan.

"It's dangerous," said Hsiang-shan, my foremost commander. "The Mandarins will kidnap all of you. They want us to grovel at their feet."

"Don't go," begged Mo Jo-k'uei. "The officials will think we're cowards if we send women and children."

"Madam Chief." Hsiang-shan held out his hands. "Please reconsider. We need you. If something happens to you, we're all doomed."

"I beg you." A young squad boss dropped to his knees. "Don't ask my wife and sons to go with you."

Nephew Pao-yang stepped forward. "There's no one I trust more with the lives of my wife and children."

"Thank you," I said to nephew Pao-yang before addressing the others. "To send the same people to negotiate the same way is foolish. I'll take whomever I choose for my own good reasons. I ought to punish you all for your collective lack of faith."

"Don't mistake our concern for lack of faith," said Headman Hsiang-shan. "We're all rich because of your excellent insight and judgment. We stand here as worried servants for our gracious leader.""

"Worried for my safety? How irrational. You trusted me when I took command of the fleet. Trust me now." I stretched my arms wide. "I've never let you down. I won't now. There's no greater force than that of a dragon."

Bao, silent all this time, shook his head in resignation.

"Return to your ships," I said. "I have work to do."

THE FIRST TWO weeks of April were busy. I visited every woman taking part in my delegation. I selected wives for their beauty, young sons for their obedience and bright-eyes, young daughters for their ruby-lips and shy smiles, babies for their chubby-cheeks and lyrical laughter. I chose two forty-year-old first wives with a glint in their eyes and three virgins with sensual mouths and submissive expressions.

I told the women to dress as though they visited Empress Xiaoherui, the Imperial Noble Consort, at the palace. I reminded them to washe in fresh water—not the saltwater baths in our ships—and to sweeten their breath. I told mothers to feed their babies before we entered the governor-general's chambers.

The women required little convincing. They wanted their husbands to leave the world of piracy for lawful work, to abandon the cramped cabins for a home with a courtyard. They knew the legitimacy of a government post would raise their social standing and improve their children's future.

I had shared meals with these wives, held their babes in my arms, and sent physicians to heal their children. They trusted me as only women who share the burdens and delights of motherhood could. They respected me, saw themselves in me, appreciated my humble beginnings.

"You command like a man but think like a woman," said the wife of Chang Kuang-ch'i. "I'm honored to be part of your delegation."

"Your courage gives me strength during frightening times," the wife of Fang Wei-fu confessed.

"I see you stand on the bow, determined and bold, and yet you take your babe in your arms with exceptional gentleness," a second wife told me.

"My husband says, 'I'm glad you're not like Zheng Yi Sao', and I think, 'I wish I were'," confided another.

"I told my daughter if Zheng Yi Sao can command the greatest fleet in the South Seas then a woman can do anything she sets her mind to."

"I want my son to marry a woman like you. A powerful couple has no limits."

"I pity the idiot who crosses you," laughed the forty-year-old woman in my delegation.

MY ENTIRE FLEET sailed up the Pearl River and anchored at Guangzhou on April sixteenth.

The following morning, I studied my face in the mirror while a servant girl arranged my hair. My skin was still tight and smooth. My eyes, however, revealed too much eagerness, too much pride. I closed them, concentrated on humility. It was unwise to negotiate with an adversary when my face exposed desperation.

Bao entered the cabin. "You don't have to do this."

I opened my eyes. "I've never shirked from my responsibilities."

Bao crossed his arms. "Your women's delegation caused a lot of trouble between the officers and their wives."

"More women should argue with their husbands instead of being treated like slaves. If those men wanted obedient women, they should have married a respectable Guangzhouese girl and lived in a village. A squad boss cannot expect his wife to wield a sword, throw stinkpots, and row a sampan without her wanting an equal say."

Bao grunted his agreement. "What will you say to Governor-general Bai Ling?"

"I'm not sure." I tilted my head to admire the pearls in my ears and exquisite turquoise hairpin. "How do I look?" I ran my hand over my silk *hanfu* embroidered with cranes, lotuses, and, hydrangeas.

"Like an empress."

"Good. Perhaps my appearance will sweeten my demands."

"I almost feel sorry for Governor-general Bai Ling," said Bao. "He has no idea who he's dealing with." Bao followed me from the cabin where sixteen women and children waited on deck.

After the *amah* set Third Son in my arms and the grim-faced squad bosses wished their wives best luck, we boarded two elegant long dragons and rowed toward our destiny.

70

Guangzhou was loud. It teemed with people and rickshaws. Villagers, scholars, merchants, foreigners, and men of every shade of skin with unusual headgear and curious clothing bought, sold, strolled, and lounged.

We heard a hundred different languages. Inhaled a hundred different smells. Passed a hundred shops selling silk, paper, lanterns, silver, jewels, tea, and medicines.

With high hopes and confident steps, we walked into the newly painted government building.

Governor-general Bai Ling was an old man with a fresh-shaved face and a long white queue. He was dressed in the garments of his esteemed office, the wide winged collar and headpiece giving him an intimidating and too-wide appearance. I suspected a frail thin body hid under all the brocade.

All the women, and even the children, bowed low.

"Greetings, governor-general," I said. "I am Zheng Yi Sao, commander of the Red Flag."

Governor-general Bai Ling and the other officials looked at each other in surprise.

"Where is Zhang Bao?" This question came from a smooth-faced official.

"Wherever I tell him to be." I used my chieftain voice. Soft. Controlled. Arrogant. Humorless.

"This is unexpected and unusual." The governor-general frowned. "We wish to discuss the new conditions for amnesty with the Great Generalissimo."

"I wish to discuss it with you directly. No middleman. Just two powerful leaders."

The officials exchanged looks again. They reached some agreement to continue the meeting by some secret signal.

"This is unprecedented, yet I will not be rude by refusing such a beautiful delegation." The governor-general leered. "What are your conditions of surrender?"

Making the first offer was never wise, a foolish negotiating technique. Besides, I did not know if the governor-general's attitude might have sweetened or soured since the last meeting with Bao.

"Our conditions are as flexible as young bamboo," I said, "and rest wholly on the favorable proposals of your esteemed office." I pretended to frown. "Forgive me, I can't seem to recall the specific terms."

Governor-general Bai Ling consulted a document. He recited the lengthy list of demands and then regarded me with an expectant look.

My face revealed nothing. Not so much as a wince of irritation marred my calm composure. I met the eyes of each official, and then lowered my gaze to the floor. Silence is an effective tactic, one I had used many times to gain advantage.

After several uncomfortable moments I summoned the wife of Fang Wei Fu. She presented me a paper with our counter offer. I stared at the list. Finally, after an extended period of pretend consideration, I gave the governor-general a pleasant smile. Another moment of silence passed. The governor-general and his officials grew restless.

"Our conditions for amnesty are generous," he said.

The tongue paints what the eye cannot see and so I chose my words with care.

"Your conditions benefit no one. Neither the Red Flag nor the imperial forces will be advantaged. There is no point in continuing negotiations when your terms offer no success or security for either party." I bowed low as though to leave and backed away.

"You will resume piracy?"

"I have led the Red Flag for three years. In that time, I've expanded the fleet and made all of my squad bosses wealthy. We are not rebels or petty thieves but outcasts. Made outcasts by our own people, by merchants, landlords, and officials. Our only desire is to earn wealth enough to join the respectable people of the Great Qing. Your offer of pardon is a timely gift, yet it's one you're not ready to bestow."

"We do not trust the Red Flag." The governor-general squinted at me. "You looted and burned many villages since we last spoke to Zhang Bao."

Trust is a vital component for successful negotiations. If I failed to prove our sincerity any further discussion would be futile.

"We're sincere, governor-general."

I nodded to the wife of Fang Wei Fu, who transcribed our conversation. I spoke slowly, as though giving her ample time to write, when it was actually to give my words weight.

I told the officials our unarmed delegation proved our respect and trust. I reminded them we stopped accepting protection money. I expressed dismay over the rogue crewmen responsible for the brutality and destruction of the village and promised punishment.

I saved the best for last.

I told them about our treaty with the English. When I finished speaking, Governor-general Bai Ling conferred with his councilors.

"You speak of mutual benefits," said the governor-general. "Explain how my terms are not already a benefit to all those living in Guangdong?"

His question opened the door for compromise. Negotiating is a studied art form. Madam Xu gave me my first lessons. Zheng Yi made me a master.

I pointed out the disadvantages of the government's conditions and explained the monetary and military advantages of my counter offer. We spent hours debating the virtues and vices of each proposal.

Governor-general Bai Ling and his councilors showed signs of flagging. Weariness was a good sign.

"We are close to being finished, yes?" Governor-general Bai Ling said to the man on his right.

I suppressed a smile. The g-governor-general was eager to finalize an agreement. Perhaps it was because I had labored many hours in childbirth that I had more stamina than he. Or perhaps it was because of my younger age. Or perhaps his own indulgent life had weakened his mind and body.

"To show our sincerity I would like to give you the men responsible for the raid on the village," I said. "Punish them as you see fit. Any punishment you deliver will not be worse than our penalty for insubordination. More importantly, it will appease the villagers we wronged."

Governor-general Bai Ling agreed. "It is settled." He gestured to his secretary to record the agreement.

The wife of Fang We-Fu wrote the same terms, and together both parties reviewed the each other's to check nothing had been added or removed.

"The same," said Fang We-Fu's wife.

"Identical," agreed the secretary.

The governor-general sighed with relief. "It is done."

"No, governor-general, it is not. Although I'm the chieftain and answer to no one, it's in our best interest that I discuss the terms with my squad bosses. You understand, of course, their total agreement means you receive the Red Flag's complete commitment during the transition process, one without violence or disloyalty."

Governor-general Bai Ling and I arranged a time for the next meeting. We agreed that Zhang Bao, my squad bosses, and two moderators would finalize the contract at a small pagoda just outside of Macao.

I left the building, weary but excited, and hoped Bao would show the proper attitude necessary to complete the deal.

71

Zhang Bao and the squad bosses wore big smiles as they approached the flagship. I pressed my hands to my singing heart.

"It's done," Bao said from the long dragon.

"No exceptions? No changes?"

"None."

The governor-general granted a complete pardon to every person in my fleet. More than forty thousand people.

"Amnesty," I shouted.

The shouts of thousands of voices unfurled from a hundred boats as they whooped and laughed and hollered with relief and joy. The gong signaled our triumph.

Deckhands strung red paper lanterns, hung flags and streamers, and tacked up paper cuttings, several I had cut while waiting. The cook prepared chicken and pork dishes. Musicians played.

Bao wrapped his arms around me the moment we were alone in the cabin.

"The transfer takes place tomorrow." He nuzzled my neck.

"A full pardon?"

"Yes, just as you discussed with Governor-general Bai Ling. In exchange, we give him two hundred and twenty-six junks, one thousand three hundred and fifteen cannons and two thousand and eight hundred assorted weapons. And our men will be allowed to join the army."

"We retain the rest of our boats, our wealth—all our treasures?"

"All." Bao smiled mischievously. "Before entering the pagoda where we signed the document, I told the Portuguese leader, Arriaga, that it was the Portuguese's superior naval weaponry which convinced us to surrender."

"Bai Ling heard this? Was he angry?"

"Quite the opposite. He agreed and then made me a lieutenant in the imperial navy." Bao rubbed his hands together. "I'll command a fleet of thirty ships, and they'll give me money to find good sailors."

"It's easier to find a thousand soldiers than one good general. I reminded Bai Ling of this when we discussed a future position for you."

Bao kissed me. "You did this, Xianggu. You took forty thousand pirates and made them respectable. You saved their lives and their children's lives. You give them all a new beginning."

"I hope they make good choices."

"Maybe. Maybe not." Bao shrugged. "But *I* will. I promise to soar to great military heights. For you and for my son." He nibbled my neck. "What will you do with your newfound respectability?"

"I'll open a gambling house."

Bao pulled away and stalked to the far side of the cabin. "Where?"

"I haven't decided."

Bao crossed his arms and his nostrils flared. "Then it was all a lie."

Dread dropped like an anchor into my stomach. "What do you mean?"

"You tell me you love me, but you don't. You've only pretended to love me so you can keep me tethered like an obedient dog, so you could keep me from becoming chieftain of my own flag fleet." Bao scooped up the celadon bowl, brought back his arm to hurl it across the room, then stopped. "Beauty is deceiving. All this time I thought…I believed your words—your reason for not marrying me. Or anyone. I thought once you weren't chieftain any more your heart would soften towards marriage. But now it's clear you used my love for your own purposes." He set down the bowl. "I'm a fool. All this time my love for you blinded me to your true nature. The foreign devils call you Dragon Lady. I was too smitten by the warmth between your legs to see the truth in the name."

Bao left before I mustered a reply. I loved Bao. But marrying him meant submitting to a husband.

I sank into the chair, weary and miserable. This day should have been my greatest triumph. Instead it was a defeat.

I lost the man I loved because I refused to surrender my independence.

BRIGHT FIREWORKS LIT THE SKY. Merriment filled the air. I watched the festivities from poop deck and occasionally cast a miserable glance at Bao's vessel anchored nearby.

He also watched the celebrations. Did he feel the same heart-hurting ache? The same crushing weight on his chest?

Was his heart, like mine, too empty and too full at the same time?

I never felt this torment when Zheng Yi died although I had loved, admired, and respected him. My love for Bao was different. It permeated mind, soul, and body. My love felt like a great banyan tree, its branches spread high and wide over the ground, its splayed roots clutching the ground beneath. Bao was my sky. My earth. My link between the two.

He was a rare man. One loving me at the expense of his own ambitions.

Perhaps the responsibilities and prestige of being a chieftain made me hard-hearted. Perhaps power corrupted me. Perhaps I was no better than an emperor on his throne who displayed his plumage as proof of his might. Perhaps...

The gong's reverberating boom interrupted my brooding. Its sound rumbled deep in my bones. Thundered in my ears. Resonated in my heart. Quickened my blood.

I stood still until the gonging stopped, yet my ears still felt its vibrations, and in its echo, I heard a whisper.

It might have been Mazu. Or my dragon spirit. I don't know which and didn't care because the voice told me what to do.

I hurried to the lower deck, descended the ladder into a tiny sampan rocking in water made effervescent with reflected moonlight and fireworks.

"Madam Chief, let me take you," said Mountain from above as I wrapped my hands around the oars.

I waved him off and rowed. I glanced over my shoulders to make sure I went in the right direction. I saw Bao climbing down the side of his ship.

I rowed faster.

"You forgot to ask me an important question before you left," I said as my sampan bumped his.

Bao, looking both amused and surprised—eyebrows diagonal lines across his forehead—waited in a small sampan tied to his boat. "What question?"

"An important question."

Bao crouched down and tethered our together. "A question about the terms of the surrender?"

"Not our surrender. My surrender."

A slow smile slid across his face and lit up his eyes. "Will you, Xianggu, the most powerful chieftain of the South Seas, marry me?"

"I do, Bao. I surrender."

AUTHOR NOTES

The story of Xianggu and the other pirate chieftains does not end here although the novel does. The infamous Zheng Yi Sao really did wed Zhang Bao after she secured amnesty. She gave birth to a son in 1813.

Zhang Bao teamed with Guo Podai to destroy the Green, Yellow, and Blue fleets. Unable to convince Wushi Er of the benefits of surrender, Zhang Bao captured the wily old chieftain during a battle near Tan Chou. Governor-general Bai Ling had Wushi Er and seven squad bosses decapitated. Eleven-finger Wu escaped execution—just barely—by convincing the governor-general that he was prevented from surrendering because Wushi Er threatened his family. As for Guo Podai, after obliterating the pirates of the Guangdong region, he retired near the White Cloud Mountains and lived a peaceful life with his wife and children.

Zhang Bao rose swiftly in the military ranks, the same charisma and successes making him a favorite of his superiors. Though illiterate, his swift ascent far exceeded that of men born into wealth and privilege. He died of natural causes at the age of thirty-six leaving Xianggu a widow for the second time. Always ambitious, she opened up a gambling house in Guangzhou. The Dragon Lady died at the age of sixty-nine.

The battles, skirmishes, blockades, pirate code, punishments, victories, losses, tactics, strategies, and the raids are well-documented. Even the siege when Xianggu went to visit her sick child. And especially her unarmed contingent of women to negotiate with the governor general.

To make nineteen-century China more accessible to modern readers I simplified and altered several components. Perhaps most important, is the anachronistic term Dragon Lady, which is a Western term first used in the early 1930's. For names and places, I used pinyin Romanization. *Divine Dominion* and the *Great Qing* was how Chinese people referred to their country at the time. For convenience, I used *Vietnam* because Emperor Gia Long referred to his country that way from 1804 -1813. In an effort to simplify the appellation for the pirate's chain of command, I shortened or combined their titles. *Chieftain* or *chief* designates the head of the fleet. Their crew would have called them *ta-lao-pan* or *branch boss*. Qing officials referred to them as *great pirate heads*, *great heads of the fleet*, or *chief pirate heads*. For the men leading a squadron, I use *squad boss* instead of *ta-t'ou-mu*, translated as *great head.* An officer in charge of several boats within a squadron is called a s*kipper.* The pirates would have referred to them as *lao-pan.* Each vessel was managed by a *t-ou-mu* or *headman.* A helmsman was called *to-kung.* Below them were four in charge with various deck duties. The pirates called them *huo-chang.* I merely refer to them as deckhands and gunners.

One of the joys or confusions about reading historical fiction is knowing who's an actual historical figure and who is a product of the author's imagination. Here's a list of who's 'real.'

Xianggu: Red Flag chieftain, also known as Cheng I Sao or Zheng Yi Sao.

Zheng Yi: Red Flag chieftain. Alternate spelling is Cheng I.

Zhang Bao: Red Flag Great Generalissimo. Alternate spelling Chang Pao

Guo Podai was a nickname. The Black Flag chieftain's name was Kuo Hsüeh-hsien.

Wushi Er was a nickname. The Blue Flag chieftain's name was Mai Yu-chin.

Eleven-finger Wu was a nickname. The Yellow Flag chieftain's name was Wu Chih-ch'ing.

The General: The White Flag chieftain was named Liang Bao.

Toad Rearer was a nickname. The Green Flag chieftain's name was Li Xiangqing or Li. Hsiang-ch'ing. He was also called Son of a Frog and sailed with Wushi Er.

Cai Qian: Pirate chieftain plundering the Fujian coastline.

Zu Phen: Pirate chieftain plundering Fujian coastline with Cai Qian.

Zheng Qi: Cousin of Zheng Yi

Zheng An-pang: Nephew of Zheng Yi

Zheng San: Brother to Zheng Yi

Hesheng: Sister to Zheng Yi

He-Song: Squad boss for Cousin Qi

Liang Po-pao, Hsiao Chi-lan, Hsiao Pu-ao,Chen Kuo-hua, Ya Hsüan Sao,and Ta P'ao-fu:

Red Flag squad bosses

Wu Shang-te: Secretary drafting the pirate code

Governor-general Bai Ling

Squad boss P'o-pao: Squad boss under Zhang Bao

Huang Cheng-sung: Headman for Zhang Bao

Hsiang-shan: Squad boss for Red Flag

Chen Yasheng: Skipper killed by a female hostage

Lieutenant Ho Ting-ao: Imperial naval officer

Chou Fei-hsiung: Longtime friend, self-proclaimed physician, and emissary

Lieutenant Colonel Lin Fa

Magistrates Peng and Arriaga

J. Turner: Captured by the Red Flag

The Armenian and Afoo: Friends and interpreters for J. Turner

R. Glasspoole: Captured by the Red Flag

Little boy given to English captain during a treaty

ABOUT THE AUTHOR

Autumn Bardot is an author of historical fiction and historical erotica. Her debut historical fiction is *The Impaler's Wife*. Her debut historical erotica is *Legends of Lust*. Autumn, a pen name, has worked as an educator for over fifteen years. She has a passion for history and has a special affinity for the unsung courageous females that history has neglected. Autumn lives in Southern California with her husband and ever-growing family. She wishes she was one-tenth as brave as the women she writes about.

Need another decadent and delicious story by Autumn Bardot?

There's more!

Never miss sneak peeks, giveaways, discounts, and opportunities to read Advanced Review Copies. Subscribe to Autumn's newsletter at: www.autumnbardot.com

The Emperor's Assassin
History paints her as the first female serial killer.

Locusta is the daughter of a winemaker in the Roman province of Gaul. She enjoys the indulged childhood of the elite, her concerns only about the day's amusements. She rides gentle ponies, attends parties, reads Ovid, and learns the herbal arts from her servant. But the day after meeting her betrothed, Locusta discovers the consequences of possessing such dangerous knowledge.

Ordered to leave her pastoral life, Locusta is thrust into a world of intrigue, scandal, and murder—where treason lurks behind every corner and defying an emperor means death. Locusta's life changes forever when a young Emperor Nero requires her herbal expertise. And commands her to be his personal poisoner. Caught in an imperial web, Locusta must embrace her profession or die.

Or is there another way out?

History paints her as the first female serial killer. Or is she yet another maligned woman in history?

Read Now

Connect with Autumn and visit her at::
www.AutumnBardot.com

Facebook
Instagram
Twitter
Goodreads

Hankering for some erotic fiction?

Legends of Lust, Erotic Myths from around the World **is fourteen romantic and erotic tales of Vikings, goddesses, shape shifters, jinn, and fae that are sure to take your love of myths to a whole new level!**

Start Reading Here

Historical Fiction available now:
The Impaler's Wife.

Excerpt:

ONE

FOREST IN HUNGARY

Seven men in gray robes circled the fire near a frost-covered riverbank. Their chants rose above leafless ice-glazed trees into a frigid starry sky. One man threw back his head and howled. From a distant hill, a lone wolf answered. A second man howled. This time the wolf pack joined, men and beasts united, their wail a bestial invocation.

Nearby, a mist thickened over the river and gathered into a half-formed specter. The breeze shifted. The murky apparition crept forward, advancing like a lynx stalking its prey until it enfolded the men in a vaporous blanket. It swallowed their chants. Devoured their howls.

The phantasmic fog stretched its ether arms into the forest, curled around trees like an embracing lover before it thinned, faded, and dissolved.

The men were gone. Not so much as a footprint remained.

From behind a dense thicket not far away, a man watched the ancient ritual. He pulled a worn book from his cloak, ran his hand over the familiar cracked leather cover with reverence, and opened to the page marked with a red silk ribbon. He read one passage three times.

"I *will* discover your secrets." Vlad Dracula closed the book and pressed it tight to his chest.

TWO

Ilona

Spring 1464
Székesfehérvár, Hungary

"That's my future husband." My sister Margit jabs me
with her elbow. "Prince Vlad."

Stunned by her announcement, I scoot forward on the
bench and crane my neck. The cathedral is packed with dignitaries for cousin Matthias's coronation. Getting a clear view
of Prince Vlad seated with all the other nobles across the aisle
proves difficult. I lean forward but it's futile, a stout
nobleman blocks the way. Another inch forward…my bottom
teeters at the edge of the pew.

Vlad Dracula is a mystery. Courtiers debate his virtues
and evils. Even Aunt Orsulya and Aunt Erzsébet argue over
the truth of his fierce reputation. Is he really as ruthless as
people claim? His nickname, the Impaler Prince, certainly
suggests as much.

"Ilona, stop staring." Aunt Orsulya turns her hawk-like
eyes on me.

I love my aunt, but her diligent guardianship of my

earthly behavior and eternal soul is rather excessive. She takes deathbed promises seriously, especially since it was my dying mother's wish that her daughters obey every royal rule and Catholic creed. "Why is Prince Vlad here? Since when does cousin Matthias–"

"King Matthias."

I roll my eyes. "Since when does King Matthias allow political detainees to attend coronations?"

"I don't know and don't care. Prince Vlad is of no consequence, his imprisonment is nothing but a diplomatic problem."

"Father spoke highly of him," I remind her.

Aunt Orsulya creases her brow. "Unless the diplomatic winds shift Vlad Dracula will remain little more than a condemned potentate with a notorious past." She digs her bony elbow into my side. "Do not catch his eye. He wants to solidify his ties with Hungary by marrying into the Hunyadi family."

My younger sister married before me? And to a prince?! Why am I not considered first? I look down to find my nails digging into my palms, a myriad of questions simmering in the pit of my belly. I sneak a peek at Vlad Dracula seated among members of the Diet. Aunt Orsulya is mistaken about Prince Vlad's insignificance if King Matthias sits him with such distinguished nobles.

Another peek later and the stout noble blocking my view settles back in the pew affording a good long look at Prince Vlad.

He is handsome, although not classically so, his face being much too intense. He wears a plumed cap and mink *baveri*—very rakish—and yet his straight mustache, almond eyes, and long thin nose give him a stern air. He turns to speak to the nobleman next to him, and the severe set of his mouth vanishes as his lips curl upward. His smile is wide and slightly lopsided, all grimness vanishing. I suck in my breath. Smiling Prince Vlad is very handsome and roguishly elegant. Not only that, he is certain to be far more interesting than all those simpering and dull courtiers who stride like peacocks about the palace.

Aunt Orsulya tugs on my sleeve. "Stop gawking and watch the ceremony."

I give my aunt an innocent smile before pretending to be impressed by the dignitaries in the chancel.

Aunt Orsulya narrows her eyes, frowns, then resumes watching the coronation.

She sees through me but because false smiles are more a courtly grace than a sin I do not worry for my soul. I used to worry about the state of my soul but after listening to the archbishop discuss Eternity and Grace and Penitence the more I think those notions are a way for ecclesiasts to control unschooled farmers and guildsmen. The conniving courtiers and scheming diplomats I know practice a much different creed. One of duplicity, ambition, lust, and cruelty. But of this I must remain silent and hide my understanding of highborn hypocrisy under courtly manners and layers of silk.

Aunt Orsulya pats my arm and leans close, her lips hovering over my ear. "People are watching. At least pretend to be interested."

I am interested in the coronation, just not with the details of every little ritual. The stout noble once again blocks my view of Prince Vlad, and I shift my attention to the ceremonial pageantry.

Dressed in a brocade dalmatic robe and gilded mitre, the Archbishop of Esztergom passes the Holy Crown to the Count Palatine. "Do you accept Matthias Corvinus as King of

Hungary?" He lifts the glittering gold crown high in the air for all to see.

"Agreed. So be it. Long live the King!" A chorus of voices rises in the basilica's vaulted nave.

Cousin Matthias's voice booms with confidence as he promises to protect the Holy Faith, Holy Catholic Church, and the kingdom of Hungary.

Archbishop Dénes Szécsi lowers his head and bestows an exceedingly lengthy blessing. After listening to too many 'exalted this' and "heavenly that" my gaze drifts past the ceremonial-robed nobles to cousin Matthias, Hungary's twenty-one-year-old sovereign. He holds the keys to the kingdom. He alone will decide my destiny and fortune. I ought to be nicer to him.

The verbose prayer ended, I snap back to attention when Matthias prostrates himself at the altar as the choir lifts their voices with the "Litany of Saints."

I do not remain statue-still for long. My feet tap with impatience under my dress, my meandering thoughts like a huchen fish jumping from the Danube. Every noble of any importance is here. In all likelihood my future bridegroom is in this cathedral. My feet stop tapping as prickles of anxiety skitter up my spine. Is my future husband sitting across the aisle? In the pews behind? Who will Matthias choose? A wrinkled old count or a handsome young duke? What treaty will my marriage guarantee? What alliance will it forge? Though the cathedral is heated by hundreds of guests the chill of reality runs through me. I will have no say in Matthias's decision. None at all.

And then I see Aunt Erzsébet, Matthias's mother, sitting two pews ahead. She wields more political influence than any woman I know. Maidservants tremble in her presence. Her ladies-in-waiting bow to her every whim. Even her son the king respects her ideas. Though she's fearsome, I admire her.

Boisterous hurrahs interrupt my grand ambitions, and I join the others in joyful whoops as Matthias brandishes his sword three times.

Margit squeezes my fingers. "Do you think my crown will have diamonds, rubies, sapphires, and emeralds?"

I wiggle my fingers from her too-hard grip. Margit wearing a crown! A knot of envy gathers in the pit of my stomach. "The crown of Wallachia?"

Margit's brows shoot to her forehead as her head bobs eagerly. "He wants a wedded union with our family."

"He's Matthias's prisoner. Prisoners cannot wed." Can they?

"They do not attend dinners with visiting kings and sultans either, but *he* does. What kind of prisoner is that? Matthias will not detain him forever." Margit flutters long dark eyelashes. "Won't I make a pretty princess? Aunt Erzsébet thinks so."

My foot flinches beneath the voluminous folds of my velvet brocade dress. How foolish of me not to suspect Aunt Erzsébet had a hand in this. "Pretty yes, but beauty has nothing to do with making a strategic marriage."

Margit's finger wraps a blonde tendril that had escaped from her tall hennin. "Aunt Erzsébet thinks Prince Vlad and I are well suited."

I swallow my surprise. "Why is that?"

Margit leans into my shoulder. "Don't make me repeat what everyone thinks."

I roll my eyes but her comment burrows into my gut. Everyone thinks Margit is the prettier sister. With her milk-colored skin, flaxen hair, doe-shaped blue eyes, generous bosom, and high forehead she is the picture of coquettish beauty.

I do not take after the fair side of the family. My looks are inherited from the Báthory clan on my mother's side. I have hair the color of a raven, ash-hued eyes, and fist-sized breasts. I like to think my features convey wit and intelligence. My name, however, suggests altogether different traits. Ilona means 'torch.' Aunt Orsulya claims I must surely harbor the twin sins of lust and rage deep within me, which is another reason she remains diligent about protecting my immortal soul. I disagree. I am neither immodest nor prone to anger.

I steal a look at Margit. She is uncommonly pretty but I think she prefers flattery and allure over instinct and intellect. Pretty only gets a woman so far in court. Aunt Erzsébet is proof. And while Margit has never shown any ambitions until today, I find myself thinking more and more of Aunt Erzsébet's influence.

"Don't believe everything Aunt Erzsébet tells you," I say. "We are just pawns in Matthias's chess game."

Margit lays her pale hand to her breast. "Call yourself a pawn but I plan on nights with a prince."

"Only if you don't spread the entrance gate to your rook."

Margit's cornflower blue eyes narrow into slits. "I am a virgin and will remain so until the archbishop bestows the marriage sacrament."

I give Margit's forearm a squeeze. "Your witty repartee is improving."

"Oh, you're teasing me." The tightness in her mouth melts. "Mmm, I must respond to 'rook' then." She taps her finger on her lips. "I would never lower my drawbridge before the nuptials." Her lips press together in a triumphant smile.

We giggle until Aunt Orsulya throws us a stern look and directs our attention to the chancel where King Matthias rides his horse up a small earthen mound of soil collected from all across Hungary—impressive since he's doing this while balancing the crown on his head and holding an orb— points his sword in all four directions and vows to protect his land and people.

Coronation now concluded with spectacle and pomp, I am impatient to leap to my feet and stretch my legs. Aunt Orsulya stays me with an outstretched hand.

"Piety becomes a maiden better than eagerness to depart," she says between lips that don't move.

Margit and I exchange an exasperated look. Fortunately, we are rescued by Aunt Erzsébet, who breaks free from the throng of well-wishers to pause at our pew and scowl at us.

"Why are they dawdling?" She aims her caustic tongue at Aunt Orsulya before returning her irritated gaze on Margit and me. "Go to the palace and pay homage to my son the king." As Margit and I exit the pew, Aunt Erzsébet sidles next to Aunt Orsulya. "The pretense of piety does not benefit our unmarried cousins unless they become brides of Christ, which will never happen while I draw breath." Her velvet-clad arm snakes out and latches onto Margit as she passes. "I need to speak to you at the palace."

Margit gives me a smug smile the moment Aunt Erzsébet rejoins her doting entourage of ladies-in-waiting and flatterers. "Told you."

Envy and frustration congeal in the pit of my belly. I am next to marry. Not Margit. Have Margit and Aunt Erzsébet grown that close they now conspire in secret? What else does Margit keep from me? I look at my younger sister with fresh eyes and wonder if her innocence is a ruse. Perhaps, she is not as innocent as she appears, and takes lessons in scheming from Aunt Erzsébet.

"Have you and Prince Vlad been introduced?" My voice drips honey, my question sweetly harmless.

"Not formally." Margit leans in. "I was passing through the small chambers when I came upon him admiring Father's portrait. After introducing myself as Mihály Szilágy's youngest daughter we exchanged a few pleasantries. He even confessed to being struck by my beauty."

"I heard he's very courtly." My voice is tight with envy.

Margit looks down her nose. "I heard he has an eye for beauty." Her mouth presses into a superior smirk before stepping into our garland-festooned royal litter.

I climb in after her and take a seat by the open window.

Aunt Orsulya, sitting opposite, presses a handkerchief to her forehead. "A magnificent day." She peeks through the curtained window at the long line of litters in the courtyard. "It will be a tediously slow ride up the hill."

"Should we walk?" I smooth my dress.

"Walk?" Aunt Orsulya's nose wrinkles as though she smells rotten food. "Among the rabble? You are a saucy girl, Ilona." Aunt Orsulya flutters her gilded fan in front of her flushed face. "Pull back the curtains. It's much too hot in here."

I peer out the window. A warm breeze caresses my cheek. The streets are alive with music, a thousand merry celebrants singing my cares away. The basilica bells peal, the tuneful clanging rising over the boisterous crowd. Street musicians play. Common folk dance jigs in the street. Merchants hawk trinkets. Peddlers tout their wares. Fresh figs! Roasted pork! Honeyed pastries! My heart squeezes tight with longing. I would rather be among the common people sharing their honest merriment than ensconced in this festooned carriage.

"Look at all the people." Margit nudges me sideways to

look out the window. "Every Hungarian in the land must be celebrating Matthias's coronation."

"Maybe it's because Matthias promised free food, ale, and entertainment for everyone," I say.

Margit wrinkles her nose. "Do you have to be so cynical?"

I flinch. "I'm just stating the obvious."

Suddenly, an old hag's face fills the window. "Princess!" Her withered hand clutches the casement as she flashes a toothless grin. "Do not seek the book."

THREE

I recoil from the carriage window, away from the garlic-laced voice, away from the dirt-ragged nails, away from the filth and stench of poverty. "I am not a princess."

"You will be." Dun-hued eyes glazed with madness, the hag cackles, and thumps her fist on the carriage before disappearing into the throng.

Aunt Orsulya dabs at the sweat beading above her lip with an embroidered linen handkerchief. "A gypsy." She waves her hand across her nose as though dispelling the odor of the poor. "I wonder how she eluded the royal guards?"

"I want to meet a gypsy." Margit unfurls her fingers and stares at her palm. "A courtier told me they predict the future by reading the lines in your hand."

"They're more likely to snatch off your rings." Aunt Orsulya sniffs with disapproval.

Margit tilts her head into mine, and whispers, "The gypsy is prophesying to the wrong sister. I will be a princess, not you."

"Pagans and infidels," continues Aunt Orsulya. "Doomed

to wander the world for seven years for crimes against the Christian faith."

"Aunt Orsulya, you must not condemn an entire group of people." My voice tightens in my throat. "Anyway, if that were true then the gypsies' seven-year debt would have been paid hundreds of years ago."

Aunt Orsulya squints at me. "I do not appreciate your insolence, Ilona. Be mindful, excessive intellect in a maiden is not appealing to a man."

I cross my arms and look away.

"I don't care if gypsies are heathens," says Margit. "I want one to tell my future, my royal future."

"Only God knows your fate." Aunt Orsulya wipes away the sweat trickling from her heavy headpiece.

From my window seat I watch the troupe of acrobats bounding by, their joyful leaping and tumbling like a salve to Aunt Orsulya's hurtful comment.

The townsfolk stop to watch, blocking the street and waylaying the long line of royal litters, including ours. The acrobats take advantage of their captive noble audience. One colorfully dressed troupe member bows low. The second leaps on his back. A third, a nimble slight youth, springs onto his shoulders, shakes his head, jingling the bells on his striped hat.

"Long live King Matthias!" He shouts.

"Bravo." Margit laughs and stretches her coin-filled hand through the window.

But it is not one of the acrobats who takes it.

A young wench in a dirty shawl plucks the coin from Margit's hand. "Pain will be your pleasure, princess."

Margit jerks back, her hand clutching mine.

"Pay no attention to the wench." I give Margit's fingers a sympathetic squeeze.

"Not you, golden locks." The wench, flashing a crooked brown-toothed grin, aims her stony black eyes at me. "The dark-haired one."

The carriage lurches forward, the wench left behind. I scratch my palm while my heart hammers against my chest. Two mysterious and ominous prophecies in one day!

Do not seek the book. What book? Pain will be my pleasure? How horrible!

"I hate gypsies." Margit fluffs her skirt. "Such repulsive people."

"They do not have the benefit of our privileges," I remind her. "They do what they must to earn money. Anyway, she did not have the dark features of a gypsy." I smile despite the worry knotting in my belly. "I think she was just a mean-spirited wench bent on having fun at our expense."

"Commoners should take a different road to the castle." Margit sniffs with superiority.

My mouth drops open. "Commoners are the lifeblood of Hungary. They are Hungary. Without them who would Matthias rule?" I turn to Aunt Orsulya in hopes she will scold Margit for her snobbishness.

Instead Aunt Orsulya presses her hand to her flower-embroidered bodice. "This is all most vexing, Ilona. You had two dreadful prophecies today." She takes several deep breaths. "It is a sign from God. I will say an extra rosary tonight. So should you."

My hand slips into my dress pocket, my fingers curling around the smooth amber beads that Aunt Orsulya insists we keep on our person at all times. They never provide me the reassurance they give my aunt. "Maybe the prophecies were done in jest." I gesture to the window. "Look how happy everyone is."

"Two prophecies done in jest? I think not." Aunt Orsulya

adjusts her hennin. "And even if they were, that type of fun is the work of Satan."

"I thought you said it was a sign from God." I puff out my frustration, shake my head, and try another tact. "How could that old woman—so feeble and bent her wits are gone—discern a princess from a gentlewoman? All her blurry eyes see is a grand carriage taking well-dressed ladies to the castle. To her ilk we are all princesses." I pat the space beside me. "If Margit had been sitting here, she would have received the prophecy."

"And the warning about the book?" Aunt Orsulya pushes her hennin further back on her forehead. "What witty explanation do you have for that?"

I flitter my fingers across my knuckles while thinking. "It's a pagan's warning against the Bible."

Margit crosses her arms, dimples punctuating her smug grin. "What of the wench's prophecy just now about enjoying pain? That prophecy was for you, not me."

"Mmm…" I brush my fingertips across my knuckles again, back and forth, back and forth. "She spoke the truth."

Aunt Orsulya clutches the gold cross at her neck and squeezes her eyes shut. "*In nōmine Patris et Fīliī et Spīritūs Sānctī.*"

I gesture to Aunt Orsulya's new hennin, a towering beaded headpiece adorned with a waist length veil. "What's wrong with your new hennin?"

Aunt Orsulya opens her eyes and shifts the headdress back, which leaves a rosy indent in her forehead. "This style is heavy and pinches my skin."

I nod my head in sympathy. "It's painful and yet you get pleasure from its craftsmanship and elegance."

Margit claps her hands. "I receive pleasure from pain too.

These sleeves," she lifts one arm, the silk cuffs dragging to her knees, "are bothersome."

"We all derive pleasure from pain." The knot of worry in my stomach begins unraveling as I untangle the cleverly worded prophecies.

Aunt Orsulya and Margit exchange unconvinced glances.

"Lent is another example," I say.

Aunt Orsulya's eyes flick upward at the slated wood ceiling as though God is listening. "Mind your tongue."

I don't. "Isn't Lent a time when we are supposed to experience spiritual delight from the pain of foregoing some physical pleasure?"

Aunt Orsulya reaches for the crucifix hanging from the blue silk cord around her neck. "I suppose."

"Don't you see?" I splay my hands. "It was wordplay meant to confound us, nothing more. Had that wench been a lady from Matthias's court we would have praised her mischievous wit."

Aunt Orsulya narrows her eyes and lifts the crucifix to her lips. "Finding a husband for you will be difficult if you insist on flaunting your intellect."

I tap my chin pretending contemplation. "Then you and Aunt Erzsébet must find me a very intelligent man."

"Or else a very stupid one," giggles Margit.

"The Hungarian court has no shortage of fools." Aunt Orsulya bursts into laughter.

Ensconced in our litter and free from prying eyes, we laugh loud and long. Aunt Orsulya wipes away merry tears and I puzzle—not for the first time—over her misfortunes. Widowed before she conceived a child, Aunt Orsulya always behaves with proper courtesies and shows a zealous devotion to God. In private, another side emerges, her disdain for men revealed through quips and criticism.

The litter stops and our heads swivel to the window. A boisterous and jolly crowd is amassed outside the castle gate where celebrations are already begun. Troubadours play lute, fiddle, vielle, and tambourine. Castle servants set large platters of bread, meat, and casks of wine and ale on long rough-hewn tables. A troupe of thespians struts across a raised platform with bows and curtsies mimicking lewd acts.

"King Matthias spared no expense." Aunt Orsulya picks off a bit of lint from her sleeve.

The liveried guards wave us through the entrance gate and into a courtyard bustling with servants, gentry, and even more entertainers. Jugglers leap through hoops and toss plates. A tiny monkey wearing a top hat rides a large hound. A jester on stilts walks a man on a leash.

I step down from the litter and rush into the welcoming arms of relatives, some who traveled great distances to attend the coronation. Pausing only to hug nephews, kiss nieces, and embrace friends, I wend my way through the crowd intent on reaching my oldest sister Jusztina—married and living far away—when Aunt Erzsébet, her face pinched with disapproval, blocks my path.

"Pay homage to King Matthias first." Aunt Erzsébet's voice is a clipped whisper. "Together." She nudges Margit, also conscripted into this most urgent duty.

I flash sister Jusztina waiting nearby an exasperated look. She rolls her eyes.

"I suppose as a pair we are more impressive than either of us individually," I say to Margit as we join all the other sumptuously dressed and decadently jeweled well-wishers in line.

Ahead of us and dabbing her neck with a handkerchief, Aunt Orsulya waits with her good friend, Lady Zsazsa. I like the woman, she is funny and honest, but her dresses do tend to be scandalous. Today is no exception. Her cleavage-baring brightly colored frock is better suited for a young unmarried maiden, not a middle-aged widow. The prude and the voluptuary: their friendship defies my understanding.

Margit squeezes my elbow. "He's coming this way."

Returning from his audience with King Matthias, Prince Vlad works his way down the receiving line, pausing to greet nobles and diplomats. His swaggering stride is equal parts warrior and prince. My heart races as he draws near, his arrogant manner both intimidating and enticing. Dressed in green velvet with a floor-length robe draping from his broad shoulders, he turns his head as though he feels he is being watched.

I am caught! My face blooms with heat and I drop my gaze to the floor.

I hear Margit's quick inhalation and the air crackles with expectancy as we wait for his approach.

"Lady Margit." Prince Vlad bows low. "It is an honor to see you on this joyous occasion."

Margit smiles wide, all dimples and doe-eyed beauty. Prince Vlad's own smile is composed and tight, the slight curve of his lips visible beneath his straight chestnut-haired mustache.

Margit curtsies. "I cannot recall a more celebrated day in my life, but then I am only sixteen years." She bats her eyes. "Have you met my sister Ilona?"

Vlad bows, I curtsy, and our eyes lock. A thousand butterflies beat against my stomach. His moss-green eyes sparkle with something beyond polite interest. His gaze, focused and intense, ensnares me. I cannot look away; his eyes keep me as pinioned as the exotic butterflies Matthias displays in his library. My body leans forward, pulled in by a man who feels like a force of nature. I swallow, my mouth filling with moisture as though a delicious supper waits. No wonder Margit is enamored.

"Delighted to meet you." Vlad Dracula's gaze travels down my neck and lingers on my bosom.

My body warms, the layers of silk feeling transparent with the prince's brazen study of my pearl-encrusted bodice. Even as my skin burns with the thrill of his attentions, I sense something beneath his emerald scrutiny that sends the chill of danger into the heated caldron in my belly. The steam it creates within me is a singular sensation, the vapor of seduction awakening both skin and soul. My breasts heave of their own accord.

"Your sister found me admiring a portrait of your father." Vlad Dracula lifts his penetratingly clear eyes to mine. "Mihály was more than my mentor, he was like a father to me." His gaze is hypnotic.

I can scarcely breathe and yet my pulse beats double time. "It's my favorite portrait of him."

"It looks exactly like Father." Margit's interruption breaks the spell between us.

"Really?" Prince Vlad's brow furrows. "I must confess, I do not think the artist truly captured his valor and wisdom."

"No artist would be capable of such a feat." I nod with eagerness. "Father's qualities transcend mere daub and brush."

"Well stated." Prince Vlad tilts his head to take measure of me, his studied look appearing as though he is trying to determine if I am a flatterer or a coquette.

"I think," says Margit too loudly while squaring her shoulders so her generous bosom strains against her flower-embroidered bodice, "the artist did a wonderful job, especially the mustache. His mouth is a little stern though."

Prince Vlad looks sideways at Margit with amusement—or maybe disappointment—and I realize in an instant that

Margit and the warrior prince are terribly mismatched. I would be the worthier helpmate.

"Father's cruel death still haunts me." I press my hand to my heart and swallow the lump of grief that returns whenever I remember the horror that befell him. "I pray daily for his soul."

"I pray too." Margit shifts her body forward.

Prince Vlad does not acknowledge her comment, neither with glance nor words. He focuses on me, and I, him. The crowd blurs, conversations mute. I see and hear only him.

"I promise to avenge the sins of Meḥmed-*i s̲ānī*." Prince Vlad's face is grave, his eyes hardening into stone.

"That time cannot come soon enough." I speak quickly and honestly, my blunder unrealized until the last word slips from my lips. I open my mouth to soften my mistake, to rephrase or clarify but it is too late. I see it in Prince Vlad's eyes and my body shrinks into itself.

Prince Vlad's smile stiffens, and his liquid green eyes freeze into emerald ice crystals.

Margit's eyes light up upon hearing my gaffe. "Matthias and I are very close," she lies. "I will explain that your talents best serve Hungary if you are released from your imprisonment and free to destroy Sultan Mehmed."

A shadow passes over Dracula's eyes. He smiles at Margit like a parent does to a silly young child. The folly in her words—her political ignorance and obvious flattery—exposes a charming naiveté. Which may be her intent.

Margit aims a pointed look at me, her eyes gleaming with friendly competition.

"I agree, my lady, however, I think it best if someone other than a sweet innocent cousin reminds him of my considerable talents." He looks away and down the line of well-wishers, then gives us a tight nod. "Enough of politics and vendettas, Matthias's coronation deserves nothing less than jubilant celebration and happy thoughts." Prince Vlad bows low. "I humbly beg your leave. Lady Margit and Lady Ilona, it is an honor and pleasure to make your acquaintances. I can now say with all sincerity that King Matthias's cousins are the most enchanting ladies in all of Hungary."

Margit blushes and dips in curtsy. I curtsy as well, his gaze like hot coals on my skin. At that moment I know I want him. It is a foolish thought. I have no say in the matter of a husband. But reality does not matter to my pounding heart and enraptured soul.

"He will wed me," Margit says when he is out of hearing. "Aunt Erzsébet will make certain of it." She turns to me, bright pink spots on her cheeks. "Why were you making eyes at him?"

"I was being cordial." Though the heat of Prince Vlad's gaze still warms me, I tell a cold but necessary lie. "Don't you want me to be nice to my future brother-in law?"

"Not that nice." Margit's lips pinch together.

Unable to meet her accusatory glare, I look over her shoulder to check our position in the receiving line. "Only Lord and Lady Magyar are ahead of us. Look, you can see the jewels on Matthias's crown sparkling from here."

Distracted by royal gems, Margit's pursed lips melt into a giddy smile.

Our cousin king sparkles as well in a sumptuous red brocade robe with a white ermine collar that emphasizes the flaxen hair grazing his shoulder. Sitting tall on his throne, he beams with majestic munificence despite his recent tragedies. Only a few months earlier we wept over the untimely death of his bride and newborn babe. Today, however, Matthias sits ramrod straight and content, his wife's and child's passing hidden under his royal vestments.

What fortitude and control it must take to rally oneself for a public function.

"I heard Aunt Erzsébet wants Matthias to wed Emperor Frederick's daughter," I whisper as we step closer to the dais.

"What? So soon? Our aunt has no compassion," Margit whispers back. "He's still grieving."

"Political alliances come first." Like all noble maidens, Margit and I desire a lucrative marriage, dream of a love match, and worry about producing a male heir.

Mother took to childbed five times. Only three daughters survived. Mother died soaked in blood, the yearned for male heir breathing his last a day later. I often wondered if Margit and I inherited Mother's only weakness, producing daughters. It certainly is not a family trait. Aunt Erzsébet birthed two sons. The first, László, was beheaded by a vengeful Habsburg king a few years ago. Matthias is her second. And had it not been for Father's clever political maneuvering, Matthias would not be king of Hungary.

I step up to the dais with Margit.

"King Matthias." I curtsy low. "Hungary will soar to new heights under your excellent leadership."

Ignoring protocol, King Matthias holds his arms wide for a hug. "I will accept nothing less than a kiss from my favorite cousins."

We kiss his cheek and then proceed to praise the music, commend the choir, and applaud the pageantry, extolling His Highness until he flushes with pleasure.

"Margit," says Matthias with an impish grin, "you stare at my crown like it's a fig-stuffed capon. Have you an appetite for ambition?"

"Ambition?" Margit's brows lift in surprise. "Only for a good marriage, but I dare say your crown is nothing less than a banquet of jewels."

Matthias chuckles before glancing at the Roman diplomat waiting behind us. "Will you make me a promise, sweet cousins?"

"Anything," Margit and I reply in unison.

"Promise you will dance until dawn to prove your love of sovereign and country."

We vow to have fun, curtsy, and depart. Our duty dispatched, Margit and I stroll back down the line, stopping to chat with relatives and friends.

When we reach the great hall a red-haired stranger bars our entrance.

"May the Lord bless King Matthias with a long and prosperous reign." The woman lifts her pointy chin in the air.

"Thank you for your kind words," I say. "Who do I have the pleasure of speaking to?"

"My name is not important. You have little use for it." She clasps slim pale hands in front of her and lowers her voice. "I come bearing a prophecy for you, Lady Ilona."

My breath catches and my skin prickles with fear. Three prophecies in one afternoon cannot be good. I make a quick study of the woman's credibility. She wears a simple yet artfully draped pink silk gown with a large ruby pendant against her alabaster throat. Her delicate hands are smooth and soft, unblemished from fieldwork and labor. Nothing about her elegant appearance suggests she is a guildsman's wife, gypsy, or common wench.

I take a slow calming breath and present my most polite smile. "You're not the first."

The woman's ginger eyebrows lift. "Then you will not be surprised when I tell you my prophecy concerns your future husband."

Read more at Amazon.